MR. MADDOX 1953

THE CREEKSIDE SAGAS

MR. MADDOX 1953

ED MIDDLETON

Published by Skipjack Holdings LLC

ISBN: 978-1-7330258-1-2

Also by Ed Middleton
Skipjack Maddox 1859
Riverboat Bill 1961

Dedicated to Fred Chappell, John Lee Hooker,
and Albert Mohler Jr.

"A man of many companions may come to ruin,
but there is a friend who sticks closer than a brother."

PROVERBS 18:24

THE CREEKSIDE SAGAS

MR. MADDOX 1953

CONTENTS

AUTUMN '953

Maddox lay in his bed.

"The Lord's bed," as Ruby Woods had put it.

Snoring, which was good, and coughing, which maybe wasn't, but at least under blankets, with folks, and off that boat: almost sunk, freezing cold, and all alone.

The Lord's bed she called it, even before they fetched him and stuffed him in. First, she said she'd just soon he sunk, but some neighbor's dog barked slow over and over. "What else can we do?"

White trash hauled in a blanket. They slid him in. Drove away like bandits. Controlled drowning; might have been pneumonia. Ruby had known for two days and still Bill stubbornly smoked. He drank some soup at first, but no meat and more beer, then a coughing that drilled deep. No talking to him. He wanted to die. She knew he wanted to die and why.

Stalemate.

CHAPTER 1

MAY 1953, LOUISVILLE, KENTUCKY

All through the arraignment and trial of his wife's murderer, it seemed something sustained Bill, almost as if he had been as certain as the puffed-up lawyers, clerks, and jowly judge with his expressive but sadly ineffective eyebrows that popped up and down and slanted, curled, and questioned conspiratorially. Neither they nor he could do a damn thing to bring Sarah back. All the talk of the horror of the crime, the rape, the murder, the torching of the house—nothing anyone could say, think, express, or do could change one jot. Yet somehow, he sat and followed the tedious ribbons of procedure that somehow shepherd law into a courtroom. He had not flinched, for he felt it was his duty, for Sarah and even for the one who had killed her, Ronald. That monster, born of humankind, had slumped in front of the court, in front of his own mother, brother, and sisters like he was being scolded for stealing milk and was mildly disturbed by all the fuss, yet somehow defiant and apparently proud of the fact that at least he was somebody.

Oblivious, that must have been what Bill was, and yet he had never felt more alert. Every speck on the sidewalk leading up to the courthouse steps suggested it concealed meaning. He had even driven himself to court, parked his own car, and only once knocked out a taillight while parallel parking. Something had held him up.

Although in ways, he had never felt so alone; Sarah was gone and who else was there? No sister or brother. No mother, no father, cousins too distant and far removed to know. Her family, you could say, was broken, except that it had never been together, not even for one night, save the night she had been conceived. Her grandmother dead and her grandfather dead, her mother in some kind of sanitarium, nuts. His, dead, right after the war, first one, then the other. Alone, yet upheld as if some great cloud had descended, surrounded, and buoyed him through the ordeal of faces, black and white, the nonsense of what passes as reason. Then one morning, on sentencing day, the last day of the trial, it was gone.

He woke up to a ringing between his ears, but that was all.

He looked in the mirror but hadn't shaved. The face that stared back hadn't deserved it. What did sunken eyes, red-rimmed and bloodshot, have to do with a razor? And the mouth surrounded with cheeks, drawn and stubbly? He couldn't even look. His nose, his blotchy skin, eyes glassy, teeth almost brown and one broken. Who could ever have loved such? Who could have ever?

When he walked into the courtroom late, someone gave him a seat. Someone else was talking and Bill was thinking about Sarah, punching a tune into the jukebox, and her smile when he knew what that song could mean. He squinted and saw a watery fat boy and a man in a slippery gray suit gesturing. He closed his eyes to see her again and then the whole room, the bailiff, the judge, the stenographer, the mother, the brother, the sisters, fell down on him—the whole damn building and he heard nothing, because it was silent where he was: quiet as a tomb. Dead as the moon.

"Guilty as charged, of first-degree murder, rape, arson . . ."

A gavel pounded. The one being addressed and sentenced understood little or nothing of the pronouncement and stood beside his shark-skinned lawyer as if being informed that the lawn needed mowing or that the truck was still a bit grimy here and there.

The boy swayed as the judge droned. It became obvious to Bill—Mr. William G. Maddox, the victim's widower—that the judge was grandstanding. He was trying to make a point, to set an example; he was not sentencing the under-twenty individual before his bench. Instead he was demonstrating the law's power to potential miscreants, like Ronald's siblings and the heartbroken mother, who sat in the row behind Ronald, while he swayed and smiled like he was behind the wheel of the biggest rig that had ever been. The press scratched away, and the judge gave a nod and avowed something about how charity and lawlessness had collided and that . . .

Bill stood, slowly, but felt he was staring down on this room. The judge hesitated. Bill raised both hands, aware of the boy's mother, Ruby Woods, her children, even the one who had taken Sarah, and without even thinking, said, "No!"

The judge blinked, leaned back, swallowed by black robes. After the gasp from the courtroom, pencils could be heard troubling notepads, and the only two people who seemed steadfast and un-perturbed were William Maddox and the defendant Ronald Woods. One understanding what he was not yet ready to fathom, and the other, swaying, yet standing stock-still, fathoming everything he would ever know and yet understanding nothing.

Bill Maddox looked down, clasped hands, and said no more. His pulse was pounding, and he felt he was standing in two places at once. He dared not listen. Had he opened his eyes, he might have seen the hope-filled face of Ruby Woods or some of the con-sternation on black and white faces, even on the judge, who had started to lean forward to plant his elbows on the bench. His face retained a smear of bemusement. Bill said nothing. Ronald grinned and swayed.

Judge raised his gavel as if to demand order but seemed to realize that there was no disorder. Bill stood, or floated, staring at scuff and traces of river mud on his shoes.

"You tell 'em, Pops," Ronald said with a heartwarming smile, arms spread so wide he could have embraced the room. "I love everybody. Tell 'em, Pops, I'm your man behind the wheel."

Who knows what went through anybody's head when Ronald Woods said that? Fred Ruby said years later that he thought that the boy should have been put in the place they put folks that weren't right, but all had expected him to get the chair. Hell, it had been rape and cold-blooded murder of a white woman, a good-hearted woman, and the house burned, but mainly her, found strangled, stabbed, dead and charred in the basement. The boy, twenty, strapping big, black, an employee who had been given more chances than a second and then had repaid his benefactors with rape, murder, and arson, and supposedly confessing it, sitting in the front yard while flames toasted his back, clawed and bloody, eyes glistening. Everyone had known he would fry.

Ruby Woods and her kids stared straight ahead. Miss Hays stroked Ruby's hand. How could you defend this? There had been no defense, not really. But what to make of what Ronald was saying?

"Just tell them, Pops."

The judge raised his gavel, but again there was no need.

"Mr. Maddox, did you wish to address this court?"

Bill shrugged but did not look up. The rustling and whispering continued. After a moment, he spoke.

"My heart is broke. My name is Bill Maddox. My wife, you know, was beloved to me, and she's gone, and nothing can bring her back. I hate that. I hate that cold fact more than anything. I loved her and love her still more, God forgive me, than anyone else or life itself. I know what was done, and I know what took her, but I got to say I will never, ever understand why."

"Tell 'em, Pops. I'm your man!"

Bill said, "If God helps, I will, boy, but please hold your tongue." He paused. "Listen. There is no point in making things right or showing what's what. Because it's done."

"Listen to the man. You tell 'em, Pops!"

Bill nodded at Ronald, now gently constrained by two deputies. Bill shut his eyes and his frame seemed to shiver. He fixed on the judge and opened fire.

"I'll say it quick. Hurting that boy," he pointed at Ronald, "won't do no damn good. Hell, truth be known, it would kill Sarah all over again and that would double kill me. Listen, I fought in the war and did what I did. Killed and sure ain't no saint. I got no right to tell anyone what to think or how to act or what to do, but I do have some stake in this matter, which I suppose everyone present would agree on."

Everyone was silent. The boy smiled and nodded at the deputies clutching his arms. Bill swallowed and looked down. He seemed to shrink as he slowly sank into his seat. He said, "For the love of God and Sarah and me, please, may this court have mercy on poor Ronald Woods. Central State, until something better comes. He don't even know what he's done. I don't know why, but neither do you. I've had enough. Put him in the institution; spare that boy's life or kill me. I can't take no more."

Some say he had to be helped out for disrupting the proceedings. Others remember only the moan. The boy, Ronald, some say, tried to break free to embrace him, but most agree that they just led the defendant away, mouthing words no one could decipher. After a retreat into his chambers, the judge returned, stroked his gavel, and sent the boy to the state hospital, Central State, which was sort of a first for a black boy convicted of rape and murder and arson in Kentucky in 1953, where consideration of mental health was not the norm.

For some, it was the last straw. They tried to latch on to Mr. William Maddox and make him into some kind of poster boy. Those were the extreme ones, the Klan and such, but also there were others, like the newspapers—not only the locals, but the Chicago papers, the Nashville papers, a whole bunch of them. It was a big deal, you see, because no black boy had ever been delivered from this kind of evil so easily, and these ones under the guise of being amazed about the charitable nature of this thing that had happened, did their very best to stir the pot and bring the whole damned thing to a roiling boil.

They tried to stir it up and got some pretty good white quotes, but they had a problem, because Bill was nowhere to be found.

Their own damn fault they had no clue. Bill hadn't hidden. The press, like a hungry pack, had chased the hottest scent out of the courtroom. Ruby Woods and her family were simply amazed and so relieved that Ronald had escaped execution that they hugged their friends and paid no attention to reporters, who hadn't expected to talk to those folks anyway. They stood aside, awaiting some kind of spokesman, while overlooking the clear fact of Mr. William Maddox being coaxed into a black Cadillac.

Bill had driven himself to the courthouse, but he had not been alone. He hadn't been alone the night the house burned down either; Old Man Green had been on the case. Green had affection for Bill, grounded in common military service, basic values, and love of truth. Rich as he was, Green was a charter member of Creekside's Fire Department, and on the night of the fire, he had taken Bill home to his own house and swilled whiskey with him until dawn.

Of course, Bill was in shock, deranged and crazy. Nothing he said about the terrible tragedy made a lot of sense. By the time he had returned from his road-hauling job for the Commonwealth of Kentucky and got back to his home, they were hosing it down for the last time. Bill drove up to his house and there was no house. Smoke and mist coming out of a hole and a bunch of funny-looking people standing around, wearing big red hats and long black coats. There were flashing lights that shouldn't be there and nobody to tell him that he might as well not bother because he no longer had a home and his wife had been murdered. Nobody told him anything when he jumped out of his shiny red truck. Nobody said anything, but Old Man Green came up quick, tackled him, wrestled him to the ground before he had thrown himself into what had been the cellar.

Blurred. That night and day and everything stacked up on either side. Never could he be sure that he remembered. Not really.

Night of the fire, Green had driven Bill away and also after the trial. The same black Cadillac nobody saw had slipped up close.

No way Ruby Woods had known this.

On the night of the fire, when Green had hauled Bill to his house, Bill had been soft as putty once he had known she was gone. His heart broken, the soft Cadillac ride had overruled his protests. Hell, he had no home! Green, his former Marine Corps buddy, with one hand on the wheel and the other on his wrist, made it clear there were no options as they slid down River Road and up the hill to Green's. When they lurched to a stop, Bill launched his final protest. That's when Green had simply asked where he wanted to go. Bill folded and retched. Green had to get his man, Marcus, to help.

No point in trying to flesh out that night. There was so little. Every bit was an escape valve from the brutal savagery of what had happened.

Marcus, a black man, who was quite light skinned, almost fair complected, was only twenty-eight years old. He had a gimpy leg, which kept him out of Korea. Green then weighed about 280 on a frame that might have been more comfortable supporting a body weighing a third less. Bill slumped like some tossed-aside garment. He was in his mid-forties, same as Green, but when Mrs. Green walked into the back room off her kitchen at six thirty in the morning, her face mirrored the scene that presented itself. She saw a grinning cadaver approving an arm wrestling contest between her husband, stripped to the waist, and Marcus, diminutive, yet fully dressed, screaming "uncle" as his boss, her husband, seemed to press the back of his hand into a sputtering candle stub. Air thick with cigar and cigarette smoke, glasses and whiskey bottles everywhere. Green's fire hat was on top of a lamp, fire boots muddy splayed on the floor.

"Enough."

That was all she had said. Green let go of his adversary's hand, which Marcus rubbed with an ice cube that he plucked off the table. Green appeared indignant. Marcus studied the back of his hand.

"Put your friend to bed and not another peep."

"Yes ma'am," said Marcus. Marcus and Green lifted Bill onto an old couch reserved for the dogs and covered him with a blanket that the dogs loved.

Green staggered off to his "snuggle room." A place for afternoon naps adjoining his home office, a sanctuary with low lighting, books, a few chairs, but best of all, an oversized couch. Green, fully clothed, but belt loosened, was soon asleep.

Marcus, who lived over the five-car garage across the pea gravel turnaround off the back of the house and kitchen, wished the birds could forget morning. Young as he was, he was pooped. The boss had worn him out and the missus would grill him later, at least he hoped later. Marcus could not believe what he had heard that night. He had known that boy, the whole family. He felt sick and wanted sleep but felt so restless and dirty he took a bath, then woke up shivering, to persistent knocking.

He wrapped in his robe and saw it was seven thirty. Opened the door to see Mrs. Green with Bill Maddox nodding behind. She looked purposeful. Bill, apologetic, seemed to make an effort to stand steady and not roll jittery, bloodshot eyes.

"We need to take the flatbed to Bill's."

Bill shook his head.

"Now," she said. Marcus nodded, shut the door, and put on the same old clothes.

After Mrs. Green had heard Bill's story, they walked across crunchy pebbles until she was tapping on the door to Marcus's apartment above the garage. She knocked like a landlord. Bill stood there, clutching his coffee mug, and looked off to the side. What the hell was he doing here? Sun so bright, yet cool on the plants and white planks of the garage. Why was it shining? Why was he waiting behind this woman tapping? There was no door that could open on this. No way. He was not thinking so much as erasing thought as fast as the knocking: tap, tap, tappity, tap, tap. What kind of fire is this? Dew in branches, leaves collecting light like things broken early and nobody screaming get back or out of the way. Tappity-tap and why is she knocking? In this damned cool morning, why doesn': she just call his name?

Marcus, wrapped in something that looked like carpet but was likely a robe, peered from behind the door as if expecting bandits. Mrs. Green, if she had continued tapping, would have tapped him squarely on his nose.

"Take the flat bed over to Mr. Maddox's."

Bill shook his head no. She nodded her head yes. Marcus rolled his eyes and shook his head side to side and shut the door. She tapped and said he was to hurry. Some sort of compliant sound escaped from behind the door. It was settled. Bad as it was, it had to be done.

If it hadn't been for Mrs. Green, there's no telling what would have become of Mr. Maddox. Bill went along, never knowing that Mrs. Green had taken Marcus aside, warned him shock had set in and Bill had to be watched like a hawk, that he was as dangerous as a wounded animal. Mrs. Green didn't actually have to tell this to Marcus because he knew. That is exactly why she had hired Marcus, young as he was; he knew things off the top of his head and not only about tough stuff, but with her kids, her husband, and the hired help. He was her right hand and her left, if necessary. When she told Marcus to look after things and take care of Mr. Maddox, she hadn't had to spell it out or make any secret signs or wink. Marcus knew. Look after Bill. Walk him through it, bring him back whole, cover his ass (she could be salty). Marcus understood and so did Bill, though he didn't understand it at the time. How else can you explain why he let Marcus drive him straight back to his burned-down home?

Though it was early, the liquor store was open, and Bill stumbled in for Pall Malls and Falls City Beer. Marcus said nothing, just sat in the truck. The weight of the thing crushed him into his seat. To him, Bill looked like a character who had walked off the big screen onto the wrong set.

Bill opened a beer before he even stepped into the cab. He offered Marcus one, but he refused.

"Damn this is hard," Bill said.

Marcus said nothing; Bill understood.

In the mile or so that they were driving, Bill croaked down the first and then another. He had two cigarettes lit. One in his hand and one in the ashtray and never even noticed, because Marcus took one and pretended to puff.

"Am I dreaming, Marcus? God knows I ain't, but no way this son of a bitch is real."

A yellow school bus picked up a gaggle of urchins, and the old truck screeched to a halt.

"Needs brakes," Bill said.

"Sure do," Marcus replied.

"This ain't a dream. I'm not gonna wake up happy, am I?"

Marcus flipped the cig out the window as the bus rolled off and turned onto Bill's road.

Clouds floated over the river, bunched up. Drizzle. Marcus had to flip on the wipers. Short drive, only two beers, two quick ones, but when they pulled close and Bill saw the bleary, sunken hole of what had been his house, his head banged against the window. His truck, all shiny as hell, was across the street. He moaned, and people parted as the flatbed pulled in. Smoke was still wafting up out of the cavity that had been the foundation. A fireman was there scribbling on a clipboard.

There was no good thing to do. Could have stayed in the truck with the wipers flicking. Maybe pull off like curious folks do, but Bill sat up and said, "Stop!"

He gave a look that Marcus would never forget, took a swig of beer, carefully set it down on the floor, and got out of the truck. Marcus followed. Bill walked toward the fireman with the clipboard, but before he got to him, Mr. Fred Ruby, a neighbor, motioned. Marcus overheard that they had done what they could. With a hand draped on Bill's shoulder, told him that whatever had been dragged out of the house was in his garage, shielded from rain.

More of a mist than rain, but the people glistened. The place stank of burnt scorch, dank wood, something indescribable, plain awful.

Bill didn't seem to notice. Marcus was so busy watching Bill, worried that he would fall into the rubble, that he ignored the god-awful until they were back in the truck.

He was amazed and puzzled by how Bill had carried himself and interacted with the folks who milled around with no apparent purpose and with those like the fireman and the two men, obviously detectives; the lot of them appeared to be all the same to him. He wandered about, followed by this one and that one, calmly answered questions from a reporter from some radio station. Took a card from a fellow who turned out to be a preacher. Fred stuck close by Bill and Marcus followed, but he walked unaided all around his property. There was nothing left of the house. Hard to believe anything had ever been on that ground except for charred, smoldering mess.

Fred and one of the detectives took Bill aside and Marcus watched as they gave him assurance, then Bill climbed back into the truck. "Home," was all he said.

Home, Marcus knew, meant back to the Greens and he was further amazed at the calmness of the man. Now it was Marcus's turn to sleepwalk. He said nothing. His passenger didn't even look tired, yet there he was, as good as dead. Marcus tended to the business at hand. He steered the truck. Bill sucked down beer and smoked.

SANCTUARY

Bill spent that first day between tipsy and asleep out on the sunporch. All the servants and even Mrs. Green tiptoed around and gave him wide berth. At dinner, he sat at the table. They had steaks and potatoes. Bill shoved his food around and favored the whiskey that Old Man Green poured generously.

With Bill's permission, Mrs. Green saw to most of the arrangements. It was a simple matter. Bill didn't care about any of the details. Pine box. Lot at Cave Hill Cemetery. Funeral director took care of the rest, all except for the preacher and that did stump Bill. A preacher?

"Who's he gonna preach to and about what?" he asked.

As he said it, he knew it didn't sound right.

"A preacher?"

He should have let it lay. That's what he thought after he had said it and Mr. Green agreed. He could tell by the way his face contorted and quivered. Mrs. Green clanged her fork down and said nothing, but the look in her eyes denied response. She laid down the law. Reverend Stephen Rucker had already agreed to preside. Bill recovered a bit of his balance. He nodded in compliance.

He and Old Man Green tippled into the wee hours. The next morning early, after Marcus had gently poked his shoulder and wafted coffee fumes under his nose, Bill, bleary and still blank beyond comprehension, soon discovered that the preacher man had a lot to do with everything because the reverend had told him so. Mrs. Green had backed him up, every word.

Bill wanted to keep it simple, but the whippersnapper preacher coyly patted his hand and instructed him that simplicity was his starting point, and the entire ritual for dealing with this phase of the human journey toward the Creator was best served by time-tested rites that engendered grace and acceptance. In other words, Bill owed it to Sarah.

They chose "Amazing Grace" for the main hymn. Bill was unable to think of any other hymns except "Onward Christian Soldiers." His mind went blank and when Reverend Rucker consolingly suggested other titles, they meant less than nothing to him. After about an hour of this drudgery, he was left with a blessing, some condolences, and a hymnal to jog his mind. Why he was hungry, Bill couldn't say, but he was hungry, and he wanted a beer.

Mrs. Green was glossing up the preacher at the front door and handing him a check that made him shuffle in his dark suit like some pale mockery of spring. Bill motioned to Marcus and whispered that he wanted a beer and that he was hungry. The preacher tucked the offering into his pocket and both he and Mrs. Green nodded at Bill with lots of teeth showing and eyes glittering. He nodded back as he urged Marcus into action by tapping his elbow.

The preacher left, and Bill saw him climb into a respectable old car. All were nodding and waving when Marcus reappeared and handed Bill a frosty beer wrapped in a fancy cocktail napkin. It probably wasn't the beer that set off Mrs. Green. Most likely, it was the napkin; after all, it was only ten thirty in the morning. She was no prig and her own husband was still sleeping one off, but still she felt she had to stand on decorum. She started to reprimand Marcus and cast a disapproving glance at Bill, when two things happened. Bill burped. Enjoying the release, he took the beer from Marcus and thanked him with twinkling eyes. This had the dual effect of temporarily infuriating Mrs. Green and endearing Bill to Marcus. Marcus had formerly thought of Bill only as Mr. Maddox, so he was pleased when Bill said, "No offence, but I asked for this beer and Marcus was only serving me, your humble and grateful guest, as he must have assumed you wanted him to do, Mrs. Green, for I was thirsty." This said, he took a swig and added, "I thank you, but that minister fellow and all that's happened, you understand, has got me plumb tuckered and would you believe hungry? Because if you can believe it, please believe it for me, 'cause I can't, except for the fact that I didn't eat last night or lunch either and you know the rest. Please, leave Marcus out of it. I asked for a beer. If you don't want me to drink it here, I'll leave and say thanks for everything all at once."

Of course, that hadn't suited Mrs. Green and she ordered up a country ham and cheese sandwich for Mr. Maddox. Turned out that before noon, Mrs. Green and Bill were hitting it off. Marcus was sent to fetch a bucket of ice, glasses, and the special reserve, a whiskey made back in prohibition times for medicinal purposes and it proved medicinal indeed, for it healed the rift that threatened to open between the two. When Old Man Green sauntered out onto the porch and sampled a few swigs, he seemed instantly to become healthier himself. Marcus was even offered a taste, but politely refused. He was a Baptist and, as a rule, did not drink whiskey, only brandy or an occasional beer and usually when no one was looking.

Before Mrs. Green sent Marcus for the special reserve, she asked Bill what he didn't like about Reverend Rucker. Bill stared blankly, not wanting to cause insult. Now, at least, he had a beer in his hand and if he played it right, a driver, more beer, a place to sleep, and a meal. He also liked Green. He didn't want to screw that up, so he did his best not to answer. He stared off into the trees and made some remark about tree frogs and how they could predict rain, but she pressed him until he had to answer.

"It's your funeral," she said. "Sorry, I mean Sarah's, your wife's. But if you don't want Mr. Rucker . . ."

"No, he's all right. It's just . . ."

"What, Mr. Maddox?"

"Ma'am, would you please call me Bill?"

At that moment, Marcus delivered Bill's sandwich and another beer. "Here you are, Mr. Maddox, sir, and here is your napkin."

"Ma'am, is it okay if Marcus calls me Bill, too? I ain't fancy enough for Mr. Maddox and besides right now, it don't seem all that friendly, if you know what I mean?"

Mrs. Green's eyebrows raised. Bill accepted the beer and pointed to a table where Marcus placed the plate and napkin.

Bill opened his arms wide, cigarette in one hand, beer in the other and winked.

"Can't we cut the crap and please be real?"

Mrs. Green was very real. She fired back.

"All right, Bill. You call me Theodora and I'll hold you to it." She stared at him until Bill lowered his hands, settled comfortably, and agreed. She looked up at Marcus, who looked away. "Marcus can call you polecat if he wants. What I want to know is, what the blazes do you have against Reverend Rucker?"

"That's easy." He laughed. "The man is as sanctimonious and phony and heartless as a politician. I ain't trying to take a swipe at the God he claims to represent, but his hands are a bit too soft for me, and when he touched me and lowered his voice, I felt like vomiting, if you want the truth."

"Marcus, please bring the bourbon. You know what I mean."

"Yes, ma'am," Marcus said. "And a glass for Mr. Bill as well, ma'am?"

"Bring four glasses, Marcus."

They were on their way. Mrs. Green, henceforth known as Theodora, was a straight shooter, for sure. Rich, yeah. She was rich and married to Sam Green, she would always be so, but there was a streak in Theo, as she liked to be called, that could come down as hard as a hammer. Her daddy had been a carpenter and eventually a builder of some fine houses. She had never been impressed by social mores, married Old Man Green for love, and took snubs in stride as he had.

"What clued you in that the man was, shall we say, a bit less than honest?"

Bill took a deep drag on his smoke. Mrs. Green waited for his answer.

"Theo, may I call you T?

"My friends call me Theo. You can call me T or anything you like."

"All right then, I'll tell you, Theo, if you won't take offence. The Rev wants to do good and that right there is problem number one. That blinds him, no doubt. Two, he is holier than thou, and that doesn't help his vision one bit. Three, did you happen to notice that he seemed to pay a tad more attention to you than he did to the bereaved, namely me? Four is so obvious that if you don't already know, then most likely it won't ever be apparent, but he treated Marcus, a good man, like a coatrack with hands and legs to fetch things with. Now what else do you want this man to say? I don't like him."

"They're building on to the church—a congregation hall and a kitchen."

"Why don't he go into the hotel business?"

"You sense that he's only after the money?"

"Theo, how the hell would I know?" Bill said. "Tell you the truth, he seemed right nice for a man with his hand out."

"You think he's doing this only for the money? The donation I gave him?"

"Why else did his eyes light up? It wasn't me he was concerned with when he hightailed it out of here."

Marcus walked in with the bourbon.

"Please don't take offense. Maybe you know the man differently, but I would bet you they're gonna name some part or maybe all of that new-fangledness after you."

Green walked in and, turned out, Bill was right. The complex would be named for them. Green said it was a good cause. He allowed he didn't much care for the reverend either, but that was beside the point.

Bill felt like he was tiptoeing. Mrs. Green sipped her bourbon and soda, and Mr. Green launched into some theory about the civilizing effect of the church on society; how it was an ingredient in the balm and fuel that propelled society away from the abyss of chaos and steered it toward the loftier goals of human endeavor. Not this quick and not this short, but that was the gist. While Bill was sinking back into the couch and thinking that all of this information was the product of one drink, without meaning to, he rolled his eyes and glanced at Mrs. Green, who sensed his pain and suggested a stroll before lunch. Glasses were replenished and off they went.

Bill was dazed, and everyone knew. Mrs. Green was a light drinker, so it is not hard to understand how she kept her mouth shut. Marcus, who seemed to appear by magic as they began the stroll, did not drink a drop most days, so it is not difficult to understand his cool. But Old Man Green was a barrel for whiskey and his tongue not easily restrained, and yet on that day and in the days that followed, he was. He never blurted out, "Bill, let's kill the bastard!" or "How can you be so stinking calm?" He didn't say anything close. Nobody wanted to be the one that woke him.

Spring. It was spring. Hostas were sprouting beside the driveway; the last daffodils were withering while lilies were marching toward bloom. Mrs. Green pointed out her columbine bed, which was ready to sprout buds. Mr. Green's tomato plants were already staked, though less than a foot tall. Marcus walked behind within earshot of course, in fact close enough to catch them if they fell and yet as invisible and as silent as a ghost. Marcus showed nothing, and Bill understood.

Marcus could not understand how this man was standing. Bill crunched pea gravel calmly as Mrs. Green strolled with her soda, as she called her drink, and pointed out a red-winged black bird to praise its song. Marcus had found that unsettling. He also could not understand how the scent of viburnum hedge—fragrant as it might be, buoying up the scentless dogwood blossoms—would not sicken Mr. Maddox with the specter of death. It worried Marcus, to tell the truth, to see the man point out flowers and snowflake-like remains he admitted to having learned about from his wife who would never garden again.

Mr. Green was easier. For one thing, his bluster was fake. Marcus knew that was true on a personal level. At times, Green had come through for him for no other reason than motives coaxed out by his Creator. The only reason Marcus had this job was due to some faith that the Greens had in him and particularly Mr. Green. As tough she was, when it came to nut cutting, Mrs. Green let the old man take the lead. Tough, but Green was the blade and she always let him know it. Marcus knew it, too. After they had helped him through a teenage scrape, he never entertained trouble.

They strolled through boxwoods that bordered the path leading past a man-made pond stocked with koi lazily fanning green water. There was a young black man mucking out winter debris. There was another fellow across the garden snipping a hedge that blocked an outbuilding. In fact, if Bill hadn't been sleepwalking, he might have noticed that everywhere you looked, there was industrious activity. There was a man lugging mulch in a wheelbarrow and another shoveling mulch carefully around shrubs while he joked indecipherably with a fellow as old as Moses, who was bent over like the redbud tree blooming behind him while he edged a flowerbed with a spade.

Old Man Green waddled, down to the finger stream that flowed into the creek that led to the river. A big man to be sure, as big in his own way as Mantar the Black Angus champion bull that they skirted past in the pasture.

The four straggled down the slight incline beside the small stream—air soft and spring sun forgiving. Foliage flickered. Birds skipped and swooped. Two drakes chased a suzie in a wild aeronautical mating ritual.

"A little bit of heaven," Bill said.

Everyone nodded.

"Let me show you my hideout," Green said.

"What you hiding from?" Bill replied.

"Nothing I can discuss, but seriously, I have an idea. Do you like to fish?"

"Fish?" Bill queried. "Fish?"

His eyes turned inward as he was asked this and both Theo and Marcus saw. He was thinking. He was remembering, swimming inward. Mrs. Green looked at Marcus and returned the nod. With a flourish, she took over and interrupted this exchange. She sent Marcus back for the jeep and "reinforcements," which consisted of country ham biscuits, a bucket of ice, and a "measure of whiskey." Green looked at her with puzzlement.

"Just trust me," she said.

Bill stumbled along trying to remember why he liked to fish or if he liked to fish, but he recalled that Sarah had liked to "wet a line." Mrs. Green plucked a plant, crushed it between her fingers and held it under Bill's nose. Mr. Green actually frowned.

"What's this smell like?"

Bill gave her a startled look.

"Tell me what it smells like," Mrs. Green said.

"Damned if I know."

Mrs. Green held the weed and blocked the path.

"Tell me."

"Well, it favors garlic; sort of a mild garlic, I would say."

"Bingo," she exclaimed. "Bill you've got a nose. This is mustard garlic and not worth a damn and if we aren't careful, Green, this plant will take this pasture. Got to root it out."

Now it was Green who looked befuddled and Bill looked sharp, clear, and proud perhaps of his good nose. He took a swig of whiskey and wondered what Green was staring at down by the creek. He could hardly make it out. Sort of a big overgrown shed.

SQUATTERS

"Do you hear what I say, Green?"

"Of course, dear, as always, but what the hell is going on at my camp?"

Green and Bill observed two entirely different things. As they got closer, Bill saw the creek reflections beyond what might have been some kind of flat-bottomed boat propped up on oil drums and timbers. Hard to tell, but he could decipher what looked like a hull and ropes tied into trees, draped with vines that both delineated and obscured. He saw light glint off a pane of glass, smelled smoke and bacon frying.

Green saw a problem. His camp was overgrown. Since the war, he had used this tub as a fishing camp, but truth be told, mainly as a drinking hole and a place of escape. He hadn't been down for a year or so, and he'd forgotten how fast nature reclaimed. That part didn't bother much. Not a lazy man and obviously, not without resources, but smoke, frying bacon, and then the clothesline! He felt violated. Whatever was left of this shanty boat that had settled there during the '45 flood had been a refuge for drink and aftermath. His own doghouse, sometimes a fishing camp, was now apparently being used for something he knew not what. He lurched down the slope, face red. Mrs. Green urged Bill on, worried about what her husband might find if he huffed and puffed long enough to arrive.

She saw mess, past and present. Loutish extravaganzas cloaked in nonsense. "I am going fishing." (Translation: See you later, alligator).

Even though she nearly always won their altercations, she hated duplicity. "Fishing, my ass!" she would say, but off he would go, and it would do no good to follow. She did not like this place that had floated off the river across treetops submerged by a great flood. She never had. Emptiness had come to rest on two felled trees, as if it had a purpose. Green had seen utility at once. Now as he charged, picking up a piece of driftwood as weapon, she gritted her teeth, clenched her jaw. No point in calling to Green. She urged Bill to stop him.

When they got to the thing, whatever it had become over the years, all they saw was a clothesline strung between straggly trees and coals beneath an iron skillet with bacon frying. Green crouched and looked left and right, standing over the fire.

Bill saw her first.

"Over there." He pointed.

"Come out, right now. Come out!" Green hollered.

And she did. From behind a bush, a young woman—earthy as creek bank, dressed in something filmy that resembled a dress, barefoot and smiling—waving a spatula, and said something like, "Would you all be wanting something to eat?"

"What's going on here?" Green asked.

"Who's asking?" She smiled in a way that suggested she owned the bottomland. She put one hand on her hip and cocked. She was defiant, held the spatula like a mace to counter Green's wand of driftwood. She smirked more than glared, then walked over to the skillet, and in one scoop, flipped bacon.

"Where you been?" she said.

Green looked startled. "What do you mean?"

She laughed. Bill noticed when she threw her shoulders back and tossed her hair that she was not quite as young as she had first appeared. So did Mrs. Green, who stared down this Jezebel. Mrs. Green was so furious that Bill considered clasping her arms, but when he looked at Green, the old man shook his head to signify that he had no earthly idea.

The large skillet was cooking up more bacon than one young woman would have been expected to prepare. From behind a cottonwood tree, two ragged, tough-looking fellows emerged.

One man held a string of fish, the other, a board and a knife. Both were grinning.

Bill clutched Mrs. Green's arm.

"Daddy man, Uncle Billy. This is the big daddy they all talks about. He owns this creek. He owns the whiskey."

It was obvious to Bill that the woman was a jokester, but he didn't know if Mrs. Green, who was straining toward her, understood that. Green looked baffled. Who was this filly out to mess him up? Her eyes were dark with mischievous passion, but her smile was beguiling and in spite of squalor, she seemed self-assured. She smiled at the two men and nodded, one dropped his string of fish and brandished a chrome-plated pistol. The other dropped the board but held two knives. The girl bent down and removed the skillet from the fire.

"Almost made me burn my bacon."

Marcus saved the day. The jeep's muffler had a hole, so you could hear him as he bounced down the path. He brought requested refreshments and ham biscuits but was even further prepared. When he saw what the mess was, he roared even faster and revved with the clutch in, then dug into brakes.

The two scraggly men glanced like it was a joke on wheels, but the girl didn't look as sure.

"What's with the jeep-driving nigger, fat man?" said the man with the pistol, but before Green could answer, Marcus leveled a double-barreled shotgun over the windshield and aimed.

Marcus stood behind the windshield and pointed the twelve-gauge and moved it ever so slowly side to side and captured their attention. The chrome-plated pistol disappeared.

"Bring that gun slow out of your pocket and throw it on the ground, you hear?"

The man did just that. The other fellow put up his arms. The young woman looked disgusted. Old Man Green looked satisfied. He turned to Marcus and nodded.

"You folks clear out right this damn minute!"

The two men looked at the ground, but the woman glared at all of them and spit.

"Whatever you have," said Green, pointing at the boat, "we'll put it off and you can get it later. Now get."

"Get out of here, now!" Mrs. Green yelled. "You have no business here. Go!"

Marcus held the shotgun. The men squirmed and started to shift their weight foot to foot. One turned and began to walk away, but the woman and the oldest, scruffiest man stood their ground and didn't budge.

"Give us a week," she said and as she spoke, she puffed up her breast and pointed it at Bill and Green. She glared at Mrs. Green, then shook her head, and looked down. She sank to her knees. When she pulled herself back up, her face was pale as ash, until her eyes flashed.

"What about the baby? What about the baby? What about *my baby*?"

Mrs. Green said, "Oh my God!"

Actually, both said it several times before Green calmly asked the young woman who was in the boat.

"Who's in there? Tell them to come out quick."

Nobody moved or said anything at first, then the older fellow allowed as how his wife was aboard tending a young one.

"Who else?"

"That's it, Mr. Green, only those."

"Have 'em step out."

"She needs help," the young woman said. "She's crippled. Can't walk. She got the polio."

Mrs. Green said, "Oh my God!"

Without saying a word, Bill walked down the slope and announced that he might have a look inside. Green started to object, but Bill waved him off. A minute later, he confirmed that the young woman's story might be true. The baby started crying and Green shook his head. Bill reported that the only thing inside was an older woman and a child.

In his understated way, Bill had left out some details, namely the god-awful, slovenly mess which wasn't discovered for about two weeks because of Green's heart of gold. After seeing the baby, only a few months old, he negotiated from the bottom rung of compassion. Over Mrs. Green's protestations and Marcus's rolling eyes, Mr. Green permitted them to stay on for two weeks, three max. He reached into his wallet, hooked a fifty and instructed Valerie—as she had wanted to be called—to purchase groceries, for he was concerned the child looked unhealthy.

The story they told does not bear repeating. It wasn't their fault. Misfortune squatted on the doorstep, took up residence, and refused to depart. Windstorms, floods, fires, failed crops. Mrs. Green, Bill, and Marcus were shaking their heads in disbelief as they saw Green suck it in as Old Testament truth. The tale cried out for plagues, locusts, and frogs.

Valerie produced tears and so did the baby. Green gathered up the pistol, a cheap .32, told them they had two weeks, and asked them to clean the place, the weeds and brush. He also offered wages, if they wanted work cleaning fencerows or painting and stuff. Of course, the Woosleys eagerly agreed.

Mrs. Green did not argue, for she knew it was pointless. Green wasn't hooked on the girl, but on her baby. She loved that about him, his unreasonable softness, but she knew his compassion was often misplaced. This was a minor battle, so she acquiesced. Marcus was disgusted. Bill wasn't sure what to think. He supposed that copperheads and vermin needed homes. The baby clouded his mind as he sucked down the last of his drink. Unlike T and Marcus, he gave Old Man Green a pass because he figured Green was thinking the same way.

The Green party piled into the jeep, but before they bounced off, Green plucked another fifty and handed it to Valerie who gushed about how grateful the baby was. She held her up for Green to kiss, but Green stroked the child's cheek instead. Through all of this commotion, Marcus, who wasn't eager to lower the shotgun, kept it cradled across his lap and glared at two white trash men in his line of fire.

They rolled down the meadow to a shady bend in the creek and sat on a slick sycamore log and Marcus served ham biscuits to fortify the whiskey. A spring cold front breezing in from the north was bracing to Green and Bill. Not so to Mrs. Green, who, like Marcus, had had enough chill just looking at Woosleys. When the old man popped off with something that ended with "there but for fortune," she said through clenched teeth, "That type will cost a fortune."

"Those people are like fleas," she said. "Easy to catch, hard to rid."

Green said he thought it might work out.

"If they spruce a bit, cut down weeds, clear brush, drag off drift and trash . . . don't you think?"

"What are they going to use for tools? You took their pistol!" Mrs. Green snapped.

"That is a point," Bill said.

"Well," Green said, cocking his big old head and looking at the sky, "we'll take them some tools after lunch. Marcus can load a saw and scythe and whatever else he figures they might need and there you go." He nodded, satisfied with his solution, and took a deep draw on his cocktail.

Bill, who was leaning against a sapling, watched Mrs. Green's eyes coolly study her husband's and then slowly settle on Marcus, who was perched in the driver's seat with the shotgun still in his lap.

"Marcus, what do you think of Mr. Green's plan?"

Marcus looked toward the boat.

"Marcus, Mrs. Green asked you a question."

Marcus tried to preserve his cool exterior, but when Green asked again, his facade fell.

"My ass ain't delivering tools without two shotguns, a .44, a switchblade knife, and General Patton. Somebody else's ass can be hauling tools to that trash. Not my black ass."

Green stiffened and the corners of Marcus's lips pulled back almost to his ears and his eyes widened and froze with the rest of his posture. Neither could believe what had tumbled out.

Bill and Mrs. Green started laughing. Old Man Green looked momentarily indignant.

"Well, Marcus," he said, "since you feel so strongly about this and since General George Patton isn't handy, I'll do it."

"Yes, sir," Marcus said. "How about a freshener for your drink, sir?" He approached with the ice bucket and whiskey.

"Dear, it's before lunch," Mrs. Green objected.

"Just a half, if you please, Marcus, for Bill and me. Our dividend."

"Yes, sir."

"Just a half? Well, I suppose a half wouldn't hurt."

"No, ma'am, a half won't hurt nobody."

HABERDASHERY, HARDWARE, PREMONITIONS

After lunch, they took naps. Around three, the tailor arrived. Mr. Green shot off to the office. The tailor was not some special man. He wasn't Green's personal tailor but was good enough for most occasions and would do, considering the funeral was day after next.

Mrs. Green ordered socks and underwear, neckties, slacks, shirts, a pair of shoes, plus the dark suit. She even threw in a bathrobe and a pair of pajamas before Bill figured out what was going on. He let himself be measured in mummy-like fashion. As he had been measured around the waist, he cracked a joke that slowed nothing, but had been so off color that it had seemed out of character even to him; that started him pondering. As soon as Mrs. Green saw this, she insisted that he must have handkerchiefs.

"Hankies," Bill snickered. "Now don't that beat all."

She knew Bill was still sleepwalking, so it didn't bother her one bit. "A blue blazer and one raincoat with a liner. That should do it," she said, checking her list. "You can't be too careful, springtime in Kentucky being what it is."

"We'll have it out this time tomorrow, Mrs. Green."

"Fine," she replied. "Please toss in an umbrella or two, both black with walnut handles. Mr. Green's looks as if it's evolved."

When Green got back from the office, it was almost dark, yet purples and pinks floated in the western sky. Bill was having a drink beside the pool. Mrs. Green was sipping her cup of tea. Green stormed in, cussing lawyers and the government, taxes, and others he clumped together as fools. He might as well have been talking to geraniums, since nobody knew what he was talking about. Marcus appeared with his highball, a touch-up for Bill, and a soda for Mrs. Green, who opened her mouth and soon wished she hadn't.

"Your Woosleys popped by for a quart of milk and were wondering about tools. The baby thought you must have forgotten."

Sharper tongues than hers had surrounded Green all afternoon. He took a long sip of his drink and whispered, "Theodora, I did not forget. I was called to town."

Rufus charged and jumped on Green, which probably saved the day. The dog was so slobbery, grateful, and rambunctious that he could have made anyone feel worthy. Green rubbed the dog's bony head and tugged his ears. He glanced at Bill and nodded.

"Let's go."

Bill shrugged and glanced at his half-empty glass. Green saw this and instructed Marcus to fortify the jeep with supplies and to load it with tools, as well. He excused himself to change his clothes and told Bill to meet him on the driveway.

Bill felt caught in the middle, but Theo smiled, told him to hang on tight, because this was one of those nights. She implored him not to let her husband out of his sight. Bill scratched his head. Mrs. Green informed him this was Marcus's job, but that he was spared tonight. Bill looked over at Marcus who was gathering the ice bucket and whiskey. Marcus grinned.

They bounced downhill in the dark, whiskey, and ice cubes

f.ying. Green wasn't too much of a driver. Besides, he was mad as hell. He mumbled under his breath, and between growls of the engine, sprays of gravel, and the jolting squeaks of the springs, Bill came to understand that the last straw had been deposited on top of Green's load. Though he cursed Mrs. Green and all of her ilk, Marcus, North Koreans, revenue agents, unions, and freeloading bastards everywhere, Bill saw through the bombast. Green needed to stretch out somehow, so he held on tight as they bounced across the field toward what—unbeknownst to either—would soon be Bill's floating home.

As soon as they squeaked to a halt, Green tooted the horn. Bill reminded him that the baby might be asleep. Green nodded. They tiptoed in their fashion up to the stepladder that served as the entrance and knocked lightly. Green knocked again, and in a hoarse whisper, asked if anyone was home. Bill nodded in approval; Green nodded back, but still there was no answer. After a few minutes, they gave up. Green wanted a look-see, but Bill pointed out that it was near dark as pitch. It wasn't quite, but Green agreed that there wasn't much point, which relieved Bill, who hadn't wanted to be around Green when he saw and smelled what it was like inside.

They offloaded tools—axe, crosscut saw, pruning saw, clippers, and such—then fixed a drink and leaned against the jeep. It was overcast with no moon. All they could hear was a chorus of frogs, some birds, and semitrucks grinding gears, storming out of the valley northeast toward Cincinnati.

As far as Bill was concerned, he was babysitting Green, and the way Green looked at it was the other way around. Mrs. Green had told him that Bill had to blow and that he should watch him, be near, close as kin. The two men stood there looking out for each other, while sky turned dark gray and frogs celebrated spring.

"Do you favor rib eyes or T-bones? Strip sirloin is all right, but I think a T-bone with an Idaho is about the perfect cap for a night."

Bill said he wasn't that hungry. Green said he wasn't either, but later they might be, and Bill couldn't argue with that. They bounced back up the hill, spun through the gravel with Bill holding on for dear life, then they raced down the driveway, Green jabbering like mad and Bill not knowing the first thing he was talking about.

What most likely saved a heap of trouble was a cop who had someone pulled over at the end of Green's driveway where it intersected River Road. The road was blocked by the patrol car. Green charged up and scrunched to a stop, and the cop dashed over, ticket pad in hand to offer to move his car. Mr. Green, with Bill tugging on his elbow, told the officer to take his time, that there was no hurry. The officer thanked him but moved the car anyway. Bill and Green slipped by and waved. This small sign of respect calmed Green.

"Nice fellow," Bill said.

"Nice enough if you're on the right side of things," Green replied, as he studiously stayed on the road. "Right side of the yellow line." He laughed, and Bill thought he heard him say, "slower than a tortoise," but he couldn't clearly make it out. The cop was back around the bend and they were charging again, rolling toward the Point. Still, Bill was happy to observe that Green was driving a bit more thoughtfully than before.

The Point was a joint close enough to the intersection of River Road and the Cincinnati highway to have earned its name. You could tell people how to get there from either road. People always found it. Some referred to a bar, some a restaurant, but it was both, and the type of crowd gathered there depended upon the hour.

CHAPTER 2

AMAZING GRACE

When Bill and Green walked through the door, it was a little late for family fare, but a tad early for the raunch some locals could provide. Green looked satisfied as he sauntered to a corner. Within moments, they were served.

The place was dark, lit by candles and dim lights mostly blocked out by shapes hunkered around the bar. Bill noticed bathrooms were handy. That pleased him. He had forgotten where they were and realized that thought like something tangible as the tip that Green slipped into the waitress's apron. He somehow let that notion waddle off as she had, twirling her tray.

He found himself wishing that it was too nice a day to be sitting in a dingy bar, but it was night. Where did he have to go anyway? Green fired a cigar. The "Tennessee Waltz" was playing on the radio behind the bar. The smoke fog softened edges. Over in the far corner, a couple stood and started to dance. Cronies hunkered at the bar, elbowed each other and nodded. They turned to watch the dance. Bill noticed the girl had long blonde hair.

"Let's go fish the creek for an hour or two."

Bill shrugged.

"Look," Green said, "I got all the gear and Marcus can seine minnows and dig worms. Not all day, of course, but we can put in down at Crabby's. Only costs three bits."

"Won't cost," Bill said, wishing he hadn't, because he didn't want to think about fishing or anything. He nodded. "Nope, not a dime," he added.

"Aw, Bill," Green said, looking somewhat concerned. "I don't care about money—want some fish for breakfast, that's all."

Bill nodded. "I can't guarantee fish, but it won't cost. I own that land; the Crab rents from me."

"I had forgotten that was your daddy's land."

"Yeah and his daddy's. That pile of rocks at the mouth of the creek was my granddad's tavern. Almost 213 acres of about the sorriest river bottom a man ever owned."

"Damn, I can't believe I forgot that," Green said.

"Forgot what?"

"That your family owned that. Ain't worth much, I'll grant, but it's almost my front yard, as you can imagine. Hell, I look down every morning when I open my bedroom curtains, the bathroom window when I shave. I see it when I drive downhill. You ever want to sell, let me know."

A baby started wailing in the far corner. The bartender turned up the radio. Bill chuckled and said, "That song tickles me."

"I'm serious," Green said. "Talk to me first before you let go of it."

"I ain't planning to sell. Pays its way, I suppose."

The baby abruptly stopped crying. Bill looked but could see nothing but shadows. Green held up two fingers and soon more drinks were delivered. Bill reached for his wallet, but Green said, "Tab." Sophie, the waitress, bowed and apologized for the baby that was making so much noise. Green shrugged. Sophie whispered something in his ear. Green's eyes widened and then narrowed as he peered into the corner. He gave Sophie an inquiring look. He shook his head and smiled. No big deal is what he said. She laughed and pocketed her tip.

"Woman's got her tits out suckling her pup," Green chuckled.

"Everybody's got to eat," Bill said.

"That's about what I told Sophie. Say, you ready for that T-bone?"

"Getting closer all the time," Bill said. He stared at his drink, which was nearly empty. "Where the hell they find these glasses, a sewing shop? They're tiny as thimbles."

Green raised four fingers. The next round leapfrogged that problem.

"Well, now this is a bit more civilized," said Bill.

"Indeed," said Green, "and it's my private stuff. This ain't for sale."

"Not yet, you mean," Bill said.

"Not tonight anyway." Green laughed. "Wouldn't want to turn the revenue man's head. He hasn't stepped on it yet, so it ain't full of water. He'd get a stiff neck, he got a whiff of this sweetness. To hell with those bastards; dealt with one all afternoon."

Bill smiled and took a swig. Smooth as silk, tingly on the lips, warm as it entered the throat, fire as it slid down his esophagus, inferno when it hit the belly. In spite of himself, Bill's eyes, then his voice, betrayed him.

"Good God!" he croaked. He cleared his throat or tried. "I'm afraid to smoke. Tell you that much."

"Let's go fishing."

"Tonight?"

"No, tomorrow. You will enjoy it."

Before Bill could reply, the blonde woman bumped as she wiggled past, which sloshed drink onto the table. Sophie was on the spot with a rag. Bill waved her off, but she insisted, grabbed his drink and had it topped off. Sophie said that she was real sorry, but after the blonde woman came out of the bathroom, she bumped into Green so hard he dropped his cigar. Bill recognized her at about the same time Sophie started mopping up once again. It was Valerie from down at the boat.

"Mr. Green, we are so sorry," Sophie said.

"Oh, howdy do, big sweet daddy man. Here, hold my baby, snaggle tooth," she said. She thrust the child at Bill and let go as she settled onto Green's lap. Bill caught the child and held her close, while Green managed to settle his drink and juggle Valerie, who was squirming like a sack of cats.

"Well, I'll be damned," he said as he recognized who she was. "What the hell are you doing here?"

"Truth is," she said, "we're celebrating my birthday, but the main thing is that the doctor said today that the baby ain't sick like he thought, so we're double celebrating." She gave Green a kiss on the forehead. "Celebrating kindness of people that give other good people a chance. Praise be, you are the Lord's own angel."

Green looked flabbergasted as she kissed him again. He looked at Bill with eyes glittering with something other than joy. Bill gave the baby's bottom a little pinch that caused the baby to whimper and squirm. He held her up for Momma, who looked as relieved as Green did when she stood and took the child in her arms.

"My little precious," she cooed, looking like an angel herself. "She says she wants to go to her table." She smiled a decidedly unmotherly smile at Green. "Say goodbye to the nice granddaddies, precious. See you soon, daddy man," she said, flashing Green a look that puzzled him. The glance she dropped on Bill did not puzzle him at all. As she turned away, she stuck out her tongue at him, but so quickly anybody would have assumed she was licking her lips.

"Cute child," Green said, relighting his cigar.

"Which one you referring to?"

"Why the one in the dress, who else?" Green chuckled. "Oh hell, you know I'm just fooling around. Now let's talk fishing. That's something we might do something about."

By the time they got around to ordering, the kitchen had closed, but Sophie fixed some hamburgers to go. She snuck them out in a plain brown sack and was tipped like hell for her efforts. The interesting corner was empty, but in the parking lot, there was laughter coming from around the side of the building that was lit by taillights—a woman's laughter, mixed with a garble of words that Bill could not catch but thought he heard that someone was somebody's angel. Bill said nothing and climbed in behind the wheel of the jeep. Green had taken on too much hooch to drive. When Bill flipped on the headlights, they lit a pickup truck and two men leaning. One held up a bundle and jiggled it beneath the moon. Bill could see that the baby was smiling.

Next morning, they were to fish. Marcus would take care of details. As soon as Bill parked the jeep, he was crushed beneath staggering fatigue. All he said was, "Whoa." Green steered him onto the sunporch, where he sank gratefully back into pillows. A few hours later, he took a bite of his hamburger, then the wee morning sparrows piped it up. He plopped back still chewing and fell dead asleep.

BASICS

Dawn brought more of Old Man Green and coffee, and Bill wasn't sure he could handle either, but did and choked down some hamburger, too. Green handed him some toothpaste and a brush, and Bill stumbled off, feeling like he had been staring into the eyes of some fat ghost. In the mirror, he saw another ghost, but this one skinny and almost recognizable. Scruffy enough to make a dog howl and children dive beneath blankets. He chuckled under his breath and had to remind himself that he was still alive, that the war, his war, was over. Then he thought of Sarah, or not so much thought of her, but felt her. He sat down on the can. His fingers dug into the back of his head. He clenched his entire body from head to toe. He might have won and stopped breathing if Green hadn't tapped lightly on the door.

They got down to Crabby's, and Green said "Damnation" when he saw the locked gate, but Bill raised a fat ring of keys.

"You got a key?" Green asked. "Looks like you've got keys to everything."

"Key to this lock," Bill said. "The rest ain't worth diddly."

Green backed the boat down the ramp like an expert and Bill tugged on the rope and the engine fired off, first try. Green parked the rig while Bill took inventory of their stuff: a basket of sandwiches, a thermos of coffee, a bucket of minnows, a can of fat worms, three fancy rods, a net, and a cooler of beer.

Bill watched Green saunter down the ramp and onto the dock. The water was still, flat as glass, but Bill felt he was tossing on the Pacific, but he couldn't understand why with the water so calm until Green clambered aboard.

"Tallyho, mate. Let's slay fish."

They putted upstream. Green poured coffee, then fired a cigar. He looked next door to heaven. It made Bill feel good to see Green like that. Bill didn't know why he had turned the bow upstream, but there were no objections, so he held his course. Green unwrapped a sandwich and offered half. Bill declined and lit a smoke. Green chomped and puffed. Just when Bill figured that Green had no destination in mind, the man pointed to the bank below the bridge they were approaching and said, "There."

They dropped the hook.

"Minnows or worms? Your choice," Green said.

"What you mean?"

"Kind of early to wager money. What you say that the first who lands a fish don't have to clean 'em?"

"What about Marcus?" Bill asked.

Green guffawed.

"That's another thing Marcus won't do. Besides he can't do it worth a shit."

"Worms," Bill said.

No sooner had Bill said that than Green pawed the minnow bucket, and next thing you know, stuck bait in the water. Bill shook his head and took his time. He hooked the old worm in such a way as to leave some tantalizing bit dangling and was satisfied with everything but the size of the hook, which was in his estimation, rather large for anything smaller than a sailfish.

As he threw the rig next to a stump, he asked Green where he had picked up his tackle. Green was so busy steering his minnow up to a sunken log he didn't answer.

"Pretty big hooks for the creek, wouldn't you say?" Bill asked.

"Not necessarily."

"Well, I've seen bigger, but these are ocean hooks, am I right?"

"Florida," Green said, "and if you don't want to clean fish, you better mind your bait."

Bill figured that Green was nuts, so he drank coffee, smoked, and let the poor worm drown. He concentrated on the mist coming up off the water. No way any creek fish could bite such a hook. That's what he was thinking when Green jerked over and his rod sank, and he said, "Wahoo wah!" Then, "Hot damn!"

The strike didn't sink the bow but did spill coffee and Green was yelling for the net over and over, but then the fish took off not fast, but steady. Green allowed as how the fish had some play. Well, this went on a couple of minutes. It was a monster fish, a channel cat with eyes far apart as a man's—then snap goes the line.

"Damn!" Green shouted. "How the hell can you say the hook's too small? What about that, fish cleaner?"

"Too bad he got away. He might have fertilized a whole row of corn."

Green popped open his tackle box, and Bill noticed that he chose a little bit smaller hook. As Green tried to poke the line through the eye of the smaller hook, Bill noticed a slight tug on his line.

"Too bad he made up his mind to toodle-oo, for he was certainly fine," he said as he gently reeled in a hand-sized sunfish. "Net," he said.

"You don't need a net for that thing."

"Hell, I don't," said Bill. "What's fair is fair."

Green scooped and Bill popped it off the huge hook and plopped it into the bucket.

A sunfish.

Neither remembered what they talked about by afternoon, but if you had been listening like some wise crow, you would have known that this trip was not for nothing.

Inside of Green's teasing was scarcely veiled kindness that said you are welcome without saying anything and as the morning advanced, Bill's responses sharpened.

Banter back and forth. Fish wouldn't bite. Green blamed it on

Bill, who blamed it on him. The little sunfish flashed and thrashed. Bill called it his little dumpling, which drove Green crazy.

"If that thing's a dumpling, I would rather starve," he said.

After a while, Bill allowed as how he was tired of sitting there, Green agreed, so Bill tugged on the starter rope and as they were about to putt upstream, they looked at each other at once.

"The anchor, marine, the anchor," said Green.

Because the motor was lucky to have all of three horsepower and Bill had gone for a slow, smooth takeoff, there was only a slight tug, which slackened as Bill killed the engine.

"Now, Green, damn if that weren't your job."

The anchor, which hadn't even set, plopped in the boat with weed and silt. Green was laughing.

"Ain't we a pair?" he said. "How the hell did we survive the South Pacific? Can you tell me? Here I captained a boat and didn't know anything. Before I shipped out, one of my daddy's friends gave me a book, *The Raft Book: Lore of the Sea and Sky*, and I can still remember the introduction. Listen. 'This book has been written for those who, without previous experience in navigation and without navigating instruments, find themselves in small craft in the open sea and who have to make their way to land.' Can you believe I can still remember that? Hell, by the time they took me in, the fact that I could read and wanted to serve, was all they needed, even my age. Didn't even check my weight. 'When full moon is rising, the sun's always setting. When the full moon is setting, the sun's always rising.'"

Bill said, "Hell, they were desperate. We all were, remember? Those things burn in. You do what you have to."

"Yeah, but I couldn't have read star charts with God helping me, yet I can still remember, saying 'Yes sir' like it was day before yesterday."

"Burned in forever. That's all I can figure," Bill said as he noticed something contrasting with the early spring foliage. Something not quite pink or white or beige or blonde. Something not stationary, moving slow. It sure wasn't a goose and it wasn't a heron.

Put simply, it was Valerie toweling after her bath. To Bill, her cover-up motions were less than convincing. They seemed to be pointing, rather than concealing, but he wasn't convinced until she bent to pick her child up and ran up the incline with the baby pressed into her breast. In a flurry of blue and pink, most of her and the baby disappeared as she stomped the steps of the boat, then turned on the deck and glared as if she had suffered grievous trespass.

"Poor child," said Green.

"Poor child, my ass," Bill said as he continued upstream.

"Aw, now, don't be so damned hard."

"No offense, old man, but it would seem to me that you are the one hard."

"That child hasn't hurt a soul."

"What you know about that, I wouldn't know," Bill said. "But listen up. Who in their right mind would hang their bare butt out in the creek for the likes of us to see?"

"She didn't know we were coming."

"No argument there. Never said she did. This sucker ain't a sewing machine. Are you saying she's deaf?"

"No, I'm not saying that," Green said.

They kept going a mile or two, when Green slashed across his throat with his forefinger and Bill shut the rig down. They drifted back slow. Used a paddle to push off stuff. Slipped up on sunning snapping turtles, wood ducks, that skittered down the creek, a heron that croaked and lifted.

Just when Bill resigned himself to a sandwich like the one that Green was making disappear, a Falls City Beer was plucked out of the cooler and pushed toward his face. He thanked Green. He picked up the church key and double-punched the can.

"Damn, Bill, did you ever, ever think we would make it?" Green squinted his eyes. It was the kind of moment that made Bill wish there was something to do with the paddle, something to busy himself with, but there wasn't anything calling for his attention except Green.

"Not really. Did you?"

Green sank in deep and reminded Bill of some hibernating creature. He peeped from beneath heavily lidded eyes like a bullfrog. A grin seemed about to precede a huge croak, but instead, his eyes flickered open a bit, he nodded, and said, "Me neither."

Then he burped one of those burps that make frogs listen. Bill laughed out loud and so did Green.

"Didn't know you had it in you."

"Nor did I," said Green, "but seriously, partner, where do we go from here?"

"Ain't sure yet but listen up. Let me see if I can recall something that might be helpful. 'A red appearance in the water, caused by minute organisms, is found in many parts of the oceans of the world but is not a reliable indication of proximity to land. A brown, or muddy, appearance in the water, however, is almost certainly the effect of silt coming from a river or estuary and consequently almost always shows nearby land.'"

"Great work, Bill, but you got it backwards. We're on a creek that leads to a river, which if we have patience, joins an ocean, but damn it, man, what the hell are we gonna do? What the hell you gonna do? Just what can I do to help?"

The spirit of play drained through the soles of Bill's shoes. He wanted to come back with something and reached in but came up empty. He stared into the bucket where the sunfish lay fighting for air.

"Mind if I throw this back?" he said.

"Suit yourself," Green said, "but we're back to even."

"Fair enough," Bill answered as he dumped the fish. Bill was surprised that Green didn't hurry to bait.

"It is surprising."

"What's that, Bill?"

"That we're here."

"No way to figure."

"Suppose we're lucky."

After a short while, they drifted past Valerie's bathing spot and eyes were peeled, but Valerie was nowhere in sight. The place, surrounded by weeds, looked desolate except for one red flower in a clay pot right next to the tools they had dropped off.

The current was slow, sun low, and it was cool. They kept drifting.

"Green, I can move up to the Melrose Inn at any time," Bill said. "Don't want to be in your way."

"Hell with that," Green replied. "I was about to say that Theodora and I would be happy if you stayed until something works out, but we want to move you off the sunporch into a guest bedroom."

"I don't want to trouble you all," Bill said.

"You don't need to be staying at the Melrose with suitcased shutouts and small-time hustlers. It is not a problem for us and if it becomes one, you can be sure Theodora will make that clear. Don't worry. You hear me? We're happy to have you. Wish we could do more."

"Thanks," Bill said. "Maybe for a few days if you wouldn't mind."

When you float down a creek with a gentle current, the breeze and what you bump into has a whole lot to do with outcome. Sometimes Bill faced where they were headed and then Green did. The whole business whopper-jawed and since no one was captain, blame for a run-in with sunken logs or low-hanging branches was nobody's fault and yet subject to debate and earnest discussion.

"What the hell! Watch where you're going," Green hollered.

"Me? Hell, it's your watch this bend."

It was jabber nonsense; both knew it. Neither was drunk, but both arrived back at the ramp with elevated moods. Crabby was his sour self and when he snatched their line and snugged it, he might have ruined their day. He wasn't called Crabby for nothing. But he was shy and when Bill pointed out that his fly was down, the Crab looked dutifully and then, of course, had to blush.

"Just teasing, Crab, now ease a bit."

Crab turned his back after securing the line and scowled before spitting tobacco juice into the creek, shrugged, and then slouched.

Hands hung dangling. Crack of ass shadow in the middle of handlebars, but then he turned his gaze back at Bill, hard and glinty like a snapping turtle. But he said nothing, just grunted.

"What's with you, Crab? Hell, we'll pay," Green said.

Crab didn't give Green a peep. He fixed his eye on Bill even harder somehow. When he spoke, Bill wished he hadn't, although what he said was, in the Crab's way, kindhearted concern.

"Mr. Maddox, I sure hope you doing all right. You doing all right?"

Bill nodded, tried not to think what he was supposed to be all right about. Green nodded that all was under control as he scrambled onto the dock, steered Crabby away and gave him the first paper money that came out of his pocket. Green whispered, "Go away."

Crabby looked pleased with the outcome. You could almost see him scrunch over and chuckle, like he might have thought the whole thing out. Green told him to get lost and he did.

This was no time for introspection. While Bill slumped in the stern of the skiff, Green backed the trailer down the incline and like magic scooped the thing up. Bill looked as mystified as the sunfish, when Green stomped down and tugged him out, dizzy, in fact, a little bit woozy.

After they had cinched down, Green tooled the rig over to the site of Bill's granddad's old tavern, which was now nothing more than stone walls and fireplace with part of a chimney.

The sun was near overhead, but not quite, so when they settled against the river side of what was left, they were shaded and that helped sandwiches slide down easily. This May, the river was up and the current swift, but both had seen much stronger. Once, Bill had seen a barn float past. Green had seen an entire three-story house. These were not tall tales. They were trying to outdo each other, but neither of them was lying. All that was drifting by now in the half-mile trudge of what looked like milk chocolate was riverbank junk—tree trunks, barrels, bottles, and cans.

Green kept his eye on a brown bottle swirling in an eddy, attempting to leave the creek and enter the larger stream, while he tried to tell Bill about the time he saw that very river charge up the creek so fast it was nobody's business.

Bill fired up a smoke, sucked on his beer, allowed as how he'd seen that too, but said, "After a downpour, a true frog strangler, I've seen this creek run out so fast it made a three-foot wall right there." He pointed at where the creek muddied the river. "If we were coming out of the creek on one of those, there would be a drop-off. Hard to imagine."

"Yeah," Green said. "Hard. Something looks so benign."

"Benign?"

"You know, gentle, like it wouldn't hurt."

"Know the word, but why the hell use it to describe this creek?"

"I meant nothing by it."

"I know."

"Bill, you okay?"

"Are you?"

When Green didn't answer, they sat in silence and didn't move until it started to sprinkle. Then it was Green who fetched two beers from the cooler. Bill thanked him when the fresh cool one touched his palm.

"Hell, Bill, I'm not used to this either. Don't know what to say and what to do."

Bill burst out laughing. He caught himself and calmed down.

"Nothing, nothing I can explain. Please, for just a minute, let's watch the river flow."

They did, which in some basic way changed everything.

After a while, Green said, "So this is your land?"

"No, not really."

"But you own it?" Green said.

"This was Granddaddy's land, not even my daddy's, much less mine."

"You own it, pay taxes, right?"

"Yeah," Bill said, "but so what? This was Granddaddy's land."

"You said that."

Bill sat puzzling, watching drift current flow south and wind pushing waves north, like nature was at cross-purposes.

"Where is harmony?" Bill said.

"Where is what?"

"Never mind," Bill replied. "Must be dreaming. The river looks to flow two directions and it's warm enough somehow to be summer, yet still bugs ain't out."

"How 'bout a beer, my friend?"

"Don't mind if I do," Bill answered and to Green's relief, sounded somewhat sane.

"How about a sandwich?"

"No, I'll pass the sandwich. I wouldn't want to spoil lunch."

Out of genuine concern, Green asked again what he planned to do. Bill allowed as how he wasn't quite there, but he supposed he might get back to trucking and find a place.

As Green heard Bill say this, he knew he shouldn't have asked.

When Bill heard himself speak, his voice seemed to be echoing.

"Sorry for prying."

"Hell, pry all you want. I'm tight as a drum."

"No, I'm sorry."

"Sorry about what?" Bill asked. "You haven't done anything. I ain't making too much sense right now."

They sat scrunched up against the wall and shut up. Maybe that helped. Bill had it in his mind he was looking out for Green, and Green still felt he was looking out for Bill. That was a lot of responsibility neither wanted, so when they shut up, it was a damned relief to both.

Mallards quacked, and frogs chattered. Tree frogs. The wake of a barge sloshed ashore and quickened the rhythm of wind-driven waves. Bill hadn't smelled honeysuckle sweetness in years, but it was beside him climbing the wall. As a child, he loved to suck out nectar. All he wanted was to smell faintly and allow it to grow.

He glanced at Green and saw that the man was catnapping. Bill kept quiet while new leaves whispered, and insects chanted back and forth. He noticed that there was no discoloration in any of the foliage. Everything was fresh in this late morning light, sparkling with springtime.

A breeze blew through and what had been a drip became light rain. The temperature dropped twenty degrees. Good old Kentucky; it was now sweater weather. Bill nudged Green who swatted imaginary flies and said, "Damn, what the hell? It's cold!"

Big eyes blinked yes when Bill pointed. Before they hopped in the jeep, the rain picked up and the day was so unlike the one they had shared all they could do was shake it off.

DRESSED TO KILL IN DOG HEAVEN

Back at the house, lunch wasn't exactly waiting, but almost. Mrs. Green instructed the two men to wash. Bill hadn't changed clothes in two days, but after lunch that was about to be remedied.

Eggs benedict with real Canadian bacon. Green ate with enthusiasm; Bill picked and sawed. As soon as his plate was scraped free of hollandaise and egg yolk, Green patted his belly and scooted off to fight wars downtown. Bill was inclined to nap, but Mrs. Green had other ideas. As Marcus cleared plates, he was instructed to guide Bill into the guest bath and to lay out a robe and toiletries, and so it happened that after lunch, Mr. Maddox had a bath.

Luxury had never been his goal. He had hoped to survive, but hard to deny that he felt special in this steamed-up tile room with sunken tub big enough for four and stretched out accordingly. Marcus had placed his wrapper, as he called it, on a bench beside a fluffy towel, but Bill was so comfortable in the lightly scented water, he was in no hurry to dry. So damned comfortable that he leaned back, braced, didn't soap, sank, and might have gone under, if Marcus hadn't pounded on the door and asked if he wanted anything. Nothing any man could bring. He said, "No," and then, remembering his manners, said, "No thank you, Marcus, but thank you just the same."

In the course of an hour, he had shaved, trimmed all nails, plucked nose hairs and even flossed. Somehow, he managed not to remember the reason. He lost himself and when Marcus tapped and called his name, he was sorry to be interrupted but eager for what might be in store.

Just before he opened the door, wrapped in his robe, he smelled fire that no soap smell could bury or cover. The rancid, tangy smell of scorch and smoke. Before he could think too much more, Marcus pounded on the door.

"Mr. Maddox, Mr. Melton, your tailor, is here, sir. Please hurry yourself," Marcus said and opened the door. Bill stood there stiff as a Roman senator. Marcus, who was in shock to see the man slicked back and scrubbed clean, hesitated before he reached out to lead him into the dressing room. As he felt Marcus take his elbow, Bill motioned at his clothes in a crappy heap on the floor. His eyes jittered when he glanced at Marcus, who nodded and urged him to follow.

He never saw those clothes again.

Before Bill was led into the fitting room, Marcus guided him to boxer shorts as soft and silky as a lady's undergarment. Then the robe came off and an undershirt went on that was slinky like pages of some French magazine. Next, socks, which were unlike any socks Bill had ever worn before. Marcus told him it would be all right and pulled up his own pant leg to prove it was so, and with that, Bill nodded and slipped into calf-high silk stockings.

"Goddamn, I feel like a French whore. Keep your distance, Marcus. Don't you get any ideas; this ain't me."

"Me neither. That's the way they are," Marcus said as he backed up a little.

"I ain't kidding, Marcus."

"I know that, boss, but you so convincing. I think I'll keep my distance."

Bill looked into Marcus's laughing eyes and shook his head and cussed.

"Where's the rest of my costume, Kilroy?" he blustered.

"That seems to be it. Now if you will follow me, sir."

"Who's in that room?"

Marcus had wanted to guffaw but didn't. As he opened the door, he said, "Ain't nobody here but us chickens, Mr. Maddox. Now if you will follow me."

Marcus could grin, and Bill stamped on his toe as he passed. Marcus was shod, and Bill was not, so no harm was done, but Mrs. Green saw the gesture and Glidden T. Melton did as well. Bill cringed when he heard G. T. suggest that he slip into the trousers.

He swallowed hard and did.

They fit. The shirt fit. The sport jacket fit. The suit fit, black as a crow. The tie fit. Red as a pope.

All worked, which pleased G. T., whom Bill had started to admire for his efficiency. The man was good. Bill looked at Marcus and could almost hear snickering. He felt his lower jaw poke out and squinted, but Marcus looked to Mrs. Green and asked if she and Mr. Melton would like wine. She declined and asked for tea.

"Oh, my God," Mrs. Green exclaimed. "We forgot footwear! Oh, my God."

"Jesus Christ," Bill said with relief. "Is that all?

"Bill, you know full well, it is not conceivable that you will wear those old boots."

"Mrs. Green," Mr. Melton said, "You have thought of footwear."

He smiled a smile that his soul dripped out of. Bill's eyes opened wide in disbelief as she nodded emphatically.

With a flourish, G. T. popped a box and the shiniest pair of black shoes that could ever be were in his hands. He put them on the floor and opened another and out came a comfort shoe, called a moccasin, with a deep cordovan finish. Melton grinned and Marcus, who caught Bill's eye before he reentered the dressing room with the tea, covered his mouth. Bill darkened; Theo lightened; Melton grinned ear to ear; Marcus didn't even spill a drop.

Thus, was Bill Maddox decked out.

It took time to get accustomed, but he had help from Theo, Marcus, and Green. For example, that afternoon he wore a blue oxford shirt with khakis and shoes without laces and all told him that he looked fine. Of course, they were right because he did.

He went through it all and ended with a drink in his hand, sauntering in front of evergreens at the deep end of the pool. From there, he left reflections of new greenery and entered a path bounded by moss-laden limestone benches that led into a fern garden.

A sturdy limestone bench carved by some local sculptor squatted, so weighty it most likely had been moved only once. Bill sat down.

There was a fountain close and water tinkled down an abstract form. Water splashed into a reflection pool that glinted with goldfish. Bill sat awhile before moving to another bench deeper into the garden. He was immediately surprised by a young boy. The kid no more than nine or ten, he guessed. They startled each other. The kid came buzzing from beneath the hedge.

"Who you?" Bill asked.

"Who you?" the kid replied.

"Well," drawled Bill, "this could go on forever, so I'll ask your name."

"Joshua."

Bill held out his right hand to the bright-eyed kid and said, "Bill Maddox. Nice to meet you, Josh."

"Name ain't Josh. A josh is a joke and I ain't no joke. My name is Joshua and aim to be a preacher. Don't call me Josh and I ain't joking."

Bill scratched his forehead. Maybe twelve? Maybe eleven? Intense beyond his years, for sure.

"All right, Joshua, so what brings you here, besides being a wandering preacher?"

Joshua shook a head that seemed too big for his body, looked straight at Bill, and said, "How come you dressed so fancy? I know who you are. Momma said you ain't nobody special. What you doing here?"

"Son, that's no way for a preacher to talk, if you are in fact."

"Might be that's so, but who are you that's asking? Momma says you eat like a bird."

"So, preacher, who is this momma that you keep talking about? And who are you to worry about what I do or do not eat?"

The boy's amused expression and shrug let on—to Bill's relief—that he was only kidding. Still Bill was curious. Who was this kid?

Joshua told Bill that his momma was Miss Laura, the Greens' cook. He said she ran the kitchen and that she knew everything going on. He said this with great pride, but his eyes kept flickering and belied the confidence he tried to project.

"Why you so dressed up if you're nobody special?"

"Who says I'm not and why your eyes poking every shadow? What are you looking for, boy?"

"I ain't a boy," Joshua said defiantly.

"I was, at your age," Bill answered. "What you looking for? What's wrong?"

"My dogs got loose," the boy blurted out.

"From where?"

"From the pen behind the barn. They dug out. If they get in the garden again, Mrs. Green will kill them."

"No, she won't," Bill said. The boy was unconvinced. Then he saw a couple of dog tails wagging in the back of the garden. He saw dirt clods fly. One of the dogs barked.

"Them yours?"

"Oh, no," the child said with a frozen expression.

"Call 'em," Bill said.

The child clenched his teeth, tensed, and shifted his weight one foot to the other, motioned for the dogs to come, but no sound came from his mouth.

"Call your dogs, son, for goodness sakes."

"I can't, mister."

"Well then, calm down. They're just digging moles."

"Mrs. Green will put 'em off. She told me," he said with pain washing down his face.

"No, she won't. I'll talk to her, okay? Will they come?"

Dirt was flying. The boy looked like he was weighing two evils.

"Damn it, child, call your dogs!"

The young preacher child looked at Bill sideways, swallowed, shrugged like he knew he was doing something naughty. As Bill shook his head, the boy cut loose.

"Honky, Cracker, Cracker, Honky! Come here!"

That's all it took. The motley rascals trotted up. The one crunching the mole in his mouth looked pleased with himself. When Bill went to pat him, he growled.

"That must be Honky," Bill asked.

"No, that's Cracker. She's a little touchy."

"Come over here, Honky," Bill coaxed in a gentle, scratchy voice. The dog walked over and allowed his ears to be stroked, and not to be left out, Cracker choked down the mole and trotted over, too.

"You like dogs, don't you?"

"Mostly, but it depends," Bill replied.

"On what?"

"On what the no-goods' names are and who names 'em," Bill said. "That's what it depends on, Joshua."

Bill stared hard at the boy, who edged back. The dogs were now licking Bill's hands. The boy smiled a little nervously, eyes twinkling.

"You're kidding."

"Can you be sure?"

"Don't know. Ain't sure, but I didn't name 'em. My daddy did before he went away."

The boy said "went away" with great solemnity and looked down.

"Where'd he go, son? Where'd your daddy go?"

"Off to Korea four years ago on Momma's birthday, but Daddy's in heaven now, and I want to be a preacher, and I'm going to learn all about where my Daddy is."

The boy nodded, his mind set. Bill nodded back. He stroked his forehead before he looked up at the kid. The boy looked straight back.

Before he could say a word, the boy grabbed the dogs by their collars and backed up. Bill slumped, swallowed, took a deep breath almost like he knew what was coming. He stared at the boy as if he thought he saw a devil or an angel and he didn't know which.

"Momma says your wife is in heaven. If she knows my Daddy, would you tell me so?"

Bill inhaled deeply and blew through his lips.

"Yes, Joshua, I would," he said as he stood. "Lord knows, damn it, I would."

"You shouldn't cuss," Joshua said, backing off.

"Momma's calling, son, and you're right about cussing. Skedaddle!"

The boy scrammed. Bill retraced steps back to the deep end of the pool and stared at the drain, chromed and clean. He shook his head like a dog with fleas and then Cracker ran up, followed by Honky, who took sloppy laps of the pool. Bill knew what was coming next, and sure enough, Joshua burst through the bushes extending one finger.

"Look what landed on my shirt, a monster." The boy held out a red-eyed, black-bodied cicada.

It was a seventeen-year locust. They were coming out of the ground after years of feeding on roots. Soon carcasses would be everywhere, the ground scattered with brown husks they discarded. At once, they began their singsong chatter, zagged and swooped clumsily through the humid spring air. They alighted on every living thing and clung in a way that looked accidental.

NATURE'S CHORUS AND THE RITES OF MAN

Seventeen years. The cicadas had come out the year he first laid eyes on Sarah. He was bothered. She was not. He could not stand the crazy, siren-like crescendo. She found it fascinating. He found her judgment faulty, which was no small thing, since the critters were chanting incessantly. Everywhere he tried to be with her that spring, there they were. She found them interesting. He found her enthralling. His attentions irritated her, but her smile and something in her voice kept him from noticing. He knew she was wonderful and the cicadas chattered and droned through a lovelorn spring. He held hands with her a couple of times. For her, the cicadas were nature's chorus. He had finally conceded that as ugly, creepy and red-bug-eyed as they were, that she was right, that they were bound to be the Almighty's chorus. He knew right then underneath old hackberry, elm, and oak trees that she was the one the chorus was singing about. That's the way he had felt, the way he felt still.

"Get used to it, son. They'll be around for a while. They don't hurt."

Bill kept on walking back to the house. Out of the corner of his eye, he saw the boy remove his belt and slip it through the collar of one of the dogs.

Drinks before dinner and Eisenhower on the news talking about reducing spending before reducing taxes and Green, florid, bug-eyed, emphatically insisting the general was wrong.

The veal was tasty, so was the Bibb lettuce. One of the Green kids, Gavin, was in town from college, and knew nothing of what made dinner strange.

The service was at eleven. The clatter of knives and forks, and talk of grade point averages, the frat house, all threaded into the conversation about how they would leave at 10:40.

The boy seemed like a good kid but kept staring.

"Gavin, mind your manners," Mrs. Green said. "Your daddy and Mr. Maddox served together."

"Fine, but he looks right through you."

"Sorry, son, I ain't myself."

Green butted in. "Don't you have a party?"

The young man excused himself and left.

"The young ones don't have any idea."

"I'm grateful," Bill said, "for all you've done. I guess I am hanging by a thread. Seems like a fine young man."

"Bill, trust that everything's going to work out," Theo said.

"Momma, ring the bell," Green said.

She did, and Marcus appeared.

"No way I could ever pay you back, but I'll try."

"I know you will," Green said. "No need to go into that now."

Fatigue clobbered Bill in the back of the head and transfixed his eyes. Before his chin touched his chest, Mrs. Green motioned to Marcus.

"I'm a stumbling fool, Marcus," Bill said as he was led through sunset-lit rooms.

Although true, Marcus assured Bill it wasn't. He opened the door to a bedroom that could have held every room in Bill and Sarah's house. He pointed out the bathrobe and slippers, the towels and washcloths. He opened the closet where Bill's new clothes were hung and opened a drawer that contained socks and underwear. When Bill sank onto the bed, Marcus offered to help him undress. Bill waved him off and sank back into the softest pillow ever imagined.

A knock on the door hit him with fear so strong he jumped out of bed. In confusion, he fell over a chair and when Marcus opened the door, Bill shouted he should keep down.

"Mr. Maddox, Mr. Maddox. You're dreaming, sir."

Bill squinted, looking side to side.

"So I am. Carry on."

Marcus gently led Bill to understand that a certain someone needed to talk to him. Bill tried to shake cobwebs out of his head.

"Who the hell?"

"It's some detective from downtown, sir. He says he needs a word."

To Marcus's surprise, Bill came to right quick. He led Bill to the front door. Green was there, carrying on, trying to run off the man by saying there was no point. Why tonight?

"I'm Maddox."

Green backed away.

It was a list of questions, each one preceded by an apology. "Where were you (sorry to be asking, sir) when the guilty party . . .? Can you verify your whereabouts, when the party in question, committed these crimes? Is it true that the guilty party was in your employ?"

"Yes, it's true. What is this all about?"

"Sorry, sir, but we've been looking for you for two days. It's routine. Have to file a report, sir."

Bill clenched his jaws.

"First time I've slept in two days."

"Sorry, sir, I have orders."

"Use your imagination." He slammed the door, then marched off like he owned the joint. Marcus and Green nodded and smiled. Bill was so pumped with indignation that it wasn't until dawn that grief dragged him under. Another knock at his door.

Not that Bill wasn't a bathing man, but Mrs. Green decided before nightfall that Bill might need encouragement to spruce up in the morning. She was right, of course.

Groggy, in a clear-headed way, he followed Marcus's softly suggested instructions. He soaped off in the shower, brushed his teeth, shaved, put one silly sock on before another, and so forth. Marcus suggested that he hold off on the necktie until after breakfast. Bill carefully sipped coffee and agreed.

He ate. He drank orange juice and more coffee, allowed Marcus to adjust his tie and button his coat. Then he sat around for most of an hour.

Bill stood on pea gravel beside the Cadillac. Mrs. Green adjusted her husband's collar. Marcus stood in his livery off to the side. The cicadas were singing much, much louder than before. The day was already hot and the singsong, zigzag, chattering, droning fools loved heat.

Their high-pitched sirens rose to a pulsing wail. Curiously, up close, individually, they simply chattered. One of the choir landed on Bill's sleeve. When he brushed away, it buzzed like a novelty shop toy. His mood was foul. Suddenly, he was more irritated and angry than sad. That puzzled him. He loosened his necktie. Mrs. Green crunched through the gravel and cinched him back. He thanked her.

Then, a funny thing happened as they rolled down the hill. Nothing anyone said or did, but as strange to Bill as if earth had become sky and sky became earth. He knew. He knew for a fact they were driving downhill, but if he hadn't known, he would have bet his last dollar that they were ascending. It was a perspective thing that puzzled him and made him dizzy. No one else seemed to notice, all looked solemn and straight ahead. Bill decided to keep this revelation to himself. Up was down and down was up. He couldn't explain what was right before his eyes.

"Oh, my goodness, Bill, please get it off."

"Hold still, Theo," Bill said and picked the buzzing cicada off her shoulder and tossed it out the window.

"They won't hurt, you know."

"I know, but it wouldn't do to take a locust to church."

Bill noticed that even Marcus chuckled. He managed a smile as they drove past the Pine Bar and Creekside Auto, where he saw Jess and Ham smoking cigarettes and talking to some green pickup guy. Business as usual, but then Bill remembered war was like that. Life goes on and on, and then doesn't.

At the fork in River Road, they passed Mrs. Robeson's, which tripled as a store, post office, and telephone switchboard. Then they left the flat and zoomed up the green-spring canopied hill and at the summit, right before the turn into the church, there were four or five men covered in white sheets or robes, holding signs: Nigras Back to Africa, States Rights Are White Rights, Impeach Earl Warren.

"Just keep on, Marcus. Pay no mind," Green said.

The men waved signs. Marcus accelerated.

"Marcus, in the name of all that's holy, stop this car and *let me out now*!"

Marcus slammed the brakes. Green wondered what the hell, but Bill was out the door.

Bill charged with fists level with his ears and the sheeted ones raised their arms, open handed. A photographer from the paper captured it on film. At first, it looked like a meeting of the minds and then Bill cut loose, reached down, scooped gravel and stones, and quick as a shortstop, let fly. The vileness of his cursing made Mrs. Green turn her head. The deadliness and accuracy of the launched stones impressed, but he did not stop charging. Like a man possessed, he seemed to be ten, and robed creatures fled the church property. Bill stood in the middle of the road, pointing to his chest.

"You goddamn fools! You chicken-shit cowards!"

Bill didn't notice he had traffic blocked. He stood and glared for a full five minutes, then when they huddled, he walked back to the Cadillac.

"Excuse me," he said. "It just wasn't fitting."

As the car crunched forward toward the church and Bill caught his breath, he was surprised to see so many cars around the circle and the young preacher in his robes walking toward them. Marcus stopped the car.

"What are they doing here?" the preacher asked, while he stamped a frail shepherd's crook.

Green said, "Bill took care of them, Reverend."

The preacher stared at the clumps of white across the road, shook his head, and walked back toward the church.

"Maybe he's all right," Bill said. "Haven't been to church since my wedding. Never seemed there was a need."

Marcus halted right before the door. The reverend caught up as they were walking up the steps. He put his hand on Bill's shoulder and squeezed gently. He leaned over and whispered into Bill's ear and hurried past.

"What did he say?" Mrs. Green asked.

"I didn't hear exactly," Bill lied.

Bill had heard him all right, but he didn't know what to make of it. Now that they were in the church being escorted to the first pew, Bill heard organ music playing and saw a whole lot more people than he had expected. He looked up at the altar and saw the cross. He lowered his eyes and saw the casket. Green clutched one elbow; Theo held the other. He swallowed hard and averted his eyes to the preacher seated off to one side. Bill was in a daze, also puzzled. What had the preacher meant, "I'll pray for you; you pray for me"?

There were flowers all over. Bill assumed that the Greens were responsible, but later discovered he was wrong. All kinds of people sent flowers, including the nursery Sarah kept the books for as well as some other clients. The Greens, of course, sent some. Miss Robeson and her daughter who worked as a nurse for some rich family, and that family sent some, too. Fred and Lucky Ruby, his closest Negro neighbors, sent some. Jim Traylor, the developer of the Negro sub-division they lived next to and that neighborhood's Baptist church sent some. So did the Creekside Fire Department. The television and radio stations sent some, along with the individual stations' owners. Hell, the mother of the boy, Ronald, who had done the awful thing, even sent some. Afterward, Mrs. Green insisted that all expressions of sympathy be acknowledged within a week, which he discovered when Mrs. Green presented him with a stack of notes to sign. At the time, he saw flowers, more than he had ever seen.

The preacher was good. He made you feel like he knew Sarah personally, but he was quick, and Bill was glad. The entire thing was over in thirty minutes. As they were walking out, Bill noticed that there were almost as many Negroes as whites. Most were in the balcony, of course, but Marcus, Mr. Jim Traylor, and a few others were seated in the back pews on the first level. There were children, too. Bill remembered how Sarah had helped the Jacob School fund-raising drive. The majority of kids were Negro.

Outside the church, everyone stood for a few minutes. The woman from the nursery, who had spoken so tenderly in her eulogy about Sarah, came over and took Bill's hand in hers. Fred Ruby approached Bill to reassure him that his stuff was safe. Mr. Traylor came over and said that the church was starting a scholarship fund in Sarah's name. Beside him stood a woman: a colored woman named Hays. She took his hands in hers and stared into his eyes.

"Your wife was a good woman. You are a good man, too."

As they drove behind the hearse, Bill could not believe how detached he felt. He lit a smoke. Mrs. Green, though disapproving, said nothing. They rolled toward Cave Hill Cemetery. Mr. Green lit a cigar. The car clouded with smoke.

"Marcus might as well light up, too," Mrs. Green said caustically.

"Yes, ma'am," Marcus replied, "but I don't smoke."

"A strong point, Marcus, if you ask me. Sam Green, if you will, at least pour us a toddy."

Green cracked open the thermos and poured into small sterling silver cups. They clinked them together; even Marcus had one.

"Happy days," Green said solemnly.

"Bottoms up," said Bill as he drained his.

"Amen," said Marcus, as he did the same.

"Please roll down the windows and pour me my dividend," Mrs. Green said, as she passed her cup forward to Green. Bill allowed he might be ready as well and, lo and behold, so was Green. Marcus said nothing at all, but Green refilled his cup and he did not complain.

On the way back from the graveside service, Green seemed more crushed than Bill.

"You're a good man, Bill Maddox," he managed to say. Mrs. Green nodded in agreement. Bill shook his head. He looked in the mirror at Marcus, but Marcus glanced away.

"I don't know for sure what you're talking about."

"What on earth made you charge those bastards? What the hell did you say to make them run?"

"The Kluckers?" Bill asked.

"They're not from around here, Bill, are they?"

"Hell, how would I know? Got no business at any funeral of mine."

"Don't think they're our county, do you?"

"Honestly, Green, I got no idea. Wherever hell is, there they belong."

"Amen," Marcus said. "Excuse me, boss."

"Forget the 'excuse me,'" Green said, as he blew out a huge puff of smoke.

Small talk ensued. Bill took part, a small part, because in his mind, things were being rearranged and stacked. He was packing up stuff he no longer had, moving stuff, but didn't know where. Fred Ruby, with his arm around Bill's shoulder, had said that his stuff was all right. His new clothes felt stiff and in the immediate present, he was thirsty. He licked his lips, but no matter how much he licked, they stayed dry.

Bill hated to ask for another drink, so he didn't. As they ascended the hill to the Green compound, he experienced a sinking feeling and drifted back to the graveside: preacher and all the surrounding faces somber, cicadas celebrating in careening mockery. One landed on preacher's prayer book, flittered off, buzzed, then crashed in the grave. Mrs. Green squeezed Bill's wrist. He wanted to scoop the critter out, not for Sarah or for his own peace of mind, but so the sorry thing could breed and somehow come back. Hard to imagine seventeen years when seventeen minutes could weigh a lifetime.

"Hate to say, but I'm hungry as a bug," Green said.

CHAPTER 3

BOAT ON BARRELS

L ater in the afternoon, Green, Bill, and Marcus drove down the hill to see how the folks at the old boat were doing. It was something to do; that's all that it was. They were drinking beer and Mrs. Green was still prettifying, so they jumped in the jeep and Marcus drove them down and across the pasture.

The cicadas were thick. They droned and whistled, flickered between the trees.

"What day is this?" Bill asked. "Damn, I don't even know what day it is."

"Saturday afternoon," Marcus said.

"Seemed like on Tuesday these rascals were chirping. Now they're screaming like the whole world's coming to an end."

Green laughed and looked back at Bill.

"Think about it, Bill. Seventeen years underground, dark as pitch, and then out into the light and your main job is to breed? Hell, you would be yelling your head off, too."

"Put that way, I suppose I would. Saturday already?"

"It ain't Sunday yet," Marcus said as the jeep bounced and came to a halt. There was no sign of the new tenants. If anything, the boat looked more abandoned than ever and the tools—in only a few days' time—were decorated with vines.

"Well, we had some rain," Green said.

Marcus and Bill held their peace.

The three of them poked around.

"Doesn't seem they've done much, does it?"

Again, Marcus and Bill held their peace.

They took a peek. Eighty degrees outside, one hundred within. Wasps flew around. The thing wasn't built right, top side anyway. It was a shanty boat that had washed up and settled. Still Green felt some wounded pride in thinking that it was somehow associated with him.

"I don't know," he said. "Bad before, but not this bad, was it, Marcus?"

"No, sir. Not this bad."

"No way," Green said, looking at dingy rubbish. They had cleared out everything but trash.

"No sir, you are right. Never this bad."

"How could it be?" Green exclaimed as he spit into a bucket that had been used for worse. "God almighty!"

"You are right, boss man," Marcus said and this time he meant it, and Bill nodded because it smelled and looked worse than two days before.

It was not hard to figure why they had left. The three of them didn't last more than a couple of minutes and two of the three had experienced wartime latrines.

Outside, the air improved with each step. Green said, "We got to clean this mess. It'll just draw worse."

They all looked at each other and nodded. Something crossed over all three faces, unspoken, yet as real as love or dread.

Bill crawled under the bottom, looked up, and was surprised to see as little rot as he saw. He poked his knife into some boards and was amazed how solid most seemed to be. Of course, there were gaps between the planks, which had dried and shrunk, and almost no caulking remained. He shaved a board. When he crawled back out into light, he saw it was an unfamiliar kind of wood.

"Damn, I know it ain't oak, but what do you think?" he said, poking the sliver out to Green.

"Cypress," Green said without looking. "What you doing carving on my boat?"

"Just checking the hull. That's where you start, ain't it? How did you know what it was?"

"I checked once myself. The guy who built this thing, whoever he was, didn't spare on materials. Rough as it is, it's built to last. Hell, I've barely touched it since '37 and look. You would swear she would float."

Both Bill and Marcus rolled their eyes.

"Well, with some work she would," Green said. "Well, damn it, I'll bet you."

Bill and Green shook their heads, but Marcus was puzzled. He saw that both his boss and Bill were scheming and, for the life of him, he could not imagine about what.

It was Saturday night. Marcus took that night off as seriously as some monks take vespers, but Marcus wasn't a monk, so it took a small bribe from Green to keep him on duty for a trip to the Point. They negotiated behind Bill's back. Mrs. Green didn't know, but had she known, would have approved.

Why she put up with Green was anyone's guess. She did though, and with a smile. If it were only money, how could that explain the fact that she was still attractive and could have jumped into all sorts of liaisons, but did not? There was something else; a deep current flowed between them. They could not have been more different.

She was straight up. He worked the underbelly. He tried to work a deal. She demanded what was right. Still, somehow, he seemed bent toward a just outcome and she knew that. She was willing to compromise a bit in deference to him. There was trust and it ran both ways.

She would have preferred that all concerned had taken a cocktail, eaten supper, and gone to bed, but even though Laura had dinner prepared, she knew that it most likely would turn into a midnight snack. She retired to her rooms and was not surprised to learn that the men were out rambling. Did she care? She cared enough to laugh and frown. There was nothing at all to be done.

Why Green wanted to hit the Point that night or why Bill went along, who could say? At least they were smart enough to let Marcus drive. Mrs. Green smiled about that. Marcus, though pleased about the extra twenty bucks, found the radio rather poor company as he waited outside in the car.

To Green's credit, he did order a steak and potato for Marcus. They meant no disrespect to Marcus. Truth was, if they had their way, he would have chowed down with them. Neither of them were what you would call prejudiced, but rules were rules. Everyone knew those rules.

Saturday night drew a different crowd; although it was early, some rowdies were there. Bill was only along for the ride and of course, Green still believed he was looking out for Bill. The joint was smoky and noisy. Honky-tonk music blasted on the radio.

Bill saw someone across the room that he thought he should be quiet about. Problem was Green saw her too, and she saw them though she acted like she hadn't.

"Let it pass," Bill said, when he saw Green flare up.

"Your ass," Green whispered as he slowly raised his bulk.

What to do?

The waitress delivered the food. As she was setting it down, something told Bill to have her box it. As he watched Green lumber to the bar, he knew why. Apparently, the waitress did too, for she did not argue. He watched Green glare into the smoky corner.

Tinkling laughter followed by guffaws. Bill watched Green swell and felt cords in his own neck tighten. Green poured down the drink he held between his forefinger and thumb. He had started to lurch toward the corner when the bartender stepped out from behind the bar with a billy club. Bill stood and was intending to move that way when the street door opened, and he saw Marcus planted there.

It happened simultaneously. Marcus stood with arms crossed. At once, somebody said, "Nigger!" The bartender nudged Green with the nightstick. The waitress handed a box of food to Bill. Green said, "Hey!" Bartender said, "Keep moving, please, Mr. Green."

"What about them?" Green yelled. "My problem, not yours," the bartender said. Then out the door on the crunchy gravel with the door slamming and commotion inside.

"Come on, boss, Mr. Bill. Been a long day."

Somehow, Marcus got Green into the car. He wasn't a big man, but his mind was made up. Green and Bill were going home.

Three cronies hunkered over steak and potatoes near the pool, with a full moon reflection jiggered by the breeze. The men attempted unsuccessfully to keep their voices down. Mrs. Green's room was directly above where they sat, so that every time one reminded another to hold it down, she turned gritted teeth into a smile. At least they were safe.

"So, where the hell are they?" Green wanted to know.

"Who cares," Bill said, and Marcus nodded.

"Stay out of this, Marcus," Green said. "What do you know about this?"

Bill looked at Marcus.

"Which do you want, Green? You want him in or do you want him out? You want him to speak or shut up? If you don't mind, I wish you would tell."

Green said, "Sorry, Marcus."

"No problem, boss."

"Sure there is. Why were they here? Why did they go?"

"They shit their nest," Bill said.

Green hoisted his glass, which was empty, rattled the cubes, and suggested a refill. Marcus excused himself and returned a few minutes later with whiskey, ice, and water.

Bill was shaking his head, saying he didn't know. Green straightened up, proffered his glass. Bill winked at Marcus and did the same. The three settled back, but within minutes, Bill didn't feel good. He fought it, but his mouth got dry and he felt dizzy. The patio tilted forty-five degrees. Green croaked like a huge frog, Marcus looked like a salamander with teeth. His own hand looked webbed. Green's voice sounded like a belch from across the swamp. Green waved his seaweed hand. Marcus blinked, nervous and skittish. Bill's heavy head, sluggish, lolled onto waterlogged arms with fingers useless; his cocktail glass, in slow motion, shattered at his feet. From a distance, Green croaked, "Marcus, Marcus."

SUNDAY FUNNIES AND TALKING TURKEY

Bill heard birds twitter, some full-throated warblers sing for joy, and damned sparrows squabbling in ivy outside the window. He stretched a leg, arched his back, opened an eye and saw what he feared: bright light on the walls. He slammed that eye shut, but the sparrow chatter wouldn't quit.

He suddenly sat up with purpose, eyes wide, searching; fingers fastening things, buttons, a zipper and such. Then he made the mistake of hesitating, still in stocking feet. He fell back into the pillow. When he awoke the second time, he glanced at the clock. This time he ought to get up, shouldn't he? A look out the window and the cicadas' ascendant song through humid glare asked, "Why? Why? Why?" When Marcus opened the door at Mrs. Green's request, he saw Bill slumped on the bed, one shoe on and one shoe off.

Marcus was spooked because Bill looked so ghastly, but when Mrs. Green poked her head into the room, he was combing his hair and seemed to be doing fine.

"Bill, I'm off to church; thought you might care to join us."

What to say didn't come immediately to mind, so he said no thanks and later wondered why. For one thing, he wasn't a church-going man. For another, he couldn't imagine what to pray for or about. His mind was tangled as the vines that were grabbing on to everything.

"No thanks," he said.

Then what? He sat on the bed. He didn't want to wander around the house or the garden.

He started to stand, then sat. He wanted this, he wanted that. The edge of the bed became his rock on which he was perched when Mrs. Green returned.

She knew what to expect. She tapped and would not have been surprised if he hadn't answered.

What she didn't know was that Laura had sent Joshua over with coffee, toast, and jam. Bill didn't need preaching. When the kid burst into his room talking about salvation, Bill pointed to the bedside table, nodded, and menacingly said, "Scram!"

With a Bloody Mary, Mrs. Green coaxed him to lunch. That and her smile, which seemed to erase doubt. When they entered the sunroom, Green was deep in the papers and Theo seated Bill in a chair next to the unread pile. Besides the local rag, the *Courier-Journal*, which Bill called "the curious urinal," there was the *New York Times*, the Detroit papers, the *Chicago Tribune*, the *San Francisco Chronicle*, and several others. Bill reached for the local funnies, which were conveniently poking out.

"Hey," Green whispered, as Theo left the room, "I've got dibs on those. Reading the papers is my job."

"The comics?" Bill asked.

"Just kidding," Green said. "Help yourself."

"Sports?" Bill asked.

"No thanks, seriously," Green said. "Keep the editorial page to yourself."

Bill ducked into Blondie and knew it was Sunday. The funnies were in color.

At cocktail hour, Green suggested they talk turkey.

"Turkey?" Bill asked.

Marcus chuckled. The suspense nearly over.

"Call it what you will," Green said. "It's best we talk."

Ice cubes tinkling and Chessie and Rufus sniffing all about their feet, they swayed in the garden in the shade of a magnolia tree, blooms swelling, while cicadas careened, thicker than flies in a stable. Marcus stood to the side.

Bill spoke first.

"I know I've got to go," he said.

Green held up his hand.

"What about the trucking business, Bill? Is that calling you?"

"No," Bill answered and surprised himself. "Look, I can leave tonight."

"No need for that, but what do you want to do, Bill?"

"If I could tell, I would, but damned if I can face that truck."

Green nodded.

"What you after? I know you want something, old man."

"No more than you."

"What you think I want?"

"Peace of mind," Green replied. "I know it's a tall order, but I believe I can help. At least my idea can, if you will entertain it."

Marcus's eyes narrowed as he watched the boss move in.

"How in hell can some idea give peace?"

"No way unless you let it," Green responded. "Listen."

At first, he whispered. Marcus could not hear a thing till Bill said, "Your ass! No damn way!"

Green upped the volume.

"Listen," he said. "Who's talking right now and all at once? But you have to admit, Bill, that your land is laying fallow and it threatens me more than it profits you. Does it profit you?"

Marcus bit his lower lip, scrunched his eyes, and wanted to say yes, to tell Bill to say yes, but said nothing.

Bill said, "Most certainly. Smith takes hay out most years and the gas dock pays handsomely, maybe not to you, but to me. What are you getting at?"

Marcus was nodding up and down like mad. Green stared off into space.

"Look, Bill, there might be some way I could help. Help us both," he added, "Realistically, how long before that land will pay your way?"

"Pay my way?"

"See, I was right," Green chortled. "You damn well thought—you and Marcus too—that I was trying to pick your pocket, but I won't and knowing you, I couldn't. Bill, if that land is worth more than a hundred an acre, it's only because I'll give two. Do you understand?

I want that land, and it ain't worth eighty, but I can rig it where you come out clean. No taxes. Hell, I don't want the gas dock. I don't even want the docks. You keep that income. I'm afraid what might happen down there."

"Which is?"

"Damn thunder and who knows! Bill, this world is changing so fast, who the hell knows?"

"Where you going?"

Green asked. "You ever heard of International Business Machines?"

"Of what?" Bill said, hoisting an empty glass.

"Of course," Green said, proffering his to Marcus.

"Old man, with respect, I say I'm just trying to figure how to live. I don't know what to say. You talking about business machines? Don't you know all I can do is stand and, thanks to you, drink."

"Look, Bill, I see you standing; where if I were in your shoes, not sure I could. Don't think for one minute I don't respect you. You have suffered—are suffering—a terrible loss. Please, hear me. I feel like I can help."

"How?" Bill asked.

"Bill, you need to start over."

Both accepted a drink from Marcus. At Green's urging, clinked glasses and warily studied each other.

"I don't plan on dying."

"Do you plan on starting over?"

"Not tonight," Bill said, light inside guttering. He waved Green away.

"I can help," Green said.

"Not this evening you can't. Damn, Green. I'm sorry, but I've got to go to bed."

"What about dinner?"

Bill's eyes started to roll, and Marcus caught him by the arm.

Green said, "Hey, get some rest, I'm sorry." Bill's eyes closed. He said nothing as Marcus led him away.

"Mr. Green is a good man," Marcus said. "In his own way, he is. Know it, Mr. Bill."

"What's this, Mr. Bill?"

"I ain't in on it."

"In on what?" Bill said as he slumped on his bed. "In on what?"

"I'm tired, too, and I don't want to talk either," Marcus said.

"What don't you want to talk about?"

"Mr. Maddox, Mr. Bill, I don't know it's my place to say."

"Your choice, damn you."

Marcus looked Bill over hard.

"Listen, you are sitting better than you know," Marcus said with a wink.

"Better than I know?"

"Yes sir, sure enough, and I swear. They want that land," he whispered.

"How bad?" Bill whispered back.

"Bad."

"Damn," Bill said.

"Say it twice," Marcus said with a smile.

"Double damn," Bill whispered. "You sure?"

Marcus nodded.

"Maybe, I'll stretch out for a few," Bill said.

"Yes, and spruce up. I could wake you in an hour."

"Could you?" Bill asked. "Then, please do, if you wouldn't mind."

"No, sir, Mr. Maddox, I wouldn't mind. I'll lay out clothes."

"You're a good man, Marcus."

"Yes, sir," he said. "I'll tell Mr. Green you'll be out in a while."

Bill laid into the pillows.

"Keep an eye on me."

"I've got you in my sights."

Short moments later, a tap sounded like a thump.

"Dinner's about ready if you are," Marcus said.

Before dinner was over, the two men were close. Mrs. Green excused herself after the main course. Green slugged down some port, while Bill agreed that there was perhaps something to talk about.

Green wasn't talking all cash. Bill had rolled his eyes. Green was offering more than that. He spelled it out: IBM, International Business Machines. Bill wasn't sure what Green was talking about. The old man smugly puffed on his cigar and told Bill that he was a fool if he didn't bite. Then he threw in some of his own company's stock.

Bill asked why he was doing this.

"Maybe I'm crazy," Green said. "No doubt, but this town was built on the river and its future is the river as far out as I can see, and damn you, some lowdown is going to snatch that property and ruin it. I want it just as is. Peaceful. Hell, Crabby's gas dock can stay and some slips, but I don't want to look down on God knows what."

"I ain't selling," Bill said.

"Not for maybe twenty years," Green said. "But it's my job to anticipate. I owe it to my progeny."

"Why you think I want to sell?"

"I can make it worthwhile. Because I can help you be fixed. Bill, where are you going to live?"

"Who knows?"

"The stock I'm offering should make you rich within ten years. You need money. I want that land. Sleep on it."

Bill was slumping in his chair. Marcus walked in. Green stood.

"What do they make?" Bill asked.

"Damned if I know, really. Their machines do the work of ten men and don't ask questions," Green said. "They are the future, bigger than the telephone. Sleep on it. I won't steer you wrong."

Bill nodded as Marcus led him off to bed.

Next morning, Bill said yes but with reservations. He asked Green to put his proposal in writing. Green agreed that he would. Then he offered to buy Bill's truck on the spot. The offer was good, and Green held out five hundred-dollar bills as a down payment. Bill waved him off, but Green insisted. The money was accepted before they sat down to breakfast.

"Just thinking out loud," Bill said, "but since you're all about the future, where the hell am I going to live? Can't build back where I was."

"I wouldn't," Green said. "Hell, it'll come. Take your time. Stay here as long as you need."

FLOATING HOME

After breakfast, Green excused himself to go downtown. Bill found himself at loose ends. He hadn't been alone since the night it happened, and he found himself out on the patio feeling suspicious, as if he were being observed. In spite of himself, he was looking into windows without knowing what he would feel if someone was actually watching.

He took a walk. Soon he was joined by Rufus, slobbering on his sleeve, then by Honky and Cracker. Bill kept walking while the dogs worked the path, sniffing and scarfing up cicadas like popcorn. They were thick as rain and several landed on his shirt before he got to the creek.

In the shade, they weren't as bad. Bill sat on a log and tried to think, but that was a joke. There was no thinking. There was worry. He told worry to get lost, but worry was persistent and sat on the other end of the log. Bill focused on the dogs that seemed to care about nothing. They crisscrossed, sniffed, snorted, ran, and barked.

Bill stood and stretched. He even tried to touch his toes. Without thinking about why, he wandered down the creek bank. He saw some deer tracks that surprised him. There were rusty beer cans and tires. All that seemed normal.

He saw large carp, way too large for the shallow water. One foot in front of the other was his uncertain progress.

Bill heard a howl and pain-filled yelping. He scrambled along the creek bank until he came upon Rufus who seemed to be troubled with something he was chewing on. Soon he was joined by Honky and Cracker. Those two were barking like the devil was at hand, but Rufus was acting like the devil was in his mouth.

Poor Rufus had chomped down on a baited hook. The line was snagged in a bush and the hook was sunk in his tongue. While Honky and Cracker snacked on fish guts and bait, poor Rufus tugged against something that would not let go.

Bill grabbed the dog's jaws and, talking softly, tried to pry them open, but Rufus snarled in such a way that changed his approach.

"Hold still, damn it!" he snarled back. He grabbed the upper jaw and somehow pried it open. He found the hook implanted in the edge of Rufus's tongue. In one smooth pull, he yanked and tore it free. The horrified dog ran off a few paces, then came right back to lick his hands. Bill shooed him off until he stuck the hook into the thick bark of a hackberry. He threw the red-and-white float into the creek and watched it bob downstream.

"Bastards," he thought out loud. He snuggled with the dogs and all four of them sank to their haunches. Rufus licked his face until Bill lit a smoke.

"Bastards."

The dogs seemed to agree and for a while, all sat and watched water flow. Rufus nodded conspiratorially.

"Dogs!" was all he said, but that seemed to be enough. They all licked him at once and nearly knocked him over. In spite of his goddamns, they did knock him backwards. It was all he could do to stand again. When he did, he was facing the hill toward the shanty boat. He tamped down the dogs.

"Damn," he said. "Hot damn!"

That seemed to please the dogs and the four of them charged the hill.

Even then, the boat looked different than it had: all brush had fallen away, and she was floating. He looked at her as the dogs scurried and rooted. She looked almost welcoming. He squinted over his shoulder down the hill toward the creek.

Inside it was foul and rank; still, he saw potential. You couldn't float it down the hill, but you could roll it down if you took out brush and a couple of trees. Then he chuckled that he, Bill Maddox, was crazy as a june bug, which pleased him so much he inspected the bottom, but this time, he was joined by curious dogs who licked at every opportunity. It was like a competition. Bill found himself laughing and cursing.

He couldn't figure out why there was as little rot as there was. Later he found out that the boat settled there in the flood of '45, not the one in '37. Still it was remarkable how sound she was. He poked with his knife. He tapped with his knuckles. The dogs crawled along with him and were especially pleased when he held his nose and they went back inside.

He drove them out and if he could have tolerated the fetid air, he would have shut the door and claimed the spot right then and there, but he could not.

Outside, he leaned against a cottonwood and smoked, while cicadas chanted, and dogs smiled. It was possible, he supposed.

Bill spent much of the day backed up against that tree looking at the boat. Would it float? How much repair was needed? The dogs sat most of the day, then got bored and wandered off. He sat by himself.

"What can I do?" he asked in a whisper that was answered by nothing but breezes and the sight of the boat perched on logs and barrels.

Later, when Green rolled in, Bill made up his mind. It was a blind stab, a leap into space. He didn't know why, but he said it.

"Throw in the boat and you got a deal."

"Boat?" Green queried, as he accepted a cocktail from Marcus. "What boat?"

Bill indicated with his head, pointed with his free hand, and blew cigarette smoke down toward the shanty boat.

"You mean my fishing lodge?" Green asked with eyes wide to bursting.

Bill turned his back and then, in spite of himself, Marcus started to snicker, but corrected with a cough.

"Do you have any idea what that place has meant? The hours I've spent in serenity?

"Afraid to ask," Bill replied. "Maybe you should sleep on it."

Marcus left the room.

"You want that boat?"

"Yes, sir, and I want it to float and I want paint and help to launch her and a tow down to Crabby's."

"You're kidding me."

"Nope."

"All you want is the boat?"

"Hell no, old man, you know better. The boat and all the rest you got drawn up."

Bill turned around and faced Green, who smiled and reached into his suit coat pocket.

"Glad to see that you're feeling like yourself."

"Thank you kindly," Bill replied. "Best to have this understanding in writing, don't you agree?"

"Tomorrow? Is tomorrow soon enough?"

"Tomorrow will suit fine, Green."

Marcus appeared with ice, water, and whiskey without being summoned though neither Green nor Bill noticed, being so busy, eye to eye that only Theo's fake sneeze broke the spell.

"God bless you, dear," Green said.

Next day, it was done by noon. Bill wasn't rich yet, but was on his way, and Green had the property he had hankered for. After lunch, Marcus and Bill drove over to Bill's old place looking for whatever was left, especially tools. In Fred Ruby's shed, they found Bill's old oak table, some chairs, and a whiskey carton full of photographs that Bill hadn't the stomach to look at yet. No tools.

"We got tools," Marcus said as they drove away. "We got tools out the ass."

Marcus knew there was nothing more to say, so he kept his mouth shut and drove, but didn't drive back to Green's. Marcus pulled the car to a halt, set the brake, got out of the car, and left Bill sitting there. He walked through spring grass, stepped over a busted fence, and sat down on a log. He stared at a gravestone with some initials and dates. He was in over his head and knew it.

A few minutes later, he heard a car door click and shut, and Bill walked over. The cicadas' song rose and fell as individual critters zigzagged around and between them.

"What's this?" Bill asked.

"Where we're buried," Marcus answered. "My mother there, father there, my brother there, my grandmother there. This is my family plot." He looked up. "Daddy was big on a family plot. No house, no car, but hot damn, always had our family plot. I sleep over there, next to brother."

"This Green land?"

"No, this is my land," Marcus said. "My Daddy's wages."

Bill nodded.

"Will you help, Marcus?" Bill asked.

"If it's up to me, but it isn't," he replied.

"It will be; you got my word."

Marcus nodded. "Then I will, Mr. Bill."

"It's plain Bill, Marcus. I can't work like that. Hear me?"

Marcus nodded.

"Deal?"

"Deal."

The two men shook on it.

———

Next morning, Bill was having coffee out in the garden, sun coming up, cicadas calming down. Bill was able to notice all of the holes in the ground that bugs had crawled up out of. Mrs. Green walked over and studied him.

"Good morning, Theo," he said.

"Did Green put you up to it?"

"Up to what?" Bill asked.

"The fishing shack part of the deal."

"No. Why would you ask?"

As soon as the words left his mouth, he knew he had said the wrong thing.

"No," he said. "My idea."

"Swear?"

"I swear," Bill said. "It was my idea. Thought I might live there for a while."

Amusement lit her eyes.

"Damn it, Bill, my imagination can be a terrible thing."

"I would imagine I don't know," he answered. "And I don't need to know, T."

She looked at him and somehow knew he wasn't lying. She closed both eyes and nodded.

Before long there was a pump: a ghastly, noisy thing squashed down on the bank. Under Green's directions (though it had been Bill's idea), it was fired up and gushing water into the bilge, which leaked like a sieve. Then after a while, the leaking slowed. Next day found Bill soaked underneath taking notes. Green knew the owners of an international wood company. Cypress was no problem to acquire though not much was needed. The decking was worse than anything and, hell, it would float without that.

At first Bill envisioned the boat being perfect and in the creek within weeks. Soon he realized it would take much longer. Sooner the better, because Green was a truthful but impatient man. Green provided money for paint and materials. The boat was launched raw from the waterline up in about five weeks.

She floated though. The pump drained the bilge for several days afterwards but was needed less and less. The damn thing floated. That even pleased Green. Some toasts were raised to that fact.

"Would I steer you wrong, Bill? Green asked.

"Only in an emergency," Bill replied.

CHAPTER 4

SNEED SNATCHER

Bill slept on the boat a couple of nights before they towed it downstream. On the eve, Green invited him for a celebration dinner and drinks, where Bill had the dual pleasure of encountering air conditioning and a brand-new car, both for the first time.

When Marcus greeted him at the kitchen door, Bill detected nothing of what was to come. The kitchen and pantry were hot as blazes, but as soon as he was led into the sunroom, he felt a chill.

"Have a seat, Bill, and cool your heels. What do you think?"

Green was pointing to a gray box stuck in a window. He felt a cold breeze hitting his face but had no idea what to think.

Green filled him in. It was the future. Then a couple walked in who didn't seem to notice. Before ten minutes passed, the gentleman offered Bill a new Ford.

Bill tried to stay off to the side, but the fellow in the bright pink shirt, yellow jacket, and green pants walked straight up to him and stuck out his hand. His face was almost as irresistible as the cartoonish cat on his necktie. His face glowed and his eyes sparkled.

"Louis Sumners," he exclaimed. "Glad to meet you." He handed Bill some car keys, while his wife nodded approvingly.

"What is this?" Bill asked, holding up the keys.

"How do you like the air, Louis?" Green asked.

"Marvelous," he replied. His wife beamed graciously.

Bill could see that she was beautiful and that she knew he was confused.

"Tell the man, Louis," she said.

Green led the way out to the driveway and there in the dappled shade of a maple was a fiery red 1952 Ford.

"What's this?" Bill asked.

"Your car," Louis said.

"Your brand-new car, Bill. A bonus," Green said. "Don't worry, it's part of the deal. Nothing has changed. This is the cherry on top."

The gift of the car made cocktail hour awkward for Bill, but as the evening wore on, the walls came down.

"Where are you going to keep our base of operations?" Louis asked.

Mrs. Green nodded to Mrs. Sumners and they left the room.

"Seriously, Bill, where will you keep the boat and more importantly, can I visit?"

"Depends."

"Just kidding," Louis said, "but damn if we haven't had some fun?"

Both men put their forefingers in front of their lips. Marcus left the room. Bill shrugged as he watched the two men swell with mirth.

Green suggested a ride to the Point in the new car and hollered for Marcus, who appeared out of nowhere and off they went with Bill at the wheel.

"Not too bad, is she?" Louis Sumners asked.

"Can't say that she is," Bill answered as Green slapped his knee. Marcus held on for dear life in the backseat because, at Mr. Sumners's urging, Bill was stretching her out, roaring out River Road.

"We can only stay a minute," Green insisted.

But once inside, he changed his tune.

It was the late-night crowd, here early and ornery. Green was ready. He wanted to talk politics. He would have squabbled with anyone and Louis Sumners and Bill soon realized that Marcus's parting groan had not been misplaced. Five minutes hadn't passed before the entire place was hanging on Green's inflammatory words.

Big as he was, he was pushing his luck as he butted heads with some fellow who had counted himself lucky to afford a few beers.

"Unions don't give diddly about the working stiff. They're communist. They want to ruin this country. They want to ruin the son of a bitch, you hear me!"

The bald-headed giant shrugged, grinned at his buddy like he figured a joke was being played. His buddy looked back at Bill and Louis and his brow knitted.

"You calling me a communist?" he said.

Green started laughing.

"I ain't in no union," the bald-headed giant said.

"Never said you were," Green said.

"Well, damn your ass, I am," said the buddy. "Pipe Fitters Local."

"Well, boogah, boogah," said Green.

Before the man was all the way off his bar stool, Louis and Bill were steering Green for the door. Green managed to turn and glare.

"A free lunch comes with a price. Good evening," Green said.

Marcus drove them back. At the table, he served dinner. When no one was looking, Bill and Marcus exchanged glances. Bill excused himself before coffee was served on the pretense of using the bathroom and slipped into the kitchen where he found Marcus washing plates.

"I could use help tomorrow. I'll pay. You want in?"

Marcus looked Bill up and down.

"You're with the in crowd now," he said.

"Can you slip away?" Bill asked.

"What you wanting to do?"

"Where you want me to start? You know how much there is. This time I'll pay."

"I got to talk to the missus."

"How about nine o'clock?"

Marcus nodded and said he would if he could. Bill stubbed out his smoke in an ashtray Marcus had already cleaned. Marcus shook his head and smiled.

"I will if I can. Join the others, Mr. Bill."

"See you tomorrow, Mr. Marcus."

"Mr. Wilson, if you're planning to be formal," Marcus replied.

Next morning found Bill and Marcus tearing off the roof. It wasn't easy. Whoever built the son of a bitch had intended it to last. The entire boat was like that. A bitch to take apart and a bitch to put back.

Marcus was a good-hearted man, but never would have helped if he hadn't been urged by Mrs. Green and enticed by extra money Bill was paying. Every time something had to be carried up or down, it was one or the other had to do it.

At night Bill slept fitfully. Often while working, prying something up or nailing something, he would catch himself wondering, why bother? He kept moving and didn't know why. Either Marcus did not see this struggle or pretended not to. They worked side by side. At the end of the week, Bill paid Marcus and that was that.

She was a small boat, but it took quite a while to bring back. Marcus took pride in many aspects of the work. He could draw a bead of caulk, for example, and after watching Bill's clumsy efforts, waved him off and insisted that he seal all the windows. He was a better painter and a better designer, too. In fact, it became so obvious that he was better at this kind of stuff, that Bill unabashedly let Marcus take charge. There was no shame. She was his. He knew that, but it became Marcus's project. Marcus knew it and he knew Bill did, too. Marcus cared more about the living outcome. Where would Bill sleep? Where would he pee? The basics. Marcus got into it and the process changed both of them.

Of course, Marcus knew about the struggle going on inside Bill, but years of holding back what he knew served him well. If he had discussed issues confounding Bill, it would have done nothing but harm. Bill would have run him off and mere words wouldn't have put a dent in Bill Maddox's armor. Not only did Marcus need money, but he also liked Bill and knew there was no way he could probe the motives of why he was doing what he was. Marcus laid low out of respect and self-interest.

Not just for Bill, mind you, but also for a certain woman, Laura, and begrudgingly, the would-be preacher, Joshua. The kid was a pain with his Bible-thumping sanctification of Daddy, who had caught a bullet somewhere in Korea. Marcus had known the man, and instinctively never liked him, particularly when just before shipping out, he had married Laura, Marcus's first love. Marcus abhorred him, but now Laura seemed to show new interest in him. Marcus was building his nest egg.

Bill knew nothing of this but found it strange that Marcus became so upset when Joshua came down to the boat one afternoon and started preaching from atop an old piece of bleached driftwood, about the folly of a house built on sand.

"And I say unto you, that though sand is closer to rock than water will ever be, man must cleave to rock! The rock of the Lord God . . ."

Marcus jumped off the boat and landed on shore. He ran toward the kid and with gestures more than words drove him away. For certain, the kid ran. Marcus walked back slowly.

"Sorry, Mr. Bill, but there's a time and place, if you know what I'm about."

"Can't say I do, Mr. Wilson."

Marcus looked up at him with a truly exasperated look. The kid was still preaching from the crest of the creek bank.

"How the hell would you like preaching first thing in the morning? Door flying open and some child spouting off about the tower of Babel and momma saying shush, putting her hand over your mouth, whispering a child needs understanding, saying, "You tell 'em, Joshua. Yea, Lord!""

Bill shook his head and smiled in spite of himself.

"Tough being a kid. Tough being a mother, too," he chuckled.

"Ain't funny, Bill," Marcus said. "That boy ain't mine."

"Might be soon, seems like."

"Go on."

"Where you expect me to go, Marcus? I'm stuck up on the roof. Want me to fly? You kicked the ladder over when you took out. She's hung on that piling over there." Bill pointed down creek.

"That boy is a mess," Marcus muttered as he went for the ladder.

"Where is home, Marcus? You sent the boy home."

"Mr. Bill, sir, please get me started."

"The ladder and I'll shut my trap. Beer time, anyhow."

Barring a frog strangler that night, roof was watertight. They would finish the next day. Climbing down without thinking, Bill hollered out something about heading to the Point and having some beers. When he faced Marcus, he looked into a face that told him he was crazy.

"I ain't thinking right. Sorry, Marcus," Bill mumbled sincerely.

Marcus put his hand on Bill's shoulder.

"I know a joint. Polecat's joint."

"Polecat Green's?"

"You know it?"

Bill nodded and off they went.

POLECAT'S

It wasn't far, but as they rolled, Marcus wanted to discuss everything about the boat. He talked about a floating palace, instead of the tub it actually was.

Nice was the word he used to describe its future. Tolerable would have been Bill's definition. When they had scrunched to a stop outside of a hashed-together concrete block and wooden shack with a rusty tin roof, Marcus was talking about the stateroom and about all Bill could do was keep from laughing.

"How can you call that hole a stateroom?" he asked.

"Why can you not, seeing as how you're the one living there?"

Bill didn't know how to answer.

"Seriously, Mr. Bill! It's where you live."

"Let's go in, Marcus."

"It's Friday. Pay or I ain't."

"Mr. Wilson, you drive a hard bargain. What if I dock you?"

"No way, Mr. Maddox, I want cash money. I pay my way."

Bill paid him. Good as his word, Marcus bought, and Polecat served. This was a late-night joint and it was barely five, so there was hardly anyone there—only Polecat, a woman who waited tables, and some silver-haired fellow who strummed a guitar absentmindedly.

Although the place was dark, Bill could see that the guitar man was not so old as one might have expected. There was a young boy messing with the strings and the man would pull the instrument back away from him and smile. The man would then pick out something that sounded good and the boy would laugh like it was a game and stick his fingers back into the strings and screw everything up. The man was patient. Bill called the boy over to the table. The boy walked jauntily over. The silver-haired man smiled and nodded. The boy stuck out his hand open palmed. The man commenced to play. Bill dropped an unshelled peanut in the boy's hand and then shelled one for himself. The boy's hand did not move or acknowledge the peanut. Bill snatched it back and ate it whole, shell and all. He acted like the boy wasn't even there. The man stretched out on his guitar and sound filled the room. The boy turned to listen. Bill tapped him on the shoulder and handed him a buck. The boy took off toward the bar. He reappeared a minute later with a Coke, peanuts, a handful of change and a gotcha smile.

A few minutes later, the silver-haired man walked over and extended his hand. The boy, reluctantly, dropped the change into it.

"He bothering you?"

"Not yet," Bill replied.

The man smiled. Shook his head at the boy and put the coins on the table in front of Bill.

"Say 'thank you, mister.' Don't shame yourself. Say 'thank you, mister.'"

"Nobody meant anything, Hawk," Marcus said.

"Don't care who meant what. Say 'thank you, mister. Thank you for the Coke.'"

The boy did as he was told, and the man commenced to playing blues so loose and rich that you would have never known there were only six people in the place. The boy ended up at his daddy's feet, and his enthusiasm made up for the lack of a crowd.

Bill noticed that the man had harmonicas on a table beside a water glass and after a few beers, something told him it was his turn to play. He walked up and grabbed one and, sure enough, it was the right key and he blew out the best riff he knew and the man double strummed and nodded. He cut loose in a way that loosened Bill from scalp to soles of his feet. He was careful to lay back and not override, still he punched and accented and felt so good that it was even infectious to the little boy.

When the song ended, Hawk shook his hand and Bill felt like a million dollars. Hawk laughed, launched into another, and Bill didn't let down. Hung right with him and kept on going.

There was laughter all around when that one blew through. The boy was grinning ear to ear. Marcus was amazed, and Polecat served them both a free beer. Nobody was there, so they took a break and shot the bull.

"You play, without a doubt," Hawk said.

Bill shrugged.

"Seriously, what you lack in chops, you make up in taste. Don't overplay, if you catch my drift."

"Well, thank you," Bill said. "Short and sweet is where I'm aiming."

"Good target," Hawk nodded.

Things were looking good. For the first time in a while, Bill felt good in his shoes, but then things turned. Two cops walked in. They walked up to the bar and quiet got quieter. Polecat was talking behind his hand, but the cops were laughing.

"You going to play, you better pay."

"I paid," Polecat said.

The little cop flipped out a notebook and his buddy peered over his shoulder. Both shook their heads.

"Don't look like it. Nope."

"Aw, man," Polecat said. "How in the world can you say that? Last week and week before, too."

"You should have signed. No record in the ledger."

"Never mind, then," Polecat said. "What you officers want?"

"Two beers to start. Then Molly and barbecue with potato salad, corn bread, and coleslaw."

"Molly's up at VA hospital."

"Polecat, let me please buy the peace officers a couple," Bill drawled from the shadows.

The place was dingy and dark, so the cops couldn't see Marcus squirming and gritting. So dark that Bill was the disembodied voice of some pale shade in the corner. One of the officers, the big one, put his hand on his pistol. Bill stood up and as the man drew his weapon, walked to the bar and laid down a five-dollar bill.

"Well, you're a white man."

"Bill Maddox," Bill said. "Good to meet you. Polecat, I'm buying."

"You live on Shirley?" the little one asked.

"Did," Bill answered.

"Where the place burned down?"

"Polecat, please get these gentlemen a beer."

"We were only joking," the little cop sniggered.

"Just pulling Polecat's leg," the big one said.

"Sure, I catch your drift. Make it four beers, please, Polecat."

Polecat shrugged and ducked into his cooler. Both cops smiled and shuffled like they were ready to move back into daylight. The beers hit the bar and Bill picked one up and before taking a swig proposed a toast.

"Wish to God the gift he give us to see ourselves as others see us . . ."

The cops picked up their beers. They both, to Bill's amusement, looked puzzled.

"My grandma was Scottish," said the big one.

"Ain't that something? So was mine," Bill said.

Bill walked back to the table and sat down after scooting the kid out of his chair. Marcus whispered that they should go. The cops cleared out just as Hawk began to play.

On the way back, Bill was at the wheel, when a siren sounded, and a red light strobed. He pulled onto the shoulder. The short little cop with the beginning of a paunch strolled up with his hand on his gun. Marcus was uneasy. He didn't like the look in Bill's eyes.

"Get out of the car."

Bill sat.

"Out."

Bill opened the door but remained seated.

"What you want, Officer Sneed?"

"What were you up to back there?"

"Drinking a beer, same as you, Officer Sneed."

"Don't be a smart ass. How do you know my name?"

"Being smart has nothing to do with knowing your name, Officer Sneed."

"What is that supposed to mean, hill jack?"

Bill started laughing and it felt so good to laugh that he had trouble stopping.

"Want to have a name-calling contest, Officer Sneed?"

Bill slammed the door. Marcus squirmed. The cop fumed, his eyes narrowed.

"Look," Bill said, "I am a patient man and you have already called me an ass and a hill jack, but if you will not tell me what I am charged with aside from buying you a beer in a joint you were trying to shake down, then I will be on my merry way."

He popped it into gear and with Marcus imploring the Lord to have mercy, sprayed gravel and sped away. Sneed did not follow them all the way. He turned off at the Pine Bar at the bottom of the hill.

"Jesus Christ have mercy," Marcus said. "You got balls, Mr. Bill."

"Hell, Marcus, it ain't what I got; it's what they don't. What you say we hit Green for whiskey? My nerves need soothing."

The Greens had stepped out to the country club for a dinner dance. Fortunately for Bill, there was already whiskey on the boat. Marcus decided to turn in. So, early as it was, Bill slid toward the creek and his new home alone.

Before he was halfway down the winding road, he got the lonely blues. They didn't creep, they hit. He decided to go to the Pine Bar. When he got there, he remembered the cops and saw their cars parked out back.

He was turning around, feeling like a fool, when he saw Valerie sitting on a stump holding her baby. He hesitated a second. She waved. He nodded. She ran over.

VALERIE

"I need help. Please get me out of here."

Before he could consider anything, she opened the passenger side and jumped in.

"Please. I'll explain."

He punched it and headed toward the boat while she sniffled, and the baby cried. He needed a drink and was glad to have ice stashed in his cooler. Before the night was over, he wished he had more than ten beers in there. Lucky the baby didn't drink. The momma could.

She had a lot of explaining to do and that required lubrication and the beer slid down her throat and the whiskey eased his mind as he tried to respond to her queries. How do you deal with people like this? How do people ever turn out like that? And Sneed, who it seems, was her second cousin somehow, how could he ever think he could make such demands? Who did he think he was?

By the time Bill's third glass of whiskey was half drained, he was so confused about the second question that he forgot her first. The next morning, when he stirred and looked into her face beside him, he confused her for an angel. She smiled as if she understood and yet she was clearly asleep. Then he remembered the baby and slipped out of the bed, tiptoed in morning light, and found the child curled up beneath his table wrapped in mother's clothes and covered with a towel.

He peed into the head and pumped it into the creek. He looked into the dark mirror and saw a man snuck past forty, beat up and eyes glazed. Part of him stirred and he decided to blindfold thoughts, so he tiptoed back to bed, slipped in, and she wrapped her thigh over his while licking her lips. He could not believe this was happening. He tried to sleep in self-defense, but he could not. Not for anything. She smiled like a contented child as her hand rested on his waist.

Suddenly anxiety crawled over his skin like a colony of ants. What the hell was he doing? What the hell had he done? He couldn't remember going to bed. He glanced over at the chair where he usually piled his clothes and there they were in dawn's light.

He tried to breathe easy, but it was a forced effort. He remembered the bit about Sneed, the cop. About how he told her that he had wanted a cut of her action, money and otherwise. Sneed had said he would give her a day or two to decide before he took her down. Bill remembered that part and also recalled telling her that she was a fool if she went for it. Then there was something about calming her and promising to help, before everything went bleary.

What had he done?

He seemed to remember her saying, "Why are you pushing me away?"

But who? Was it Sarah? Was it Valerie? Then he remembered. She kissed him, and he gently pushed her away, thoughts of Sarah forcing him to grimace.

"What's wrong with me?" she had said and then the baby started crying. She scooped up the baby and plopped on the ratty sofa. She rocked the child and glared at him. "What's wrong with a little comfort?"

"Nothing and nothing," Bill said.

"Now, what's 'nothing and nothing'?"

"Just saying," Bill said. "Please forgive me; I ain't ready. Nothing wrong with comfort. God knows and nothing wrong with you I can tell."

He started off to bed. She was still rocking the child but looking at him like she was trying to turn him inside out.

"Would you feel better if I made you pay?" she asked. She made no attempt to hide her breast as the baby suckled.

"No, I reckon not. Make yourself easy. I got to hit the hay."

He remembered her shaking her head and turning away.

The boat swayed and groaned on her lines. He had opened the flag that served as the door that separated "the stateroom," as Marcus called it, from "the salon." He had stumbled down the three short stairs, but then what? He must have removed his own clothes. That was the way he always stacked them. Valerie's hand reached directly for his penis and all of a sudden, Bill remembered. She chuckled and nuzzled into him.

"Feeling a bit frisky, are we?" she drawled.

They had.

"What's the matter, cockle-doodle-do? Forgot how to crow in the morning?"

"What?" Bill stammered, pretending to be asleep. "What?"

"I believe you are separated from your true self, sweetness."

Bill felt himself swell in her hand. A torrent of thoughts was silenced as she stroked him and then kissed him head to toe and someplace in between.

It was confusing to him, but not to her. As soon as everything settled down, the baby awakened, and Valerie tended to her child as tenderly as she had tended to him. The baby was content. Bill was disoriented.

"What was she like, your Sarah?"

Bill didn't know what to say.

"I know she was pretty," Valerie said, "but what was she like?"

The baby seemed to nod at Bill while she slurped applesauce off a little spoon. The woman asking these questions was naked as a jaybird. He didn't feel bad, and that felt weird. Here it was nearly noon on a Saturday and still in bed, propped up, like this sort of thing happened every day.

"What was she like?"

"She meant the world. What's to say?" Bill said. "What about your baby? Tell me about her."

"She's my baby!"

"Rest my case. You want breakfast, beer, or both?" Bill asked.

"Both," Valerie replied. "You really loved her, didn't you?"

"Beer or not?"

"If it isn't too much trouble, a beer would be good."

"No trouble at all," Bill replied, surprised at himself when he didn't put on his pants.

Before she left two days later, Bill was not only smitten, but had a full diaper pail, plus another full of beer cans. It was unbelievable how aware he had become of plumbing.

Valerie asked a whole lot of questions but offered few answers. She never explained anything. Bill spent two days blissfully attempting to answer questions without answers and puzzling over geometries that kept him baffled. The baby was no help at all unless she cried out when a query got too close to the bone. At those moments, the adults smiled gratefully. Once the child dozed off, they resumed their pleasures. The pendulum was swinging back and forth; a strange two days to be sure. Then on Monday, she was gone without a note or any sign.

At first, Bill thought it was a good thing.

Several nights later, when she stepped on the deck about ten o'clock, he felt the boat roll and heard the baby cry and jumped out of his bed and half crawled up his steps into the front room. And there they were.

"You all right?" she asked.

"Suppose so. You? I was worried."

"About us?"

"Who else?"

She turned her back.

"Taking care of some business, if you can understand."

He moved toward her and resisted the urge to spin her around.

"What kind of business?" he said.

"None of yours," she said.

"Fair." He turned back toward his bed.

"Wait," she said. "Just wait a damn minute. I ain't through with you. Listen."

She walked toward him and handed him the baby. She nodded and stepped into the head. The baby started to fidget and whimper. He heard her pump the lever as the baby broke into a full-blown howl. She walked out, smoothing down her skirt. The baby was bawling. Valerie took her back.

"What did you do to her?"

"Nothing."

"More of your nothing," she said, cradling her baby. "Why don't you bring in the stuff off the deck?"

"What stuff off the deck?"

She was acting somewhere between ornery and scared. The only thing he could make out in the dark was something that looked like a small jail cell and indeterminate shapes.

"I had to do something. Don't hate me."

"What's hate have to do with anything?" Bill asked.

"Just bring the stuff in. Please. I'll explain later."

With Valerie directing, he unfolded the playpen, which was hinged in some mysterious way, and slid it into the salon, where she positioned it, while he held the baby. Then, he was dispatched for the boxes, which contained all kinds of things: diapers, ointments, powders, baby food jars, oatmeal, animal crackers, clothes for both mother and child, plus two boxes of books and some pots and pans, and baby bottles.

He held the child who whimpered and squirmed, while Valerie stashed. When he tried to ask her anything, she raised her hand and asked him to have patience.

"Fix me a drink then, if you want patience."

She saluted and ducked down into the stateroom where he kept the booze and an ice chest stored beneath the water line where it was cooler.

"Hey, thanks for the beer," she called up, while chopping off ice chunks with the ice pick. "How did you know we were coming back?"

"Didn't know you were leaving."

"What?"

"Nothing," Bill growled, and the baby started to bawl. Valerie ran up with a glass of ice and a cold beer. She handed Bill the glass of ice and took the baby.

"Where's my drink?" he asked.

"Down below. Apparently, you're not so good with babies."

"Well, I'll be damned," Bill said.

"Don't get me started, Bill Maddox. I've had a day," she said and then added. "Watch that cussing! It ain't right to cuss during the formative years."

In spite of himself, he found himself chuckling as he poured.

"Why do I have to do everything around here, anyhow?" he asked.

"You don't."

Bill laughed. She responded with a wink.

"Fetch me a diaper."

"There's bound to be a better way than diapers," Bill said. "If a man hit on that, just imagine."

"No kidding," Valerie said, "but please just hand me the thing."

"Seriously," Bill said. "Can you imagine how many . . ."

"Watch your language," Valerie insisted.

She stayed for a while. Bill could never remember how long. When she was there, she was there: a wife. When she wasn't, she wasn't anything and he was baffled by her absence. She seemed baffled by his concern. That, in turn puzzled him.

Everything was fine for a while. She got along with Marcus. She helped choose paint colors. She was smart as could be and Bill deferred to her again and again. She was feisty, but he was surprised one day when she announced that he was impossible and that right after one of their best nights ever. She stormed out and failed to return.

She didn't come back this time. Not the next day or the day after. There was no one to ask about it. Days and nights dragged on.

He slept alone and awakened alone. Marcus showed up and they finished painting.

He had one dream of Valerie to ten dreams of Sarah. In the Valerie dreams, there was blurry vagueness, but in Sarah dreams, details so defined he awoke with particulars.

His belly hurt. His arms ached and felt heavy. What could he be betraying? He knew Sarah wasn't coming back.

Valerie was so young compared to him. He decided it didn't matter. Then she showed up, slipped into his bed while the afternoon sun was still high, and he had been pretending it was midnight. Eyes slammed shut, darkness his destination..

He hadn't said anything at first. She snuggled into him.

"Damn," he said.

"Damn, yourself," she said and giggled. "Don't ask what I'm doing here."

"So, what are you doing here?" he drawled.

She snuggled into him.

"What are you doing here?" she whispered.

He could feel his pulse quickening and wanted her there. He loved the sound of her voice, the warmth of her smooth skin.

"What are you thinking, scratchy face? Relax, I won't bite," she said.

He wasn't so sure what anyone was thinking, as warm as her thigh was, her touch felt as deliberate as a move in a chess game. He worried over that quietly. She started to snore.

When he was sure she was asleep, he slipped out of the bed, looked down on her face and saw a puffy-eyed angel with parted lips. He walked up into the front cabin and expected to see the baby in the little jail-like crib, but there was no baby. A bottle of bourbon, partially drunk, lay there half covered by the pale blue blanket.

At first, he had wanted to laugh, then he was worried. Where was Alexandra? He plucked the whiskey out from under the blanket and took a swig. What had Valerie done with the child? He decided he needed ice and smokes, so he turned back toward the stateroom and there Valerie stood with the flag that served as a curtain draped around her. She smiled and held out his smokes. He walked over, took them, and accepted her offer to fix him a drink.

SNATCH

Turned out Alexandra was with her mam maw. It was the only way Valerie could find time to hatch her plan.

"What plan?" Bill asked.

"The Sneed snatcher!" Valerie pretended to be surprised Bill hadn't guessed.

"Oh, I see," Bill said, feeling hairs rise on the back of his neck and cool goose bumps slide down his arms. "The Sneed snatcher plan. Are you sure you want to let me in on this?"

"Not completely," she replied, "but do I have a choice?"

"I don't even know what you're talking about."

She dropped the curtain and Old Glory unfurled and hung straight down. As Bill scratched his head, he heard scurrying around, and when she next appeared, she burst through the curtain naked as a jaybird with Bill's flash camera in her hands.

"It works, doesn't it?"

Bill had kept it in the cab of his truck. Sarah had given it to him, so he could take pictures when he traveled. Sarah had always complained that Bill's descriptions were inadequate. Actually, she had said cheerfully that they stunk. She gave him the camera on a

Christmas morning. It was a standing joke, because he overexposed, double exposed, and sometimes failed to load film. The Bill Maddox photographs were so poor they made her laugh. Lousy was the word she used to describe his efforts, but she had hugged him close, so it was disconcerting for Bill to behold Valerie brandishing the camera.

"What's the matter? You can make it work, can't you?"

"Matter of opinion," Bill said.

"Can you make it flash? We ain't talking Hollywood."

Bill started laughing but stopped short, Valerie looked so intent.

"Can you make her flash? To hell with pictures. Bill, I am dead serious."

Bill nodded. She held out the camera.

"Prove it."

"Fetch me the flashbulbs."

She ducked through the curtain and reappeared clothed, carrying the cardboard flashbulb gizmo.

"What's with clothes?"

"In case you get ideas. Not made up for photographs," she said as she handed him the flashbulbs, took a gulp of beer, and smoothed her hair in almost one motion.

"Just prove it. Make her flash!"

Pop!

"There, you satisfied?" he asked.

"No, not yet, but encouraged. Can't see a darn thing. When's the blindness wear off?"

"In a minute or so."

"That'll have to do, but you'll have to move fast," she said.

"What you talking about, Valerie?"

Suddenly, she looked demure and stared down at her feet.

"We have to meet Sneed in about an hour."

"What you mean we?"

It was amazing for Bill to watch her gears shift. Demure was replaced by pure logic. She had now seen the clean outcome of her plan.

"Well, he won't exactly see because of the flashbulb, but then you got to move fast, because I ain't sure we got a whole minute, unless I drive the getaway and you jump in."

"Jump into what?"

"Your car. Just keep idling and I'll scratch out before he can see and long before he's got britches."

"Now wait a damn minute," Bill said.

"We can't."

She was supposed to meet Sneed at the Pine Bar in the back to give her final answer. He wanted money and something else or he was going to bust her.

"The 'something else' is where I get him. That tree back away? The big old willow with the branches hanging like a curtain? That's where I coax him to haul me."

"Kind of close, wouldn't you say?" The tree was hardly a hundred yards from his boat.

"That simplifies things for you."

"Now wait a minute—"

"No, you wait and listen. Want me to go to jail? He won't have a chance. He'll be wrapped around my finger. Pants down, gun in the trunk along with his keys. All you got to do is flash one picture and we skedaddle like bats out of hell."

"You're nuts," Bill said, chuckling.

"So are you."

"I won't dispute that, but even if I agreed, how the hell will I know when to sneak up and pop the picture and what's to keep him from hearing?"

"Trust me, scratchy. I'll have that son of a bitch so stirred he won't see nothing except what's he's set on and all he will hear is me. Just count thirty, keep the car running, fire the camera into the backseat, and I'll do the rest."

Bill dropped her off at the Pine Bar, went back to the boat, fixed a stout drink, and waited. When an hour passed, he breathed easier. Maybe this crazy scheme had been derailed. He didn't like Sneed, nobody did, but he was more nuisance than threat. Bill couldn't believe he had been talked into this deal, yet in spite of himself, he was as excited as a teenage boy. He lit a smoke, but before he inhaled, he saw Sneed's patrol car turn in and wheel to a dusty stop under the willow tree.

The camera, loaded with film and equipped with a flashbulb, sat on the car seat beside him. Shadows long, sun about set, Bill slouched and waited. His pulse quickened. In fact, his heart was pounding. The bastard was going to get what was coming. Bill grinned. He waited and puffed on his smoke.

After a while, the doors of the cop car opened, and Bill saw Sneed look around furtively, as Valerie confronted him with hands on hips. Bill imagined her scolding tone. He laughed out loud and took a swig, then Valerie held out her hand. She turned and walked back to the passenger side, climbed in and shut the door hard. Sneed poked his head into the car and Bill figured the whole deal was off, but in one fluid motion, Valerie climbed out of the car.

Head bobbing up and down, she chewed Sneed's ear until he took off his holster and britches and handed them to her. She pulled up her skirt and pointed to the backseat. Sneed scurried in and shut the door. Valerie walked to the trunk, opened it, and laid Sneed's trousers and holster inside. Bill could not believe what he was seeing. She shook her ass and lowered the trunk gently but did not latch it; she climbed into the backseat with Sneed.

Bill gulped and counted to thirty, then slowly rolled until he was ten yards away. He opened the door, left it open, and scooped up a handful of sand and dust. With his camera at the ready, he listened to loud moans, the "oh Gods, oh yes, oh oh oh God yeses," finally a screeching howl and then a "Now, *now*! Please God, please *now*."

That's when he made his move and ducked through willow fronds, snatched open the door, flashed the picture of busily enraptured

Sneed, who screamed in a measure all out of proportion to the sand and dazzle light that filled his eyes, as Valerie turned a back flip and landed on her feet. Bill slammed the door and ran for the car, but Valerie paused long enough to press down the trunk lid. It latched. She trotted over, jumped in. They sprayed gravel and dust.

When they hit River Road, tires were squealing. Valerie told him to calm down. At first, he didn't heed her, but she insisted that everything was under control. She held up a key and shook it in front of his face. Bill slowed down as they sped through the curve that ran past the Pine Bar, slowed down out of curiosity more than anything.

"What you got?" he asked.

"Key to the trunk. Locked tight with his gun and the ignition key. Please, we don't want an accident."

"Nice touch."

"Thanks. Thought it might buy us time. What did you throw in his face?"

"Nothing but sand."

She laughed and popped one of the beers Bill had stashed.

"It's good to know a man with a church key on his dash. Two nice touches, Mr. Maddox. Say, why don't we head up to the Point and grab a steak. I'll buy."

"You think that's wise?" Bill asked.

"The right witness never hurt anybody," she said.

"I figure we might want to stash this camera."

"A place to stash the Sneed snatcher?" Valerie asked.

They stopped at Fred Ruby's, who had lived right next door to Bill. There was no sign of any fire. The hole filled; some grass had grown. Weeds had grown. Green had taken care of everything. The place looked as calm and peaceful as a cemetery plot. Bill went numb in his old driveway, which he had pulled into out of habit.

Valerie touched his hand.

"Goddamn, it's hard," he muttered.

"Bill, we got to get out of here. You can't do this right now. You know it. How do you unload the damn thing?"

"I never did it," Bill whispered. "I'm sorry, you're right. You're right as hell. Please take the rig to that door and ask the man to keep it safe for Bill. He'll do it."

Valerie hopped out, ran to the door, and was back in minutes, followed by Fred and Lucky Ruby. Bill wanted to slink out of sight but forced himself to sit up straight.

Fred said nothing. Lucky touched his hand and Fred put his hand on top of hers.

"We miss you, Bill," they said simultaneously. He nodded. Valerie cheerfully offered to bring back some steaks. Fred and Lucky laughed and waved goodbye as they backed away, saying thanks, but no thank you. Both were bowing gracefully. Bleary eyed, Bill gunned for the Point.

"We got him, didn't we? Wonder if he's got his pants on?"

"Most likely. Let's get us a witness," Bill said. "That is, if you're still buying."

"How could I refuse to buy supper for Flash?"

"Flash, my ass! How the hell did you talk him out of his gun, pants, and keys?"

"That was easy."

Valerie leaned over, breathed in Bill's ear, and stroked her fingertips up the middle of his thigh.

"Now, watch it, Valerie. I'm trying to drive."

"Easy as pie," she whispered. "Told Sneed I didn't have any money on me. That I hid it down near the creek, then told him we didn't need money if he would settle for something better. I gave him a peek and teased him, but he started to get grabby and said he needed both. I told him he drove a hard bargain. I acted real hurt and told him I would take him to my stash. Then about halfway there, I arranged myself so the road wasn't as interesting and told him I liked a man could drive a hard bargain. He promised he was that man, so I reached for his belt buckle. He slapped my hand away and put his hand on his gun. That's when I knew. When we pulled into the creek road, I told him deal was off. Nothing, no money, no loving, nothing.

I told him I knew he was going to rob me and rape me at gunpoint. He practically started to beg. After that, it was easy. I whispered he had to promise not to hurt me. When we were outside of the car, I made him prove it. All it took was a couple of peeks. The man is starved. After I got the pants and gun, I was tempted to make him crawl, but thought better."

Bill turned into the Point's parking area.

"I never heard a woman moan so. What the hell you have him doing?"

"Warming me up. I told him I got really fired up when a good man licked the back of my knees. I figured that would make the best shot and besides I knew where his eyes would be."

"You think of everything. Did it warm you up?" Bill chuckled.

"Hotter than hell. Believe I owe you one."

"Don't owe me anything."

Valerie leaned over, whispered in his ear.

Whatever she said led to the backseat. Valerie wasn't kidding when she said she was hotter than hell. While Bill protested, she took his cigarette and sat in his lap. He was laughing so hard at the absurdity of the situation, him protesting and her urging him on that he forgot about his driveway, Sneed, Fred, and Lucky. He forgot that it was not fully dark and that he was in a public place. All he could do was hold onto Valerie and trust the shock absorbers. Minutes later, they strolled toward dinner.

"That was the first course," Valerie said as they walked through the door.

THE SECOND COURSE

When they walked into the smoky room, heads turned. Somebody whistled, though it was quiet as they walked to the bar. Bill ordered whiskey; Valerie asked for beer. The jukebox was playing Hank Williams. The conversation resumed as they sat down.

Bill's ears were ringing from backseat boogie. Valerie was looking at reflections in the back bar. Three guys seemed to command her attention. Out of the corner of his eye, Bill could see that one was talking behind his hand and that the others were laughing silently. He couldn't hear, but Valerie could. She put a finger to Bill's lips and her eyebrows arched. She shook her head. Minutes later, some fat old guy with red suspenders walked in, laughing like Santa Claus. Bill knew the guy. He ran the wrecker service. The man was laughing out loud as he walked up to the whispering men.

"Damn, you ain't right," he bellowed. "Sneed done walked into Pine Bar in skivvies. Shoes, shirt, and badge, no pants at all. Wouldn't have believed all the saints. I just busted his trunk. Claimed he was overpowered by a gang of some kind. Made him take off his pants and gun."

"Junior, ain't kidding then?"

"He might be, but I'm not. Amazing to see a cop with no gun and no pants. Vouch for that and I busted his trunk, and swear to God above, the man's got more booze than Don's. Car keys right on top like he placed them for safekeeping. If he's right, we better lock our doors."

His laughter was loud and infectious. Bill tried to suppress a grin. Valerie coolly asked for menus and another round.

They moved to a more secluded table and ordered. Dinner was good, but anticlimactic. Valerie wanted Alexandra more than dessert, so after they ate, he drove her to Mam Maw's where she decided to stay. She promised to come by the next day. He drove away from the little corncrib of a house with one eye open and one eye shut.

When he wound down into the valley, the road turned into four lanes, making his driving task easier. Somehow, he felt he would never see her again, and though it bothered, he realized he had suffered worse. He felt resigned. He held the steering wheel with both hands and sucked in fresh air pouring through the window, glad—at least he thought he was—to be alive. He turned off the highway back on to River Road and hadn't traveled a hundred yards before the red light of a cop car lit his back window. He pulled over to let the man pass, but he did not and stopped behind his car. Bill saw it was Sneed.

"Aware of the fact you're weaving? License."

He pulled out his license. Sneed hesitated. Bill could hear Sneed's radio crackling. Sneed noticed and excused himself. Bill contemplated driving off but decided to keep his cool. He fired a smoke and listened to yes sirs and no sirs until he felt like it was an accomplishment he didn't laugh.

Sneed walked back, raised his clipboard, and asked Bill where he had spent the evening. Bill told him he had dinner at the Point and taken an evening drive.

Bill could see that the wind had left Sneed's sails, so he came right out and asked.

"Are you worried, officer? Anything at all I can help with?"

Sneed looked uncomfortable. Bill waved his driver's license.

"What do you know about Valerie? Tell and there might not be no trouble."

"Trouble?" asked Bill. "Is sweet Valerie in trouble? Lord knows, I would sure love to help."

"Look, Maddox! What do you know about this?"

"Excuse me, sir, about what?"

"I know you took the little bitch to dinner and know you taken her home."

"Actually, officer, she took me to dinner after."

Sneed turned red. He put his hand on his gun. A car's headlights lit him. Bill could see sweat on his upper lip.

"Were you there?"

"Pardon me, officer, was I where?"

"All right, be cute. I can take you in," he said with glittering eyes.

Bill knew to go for broke, gaze steady, license in reach.

"Don't push too hard, big boy. Ask and you might receive," he said.

Sneed tightened his grip on his gun, but suddenly Bill didn't give a damn. He saw the bastard for what he was. He didn't care what happened. Sneed rocked on his heels like he was goosed.

"Who has the film?"

"Film? I'm not a photographer."

"Look, I need that film. If you know where it is, I'll make it worth your while."

Bill put his license back into his wallet and said nothing.

"Well?" Sneed said.

"Deep subject, Sneed. I am a peaceful man and don't want trouble. You want trouble?"

"No, sir. I want no trouble."

"Now we both understand, may I make the point that Valerie does not deserve trouble either?"

"I would never hurt anyone."

"Promise me. You never will hurt anyone."

"The film. You've got it. I know it. Where is it?" Sneed tightened his grip on his gun.

"Neither one of us have it. Shoot if you want and you'll never find it. Calm yourself, there will be no trouble. Everything is under wraps. Entirely up to you, Sneed. Entirely up to you. Understand."

"I got money."

"No, you don't, Sneed. Not near enough and if anything happens to Valerie, your ass is grass. Do you understand me? Toodle-oo, Sneed. You are a charming man."

Sneed hesitated, started to say something, but then did not.

"Aw, never mind," Bill said, as he eased away.

As he left Sneed behind, he felt amused, but then noticed a car tailing him. When he turned onto his road, he knew it was Sneed. He drove to the boat like always, but he stayed in the car. It was Sneed all right. He pulled beside him.

"We got to talk."

"Talk."

"I need the film."

"Don't have it. Neither does Valerie. Case closed."

The idiot was pointing his gun. Bill grinned and slammed the car into first and spun around, left him in the dust, and never even saw headlights. He hid out at Green's for an hour or so. When he got back to the boat, he found a mess. The bastard had torn the place apart, but there was nothing missing. The next morning Bill called the cops and reported a break-in. That calmed Sneed down, for a while.

But only for a while. The cop who followed up on the break-in was so matter-of-fact the whole thing was pointless. He yawned and slouched, took a few notes. Nothing missing except a camera.

That same afternoon, Sneed cruised by. Bill saw him and made a point of putting down his paintbrush to walk out and wave. He was real cheerful. Sneed looked glum.

"Look, Maddox, I ain't kidding. I don't want trouble."

Bill assured him that trouble was not on his mind.

"So make it easy," Sneed said. "The bitch ain't worth it, Maddox."

"What are you so worried about?"

"I've been investigating. You got no idea where she's shacked up, do you?"

"Sneed, I not only don't know, but don't give a damn. I got no film handy and got no camera since the break-in, which as you must know, was reported to the proper authorities."

"I know more than you want to think, Maddox. Word to the wise."

He turned his head and slowly rolled away.

Bill went back to painting his trim Calvary Blue. Valerie had chosen the color. The close trim work eased his mind.

———

Bill got industrious and measured out potential new boat docks. He figured he could probably put up fifteen, maybe twenty more boats. He was sure Green would go along with that.

He was finishing the last exterior trim around the aft cabin window, when Sneed rolled up. Sneed's face was beet red. Bill stayed cn the catwalk. Sneed remained in his car with the engine running. Bill waved, then turned his back and resumed painting.

"Maddox," Sneed said deliberately, "turn around slowly. We have to talk."

"Just give me a couple minutes, Sneedy. I'm about done here."

"You got that right."

"Would you be threatening me, Fatso?"

"Not hardly, but your behavior is threatening Miss Valerie."

Something snapped in Bill. Suddenly in the clear light of that late afternoon, he didn't give one damn. He laughed.

"Ain't no laughing matter, Bill Maddox."

Bill dipped his paintbrush into the paint pail.

"Never said that it was," he said, then jumped on the dock, then onto the bank, and walked straight up to squinty-eyed Sneed.

"Your girl's with a bad bunch, and I got my finger on them," Sneed said with a smug grin.

"So?"

"So, if you are concerned, might want to understand some facts of life."

"Such as?"

"Such as the only thing keeping that crowd from time is a good relationship with me. Burglary, possession of stolen property, assault and battery, statutory rape, all the way down to arson and extortion. They love me, Bill, like they would love their big brother. Understand me? She's a peanut. Catch my drift?"

Bill's hand was shaking, but he held his ground and let Sneed speak.

"She hasn't talked yet, but she will soon as they start in on the baby." Sneed chuckled.

"Well connected, aren't you, Sneed?"

"Better than you know. Can I call you Bill?"

"Anything you want."

With what almost sounded like genuine emotion, Sneed said, "Now Bill, we both know that you've seen trouble and don't want more."

"Officer, I'm amazed you recognize this fact."

"All I need is film. Needn't be trouble."

"You're right, Sneed," Bill replied as he shut his eyes and a genuine tear rolled down his cheek. "I want no trouble."

Bill inhaled several times.

"The film."

Bill, eyes closed, bowed his head, leaned in on the window with his elbow. He shook his head and sighed so deeply, he stirred up phlegm. He coughed, spit, and excused himself. When he opened his eyes again, they were red with tears.

"Sorry," Bill said. "Guess I forgot my place."

He shut his eyes and shuddered, leaned in closer. He heard Sneed unsnap his holster strap. Bill stuck the paintbrush bristles in Sneed's eyes. Struck like a snake. The fat bastard shut his eyes. The bridge of his nose, his forehead and both eyelids were Calvary Blue. Sneed struggled with his gun, but Bill pushed the handle of the brush into his ear and told him to put his hands on the steering wheel and keep his eyes closed if he valued his eyesight. Sneed complied.

"Smart move," Bill said. He put the fingernail of his forefinger on Sneed's neck and said, "When I open this door, you will step out. Keep your back to me or you will die. Do you understand?"

Sneed hesitated, so Bill gave him a blue mustache and goatee.

"Don't cut me," Sneed pleaded.

"Nobody's going to cut anybody. Hand me your keys," Bill said as he painted Sneed's Adam's apple and then daubed his badge.

"Maddox, my eyes are killing me."

"Keep tight, Sneed, and undo your holster," Bill said, while dragging his fingernail about a centimeter down Sneed's neck.

Sneed opened his mouth to yell. Bill stuck the brush into his mouth. "Loosen the buckle and get out."

Sneed did what he was told, but then he grabbed at Bill and made the mistake of opening his eyes. Bill kneed him in the balls, then in the throat, grabbed the pistol, and cocked it.

"Get up."

He made him climb in the trunk. As Sneed was climbing in, Crabby drove past and waved. Bill waved back.

"Damn it, Maddox, my eyes!"

"Keep 'em shut and tell me where Valerie is."

"Quail Hollow." Sneed whimpered. Bill shut the trunk. Sneed screamed. Bill fetched the handcuffs from the front seat and walked back to the trunk and tapped. The screaming ceased and was replaced by moans. As Bill opened slowly; Sneed banged his head several times before it was fully opened.

"Oh my, you are nice in blue. Hold out your hands, now. Unless you would rather I blow your head off."

Sneed complied.

"Good boy," Bill said, as he clasped the cuffs. "You're quiet, I won't drive around long."

Bill shut the trunk and tried to decide whether to take the cop car or his own out to Quail Hollow Road. He decided to fix a triple decker in his biggest glass. Then he soaked a rag in mineral spirits and filled a paint pail with soapy water, grabbed a clean rag as well, and walked back out to the car. Sneed was still moaning. So pitiful that part of him felt sorry. Bill knocked on the trunk. The moaning stopped.

"Lay back. Help is on the way, but lay back or so help me, I'll kill you."

Bill opened the trunk and handed him the rags and the pail of soapy water.

"That should help," he said, as he gently closed the trunk. He had to drive only about four miles to Quail Hollow. Sneed could make it. He put the gun beside him on the seat and tore out. The damn thing was full of torque.

Sneed was noisy, but then got quiet. So quiet, in fact, that Bill pulled over to the side of Dove Flight Road. Quail Hollow was just ahead but he wanted to make sure there were no surprises. There weren't. Sneed was woozy and smeared with blue paint, but definitely conscious and that was the main thing. Bill jumped back behind the wheel and moved slowly up an incline, more dirt than gravel, alongside a cornfield and then down through a dry creek bed and over to some kind of shack in a stand of trees.

HOEDOWN MASQUERADE

It was dark now and Bill had never turned on emergency lights in a cop car. He yelled out to Sneed and asked where the siren was, but what muffled through was unintelligible, so he experimented with great success. Soon he had the siren going and the red light flashing. He picked up the pistol and took the shotgun down from its mount and yelled he would be back. Sneed was so quiet that Bill considered checking but did not. The element of surprise was important.

He marched through a pack of dogs more interested in sniffing than biting and stomped onto the porch, then banged on the door. Nobody answered. He banged again and again. Nobody there.

Bill was pissed and thirsty, so he walked back to the cop car, took a slug, then opened the trunk. Sneed was near passed out, so he let him take in air before he gave him the third degree.

Bill was in no mood to fool around.

"Where is she?"

"Maybe at the barn dance the next road down."

"Hope you're right."

He was right. Bill could hear fiddle before he crunched gravel. A few trucks and jalopies were parked outside a barn lit by lanterns. He parked the cop car in shadows, slinked to a crack in the barn siding, and peered in. The music was mournful, then suddenly spirited. Some people were dancing. Some sitting around. Bill heard voices approach, moved into darkness, stood absolutely still.

"You maintain you have no clue who?"

"Sure thing, Uncle Lacey. Have I ever, ever lied?" Bill heard her voice. "Must I tell you again? Must have been a pervert. One of those guys in bushes. What about Cousin Sneed? He tried to force me."

"Let's kick ass," said another.

"Not yet. Let me ask little Valerie." He cleared his throat. "You have any idea what you're doing to this family? I'm serious, you have a notion?"

"Never tried to hurt anyone I just—"

"Do you have an idea?" The voice insisted. "You have ruined this family. You understand? Know what it means to crawl through dirt? We fought for ever' inch. Ain't no poor man's world, girl! You have a clue how long it's gonna take to rebuild? We could kill you, your baby too, and not do harm you may have already done, God rest you."

Uncle Lacey said, "Pap Paw Hawkins, please let me."

"Ain't finished but go on."

"Honey, no one wants to harm that baby, whose ever. I sure don't blame you for holding Alexandra close, quiet and peaceful," Uncle Lacey cooed. "It's amazing in a way you don't catch our view. See, darling, we like peaceful, way you do, way it's supposed to, but facts are facts."

"That's correct," said the old man. "Facts are facts!"

"I don't know about film," Valerie insisted.

"Aw, honey, we done round and round. Why would cousin lie?"

"Uncle Lacey, God is my witness, the man tried to rape me."

"Who took the damn photograph?" Mam Maw chimed in.

"Know nothing about no photograph."

"She's lying, Pap Paw," Mam Maw said. "Gnat don't have the guts to lie."

"He's a Sneed," the old voice insisted.

"Might be, might not, but for sure he's a gnat, Oliver. Will you agree?"

"Put that way, I agree." The old man guffawed.

Bill heard what almost sounded like gentle laughter. He decided to lay low to see what came next.

"Give me the baby," said a rough old voice.

"Now, Oliver, give the girl a chance," said Mam Maw.

The baby whimpered, and Valerie said, "No way."

Another voice broke in and said, "Maybe another approach."

That voice was Bill's. He pointed the shotgun and pistol at the little group less than five yards away. The baby started howling as Valerie lurched over and stood beside him.

"Stay still and enjoy the music," Bill said.

"Who the hell?" Uncle Lacey asked.

"Your new boss," Bill said. "Get down on all four or I'll blow you away."

"Not Mam Maw," Valerie protested. "She has arthritis."

"All right, Mam Maw can stand. Rest down or you won't have knees."

"Who is this man, Val?"

The old man said, "Seen him down at Green's fishing shack. He come up with that nigger and Green."

"So, you're a friend of Green's?"

"You folks are amazing. You speak good, but you don't understand. Down or so help me, I'll open fire."

They kneeled like they were in church.

"Better. Now get in a little row with your hands out where I can see. Now listen. I got no quarrel with you people and you got no quarrel with me, but a problem we share is in the trunk of a cop car over yonder."

Their heads craned toward shadows.

"Sneed's in a trunk?" the old man asked. "Dead?"

"Nope, not last I checked, but he had turned most near blue."

"Well, I do declare," said Mam Maw.

"Now listen. This film you ask about is mine, not Valerie's, but mine, and if she knew where it was and gave it to you, she would be a fool and you would be a fool to give it to that lard."

Bill let that sink in.

"Fat boy can be persistent, can't he? No doubt he can lean hard. Sometimes you most likely get sick hiding behind his badge."

"You got that right," said Pap Paw.

"Didn't have to turn out this way," said Mam Maw. "Hard to believe he's a Sneed."

"Don't blame yourself, ma'am," Bill said. "What I'm driving at is that film, which is safely hidden, is about the best insurance policy that ever was. All that's on that film, which I hope never becomes necessary for any soul to see, will terrify Sneed for the rest of his days. You catch my drift? We got him where we want. Why mess? As long as he don't have the film, he's defanged. Got me?"

"Except for one thing," said Lacey.

"What's that?" Bill asked.

"What if you in cahoots? You sell him the film?"

"Not hardly," Bill said.

Bill started laughing and tucked the pistol under the arm still holding the shotgun level. He reached into his pocket and pulled out the car keys and handed them to Valerie. He pointed toward the cop car.

"Go open the trunk of Sneed's car and ask him to join us."

Valerie walked over, opened the trunk, and peered in.

"I think he's dead," she cried out.

"Doubt it," Bill said. "Find a stick and poke him."

"He's blue head to toe."

"Give a minute. He'll climb out."

Sure enough, he staggered over a few minutes later. All gasped when he emerged from the shadows. The faint light coming through the cracks of the barn made him look worse than Bill would have imagined. His entire face was blue, his hair and handcuffed hands were blue, eyes were blood red and glassy.

"Them ain't bruises," Pap Paw said.

"No sir," Bill answered. "He messed in some paint. He'll clean up."

"Land sake's," Mam Maw exclaimed. "How could he be that careless? Hate to say it, but he might be a Beasely, the more I think."

"Oh, Momma!" The old man interjected.

"Oliver, he can't be no Sneed."

"Just don't tell me he's a Beasely. Lord have mercy!"

"I ain't saying for sure."

Sneed was so bleary and sick, Bill figured he barely knew where he was.

"The main threat looks pretty tame and harmless, wouldn't you say?"

Everyone nodded, even Sneed.

"Suppose we agree to our little deal so that I can let you folks up and I can lower these firearms. Are we together on this? All in favor say aye."

Everyone said aye except Lacey. Bill called him on it.

"You're asking us to trust you an awful lot."

"No doubt," Bill said, "but no more than I'm trusting. Blood runs thick."

"Mam Maw's right. That boy can't be no Sneed. He ain't no blood of mine," the old man said. "Come on Lacey, quit playing lawyer and say aye."

He shook his head like he didn't like it, but he said, "Aye." Bill lowered the gun and they all stood up except Sneed, who was retching.

"You know," Bill said, "he might need doctoring. He's more trouble dead than alive."

"Fetch Cousin Bertie," Mam Maw said, pointing at the barn. "He's a damn good vet."

Pap Paw motioned Bill aside and asked when he could get a picture. Bill told him whenever he needed, which he doubted he ever would, then told him to let on like he already had one and that that should do the trick. The old man looked Bill hard in the eye.

Bill had known all along that guns were a bluff. Every man there had at least one, plus a razor-sharp knife, so when he locked Sneed's weapons in the trunk, it was no act of courage, but of practicality. Fortunately, when the vet was examining Sneed, he discovered a .32 strapped to his calf. Sneed was puking and didn't even notice when Cousin Bertie handed the dainty to Bill with a look of contempt.

"Gun that gets you dead," he said. Bill nodded but stuck it into his pocket for safekeeping.

The vet gave Bill, Valerie, and Alexandra a ride home. The baby cried the whole way, so it was hard to talk. As they crossed the bridge,

Bill threw the trunk key of the cop car out the window. The baby wailed until Valerie's soft noises seemed to comfort her. A moon was rising, and silvery light streaked the river.

It was so good to be home that Bill wanted to dance. Valerie tucked the child into her makeshift bed.

"Oh, Bill," she said as she fell into his embrace.

"Oh, Valerie!" he answered, playing along.

Dawn's early light affirmed it had been a late night. They awakened toppled and grinned like conspirators until the young one cried.

"This can't work," Valerie said.

"It sure is," Bill replied, as he was shifting into position.

"Is that all you men think about?"

"Mostly."

"God help us." Valerie ran to the child.

Bill pulled the cover over his head and dozed. When he awakened, she was gone.

He never figured out how—whether she walked or if somebody picked her up. She vanished. There she was and then she wasn't.

Days passed and nights, slowly. Green dropped by one late afternoon and they drank on the deck until the full moon set. Not a word passed between them about her except when Green asked about baby bottles inside the cooler.

"The girl stayed here a day or so," Bill said.

"She isn't yours, is she?" Green asked.

Bill didn't know what he was talking about. It wasn't until later as he was stretched out that he chuckled at the absurdity of that notion and wondered why Green had asked.

CHAPTER 5

FOREVER IN YOUR DEBT

Strange, but no stranger than the basket containing turkey potpie. The note simply said, "Thank you, Mr. Maddox. We are forever in your debt." It had appeared on the deck one morning when he wasn't looking. Days later, there was an apple cobbler. No note this time. He was wary of these offerings, but both smelled so delicious that after a small taste test, he ate his fill.

Bill had too much time on his hands and knew it, but nothing he could think to do really appealed. One morning, he walked down to Crabby's, air cool and clear, and realized that it was mid-September. Onset of autumn always energized him, so Bill conjured a plan, which he explained to Crabby whose eyes squinted and mouth twisted like he had chomped a lemon. Bill realized his own voice didn't sound convincing.

"Ain't thinking straight. Pack your car and move to Florida. No damn fool builds boat docks with winter coming." Crabby spit a gob of tobacco juice for emphasis.

"Well, next spring then. We'll do her next spring," Bill said as he turned away, wondering if he was losing his grip.

"Take a look around at what you already got. We'll be damn lucky if the whole kit and caboodle don't go south with high water. Buy insurance and pray they do. They're so torn up ain't worth a diddly."

Bill waved and kept on walking back to the boat. He couldn't explain. Felt queasy and feet heavy. Surprised and annoyed, as if he could float, but that maybe his feet would hold him down. He found his eyes near shut; maybe that explained darkness.

"Get your bony ass to Florida and take out insurance."

Bill lifted his arm and saw Crabby shaking his head.

Part of him wanted to do what Sarah wanted. But as Bill watched sun slant through late afternoon leaves, knew he could never. The boat was fine for sorting out.

He was inspecting docks when Valerie slipped up behind him.

"Damn, woman!"

"Oh, chicken. Now, Bill, don't make me cuss."

Bill had a huge grin that belied feigned fear.

"Listen, we got to talk."

He would always remember her eyes and how she managed to fold into his body. He would also never forget the way she smelled: sandalwood, fresh pine, and something beyond description. He followed her back to the boat totally aware of the light that danced through her dress. When a crow mocked, he refused to listen.

She wanted to get away. Away from family, from Sneed, from every damn thing, and she wanted to go to Florida.

"Tonight?" Bill asked.

"Why not?"

Bill struggled; she squirmed.

"Tonight?"

"You can't stay here, Bill. Your life is plum over. We got to get."

"Now, wait a damn minute. What's wrong with here?"

"There's no here for me or you!"

"Okay? Where in Florida? Got a plan?"

"Do you?" she asked forcefully. "Bill, it's warm and it ain't cold. What have you cooked? You going to sit here until hell freezes?"

Bill had no answer to that question, so they went to dinner. He figured it would pass, but it did not. She, like a hurricane, was as strong in the end as at the beginning. They were at the Pine Bar when she laid it on the line: my way or the highway.

As he was digesting this, some critters she was related to walked past their table and nodded.

"Do you see?" she asked. "They don't believe in nothing."

"I ain't running," Bill said.

"Who is talking about running? We're talking survival."

They ended up in the car behind a nearby barn. They talked, smoked, drank, and did things that led to forgetfulness.

When the bullet busted the car's rear window and sprayed them with glass, they kept right on pumping. Their hydraulics stopped, and both wondered what the concussion had been. So calm, they talked about it. Valerie smoothed down her skirt as Bill insisted on lighting her cigarette.

"Damn, if that ain't a bullet hole."

"Sure is, sweetness. Better keep down," he said.

"Bill, I'm scared."

"Yes, but he missed, didn't he?"

She nodded into his shoulder.

"Listen, he's probably more scared. If he had wanted, he could have shot point-blank and didn't. Why not?"

He held her close and listened.

"What if he shoots again?" she whispered.

"He'll miss."

"How do you know?"

"He don't want to die. I guarantee."

Bill lit a smoke.

"Holy moly, hallelujah! Bill, I thought it was the saints coming in, didn't you?"

"I sure did, sweetness." Surprised by a glint of light, he gently pushed Valerie down and slipped out the door. Before he had taken a step, a car door slammed and an engine roared and dust flew.

He jumped back in the car and chased after the taillights disappearing. Valerie climbed back into the front seat.

"Where's your gun?"

"Glove compartment," Bill answered.

"This ain't no gun," she replied, holding up her cousin's .32.

"Best we got."

"God help us, Bill!"

"He does if we allow," he said as the rear end slid and cracked a sapling.

"Careful! You want to get us killed?"

That seemed to cool Bill a bit and he backed off. He noticed the right rear dragging. A flat tire sure as hell.

Didn't take long to fix, but it took most all night to extinguish the smoldering fire that ate the backseat. It was only a smell at first, unpleasant and unidentifiable. Soon as they hit the highway, headed home, it got worse. Flames didn't exactly shoot through the bullet hole; however, there was a good deal of acrid smoke. He was back in Creekside across from the post office when the backseat suddenly burst into flames. Valerie sneezed, then snored, as Bill steered into the volunteer fire department. He sprayed the flaming mess, but not before he had carefully laid Valerie aside in soft grass. She didn't awaken until after he soaked the entire outfit.

She protested gently as Bill placed her back in the front seat but did not completely revive until they came to a stop at the boat.

"Oh, my God, fire and brimstone. Jesus, what the hell's that?"

Valerie folded into his arms and he almost dropped her into the creek as he carried her aboard. He managed to steer her into bed without answering further queries. Hell, it might have been his cigarette. Moonlight laced her face as she yawned and burrowed. He grabbed his flashlight and probed his car. Pretty sure the fire was out; still he yanked what was left of the backseat. He always had heard that kind of fire could burn hours.

He sat on the front deck and drank. The moon rose like a taunting ghost; wispy clouds surrounded the slender crescent, naked and stark as a needle at both poles. Bill wasn't frightened, but worried— mainly about Valerie.

Before he married, there had been a period after the war when life was automatic. While he wasn't looking, easy street became quite desolate. Then somehow, he met Sarah. She awakened something. He never knew what, but as he rocked on the creek and studied the moon, he realized that it was basically the will to seek life. With a chill running from the nape of his neck to the tips of his toes, he felt this will slacken. He felt a tug, but he had no idea what was pulling what or where. He slumped and tried to think of Sneed and how best to deal with the fat little bastard. Bill knew that Sneed was only a minnow, quick and foolish, and that whatever he had hooked or that had hooked him was certain and determined.

He looked in on Valerie. Whatever she was dreaming made her toss. The sheets were tangled. Bill fixed another and wondered how she could have gotten drunk so fast. It never occurred to him until months later that perhaps she had never bothered to be sober.

The moonlight played across her luscious derriere, but there was no room for him, so he returned to his chair on the deck and snoozed. When he awoke, it was still night and birds were beginning to anticipate dawn. He stood, stretched, and fired a smoke. The wind blew, and trees waved goodbye to the moon that had accompanied his slumber. The leaves, drying now, clattered a bit and a few came down at his feet.

A spider had been busy as he dozed and had woven an elaborate web from the overhang to his chair. He watched the spider laboring, not deterred that with a swipe of his hand, Bill could have destroyed everything.

Bill grinned at the spider, entered his boat, and by feel and first dawn light, approached the bed. He expected her to be gone. She wasn't. She was curled up in the blankets butt naked and soon he was beside her with a companion, a darkness he could not name.

RIGHT AS RAIN

A banging at the door shook him from reverie and into his pants. It was Green and Marcus and the kid with dogs. Bill asked for a minute to make himself decent. When he looked in the mirror, he knew he should have asked for an hour.

"We going fishing, Mr. Bill," Joshua announced.

Bill nodded.

"Brought you an old skiff I found in the barn. Be good for high water," Green said.

Bill nodded again.

"You all right?" Green asked.

"Hell, yeah," Bill said. "Right as rain."

It wasn't much of a skiff: wooden, full of leaks and with a motor whose oil had likely never been changed. But it chugged up creek with Green at the helm and Joshua bailing. About all Bill could figure was that this beat the deck.

"Mr. Maddox, you okay?" Marcus asked.

"Not bad for a white man," Bill replied, wondering why.

Joshua played with worms in the can and spouted off platitudes while Green steered the vessel like he was crossing the Atlantic and Marcus pretended to be studying the heavens. It was like that all day.

Fish were caught, but most released. Bill caught a keeper smallmouth. Joshua caught a nice catfish. Marcus went zip and Green caught three bluegill that were nothing to brag about.

Bill felt dizzy all day. Green pulled out a pint of whiskey and passed it to Bill, but he waved it off.

"Bill what's eating you?" he said. "Don't turn your back on your friends."

Bill swallowed and looked down. He felt weak.

"That's right, mister, we're here for you, for that is the Lord's way," Joshua exclaimed.

"Thank you kindly," Bill replied.

"Why don't we get you a phone?" Green asked.

"What do I need a phone for? People come and go."

Marcus raised his eyebrows. Green asked Bill what he was talking about. Bill said he wasn't exactly sure. Joshua said, "The Lord works in mysterious ways." Marcus put his hand on the child's knee.

Bill slumped on his deck and drank. He couldn't figure out whether he was trying to get warm or cool. A sunny October afternoon, but the breeze off the creek had a bite. Soon he was in shade and when the sun set, he welcomed darkness. He drank, smoked, and waited for nothing.

Weeks passed before he realized Valerie wasn't coming back. At first, he waited. At one point, the colorful autumn leaves rustling on the deck made him twitch, anticipating footfall.

Green ordered a phone. After it was connected, he dropped in and, over whiskey, suggested Bill use it. His jocularity was false, however, and both knew. He gave Bill a list of phone numbers. Marcus was on the list. Green told Bill to call Marcus if he needed anything in the next weeks, as he and Mrs. Green were off to Italy and Greece. Bill thanked him. When Green got home, he scared the hell out of Bill by calling. The phone had sounded like a fire alarm.

"Just checking," Green said. "Use the damn thing, will you, Bill?"

Bill said that he would, but after hanging up, he cut the wire and the next day he fed the phone to the fish. He was sinking low. Another turkey potpie appeared on his deck one evening while he was napping; too warm for catfish, so he waited about an hour before he called them to dinner. He placed the empty dish on the deck where he found it and, without considering its origin, returned to bed.

Temperatures were falling. Bill dreamed of coal. His forehead was blazing hot and if he squinted and focused right, he found he could jam some heat down into his knees and calves. He practiced, but never succeeded in penetrating past his ankles.

He awakened one morning to find what seemed like casserole dishes everywhere and he dumped them overboard and went back to bed. Bill conquered drink for the first time in his life. And smoke. Who needed it? He was fire. He was the essence of fire. He was a diamond in the making. He was coal black. He no longer needed to open his eyes. He shook with power. He burned without being consumed. Projected heat so focused it pierced like a needle of ice. It was now November.

———————

One day, he drove to Miss Robeson's, which served as the post office, phone switchboard, and small general store. Bill inquired about mail. There was none. Miss Robeson commented that he didn't look too good, but Bill shrugged and said he never had. He bought a Moon Pie he didn't ever open. She told him something was wrong with his phone. Bill's ears perked, but when she told him that Marcus tried to reach him, he smiled. Miss Robeson shook her pasty face as Bill stumbled out. He held the door open for a black woman who was trying to enter. She looked vaguely familiar.

He climbed in his car and drove home. Horns blared every foot of the way. He passed Sneed at the Pine Bar and waved. Sneed smiled and looked away.

When he got back, he noticed the skiff was sloshing. Part of him didn't give a damn, but he bailed her out. The effort seemed to do him some good. The rhythm of bailing, dip and splash, revealed vibrant colors of leaves reflected in rippling water, a swirling, hypnotic pattern. Mesmerized, he sat and watched and did not notice his feet were cold.

Everything was a swirling blur when a voice announced that they had to talk. Bill did not respond. The voice insisted that they had to talk. Bill resumed bailing.

"I need those photographs," the voice said.

"You're in the wrong place," Bill replied and scraped up water and dumped.

"I can pay good money."

"You're in the wrong place."

"I know where your girl is. Good money, Mr. Maddox, do you hear?"

"I wish I didn't."

"What you mean?" the voice asked.

Bill kept bailing.

"I am trying civil, Maddox. There are other ways."

"Try, Sneed. This ain't working."

Bill knew who was talking, but the ache did not and could not care. Money and fear had no purchase. He waved and returned to bed with cold feet.

"Son of a bitch," he muttered before he slipped away.

There was no dreaming that night. Fever was inside the covers with a rasping cough and outside too, seeking cool and then warmth. The sloppy wobble of the boat dizzied morning steps. The light, though not blinding, was too bright. He was thirsty, but before he had taken more than a few steps, he turned and tumbled back into bed.

Whatever he dreamed next clenched his hands and curled toes. His head was on fire and throat raw. He stretched his calves and dug deep into the pillow. When he awakened next, slanting light announced late afternoon. He hit the head and thought about a drink, then went back to bed and slept until dawn. His cough so deep that it intrigued him. Shaking chills made him yearn for a fire, but he stayed in bed conjuring cool water and heat, fire, and ice. His brains felt buttered, slippery and sliding.

It never occurred to Bill that he might be missed. Crabby and Bill gave one another a wide berth. Green was on a cruise. Valerie long gone. Bill dozed and stewed. One day he dreamed and when he awakened, he felt so refreshed that he poured a drink and lit a smoke. He went off for supplies: ice, beer, whiskey. As he stumbled across his deck he could see that he didn't need food. There were several casserole dishes lined up, untouched.

When he returned, he was puzzled to see all the casserole dishes were gone. Shaking his head as he looked in the mirror over his sink, he winked at himself. He didn't look all that bad, not half-baked dead like the clerk at the store had told him. He iced his beer, poured a drink, lit a smoke, took a few puffs, stubbed it, and passed out cold across the bed.

ANGEL AT THE DOOR

There was banging at the door.

Bill dug in deeper and ducked. When the banging did not stop, and he still wasn't dead, he peeked out, surprised to see the walls of the boat cabin. Some determined voice commanded his attention. A voice he did not recognize. He hollered something to make it stop, but it would not, so he dragged himself over and with no thought at all, opened the door.

"What?" he said.

"Lord have mercy, Mr. Maddox."

Bill saw a small black woman, a bit startled, who held a pot of soup, still steaming.

In the dark through the steam, Bill had no idea what he was seeing. Was he dreaming? Was it his time? He stared hard but could make no sense. She seemed to fight the urge to jump and stepped forward. Bill stepped back. That seemed to embolden her.

"I brought you soup that'll do you good," she said.

"Come aboard," Bill said, turning. "Watch your step."

Hard as it might be to believe, Bill did not recognize Ruby Woods, only saw a woman with dark skin, a commanding presence, and a pot of unwanted soup. He coughed deeply and poured a drink. He offered her one and she accepted a nip, but then refused another.

"Soup is it?"

"Mr. Maddox, please sit; you are looking poorly."

"I have been hearing that all day. I'm tired of hearing it."

"You might want to listen, sir. Why haven't you been eating?"

Bill looked at her earnest expression and saw nothing but vague shape and steam.

"I ate some," he said.

"Not enough. You look awful," she replied.

"Damn," Bill said.

"Now, Mr. Maddox, no need to cuss, though I don't condemn, but you must eat. You haven't most of a week."

"How you know what I eat?"

"Please sit down, Mr. Maddox; have some soup and maybe I'll clue you in."

Bill sat.

They did not talk easily. For one thing, he wanted to smoke and drink, and wasn't hungry. Publicly, she disapproved of tobacco and liquor, though she partook. She wanted him to eat. There they were, eye to eye. Bill saw blur; she missed nothing.

"You trying to die?"

"You trying to make me lose my appetite?"

"Not hardly. Why you think I'm cooking so hard?"

Bill took a sip and grimaced.

"All fresh, Bill Maddox."

"Well, I ain't used to it."

"Better had, if you want back."

"To what?" Bill asked. "What do you care?"

Miz Ruby coughed through that remark and asked permission to smoke.

"So you smoke?"

"And drink too," she replied defiantly, "although I do disapprove."

"Hell's bells; let's party," Bill said.

"Please eat, Mr. Maddox. I'll take care of smoking and one more nip."

That night he ate, drank, and smoked. Next day, he woke up feeling like hell. Miz Woods woke the same as usual and started in on a potpie. Before she and her daughter stopped off at Bill's, she surprised herself when she checked out her makeup in the vanity mirror, but Bill was asleep when she banged on the door.

When he finally came to the door, he looked a bit worse.

"What you staring at?" he asked.

There was a November chill in the air and with Bill's permission, she built a fire in the stove. He fixed a drink as the fire popped and crackled, but before she had ladled out his portion of pot pie, he was asleep in his chair.

"He looks like death," she said to her daughter, Amelia, as they slowly drove away.

"It ain't right. It ain't right, Amelia. I'm saying it ain't right!"

"You done what you could, Momma, all you could."

While Bill snored, her food cooled. Miz Ruby knew it and felt terrible inside.

That night as she said her prayers, she vowed she would never quit. She and Bill made a strange pair and fought every inch. Bill did not know he had made up his mind to die and Ruby wasn't altogether certain. Her helpfulness made him crazy.

As November inched toward December, they fought. They fought about soup. They fought about stew. They fought about politics and health regimens.

They fought about everything. They never mentioned Ronald or Sarah or anyone either had personally known and it finally dawned on Ruby that she was nothing more than a foil to a death wish. She wouldn't have put it like that. Most likely, she would have said the man likes to spite. She didn't know yet that he was almost totally out of his mind.

That's all they did, spar and snarl. Bill was drinking more, eating less, and coughing like he was heaving up an anchor. It wasn't working. Her food that she watched him take was nothing compared to what she left and what he claimed to be eating but wasn't. He was feeding fish and she caught his skinny ass. She gave him hell. He gave it right back and she went home indignant and didn't return for two whole days. When she did, she dropped off a small pot of soup and knocked on the door. She felt bad about driving away, but that's what she did.

The next day she brought nothing, but when she drove by, she saw the pot undisturbed. She went home and before dinner, she asked her children to pray with her. She was stumped and did not know what to do. The cantankerous old goat had her stymied.

"Cory, Amelia, John, Jason, Ava. Lord, please Lord, join us in prayer . . ."

She prayed for Bill Maddox. They all did. She asked for his health to improve and begged forgiveness for whatever responsibility her family might bear for its failing. She pleaded for an answer.

Her youngest spoke up right after the amen.

Jason said, "We need to go get him, tonight, else he might die."

A squabble broke out around the table,

"Dinner's getting cold." said John.

"We got no room for no one else."

"He's sick. We don't need a sick man here."

"Where we gonna put him?"

"He's a white man. Let them do for their own," John said.

"Yeah, he ain't none of us," Ava chimed in.

"Hold it. Eat your supper," Ruby said. "What do you say, Jason?"

"Blood is on our hands already. Get him tonight or he will die."

"Hear your brother," Ruby said. "Eat your supper, now. We got work to do."

Who knows what Bill was dreaming? The rocking of a small boat is confusing. He was fevered and near death, when they rolled him into a blanket and managed to cart him off. It took all of Ruby's children to do it and they almost dropped him overboard. He was dead to the world, way beyond soup. They bumped his head on a piling when they stepped on the shore.

"Thank you, sugar," Bill said, as they trudged up to the car.

"What's he saying, Momma?" Amelia asked.

"Boiler maker. Rummy baby. Drop the skirt, sweetie pie!"

"Just put him in the car," Ruby said. "Never mind what he's saying, he's out of his mind."

"How do you get out of your mind, Momma?"

"Hush and load him in. Do what I say."

DEATH'S DOOR

Ruby's was a small, well-kept house. Bill was tucked into a fold-out, makeshift bed that the grandmother slept in when she dropped by. He was pale as a ghost. His cough scared everybody. Ruby had a doctor; though she didn't believe in them, she called anyway. The doctor gave Bill penicillin, frowned, and asked Ruby what she thought she was doing.

"If he ain't better tomorrow, put him in the hospital."

Amelia nodded like she agreed.

Bill had turned gray by morning but wanted a drink by mid-afternoon. But there was no whiskey. That was no problem, because he was dead asleep within an hour and stayed that way for most of two days. Ruby made soup, but no one drank it. Even the kids lost their appetites. Bill was dying. There was no doubt. Ruby was scared.

"What if he dies on us, Momma?"

"Don't even talk like that, child," she said, knowing in her heart no hospital could save him.

"But what if he does?"

Somehow he didn't.

They prayed over him. He coughed and sputtered.

They bathed him and cleaned up his mess. For a few days, he was nothing but mess. They cried over him. He became something of a pet. To the kids, he was like some lost animal; to their mother, he was something more. He still did not know that this was Ronald's family. He was totally out of his mind.

After a few days, they got used to his retorts.

"Your love pleases more than anything."

A child wiping his brow with a cool cloth.

"Come now to paradise, my dear angel."

Someone performing a necessary ministration.

"Thank you for coming, my child."

Giggles and laughter. Children as nurses, mother as cook.

Ruby called the doctor back in and Bill was given another shot. The doctor wasn't hopeful. But Bill fooled them all. He was a tough bird and woke up singing "You Are My Sunshine," which startled everyone.

Amelia was there first, followed by her mother and both were horrified. Bill's voice was so bad that it would have frightened anyone. Ruby had never heard him sing and Amelia saw his eyes open for the first time. It was easy to understand their consternation. They tried to calm him, but he was like a springtime bird and would not stop.

He sang for hours, and at first, it was funny, until he would croak he was dry and needed whiskey. Ruby did not know what to do. She attempted to calm him with no success. She sent Jason for Polecat Green and some of his whiskey. She already had honey. She figured a tonic might do him good. About the time Polecat and Jason got there, Bill was wobbling on elbows, eyes wild. Polecat, who was a huge man, looked frightened when he saw him.

"Sure that man needs whiskey?"

"Not hardly," Miz Ruby said, "but sure needs something and I could use a shot."

"I hears that," Polecat said.

"That man needs peace," Jason said.

Ruby and Polecat urged Jason out. Ruby took the pint from Polecat and took a shot, while Bill stared off into space and sang the "Star-Spangled Banner," interspersed with snatches of "Over There." Polecat took some himself.

"Maybe a little bit wouldn't hurt," he said.

Ruby poured hot water, honey, and lemon juice into a glass and splashed in an ounce or two of whiskey. She nodded at Polecat as Bill warbled. She held the concoction under Bill's nose and he instantly stopped singing. She winked at Polecat.

"Seems to be working," she whispered. "Mr. Maddox, Mr. Maddox, something good for you to drink, sir."

She put the glass to his lips, and then one of his hands, trembling, clutched and tossed it down in one gulp. His eyes got wide; he grimaced.

"Praise God, but that is one unusual cocktail, pilgrims," Bill croaked. He coughed and slowly fell back and closed his eyes.

"Seems it quieted him."

"Not a second too soon, either," Ruby replied. "That man's voice is cross between buzzard and crow, so help me."

"Thank you, good pilgrims," Bill drawled. "One more, if you please. I feel a song coming on."

Ruby and Polecat started pouring, squeezing, and mixing, and before Bill had got more than halfway through "Danny Boy," they had the concoction to his lips. Ruby and Polecat finished what remained of the pint. Bill fell back satisfied and licked stubbly chops.

"How much do we owe you?" Ruby asked.

Polecat said, "This one's on me. Sure you be needing more."

They did, but not right at first, because Bill almost immediately took a turn for the worse. In fact, he sank so low the preacher was worried as he had never blessed a white man in a black person's house. He knew of Bill and, like everyone else, knew what he did for the boy, kept him out of the chair, but after all, he was a white man. Strange—though he never would have admitted it—to pray for his soul. Bill guttered and spewed on the edge of what is called con-sciousness and garbled wisecracks no one could decipher. He was a goner, and even Ruby knew.

At night and even sometimes during the day, he screamed outrageous threats. Some were intelligible, relating to the war; most were not. Polecat became a frequent visitor and his medications seemed to provide a glimmer of hope.

"How could I have done this without you?" Miz Ruby asked Polecat one day when Bill was starting to sit up and sip soup.

"He be all right, Miz Ruby," Polecat said. "We done what we could."

Later on, Jason tried to claim that his and Joshua's prayers had done it, that Mr. Maddox had found the peace of the Lord. Miz Ruby smiled and looked up to the sky and said, "You children don't know the half."

———

Amelia, who was seven, turned out to be Bill's favorite. Tiny, she was, and bright as a button. Her eyes flashed with amusement at almost everything Bill did, so naturally he was taken by her. She was quick and nearly anything he uttered tickled her funny bone.

"So, Amelia, why did the chicken cross the road?"

"Who can say, Mr. Bill?" she would answer, laughing her head off.

"To get to the other side."

"Oh, Mr. Bill, you made that up to make me laugh."

"Did not, ever."

"Did too, ever."

"You're pulling my leg," Bill would say.

"I am not. I'm not pulling your leg, you old rooster!"

"You calling me an old rooster?"

"No, no, Mr. Bill. I call you a poopy cock; Momma calls you an old rooster."

"She does?" Bill would say, making the small girl's eyes large. "What else does she call me?"

"She calls you a whiskey-guzzling nincompoop."

"A whiskey-guzzling nincompoop, does she?"

"Yeess, she does." said the little girl, backing away and smiling.

"Praise the Lord, must be getting well."

"That's what Momma says, old fuddy-duddy, you!"

"Come back here, whippersnapper." Bill made as if to grab her and she giggled out of the room; he laid back onto the pillow and thought better of getting well.

He smiled as he drifted back, but then made a mistake. He asked why.

Why? What for and why should he get well? It was the wrong question; that didn't stop his mind churning. What was the reason?

Bill sank again, and this time wanted to die and knew it. Previously it had been a feeling. This time was conviction.

Good thing Amelia didn't sense it. When she traipsed in with her yellow rubber duck toy, Bill was asleep, and she poked him in the nose. He coughed so loud that it scared her. When his eyes opened, he saw Ronald and grabbed her and shook her. Amelia screamed for Ruby, which brought Bill to his senses. When Ruby walked in, Bill was weeping and tenderly holding the child's fingertips.

"It's okay, Mr. Bill," the little girl said.

"No, it ain't, young one. I am forever sorry. I was asleep, child. I'm awake now. Please understand."

So many thoughts jiggling, Bill was reminded of the house of mirrors at the Fontaine Ferry Park on the other side of town. He couldn't conceal the dread and confusion he felt as he stared from the frightened child's face into the eyes of her mother.

"Mr. Maddox," Ruby said. "Please do not blame the child. Do you hear me?"

Bill saw enough to know where he was and who had been looking after him, though he didn't know quite why. The child clutched her mother before she ran from the room. Ruby said nothing. Neither did Bill.

Amelia and Jason peeked in, brother John looked over their heads. Bill stared wild-eyed with his mouth open. Ruby shut the door without saying anything and the children disappeared.

"I didn't know," Bill said. "God almighty, I didn't know."

"You've been sick, Mr. Maddox," Ruby said. "Be still, and I'll try to explain."

"I don't know if I can be."

"Want to die?"

"Who the hell knows? Do you relish a nightmare? What am I doing here?"

"Getting well, for one, you didn't know your name two days ago."

"Is that so?"

"You want some whiskey? I got a pint."

"Do you think it's wise?" Bill asked with a grimace.

"Not hardly, but I do think it's called for," Ruby said.

Bill consented and after clearing his lungs, asked for a smoke.

One sip and his lips were burning. One puff and his throat was raw, and he coughed so hard that he put it out. In fact, he only half finished the drink, but it seemed to comfort. That he had just about died was about all he could take before fatigue grabbed and tugged. He held his half-finished drink.

"Why?"

Before Ruby could answer, he snored.

———————

Almost well, he was even more of a curiosity, especially for the young. After all, they had carried him off that dingy old boat, in drizzling chill in a blanket. Finally, they got to see what was inside the head that they bumped while they dragged and lugged deadweight. Now there he was, some strange old bird hatched out of scratchy blankets.

He sang for breakfast: a piece of toast with jam.

At lunch he piped up: soup, saltine crackers, and ginger ale.

Cocktail hour brought forth an aria: Bill's voice, demanding, but not insistent.

He crowed for his supper while the family dog, Brutus, hid.

He was, indeed, getting better. At first, it was gratifying and then amusing, but at last, it was Ruby's family's turn to ask why?

Bill, for his part, was glad to be alive. He wasn't sure yet what for, but unlike his saviors, was not asking many questions. The cool December light poured in before the children got home from school and Ruby returned to tend them. He probably did some contemplating, but not much and was amazed to be able to scruff to the toilet and doubly when he realized that other people had taken care of all this and he couldn't remember a damned thing.

One afternoon, he found Ruby's pint in a cupboard, and minutes later, she walked in to find him on all fours drinking whiskey and smoking one of her smokes. She said nothing at first. Bill tightened his bathrobe sash and cleared his throat. She placed grocery sacks on the kitchen table.

"So how was your day?" Bill asked, trying to sound normal.

"We needs to talk, Mr. Maddox, that's how my day goes."

Bill said he was all ears.

"Mr. Maddox, I emptied your pockets when we carried you here, but I did it for your life's sake. I felt an obligation," she said, standing as tall as she could. "The money's long gone and the doctor's bill is due and I don't mind feeding, but you're drinking my whiskey."

"And smoking your smokes and God knows they're awful things," Bill allowed.

"You shameless man. You done finished them," Ruby exclaimed, throwing the empty, wadded-up pack into the trash.

Bill started laughing and Ruby scowled.

"What's so damn funny?"

"You got my shoes here?" Bill asked.

"What would anybody want with your shoes?"

"Hell, nobody wants my shoes, but was I wearing them?"

"Along with the rest of your stink."

"If you didn't throw them out, please bring them to me."

Ruby brought him all his stuff. Washed clothes, folded. His shoes even shined. She presented them to him like a crown at a coronation. Bill laughed and took one of the shoes and reached inside and dug out a small sheath of greenbacks.

"What do I owe you?"

She laughed.

"Well, at least one quart of whiskey and the doctor's bill, plus a pack of smokes."

Bill handed her some money and she asked him if he wanted

some provisions, as well. Bill doubled up and that brought a smile to Miz Ruby, who dashed out the door. Bill took a quick bath and when she returned, was dressed, clean, but not shaven. He rubbed what must have been weeks of stubble.

"I couldn't find a razor," he said.

"Leave my razor alone."

"Right."

"How about a drink, Mr. Maddox?" she said, as she handed him smokes and matches.

"Oh, perhaps, a short one," he replied, as he fired up a Pall Mall and lit Ruby's Kool Menthol.

"Knew you were a gentleman."

They clinked glasses.

Ruby suspected Bill was fragile as eggs. Bill knew he was.

"Damn it, Ruby, what's going on? God help me, I swear I con't know."

Ruby raised her hand like a traffic cop.

"In the morning. Take another taste," she said, offering the whiskey. "Mr. Maddox, please believe, no one here means harm. You're tired now. Sit back and rest."

A few minutes later, halfway through his drink, he stumbled to bed and sank into his pillow, managing not to spill a single drop.

"How you like that?" he asked, before he dozed.

Miz Ruby took his glass and shook her head. How the hell could she tell a story so confusing? Bill snored. She poured another whiskey. She wanted him stronger. She feared driving him crazy. She would somehow have to tell and knew that sure as hell. She dreaded that moment, but as Bill snored, Ruby sipped whiskey gratefully.

CHAPTER 6

GRATITUDE

To Ruby, Bill did not seem filled with prejudice, but bitter experience had made her wary. Everything that she wanted to reveal to him had happened a long time past. Still, she was concerned. You never knew about these crackers and she hated to think of this man that way but couldn't help it. What if she was wrong about him and he took offense? She knew that by all rights, after what Ronald, her firstborn, had done, that any natural man would have wanted monstrous revenge. She balanced her need to protect Ronald, whose safety she credited to Bill's intercession on his behalf, with her deeply felt desire to explain why she felt a further strong bond with Bill and his people.

What if telling him the truth of what had happened nearly one hundred years before drove him into an even darker place, a mood turbulent and incomprehensible? She knew he had forgiven Ronald officially, but what if he concluded that his people back for one hundred years had been deeply betrayed? Ruby left him snoring. In her bedroom, she sat down with the family Bible.

She lugged it into bed. Ruby stared at it like it was a closed casket. When she opened it, neither the Old nor New Testament struck her eyes. Instead she gazed upon entry after entry of family history. It was to the ones whose names appeared in mostly purplish ink that she made her appeal. She turned these pages reverently.

Vision blurred, her hand caressed, seeking assurance. Apparently, none was forthcoming. It was dark when she closed the book. Amelia peeked in and asked her mother if she was all right. Ruby said she would be in a minute. Then she knew what to do.

First, she called up Mr. Traylor and talked it over with him. He agreed that Bill had to be told. He suggested it might best be done in a group setting. He told her to touch base with Miss Hayes, which after thanking him, she did. Miss Hayes soothed her fears some and said something that should have been obvious. "Even so, what can he do about something long ago?"

Miss Hayes suggested Miz Ruby call Fred Ruby, who had been Bill's neighbor and pretty near friend, who happened to be her second cousin once removed. Miz Ruby called Fred and he agreed to be part of the group. He proposed that she call the Reverend William, who was his first cousin and also Polecat Green's cousin.

Miz Ruby liked the idea of the preacher being there, but she was troubled by the mention of Polecat.

"Fred, why you want Polecat there?"

"Well, he's a relative and reckon we might all need a drink after, no matter which."

"Fred Ruby, you're still a devil."

"I prefer practical," Fred said.

Once it was settled, Miz Ruby felt so much better that she whistled around the house and not only did the kids notice, but Bill did as well. He sat in bed as she spruced and dusted. She put her brood to work, scrubbing and such. They complained and asked what was going on. She shushed, and they complied.

Polecat was first to arrive that Friday evening. He commented that the soup smelled good as he put about five pints of whiskey on the counter.

"How you be knowing it's soup, Polecat? Might be a roast," Miz Ruby said.

Polecat was about to agree when Bill sauntered in, looking three or four paces further from death.

"Howdy do, pilgrim," he said.

"Fine, indeed, Mr. Maddox."

Bill seated himself. Polecat poured him a drink. Bill thanked him graciously. Polecat thanked the source of all grace that Bill was not singing.

"Well, perhaps you're wondering what summoned you here," Bill said.

"Yes, indeed," Polecat said, raising his glass.

If Miz Ruby hadn't been so nervous, she would have shooed Amelia and Jason out of the kitchen before she said what she did.

"Neither one of you turkeys knows why. Drink your whiskey and hold your fire."

Both men looked at each other with consternation, but before they said anything, Miz Ruby was scattering kids and there was a knock on the door. It was Mr. Traylor, followed by Miss Hayes. Then minutes later, Fred Ruby walked in with Reverend William.

Bill was in the mood to check his pulse. Polecat's eyes were bulging. They looked at each other and shrugged.

Mr. Traylor and Reverend William were served coffee, but Bill noticed that Mr. Traylor added a dash of Polecat juice. Miss Hayes asked for water and old Fred accepted a glass of bourbon and water, the color of strong iced tea. There wasn't a lot of shooting the breeze. Miss Hayes and Ruby gabbed it up about how nice everything looked, but the rest of them sipped beverages and looked apprehensive, even Mr. Traylor, who sat in his chair tapping his foot.

"You looking better than I feared," Fred said.

"Better than I deserve, I suppose," Bill replied. "Thanks to Miz Ruby and Polecat Green."

"Now, now, I ain't done nothing," Polecat said.

Reverend William drained his coffee cup, set it down on the kitchen table, and asked Miz Ruby for a glass of whiskey, straight up. She proffered it with shaking hands.

"Aw, come on folks, I ain't that bad. Reverend, you look so grim, it looks like you're preparing to send me off, and I'm warning that in spite of all prayers that it most likely will not work."

Miss Hayes drew in her breath, but the Reverend laughed and took a sip of whiskey. Mr. Traylor chuckled and suggested that he could use a taste, and of course, Fred asked for another. Miz Ruby laughed and poured one for herself with some Coca-Cola after she had served the others.

They all lit cigarettes at once, except Miss Hayes who didn't smoke and Fred, who lit a cigar. The room was smoky instantly and full of the sounds of throats clearing.

Mr. Traylor spoke first.

"Mr. Maddox, all here are grateful you are improved and sincerely hopeful for your full recovery. Please indulge Reverend William, who has been moved to say a short prayer."

"Lord, please guide our hearts into your grace and free our minds of chains that bind to darkness so that we may be free to glorify in the love, wisdom, and forgiveness that can only be offered by Jesus Christ, our Lord."

"Amen," everyone said, even Bill and Polecat.

No one spoke. There was plenty of time to sense silence. Mr. Traylor again spoke first.

"Thanks for joining us here, Polecat. I had forgotten how good whiskey can taste. Mr. Maddox, I suppose you wonder what this is about."

Bill simply nodded. He looked puzzled, not nervous.

"I'll tell you. We in this community are deeply grateful for what you did for Miz Ruby and her son, poor Ronald. We know that no amount of gratitude could ever make up for what you have suffered and the burden you bear. It troubles us more deeply than you could ever know."

"Yes, that's true," Miss Hayes said. Ruby and the others nodded. Bill bowed his head.

"Please," he said, and he started to shake. He held his breath. Fred placed his hand on Bill's shoulder.

"Mr. Maddox, my name is Jim Traylor. May I address you as Bill?"

"Call me anything," Bill muttered.

"There's a whole lot that can't be changed. As much as we might hate that, it is undeniably true. Would you agree, sir?"

"I thought you were going to call me Bill."

When Bill said that, it seemed to squeeze something out of the room. Everyone seemed to stretch a bit.

"Bill, all of us here owe you. Not only spared one boy's life, but who knows how many others you may have spared with your wisdom and kindness. That is speculation, though all of us here are certain it is true. That boy, Ronald, faced certain death until you spoke."

"What else could I do, damn it?"

"Thank you, from a mother's heart, Mr. Maddox," Miz Ruby said.

Fred nudged Bill's elbow and Bill polished off his drink. Fred fixed him another.

"Miz Ruby, fetch your Bible and put it on the table here. Bill, all of us here have something in common," Mr. Traylor said. "That is, some of us would very likely not be here if your grandfather hadn't done what he did."

Miz Ruby opened the family Bible to the inscription part. All Bill saw was scrabbly lines, crude script, Xs and dates. Miz Ruby explained that these were her people who had been slaves. "Slaves and then free folks."

Bill looked up and shrugged.

"I don't understand why you're telling me all this," he said.

"Because the part that ain't written is the story you need to know," Miss Hayes said.

"Your grandfather, the man who owned the tavern down on the creek, saved our lives and nobody knows it. At least almost nobody," Mr. Traylor said.

"What are you talking about?" Bill asked.

"Freedom. Liberation. A chance at life. Have you ever heard of the Underground Railroad?" Mr. Traylor asked.

"Maybe we should slow down a bit," Bill drawled. "At least I should, I can tell you."

"You set the pace, Bill," Fred Ruby said. Everyone nodded in agreement. Bill shook his head and looked into every face.

"Been sick, still am I guess, but thought all the strangeness was getting better. What the devil you trying to tell?"

"Your granddad was a freedom runner," Mr. Traylor said.

"A what?" Bill asked.

"Your granddad was part of the Underground Railroad. He carried our people out of slavery across the river to freedom. He did this at great risk. Nobody knew. His people didn't know. If they had, they would have figured him crazy, risking all their lives and everything else. 'Stealing niggers' was frowned upon at the time," Mr. Traylor added with unconcealed bitterness crackling in his voice.

"There is no telling where many folks would be without him, Mr. Maddox," Reverend William said. While the women nodded, Fred patted Bill's shoulder.

Bill shook his head. "I didn't know anything about this. How do you know?"

"We know," Mr. Traylor said and everyone but Bill nodded.

"How? That stuff is history, ain't it?" Bill asked, looking genuinely confused.

"Not all that long ago," Fred said.

Polecat spoke up. For such a big man, he looked like a shy, tall boy, but his voice was strong.

"My people worked for your people, Mr. Maddox, and they were free somehow. They did gardening, some carpentry, and helped make your granddad's whiskey. That's the way I heard it as a child coming up, always in whispers. Nobody would talk about past things out loud. Did you ever know whether or not your granddad had slaves?"

"Not hardly," Bill answered with a tinge of irritation.

"Well, he never did. He paid and those he paid, he paid well enough that he made enemies with his own people, and the people he paid stashed it away. Did you know that my granddaddy had slaves? Guess what? After a time, he freed them. Some of those slaves worked for your granddaddy and then somehow their kids and relatives would turn up missing. Can you believe that?"

Bill started laughing quietly.

"Listen, Bill, it's true," Fred said.

"It's the Lord's truth, shameful as it is, but it is the truth," Polecat said. "Maybe not so hard to understand when you consider the economics. Do for me, I do for you. You understand that, don't you?"

"Aw," Bill said. "What is this—comedy hour? I feel pretty good. Don't humor me, please."

"Nobody's humoring anybody," Mr. Traylor said.

"Mr. Traylor—" Bill began.

"Jim," Mr. Traylor interjected.

"All right, Jim, what are you driving at?"

"Truth."

"Truth?"

"Bill, things have been buried so long; people have forgotten where. Polecat is not lying. His people owned slaves: Miz Ruby's people. His people built boats and needed labor. Your granddad and the others worked them hard, but then set them free. Think about it like a retirement plan."

"My people built boats, keelboats and they done every other damn thing, Mr. Bill, but they was somehow free and they could buy freedom for others over time," Polecat said. "Your daddy, I mean, your granddaddy, could fudge the situation a bit. By that I mean, as I heard it, he often sweetened the pot, which way don't matter much, but the people got paid mostly. Still it don't take away from what he done with that boat of his. If he had been caught—and nobody could ever figure out how he wasn't—some folks would have put a bullet in his head or a sharp knife across his throat."

In spite of himself, Bill harrumphed. "What you mean by mostly got paid, Polecat?"

Polecat snickered and said, "Well, he was a Scotsman and a

Presbyterian who loved to make a nickel, but also apparently, your granddaddy liked a challenge or else the way I heard it, he made it his cause. Because he went hog wild. Instead of every few months on a cloudy night in the dark of the moon, seems like he got bolder and bolder, but he never got caught. Maybe because he always employed free people like mine and mixed us up together. Who the hell knows? We all looks alike, Mr. Bill. You've heard that said a time or two."

"Never!" Bill laughed. "How do you know your grandpappy had slaves? And how in the hell do you know my granddad helped free them?"

"We just know. It's a fact. Just like Miss Hayes' great-grandpa owned a Cherokee and her mother was owned by one. No one wants to remember these things, least of all me, but I have heard these things forever. They don't go away."

"Dang."

"What you mean by that?" Fred asked.

"Damned if I know. Nobody told me anything except the difference between right and wrong. Why didn't anybody tell me?"

"Who could?" Mr. Traylor said. "It was too dangerous long ago to admit anything. Your grandmother didn't know. I would bet everything I own. If she had, she would have called your granddad a fool and she would have been right. Nobody could talk about this stuff. How could anyone remember? For that matter, why you figure there are so few of us this evening?"

"I ain't sure. What I want to know is how come you can talk about it?"

Mr. Traylor looked around the room and into every face before he spoke.

"You're right, Mr. Maddox, that has been a problem from the beginning. There are two enemies we have had: our people and your people. The very worst of both, no lie. As you must notice, we are a small group. That is on purpose."

Bill nodded.

"Thanks for including me," Bill said.

"You included yourself with deeds," Mr. Traylor said.

"Yeah, but how did people pull it off?"

"Use your imagination," Mr. Traylor said. "Some people were bought; some were sold. There were brokers, both sides making money off the middle. There were snitches and turncoats. A lot of blood was spilled, and a lot of people hanged. There was a lot of loose talk, but there were some solid people as well."

"So, maybe I'm talking to the solid people?"

"We certainly pray we are worthy," Reverend William said.

"Imagine this," Mr. Traylor whispered. "Imagine having absolutely nothing to buy anything with. Then there's a wake-up call each morning and all night, too, and none of that was going to change one iota. That is incentive, sir. Miz Ruby, please show Bill your great-grandmother's bracelet."

Miz Ruby reached down and lifted an old wooden box. She put it on the table and removed the lid. Mr. Traylor reached in and pulled out some old rusty chains with shackles. He stirred around until he came up with a key. He held it up and, with glazed eyes, shook it.

"This key cost more than a Cadillac car. This key cost more than most who would have loved to use it would have ever earned if they had been free. Do you understand the singular achievement of those folks like Polecat's who managed to purchase not one, but many?"

Polecat nodded. The rest did the same.

"No matter how many flatboats and skiffs they built, his folks could never, ever have earned enough to buy all free. The wages were not there, so people done other things, unspeakable things, just to free themselves or others. People had to look the other way. It was war, Bill; it sure wasn't pretty. You understand, of course."

Bill nodded, remembering things he wished he couldn't, and then Mr. Traylor quietly added, "Your granddaddy picked up a lot of slack. Some told he took money sometimes, but if he was in it for money, he was a fool! Not enough money in this whole world to have everybody wanting to cut your throat. That's the way it was.

Black people were tied in with white. Had no choice if they wanted to eat. Stool pigeons were everywhere, and envious people wished it was them getting out. How anybody pulled off what your grandfather did is a mystery."

"Amen."

"Everybody against you. Your own blood and not only the powers that be, as they now say. Still the same. Your race, my race: What difference? People hiding from truth! Black people bad as white. Most folks scared of their shadow. Some, praise God, were not.

"When I started out in the hauling business, my competition was white, and they were rough, but I could beat the price. They hated me, but before long, they hired me some, and I made them money and after a while, they figured old Jim Traylor wasn't so bad after all. When I started toting garbage, the white man that did it threatened my life and I carried a pistol right in my belt. We worked it out so that he could expand and then offer twice the service and enrich himself, too.

"But see, in those olden days, you could not have done that. They would have screwed you up from here to Tuesday. Let me tell you, Bill, the way things have been since Jim Crow has at times been worse. But enough—that came later. Now, the point I want to make is that all my success with my homestead development, my school bus business, and all that, is owed directly to men like your grandpa. My kind fight tooth and nail, but we could not have fought one step without men like him. You are one of those men, too."

Bill didn't have a thing to say. He raised his glass.

"What you've done by sparing Ronald is of the same cloth," Reverend William said.

"That's right," Miss Hayes said. "Tapestry is woven of many threads. In my yard, there is a stout oak I hate to look at sometimes because I know history, but it stays right where it is, and I remind myself that the limb used was innocent. Mr. Maddox, you cannot know how grateful we are."

Finally, Bill felt like he had to speak.

"Miss Hayes, Mr. Traylor, everybody, I appreciate everything that has been said, but the food smells so good. Is it possible, do you think, for a poor sinner like me to have supper?"

Bill was the only one hungry. Miz Ruby brought him some soup. He didn't mean to slurp but did. Everyone laughed. Bill was so hungry he didn't care.

"Happy to see you feeling better," Polecat said.

"Damn straight," Bill said, suddenly feeling ravenous. "Got bread?"

"Corn bread," Miz Ruby said.

Bill nodded and was served a hefty wedge.

He was exhausted. He tried to put up a front that everyone saw through. Before long, he was alone with Miz Ruby, who simply told him to get ass in bed.

Bill complied, surprised at her salty command but was so tired he did not resist. For her part, Miz Ruby fell like a tree cut at the base. She felt years of stuff sliding down through arms and fingers, ankles and toes. Hell's bells, she thought and the next thing she knew, morning announced kids everywhere.

Bill slept like a baby through oatmeal, raisins, and the Saturday morning Ovaltine. Ruby knew she was crazy to put up with this man, but something told her there was nothing else to do.

A little later, after the kids were shooed out, Bill sipped coffee at the kitchen table. Miz Ruby washed dishes. Part wanted to bring up the night before and part of him didn't. He fired up a smoke and said nothing. He started to think about his boat. He figured the old tub had probably sunk.

"You know, I should most likely look in on my boat," he said.

She said, "You ain't going nowhere until at least tomorrow or the next. Are you crazy?"

"She might need attention," he said.

"What kind of attention? Fred Ruby has been looking and he's a navy man."

"Damn," Bill said. "What's he been doing?"

"Who knows? What the hell do you do with boats?"

"Damn it, Ruby, that's home."

"Could have fooled me."

"Is the bitch sunk or not? That's all I want to know."

"Ain't you something!"

"What you mean by that?"

"You are feeling better then?"

"You're driving me nuts."

"Yes, you're better all right. Maybe, after church we'll go look."

"Church?"

"You heard me. Now drink your coffee."

CHAPTER 7

ANGEL

B ill obeyed. Ruby was feisty, all right, but she fed him bacon and eggs and potato cakes, so how could he complain? After he ate, he smoked and then fell back in his bed and slept till dark. When he woke up, the house was so quiet he thought it was about dawn but realized that was most likely untrue. He felt totally discombobulated. It was weird not knowing whether it was night or day. It was dark and quiet. Someone knocked on the door.

Bill swung his robe around him, cinched it, and was amazed at how far away the door seemed. Fred Ruby was standing on the other side of the glass. Bill flipped the latch, but the door still would not open.

"You got to lift when you push," Fred said.

Bill did that and the door popped. Fred handed Bill a beer and a pack of smokes. He had a paper bag under his arm. Fred nodded his head like he wanted to come in. Bill swung the door.

"What time is it, Fred? Where is everybody?"

"Church supper, I reckon. Figured you could use supplies."

"You ain't a church-going man?"

Fred did not answer until the bag was emptied. There were a few more beers, Bill's camera, and a speeding ticket.

"Sometimes I go, sometimes I don't," Fred replied. "But friend Sneed is on to something and the wife ain't eager to have a camera in the house."

"What's this ticket for?" Bill asked.

"Speeding," Fred said. "On the way home from your boat day before, the son of a gun pulled me over past the bridge. Pretty plain he was watching. Parked there the whole time I was pumping her out and when he pulled me over, writes the damn ticket. Then he asked, what did I know about film? I told him nothing and he said too bad; driving was about to become very expensive."

"I'll pay the ticket and extra for help with the boat," Bill said.

"Don't worry about that, but what's on this film got him so worried?"

"Nothing, probably, but he don't know. I got an idea. Next time you see Sneed, tell him to come see me. Tell him to call Miz Ruby's and set up a time. Just leave the camera. Don't worry about the ticket. We'll fix that."

"What you fixing to do?"

"Put him on simmer and make him stew."

"He's a hateful man," Fred said.

"A call from his veterinarian might tenderize him."

"What do you mean?"

"Listen while I call the vet," Bill said.

Bill punched a beer and fumbled through his wallet until he found the vet's card. When he got him, he told him that his snout-nosed cousin needed his nuts cut because his boorish ways were troublesome. He asked him to tell Sneed to come in for a visit and that the film was in the darkroom.

"What's on that film?" Fred asked.

Bill raised his hand and called Porter's Drugs. When Glen Porter answered, Bill told him he needed a favor. Glen agreed to look the other way, no matter what was on the film.

They dropped off the camera and drove toward the boat. The film was to be ready in a few days. They drove by the boat, but they didn't see Sneed. Bill got dog tired, so they cruised back to Ruby's.

Fred assured Bill his boat was okay, but as he was saying it, Bill snored. Fred almost had to carry him in. Miz Ruby gave Fred hell for taking Bill out and Bill woke up long enough to wink and so she gave him hell, too.

A couple days later, the film was printed, and Bill wasn't displeased. Sarah, God bless her, would have been horrified, but the spirit of the thing was captured, sure enough. Valerie was unrecognizable, but Sneed wasn't, the greedy pig in glory.

Glen, a slight bespectacled man, was amused.

"What do you want with this, Bill?"

Bill was looking at the rest of the pictures, which were mostly so blurry you couldn't see anything.

"Nothing really. Four or five copies will do and the negatives and promise to keep your mouth shut."

"Sure," Porter said. "I got nothing to gain by talking, but why do you want something so ugly?"

Bill paid and left. He gave the first print to Fred with the caution that he use it only if he must. Fred laughed when he saw it.

"It ain't funny," Bill said.

"Not really," Fred said, "but surprising."

"It'll surprise Sneed, guaranteed."

When the vet finally called, Miz Ruby dragged Bill to the phone. Still weak after napping, but Bill recovered quickly and told him that they had to meet. The vet guessed it right off.

"Pictures?"

When they met, Bill gave the vet three. He instructed the man to distribute them wisely. Bill wasn't packing when he said this but grinned like a man who was.

Bill was getting stronger and was eager to return to his boat, but Ruby insisted that he stay until he was right.

"We want you to stay," her kids said, and Amelia volunteered that she didn't want him to die again. Bill laughed hoarsely and said that he never had. They all said, "Yes, you did."

"Naw, I didn't."

"Yes, sir, you did. It's a miracle you're eating a pork chop now."

"Suppose it is," Bill replied. "Especially, if you say so."

Amelia nodded solemnly.

Toward the end of his recovery, the kids quit looking out of the corners of their eyes. He became more than a curiosity and they became more than a darting blur. John, the oldest, said the blessing one night. As he stumbled over the last line, Bill prompted him gently and the boy finished on his own. The next day, little brother Jason had a splinter, and John brought him to Bill, who requested a needle. While Jason looked away in distress, John studied with wonder as Bill first sterilized the needle with flame and then dug out the sliver. Cory, the second youngest, was amazed.

"You a doctor, too?"

Bill laughed.

Amelia said, "He's much more."

Miz Ruby heard that and burst out laughing. Ruby brought him a beer, said he had earned it. Bill only winked.

"He knows good stories, too," Amelia said.

"He sure can spin a yarn," Miz Ruby said from the kitchen.

"What kind of story?" John asked.

"Tell him, Amelia," Bill said.

"Tall tales. What he told me."

"How tall were they?" Ava wondered.

"Like what?" John asked.

"What is a tall tale anyway?" Jason wanted to know.

"Tell one," Amelia demanded.

Bill had no choice. He pulled on her ear gently.

"Ouch."

"You want a tall tale or not?"

She nodded. "Just don't make it scary."

He asked Jason to turn off the desk lamp and before he could, John flipped off the bulb over the door. The only light glowed from the kitchen where Miz Ruby was cooking and near silently chuckling. Bill heard but didn't let on. Amelia jumped up on his knee. He looked very serious. She drew in her breath and clutched his arm.

"Go on."

"First off," Bill said, "it was a dark and stormy night. There were no question marks prowling the neighborhoods. Dogs were curled beneath exclamation points that did not disturb them since they were all sound asleep."

"What?" Jason said.

"Let him finish," Amelia said.

"Anyway," Bill continued, "the god-awful teachers were on the prowl. They were looking for kids hiding in dark places who had not done homework."

"Oh, my God!" John said.

"There were commas swimming around like minnows and they made it hard to see what was going on. Also, there were semicolons that were as big as catfish and even though the kids were on dry land, they knew that they owed these critters, because if the teachers could see past the schools of minnows and the skulking semicolons—"

"What does 'skulking' mean, Mr. Bill?"

"I'll tell after a while, John, if you just listen," Bill said. "So, not to mention the colons, thick as moray eels, numerous as shoestrings floating in dark rooms. There are no ghostly things like sheets swirling, but there are quotation marks that haunt, periods and parentheses that surround and jiggle things up like a bucket of you know what."

"Dinner's ready," Miz Ruby announced.

"Anyhow, these teachers were slinking around like snakes on the prowl. The kids were terrified because they had no homework done yet and without that, in spite of all the exclamation points, semicolons, colons, commas, and periods, they would soon all be devoured."

"Oh, my goodness," Amelia exclaimed.

Bill drew in his breath and widened his eyes.

"There was a way out," he said. "Of all the punctuation marks, there is one left out. Whoever names it might escape this certain doom."

"Question mark," Jason said.

"Oh, my gosh," Amelia said.

"What did the question mark say, Jason?" Bill asked.

Jason shrugged. "'Have you done your homework, I guess?'"

"Right you are, my man."

"Supper's ready," Miz Ruby said again.

There was never any mention of Ronald, except for one of the last nights. Between bites, Jason asked if Ronald was coming home. Miz Ruby shook her head, and everybody looked at their food. Nobody said anything until Bill spoke up.

"Delicious, Miz Ruby. These stewed apples make the pork simply scrumptious."

"Don't they though?"

That was that.

A few days later, Bill was back on the boat and despite Fred's help, it was full of cobwebs and dust, and had water in the bilge. These were comforting things that gave Bill something to do, and Bill needed something. Blues were setting in.

He couldn't sit still or else he would start thinking and thinking wasn't fun. He would sink into funk, and funk had no bottom he could find. Miz Ruby continued to bring food a few days a week and they would talk. She suggested that Bill try out church going, and he laughed. She didn't push.

Marcus came down one day and they cooked up a plan to polish up the interior, which was still dingy. Mrs. Green was big on holidays, so Marcus was busy with dusting and polishing silver and all kinds of household stuff. There was no way to get right after an enhancement, but it was fun to talk about.

Miz Ruby came by one day with Amelia, who was dressed like a pilgrim, proud as a peacock in a black dress made of paper. She handed him an invitation that she had made at school that invited him to dinner. It was a crayon drawing of a turkey on a piece of folded orange paper. "Happy thanksgiving" was scrawled out in black with two backward p's. Naturally Bill accepted, but when they left, he sank a bit.

There was almost nothing on the boat to remind Bill of Sarah. He saved none of her clothes. They had all smelled of conflagration. Just one thing in the whole place reminded him of her. It was the very table where he found himself planted with drink in hand. They had sat there, dreamed and desired. They had had meals there, appreciatively. She was gone, and he knew it somehow deeper than before.

He made it through Thanksgiving; maybe because it never meant all that much to Sarah. He had accepted Amelia's invitation to dinner, expecting nothing. What he found was wonderful food and lots of laughter, especially from the kids who still found him amusing. Just the sound of his voice would bring laughter. All he had to do was tweak a word to push them over. He drove home puzzled by his good mood.

Christmas came close to being entirely different. Sarah had always loved Christmas. She had been such a giving person by nature that the holiday suited her perfectly. She hadn't had to shift gears. She simply accelerated a bit and her joy ran circles around almost everybody. Bill could never understand her wellspring of joyfulness. He could never understand what the hell she had seen in him and, for better or worse, she never told him.

She loved a big tree. She wanted a wreath with holly, a bright red ribbon and mistletoe; he dutifully shot mistletoe out of the top of an oak at the back of their lot. She had small presents for the milkman and postmistress and the little kids. She kept these in baskets that looked like a cornucopia of colored mysterious shapes. She baked pies and cookies with almond extract that made the house smell wonderful and she made eggnog, which they had always imbibed on Christmas day.

Bill had never been much of a shopper. Sarah was frugal and creative. It always seemed magical to him how she could manage to find combinations of small things that together would add up to more than the sum of their parts. He was tagalong, the donkey that carried the loot. He grumbled outwardly, but inwardly was amazed to see apples, baseball cards, brown sugar, and flour turn into a full-blown smile. Old folks got meat pies and cobblers. Everybody got cookies. The house smelled like a wonderful factory and he bumbled through, not understanding, and she never seemed to mind, asking nothing more than that he turn down the oven or put his finger on the foundation of a knot so that she could tighten a bow.

Christmas week hit hard. He wanted to buy presents. He knew he should for Fred and Miz Ruby and her kids. Then he thought about neighborhood people that Sarah had given things to and took out a piece of paper and was damned if he could remember even half of their names. He wanted to do something for the Greens, but hell, they had everything. Marcus. What about Marcus? And Valerie, where was she?

He had no idea something was wrong. He knew he was confused, but soon he was sinking so fast all seemed perfectly normal. Before he knew it, he was out of booze on Christmas Eve. He got to the liquor store, which was a shack just off the highway next to the Point, and the neon light blinked off as he parked. Fred was walking out the door and, seeing Bill, he waved, and the light flicked back on after he said something to the man inside.

Bill navigating from his car dragged his feet through gravel, and Fred was eying him. Fred didn't speak until Bill staggered back out.

"Bill, it's Christmas," Fred said. "Why don't we share a drink?"

"What you mean, share a drink?" Bill asked.

Fred stood his ground. Bill was surprised at the harshness in his own voice. Fred didn't say anything. He reached for Bill's shoulder and nodded toward his old rattletrap.

"What's up?" Bill asked as Fred cranked the motor.

"Nothing," Fred said. "You're drunk, Bill. Follow your usual path, Sneed will pick you off."

"Bastard."

"So, what say in the morning I bring you back to your car?"

"Damn it! What's going on?"

"Nothing. It's Christmas, that's all."

"Goddamn," Bill said.

Fred steered clear of Sneed and ducked down a side lane over to River Road. When they got to the boat, Bill seemed clear as a bell. He invited Fred in like they did this every day, but when he tried to walk, was wobbly. Fred took his elbow and most likely kept him from stumbling overboard.

"I ain't right, Fred," Bill said as he sank into his chair.

"Who is?" Fred responded.

"Kind of you to drive. I can walk in the morning."

"Why walk when you can ride? Don't be hard on yourself, Bill. Shit!"

"What you mean?" Bill asked.

"Bill, I didn't come here to hurt, but listen, if I lost Lucky, I don't know what I might do. You don't even know what you're suffering, do you?"

Bill closed his eyes.

"I didn't come here to hurt, like I said, but you got to understand what you been through and it's going to take time. You lost your Sarah, and in the worst way. Damn it, we don't need to lose you."

Fred stoked the fire and poured whiskey for Bill. Fred sat down and neither spoke. The fire crackled; the wind picked up; the boat strained against lines that held. Fred counted blessings. Bill heard echoes he could not decipher.

"Bill, one day you will look back on this and barely remember sadness. One day, you will look back and remember joy you shared. Hard as it is to believe, that is true."

Bill squinted through dim light. He said nothing.

"Do you know what Sarah once told me about you?"

Bill shook his head.

"She said you was the hardest-headed man she ever met."

"Bull!" Bill said.

"Well, damn, you *can* talk, can't you?"

"What did she really say?" Bill asked.

"Of course, she was mad, you driving out into a snowstorm. But right, she didn't *say* it at all."

"Told you," Bill said.

"No, sir, Mr. Bill, she yelled so loud all of us—even those behind closed doors—could hear over the screaming of your spinning tires."

"She did not."

"Oh, yes, she did. Was year before last and I remember plain as day, a night cold as a witch's titty."

"Year before last?" Bill asked, staring into the corner.

"Yes, sir. Just before Christmas."

"Jesus, doesn't seem possible. I mean, I know it is, but Fred, where have I been?"

"God knows, Bill."

"Lord, I hope, because I sure don't. I feel like I spent a year at Miz Ruby's, not to mention at Green's."

"I don't doubt."

"Know it was spring, but when did it happen? Jesus! This is Christmas again, ain't it?"

"Sure is—tomorrow. The fire happened in late April past, a week before derby, Bill. That wasn't so long ago. Know what else Sarah said about you?"

Bill looked at Fred like a man eager for drink and took a gulp and still looked the same thirsty way.

"Miss Sarah said you could do anything you wanted and that she loved your ass, and then she cussed most powerfully—for a woman, that is."

"She did not," Bill said. "She only cussed in private."

Fred chuckled.

"What she said was, 'I love that man, but Fred, I could wring his neck, but I love him too much to kill him.'"

Bill smiled. "That's more like her."

"She don't want you to die, Bill. Not yet. It ain't your time. Make her proud, if you can."

"What in hell am I supposed to do?"

"Wait. That's the only way. Time, that's all, just time."

"Damn," Bill said.

"You'll make it and maybe do some good, too."

———

When he awakened, the boat was freezing. A Valerie dream lingered so vividly he wasn't sure he had dreamt. He sighed and assumed he had.

It was Christmas morning and the fire was nearly out in the stove. He stoked it and jumped back into bed until the cabin was warmer. He thought about Sneed. Valerie told him that Sneed was out to get him, but Bill knew that already. She told him that Sneed had joined the Klan. He didn't know anything about that. He scratched and shook his head; who knows? After he drank a cup of coffee, Fred showed up and they went to fetch his car. Bill tried to give Fred cash for gas. Fred refused, but wondered if he and Lucky could drop by for a Christmas day visit. Bill told him he would be honored.

Later, Bill was drinking coffee at his table and thinking about how sweet and crazy Valerie was and about how maybe Sarah had something to do with it. He was puzzling over it and smoking a cigarette when the boat listed, and Green hit the door with Marcus in tow. Green was carrying a case of his whiskey and Marcus was struggling under two cases of beer.

They were drinking when Fred and Lucky showed up with ham and biscuits, scrambled eggs, sausage, stewed apples, potatoes, and corn bread. Bill was apologizing so hard for having nothing to offer anybody that he barely noticed he had everything. When Miz Ruby and the kids showed up, they brought desserts, cookies, still oven warm, and roasted chestnuts, and everything was in bowls, ready to serve. Bill kept apologizing, but no one paid any mind.

Polecat Green showed with a trash can full of ice and Theo, who was in Barbados, sent her love and a lovely Christmas card that Green presented. Amelia gave him drawings of reindeer and old Saint Nick. Mr. Traylor and Miss Hayes stopped by with some hot cider. They didn't stay long, but neither did anyone else, except for Green and Marcus, who stayed until midnight.

There were only four chairs and a handful of utensils, but everyone got fed. Along about ten o'clock, Bill looked around at the candles flickering and the hurricane lantern on the table between Marcus and Green who were arguing football; thoughts of Sarah took root, but they were happy thoughts. He surveyed the food still spread out and knew that Sarah would have approved. That thought toggled a switch that sent him down.

Next thing he knew, he was on the bed and big old Green was pumping his chest and Marcus was beside him, looking worried.

"Come on, Bill," Green was saying. "Come back and join us. There you are."

"Yes sir, there he is," Marcus said.

"Where who is?" Bill croaked.

"Yes sir, he's back," Marcus said.

Bill had passed out cold right at the table. He couldn't understand the fuss over him. He looked grumpy as a crab in a basket. Even Marcus had to laugh.

They coaxed him out of bed and back to the table, fixed him a drink and continued their battle about the Browns versus the Rams. Somehow it was important for Bill to witness.

"You don't seem yourself," Green said after a while. Marcus rolled his eyes.

"Merry Christmas," Bill said.

"Say it like you mean it," Green insisted.

"Don't push."

Green looked puzzled, but Marcus suggested to Green that it was time to go. Green protested, but Marcus stood firm, and so they left with Green promising to return the following day when Bill wasn't so indisposed and inhospitable. Bill said nothing, just nodded at Marcus. Bill fell into bed before he heard the old Cadillac engine roar. That meant Green was driving. Bill said a prayer for Marcus, and the next thing he knew, it was morning.

COINCIDENTAL ANGEL

Bill ate leftovers and took a drive. He had no earthly idea where he was going. Left or right? He turned left but didn't know why. He ended up on the Cincinnati road. He drove all the way to Carrollton, about fifty miles upstream. He bought a sandwich in some joint and drank a beer. He took the ferry across the river into Indiana and wound his way home. The river towns he passed through reminded him of a collection of dollhouses. It all seemed unreal.

He was dry. Late afternoon, he stopped at a joint that sold beer and bought six. He felt like a ghost as he carried them back to the car. He popped one and then almost turned the wrong way.

As he drove along beside the river, the sun was setting. The river, often angry at this time of year, was placid, and purple and orange glazed the surface. His mind filled with thoughts of Sarah. He felt her presence sure as if she were in the passenger seat. He didn't allow himself to look because he knew she wasn't, but he talked aloud as if she were.

"Damn it, woman, I love you so much. Why did you ever, ever have to leave?"

He fired up a smoke and took a long swig of beer.

"I mean this has been one bad joke. You always said we were one person, didn't you? So, what the hell am I doing here?"

He dodged a cat that was outrunning a dog; an oncoming car blew its horn.

"I hope I did the right thing, seeing Ronald put into the hospital.

Part of me wanted to tear him limb from limb, and you must know that's true."

A cop passed with lights flashing and siren blaring.

"Jesus Christ," Bill exclaimed. "What the hell's that about?"

A few miles later he knew.

The road was blocked. There had been a head-on collision. Bill pulled up right behind the cop car. The ambulance wasn't even there, neither was the fire department and one of the cars was on fire.

Bill jumped out and ran to help the policeman who was trying to extricate people from the mangled mess. There was a body in the road. Two men walked around holding their guts, eyes sunken and glazed, both groaning. One had a terrible gash across his forehead. Bill tried to coax them to lie down but could not.

Another car pulled up and it was an old woman. Bill motioned her over and urged her to stay with the men, but she took one look and turned away. A young woman ran up and announced that she was a nurse. She took the men's hands in hers and started talking calmly.

But there was nothing to do. Two people were trapped in the car, but they were crushed under the dashboard. The cop said they were dead. Bill heard a moan and cry and ran across the road. Down in the ditch there was a crumpled woman with her dress up over her head. Gently he rolled her out of the puddle and noticed her foot was backward and then saw her child all turned around—or so he thought—until the baby smiled and called him Da Da. The woman's eyes were shut, but she was breathing.

Bill grabbed the baby out of the woman's arms and carried the baby up to the cop car and laid it in the backseat. The cop was spraying down the wreck with a fire extinguisher. Bill looked in the trunk and found a blanket. He took it to the woman and covered her.

"Where's Melissa?" the woman asked calmly. Bill told her that Melissa was fine. The woman closed her eyes and nodded.

The next day it was in the paper. "Head-on collision on 62 kills three."

Five people were seriously injured. The baby escaped without a scratch. The mother, who suffered a compound fracture of her left leg, claimed from her hospital bed that an angel carried her baby to safety. Bill smiled and remembered the rest of the drive home. He had spent it with Sarah as far as he was concerned.

He had never been called an angel before, except by Sarah, and she had been his angel too. She wasn't, of course. She had her ups and downs. About the only thing about her that bothered him was that she had no sense of time. Bill was punctual; she was not. She possessed a whole different view of time.

He would call her from the road and say he'd be home in two hours and would arrive to find her gone. Never to some place that was questionable, but maybe someone would want her to stay to talk things over or a child might need tending, and he could never understand why that had taken precedence. He never did, and it caused a few problems. It was something they never had resolved.

She tried to tell him they were just alike, but he never could believe that. He told her he would never do her that way and she told him he did it all the time. He never had known what she meant, but as he drove home, it slowly started to dawn.

After all, he had brought Ronald into their lives. She had warned him that the kid wasn't right, but Bill insisted that the young man only needed direction. Sarah had followed his lead.

There were other things. For example, he brought home the bacon, so when he called from the road, it was always his schedule. There was never any way she could call to inform him of hers; never had penetrated until late afternoon on that serpentine riverside road. Then and there he had asked her forgiveness and somehow had felt it granted.

When he got home, the sun was set and as he swung into his parking spot, thought he saw something like a small dog sleeping on his deck. As he stepped aboard, the loll of the boat caused the sleeper to stir in the dim light. Bill saw that it was Amelia. He was alarmed.

"What's wrong, Amelia?" he said.

"I'm cold," she chattered.

He bundled her inside and sat her in a chair. He fired up his stove. He lit the kerosene lamp and rubbed the child's icy hands.

"How did you get here?"

"I walked."

"You walked here? Why?"

"I miss you, Mr. Bill."

"They know where you are?"

"No."

Bill threw a couple of logs into the stove, shut the door, and huddled the child close. She was shivering.

"You walked the whole way?"

She nodded, staring into his eyes.

"Why? Why didn't anyone stop you?"

"I don't know," she said through chattering teeth.

On the way home, she asked him to tell her a story like the elephant and the mouse. Bill figured it was better not to. He was surprised to find Ruby at home. The rest of the children were out scouring the neighborhood. She was alone and remarkably calm, but not so cool that Amelia could escape a few swats on the bottom and a shake or two. Amelia looked at Bill as if she had been betrayed. Bill felt terrible in an odd way.

"I found her on the deck," was all Bill could think to say.

"Lucky it was you found her," Ruby said as she carried Amelia off to bed.

Bill went outside and called John and Jason. A minute or two later, John ran up with Jason at his heels. He told them Amelia was safe and he left.

The look of betrayal that had shone out of the child's eyes haunted him all the way home.

THE DADBURN BOAT RULES

Green showed up with a powerful urge to drink.

Bill was low on ice, so Green sent Marcus back to the house for a cooler full and a bucket of coal. Said he wanted to heat the old tub. Bill couldn't help but notice that Marcus looked irritated.

Green was pissed off. He poured whiskey and then blasted the changing times. Said he could understand that colored folks should have their own joints, but he couldn't understand how the Pine Bar could deny him. Green claimed he had probably spent more money in that establishment than anybody. How could they deny the right to take his man, Marcus—a good man, he added, and his man too, he emphasized—into the damn place to keep him company, while he choked down one of their crappy sandwiches and drank a couple of their watered drinks. It wasn't like Marcus had just walked in by himself and asked to be served.

"With me, damn it to hell!" Green bellowed.

Bill knew better than to contradict but did anyway.

"Well, the law says the man don't have to," Bill said.

Green sloshed more whiskey into his glass and his eyes got fiery.

"So goddamn what! To hell with law! He was with me, damn it! Don't you understand? The son of a bitch was with me and besides that, he's a good man. He ain't common. You know that."

"I'll grant you," Bill said, "but there's lots of places those folks can't go."

"That's a different matter," Green huffed.

"How?"

"Well, it is, that's all. A man should be able to do what he wants, I'll grant. But damn, don't seem right to turn a man down, me vouching for him. Hell, there were no ladies present."

"So, what happened?"

"They asked us politely what was wrong and when I said nothing, that we wanted sandwiches and beer, the bartender started laughing. When I told him I didn't get the joke, the bartender calmly asked

Marcus to step outside, and then before Marcus had even left the room, offered that he would serve me and have a waiter run a sandwich out to the car for my boy. He said this like he was pleased with himself."

"So you left?"

"Hell yes, I left him with a piece of my mind."

"They're in trouble now," Bill said.

"Bill, they were being unreasonable. Ain't no way I would cause a ruckus, but damn, Marcus is all right. He's just like you and me."

"Some white men would take offense at that," Bill drawled.

"To hell with them. Do you?" Green asked.

"Nope, not exactly. Proud you admit it."

"Damn straight! No law says that they can't serve 'em, just one that says they don't have to, but for God's sake, you know it ain't right, don't you?"

"Yeah, I do, but what the hell can we do about it?"

Green slumped and all three hundred pounds of him looked concerned.

"You're right and that's what's so damn frustrating. Where the hell you start? How you keep from going too far?"

"What you mean?"

Green studied Bill over the rim of his glass for a moment, then said, "Not all are upstanding like Marcus."

"So, who's to judge?"

"Damned if I know," Green replied. "This whole business is confusing."

"Sure ain't what we fought for, is it?" Bill said.

"I never thought about it," Green replied. "Liberty, justice for all. Freedom from tyranny and I can't take Marcus for a sandwich?"

"How did Marcus take the thing?"

"Like they always do," Green said, nodding. "Cool as a cucumber, said he wasn't hungry anyway."

"Was he?"

"Damn right. He was the one said Polecat's cooking ribs."

"I know you like ribs."

"Sure, but I wanted a sandwich. Bill, I don't have to tell you that Polecat's is a real nigger joint!"

"How would you know?" Bill replied.

Green looked at Bill sly-like and winked.

"I've been there a time or two."

"Did you dine there?"

"Don't be foul." Green scowled.

"Aw, come off it, Green."

"Well, come to think, suppose I did, but what of it? She could have passed."

"Passed for what? A lady?"

"Whose side you on anyway, Bill?"

"The side of curious."

"How so?"

"What if your daughter brought that girl's brother home for Sunday dinner?"

"You've always been like that, Bill. God bless you!"

"Seriously," Bill insisted.

"That ain't fair, Bill. Different and you know it."

"Why?"

"It just is."

"What if your daughter said he was a good man?"

"I would kick ass, that's what! What do you say to that?"

Bill laughed.

"Nothing, Green. I was just curious. What might you do to your daughter?"

"Skin her alive."

"You wouldn't even give the man a sandwich first?"

"Hell no! Damn it, why do you want to complicate?"

"Good thing Marcus ain't back yet," Bill said.

"Now what's that supposed to mean?"

"Nothing, but it is logical."

"What do you mean? We need ice," Green said.

"You got that."

"You sure you're all right down here?"

"What's the alternative?"

"Damned if I know," Green said.

Bill poured some whiskey for both of them, and as he did, he heard Green's car.

"Don't worry, Green. Marcus is back."

"Don't breathe a word, you understand? I don't want to embarrass the man. At least you got that straight, don't you?"

"This mouse won't squeak."

"Promise?" Green implored. Before Bill could say anything, Marcus squeezed through the door with a cooler.

The men commenced to drinking. At first, Marcus was quiet. Bill was on guard as well, but Green was on a roll. Before five minutes passed, Green asked Marcus what he thought about what happened at the Pine Bar. Marcus declined to answer, but Green persisted and finally Marcus nodded, as if to say, okay, you asked for it.

"Mr. Green, with all due respect, I would rather say nothing, but as Bill is my witness, you have insisted, and God bless us all, speak I will. Mr. Green, I have been faithful and true, and you know that's why I'm here, but damn! There are limits! There are some places no man wants to go. I can tell you, Mr. Green, there are some spots I will no longer. Thank you so much for helping me to learn proper respect and indignation, but sir, never, never ever put me in that place again, for as God is my witness and Mr. Bill is too, I do not know what I might do. God help my soul."

"He's his own man, I swear he is," Green said.

Marcus looked at Bill with a pained expression.

"Green, you think I am my own man?"

"Of course, I do. Why the hell am I here?"

"Listen up, you're an idiot."

Green reached for the bottle, but Bill grabbed it first.

"Green, I don't give a rat's ass who brought the whiskey. You drink on this boat ever again, you will stand, turn around three times and say, 'Dadburn!'"

"Dadburn?"

"Green, it's either that or apologize to Marcus and me."

"Apologize for what?"

"You know what. Doesn't he, Marcus?"

"Mr. Bill?"

"Doesn't he, Marcus?"

"Marcus, have I offended you somehow?" Green asked.

"Damn right and on my no-excuse-for-it boat, too. Damn your ass."

"What do you say, Marcus?" Green asked.

Marcus shook his head side to side.

"Screw this," Bill said. "Marcus, speak straight or you are not welcome either. I've had it with the both of you, damn it! Speak up or ship out; I'm done!"

Green and Marcus looked down.

"I ain't kidding," Bill said. "Either talk straight or don't talk. Got me?"

Both nodded.

"Going to talk to your feet or me?"

Both looked at him. Bill raised his glass in a toast.

"Only if you're willing and able," he said.

"Damn you, Bill," Green said, then stood and spun around three slow times, saying, "Dadburn, dadburn, dadburn."

Marcus smiled.

Bill clonked his glass on the table.

"Let's get serious."

Marcus shook his head slowly side to side. Green looked puzzled.

"Where you going with this?"

"All right," Bill said, "I'll tell you. You said there were no ladies present, right? Well, what if there had been? What if Marcus had looked? How would you have taken that? What if he denied finding the lady attractive? Would you have believed him?

Because everybody knows that the black man desires the white woman. Would you have been offended if he had said he preferred his own kind? Would that have been the right answer?"

Marcus was squirming. Green looked pissed.

Green asked Bill to continue.

"It ain't right and all know it," Bill said. "There is no way to give the right answer to a kangaroo court. If the man said he didn't, he would be a liar; if he had said he did, he's a fool. That's an impossible spot. Wake up, Green. No way for Marcus to be comfortable. How would you like to wear blinders at Polecat Green's?"

"I didn't make this world, Bill," Green said.

"No, but you have more ability than most to navigate the bullshit, right? How would you like the tables turned? Walk into a joint with your damn boss and have to say yes, when you wanted to say no and both answers put you in the wrong."

"Where you going, Bill?"

Marcus offered to freshen drinks. Green held out his glass.

"Damned, if I know, Green. Hold your horses, Marcus," he added, which caused Marcus to appear to be hovering.

"Trying to stir things up?" Green asked.

"Sometimes stirring things helps to sort them."

"Yeah and sometimes it makes a bigger mess. What do you think, Marcus?"

Marcus allowed as how it might go either way.

"No shit," Bill said, "but Marcus, don't you think it could help to lay things in the open?"

"It's hard to say, Mr. Bill."

"No, Marcus, under the present rules, it is impossible, so don't worry. I make a proposal." Bill thought for a moment. "I propose that when we are on this boat, we check rules at the door. No rich, no poor, no black, no white, no old or young, no boss, no servant."

"Sounds more like an ultimatum," Green said.

"It is," Bill said and stood. "Do you accept?" He snatched Green's glass and reached out for the glass that Marcus held.

"It's your boat. Looks like we have no choice, Marcus."

"Well, I suppose you could leave."

Both Marcus and Green shook their heads.

"Don't be absurd," Green said.

"Then it's settled. I'll fix this round. Green, you'll fix the next. Then Marcus and so on unless we lose track, then every man for himself."

"Why the hell don't we start where we're going to end?" Green grumbled.

"Why not humor me? It won't kill you, will it?"

"Did you wash your stinking hands?"

"I washed them right after tea. Thank you kindly and you?"

"Screw yourself, Maddox."

"Could you teach me that trick? It sure would be handy, wouldn't it, Marcus?"

"That's your business and none of mine, sir," Marcus replied.

"You're a damn diplomat Marcus. You know that?"

"Yes, sir. Part of the job."

"Horsefeathers," Bill said, as he passed out drinks. "Another thing: No sirs or misters. You got me?"

"Know what? You're crazier than Tom Sawyer screwed on backwards, no lie."

"I ain't no Nigger Jim," Marcus said.

Both Bill and Green paused and looked at Marcus.

"Yeah, well I ain't Tom Sawyer, so what's your point?'

"No point," Marcus said. "Let's play."

"Play what?" Green said.

"Spin the bottle," Bill replied.

"I draw the line at spin the bottle," Marcus said.

"Praise the Lord," Green said.

"That's another thing," Bill said. "All discussions about the predispositions of the Almighty, as well as inflammatory political rhetoric are strictly outlawed."

"Good God, man," Green grumbled. "For someone not too high on rules, seems like you got a pocket full, doesn't he, Marcus?"

"Well, does seem a bit contradictory now that you mention, but it is the man's boat, I suppose."

"Another thing," Bill added. "Diplomacy is banished. Speak straight or shut up. No sidewinders allowed."

"There he goes again, Marcus. Can you believe?"

"It's hard, but it's plain the man loves rules."

"Don't let it trouble you, son; the man has always been a mess of contradictions."

"So you have always said," Marcus replied.

"All right, gentleman, apparently it falls to me to bring this meeting to order. Can I have a second?"

"You certainly can," Green said, struggling to his feet as he extended his hand. "But I would bet it's more like your fourth."

Green reached for Marcus's glass as well, and the meeting got underway.

As soon as they cleared the air so that the discussion could begin, it was discovered that there was nothing to discuss. There was hemming and hawing.

After a short while, they settled on women. First, they sang deep praises and then voiced complaints. They agreed on most matters, which was made easier, all conceded, because the subject was over their heads. Comfortable with that, Marcus poured the next round, and all seemed about ready to agree to anything. In fact, they praised one another's insightfulness on a host of matters.

Marcus, for example, praised Green's taste for possessing a Picasso. Bill nodded wisely, but then Green looked puzzled and fumbled his jowls and asked Marcus what he was talking about.

"Over the service bar, sir, the Picasso," Marcus replied.

"Over what?"

"Where we make drinks, sir."

"No sirs here, Marcus!" Bill said.

"All right, but there is a Picasso over the bar unless I'm mistaken."

"There may be," said Green, "but whatever is your point?"

Marcus was visibly perplexed.

"Green knows nothing about what makes a house work, Marcus," Bill said.

"I pay for the damn stuff. I know that much. Color schemes are out of my league, but I know what I paid for the damned thing, and I am aware that it matches the sofa and drapes as I was told for most of two nasty weeks."

"Mrs. Green says it's priceless," Marcus offered.

"Wrong on that point. It had a price and may the chiseler that talked her out of the Remington burn in hell a day for every penny he gouged. Damn drab woman with two eyes on the same side of her face like a dead flounder."

"Well, I prefer it to the one in the living room that looks like a drop cloth," Marcus replied.

"Pretty fancy drop cloth I would say," Bill said.

"That's the frame makes it so," Marcus replied.

"I call it de coon," Green said.

"No," Bill interjected. "I believe you commonly refer to that one as the Pollack."

"Whatever," Green said. "De coon is in the same damn room and the fellow who sold her that one looked like a garbage bandit, except he was skinnier than most and his nails weren't as sharp."

"He was peculiar," Marcus added.

"Why you say that?" Bill asked.

"Well, for one thing, he wore high heels."

"Those were Italian boots."

"Call them what you will," Marcus said. "He also wore perfume that put ladies to shame. He smelled like a whore's briefcase."

They decided a road trip to Polecat's was in order. Green praised Marcus for suggesting Polecat's ribs and Marcus praised Green for reconsidering them. Off they went with a blue moon shining above and Bill at the wheel of the Ford with the rear window shot through. They decided it would be less conspicuous than Green's Cadillac.

Marcus sat in the back and didn't seem to mind much except

for bumps that drove raw springs of the burned-out backseat into pinch mode.

"Not to be complaining, Bill, but what in blazes happened back here? Your springs are as ornery as a junkyard dog."

"Breezy too, ain't it? There was a slight fire after the window got shot out. Don't worry about it, Marcus; you'll have supper."

CHAPTER 8

WHAT YOU TREATING THE DEVIL TO

All could smell hickory and apple wood smoke before they parked, but none noticed there was only one other car in the lot. That car belonged to Polecat Green and he was inside and anything but happy.

He was alone at the bar sitting beside a candle nursing a drink. He told them his nephew had been shot to death a few hours before right outside the back door. Cops showed, and the kid ran out back. Polecat said an officer gut shot point-blank; said the kid had drawn a razor knife.

"A damn good kid, too," big old Polecat said. "Sneed said he was wanted for burglarizing a vet doctor's place. Now why would he want to do that?"

"You say Sneed?" Bill asked.

"Yeah. You know the man, don't you?"

"Yeah, I do. What veterinarian are they talking about; do you know?"

"No, don't. I don't know."

"What difference what vet?" Green asked. "Just shot him dead?"

Polecat, big as a stout oak, moaned.

Marcus said, "Have mercy."

"You got that right," Polecat said. "It'll plumb break Little Sister's heart. He wouldn't pull no razor. Something don't add up."

"Did the cop say what was supposedly stolen?" Bill asked.

"No, not that I heard. They run in and called out and the boy run out back and that was all. Ambulance came, and cops told everybody to go back home. That was about it. The boy's dead."

"Did you see the razor knife?" Bill asked.

"Yeah, right beside his hand. So what? I'm surprised there wasn't a throw-down gun."

"What the hell's a throw-down gun?"

"Mr. Green, I am surprised you don't know. Cop shoots a nigger, he's got a throw-down so he can claim self-defense. They do it to whites, too. Shit! That's the way, don't they, Marcus?"

"I've heard it said," Marcus replied.

"Hear it again. That's how they do, and you better wake up. They'll do it to you, too."

"That's cold-blooded murder," Green said.

"Yes sir, it sure as hell is."

"Well, what can we do?"

"What somebody can do, I wouldn't know, Mr. Green."

"I smell something burning," Marcus said.

"Let 'em burn. It's ribs. Ain't no one eating tonight."

"I'll take them," Green said.

"Take 'em."

Green put a hundred-dollar bill on the bar. Polecat shoved it back.

"No disrespect," he said, "but keep your money. Everything here's on the house."

"I insist," Green said.

"Insist all you want. Whiskey, beer, gin, ribs. Free. I'm closing."

"I want to help," Green said.

Polecat studied Green a few seconds, then looked at Marcus, who nodded.

"All right. Let Marcus pack it: slaw, corn bread, beans, and all. I'll give the money to Sister."

Green slid another hundred. Bill threw in a twenty. Polecat scooped it up and raised his empty glass.

"Let me pour you one," said Bill.

"Bourbon and help yourselves," Polecat said. "Damn, this is hard. It's going to kill her. Marcus, pack neat; no mess, you hear?"

"I hear loud and clear, sir," said Marcus from the smoker room.

Polecat stuffed the money. "These tough times."

"Confusing times, Mr. Polecat Green."

"Thank you, Mr. Bill," Polecat said as he was handed his drink. "Sure as hell is. Mr. Green, one day, perhaps you might give me your take."

"Likewise, Polecat, but it depends which situation we're discussing."

"Sure do. It sure do."

"I'll look into it," Green said.

"We appreciate, though it won't bring anybody back. Only God can," Polecat said.

"Can he? Do you believe that?"

"Who knows, Mr. Green?"

A few hours later, they were surrounded by cops. Somehow, they had forgotten to leave. The food had been unpacked and eaten, much whiskey had been drunk, then suddenly, red lights were flashing.

Polecat and Marcus were alarmed, but Green and Bill stomped to the door.

"What's this all about?" Green said.

Next thing, he was handcuffed to Bill. The cop raised his forefinger to pursed lips in a way even Green could understand. The other two cops stood and stared at Polecat. They seemed to have no interest in Marcus, who sat like he was in deep contemplation. After a minute, one cop threw down two small packets and a rolled-up paper sack.

"Mean anything to you, Polecat?"

"No, sir."

"Funny. We have it on good authority those packages are from here."

"I don't know nothing about those things."

"They come off your boy, Polecat. In his pocket. You got more?

We'll take this dump apart board by board. Want to save some trouble?"

"Look, Polecat, what my partner is saying is that if you want to reduce your debt to society, you might want to put your finger on the source of this shit. Peddling narcotics carries a bit more weight than prostitution and illegal sales of whiskey."

"That boy wasn't into dope."

"It was in his pocket. What's in your pocket, Polecat?"

"Don't even talk to him," Green blurted out. "You need a lawyer. He needs a warrant."

"Shut your trap, fatso."

Another cop burst into the room. He didn't say anything. He gestured. Bill and Green were set free. With his thumb, he pointed to the door. As he rubbed his wrist, Bill overheard the captain was coming. Next thing, all heard spraying gravel.

Green and Marcus wanted to clear out, but Bill convinced them that they needed a drink to steady nerves. Polecat opened his huge hands and shrugged, so they poured another round. None of them could figure.

"Like no cops I ever saw," Green said.

"Bad SOBs," Polecat said.

Bill kept quiet. He wanted to let it play out.

"That was a flat-out shakedown," Green said.

"Yes, sir, it was," Polecat said. "That ain't so unusual, but that there wasn't right. I don't allow dope on this place. I don't, and everybody knows me knows. Want to know why? Dope don't sell booze. Forget the rest, which ain't good either. If I wanted to sell dope, why the hell would I sell whiskey? Just tell why. Maybe I'm greedy."

"It ain't greedy to run a smart business and support your own," Green said.

"I sell your products proudly, sir."

"Welcome your business."

"And I yours," Polecat said.

Bill was leaning on the bar next to Marcus, who was nodding in agreement with everything, but then he suddenly placed one of the little packages on the bar.

"They dropped this on the way out. Wonder what it is?"

About that time a car stopped outside. Bill went to the door and saw a cop. Polecat wanted to stash whatever it was, but Green grabbed.

"I'll be witness," he said. "There is something doesn't smell right."

This cop knocked before he entered. When Bill opened the door, the cop asked for permission to enter and was motioned in. He came to the point quickly. He was Captain Datillo, in charge of the investigation. All he wanted was basics, but first accepted a beer and a bowl of beans. After he heard Polecat's version, he made a few notes and chewed.

"Polecat," he said with his eyebrows arched, "I don't know if anything I say will help you believe me. We've watched you for years. I know you take in all kinds of cats. From strays out back to girls who ply trades here. I suppose we've had a truce, am I right?"

"Yes sir, I've done my part and paid my share."

"Work with me, Polecat; never mind arrangements. Let me cut to the quick. Our officer Sneed found what he believed to be narcotics in the pockets of your unfortunate nephew. Do you know what catnip is?"

"Of course, I know what catnip is," Polecat said angrily.

"Now, please work with me."

"I'm trying, Captain, but tell me, did he find what he thought he had found before or after he shot Nephew dead?"

"Hostility will solve nothing. I need to know from one cat lover to another."

"Shoot," Polecat said.

"Who would be trying to set you up?"

Polecat shrugged. Green raised his hand and asked if he could speak. The cop nodded.

"Was that boy running drugs?" Green asked.

"I sure doubt it," Polecat said. "Barely sharp enough to push a broom."

"Polecat," the cop asked, "in your opinion was the boy capable of burglary?"

"Far as I know, the boy never had trouble except for usual stuff."

"Well, I know he has no record. Would you say the boy was gullible?"

"Gullible?"

"You know, was he easily tricked? Could you fool with him?"

"Yeah, I see what you mean. Folks sure played a lot of jokes. Suppose you could say he was an easy mark. Liked to think he was smart, so people pulled his leg. Plus, he fancied himself, so he fell for bull about how some honey or another needed loving, and of course, he would make a damn nuisance of himself. But I can't see him getting talked into burglary, unless somebody had something on him. I couldn't tell you what that would be."

"Me either," said the cop. "Did he fight? Was he violent?"

"Hell, no. That boy never hurt a fly. He would joke his way out of a fight most likely."

"Why do you think he ran when the officer walked in?"

"I'm not sure he ran, so much as slipped out, but officer, they didn't just walk in. They crashed the door, yelling, "Nobody move," with their weapons drawn. They was rowdy."

"You say, they?"

"Yes sir, two busted in."

"Sneed out back, correct? He didn't come in?"

"No, sir, didn't see him until it was done."

"You are sure there were three policemen here."

"At least three, seems more."

"What do you mean?"

Polecat looked at the cop, then looked at Bill and at Green before speaking.

"Officer, this joint has been swarming with cops all night."

Green spoke up.

"Officer, a few minutes before you arrived there were five patrolmen here."

"Tell me about it."

Green did.

"They dropped this on the way out," he said and threw the package on the bar.

"Did they identify themselves?"

All laughed except for Captain Datillo.

"With a pistol."

"And handcuffs," Bill added.

"Threatened to tear my place apart if I didn't own having dope."

"You're telling me there were five policemen right before I got here and that they threatened deadly force, handcuffs, and threatened this place—"

"No, officer," Green interjected. "Not saying that they were policemen. But they were uniformed, I can tell you that much and everything else is true. Look at my wrists. Look at Bill's."

"Better check his. Mine are skinny," Bill quipped.

The cop looked both embarrassed and concerned. Concerned won. He scribbled in his notebook and then double-checked. Polecat offered a beer and he accepted. Marcus fetched a couple of ribs.

"Those weren't cops," the cop said, "but are you sure about your numbers? The first time three and the second time five?"

"Dead certain," Polecat said.

"Don't like to admit it, but I can't piece this together. If what you're saying is true . . ."

All of them nodded.

"If it's true, there's something god-awful wrong."

"Blood spilled is more like it," Polecat said, and nobody told him to calm down.

It started raining, and all of a sudden, that rain was pounding the tin roof. There was nothing to say and nobody said anything. If confusion has a face, all wore it.

"I'll get to the bottom of this," the officer said. "Please, try not to talk. Something's not right."

"Cold-blooded murder. That's what," Bill said.

"Perhaps, you need to talk to your Officer Sneed," Green suggested.

The captain nodded. A bright-looking young man, Bill thought, while he weighed what he knew with what he thought he might decipher. He knew he had to be quiet for now. He could feel it in his bones.

"This doesn't make any sense. Who's investigating who?" Green said, looking at one of the cards that the cop who appeared to be good had left.

"Mr. Green, welcome to nigger land," Polecat said. "None of it makes sense."

"Start with one fact. The young man is dead," Marcus said.

Bill poured a round but kept quiet. Something told him to keep his trap shut. Green wanted to use the phone.

"Ain't a phone. Not even a bathroom; this is a joint," Polecat said.

"You need a lawyer," Green said.

"I need an army," Polecat responded. "What the hell can a lawyer do?"

"They're trying to frame you."

"Not if I get them first, they don't."

"What you mean by that?"

"Natural law, the law of survival. I got lists, phone numbers, and dates. You might be surprised, perhaps, at the citizens who have walked through these doors, Mr. Green."

"I'm saying you need a lawyer," Green said.

"Welcome aboard," Polecat said, "but so might you."

"Be that as it may."

Green didn't look too happy. He looked like a man who wanted to bark orders, but there was no one to bark at. Polecat just nodded.

"No offense," Polecat said.

"None taken, so long as we're on the same page," Green said.

"It appears we be getting closer."

"Might," Green said.

CONFAB COALITION

What was said after that could only be interpreted by geniuses or angels. Marcus was elected driver and it was a good choice. Even Polecat was stumbling as Green coaxed him out to the limousine, as he had dubbed Bill's car. Somehow, Polecat had been persuaded to accompany them into the next stage of ruminations.

Most likely, he wondered what these white men were so concerned about. His nephew meant nothing to them and, in truth, not all that much to him. The only reason he was riding along was because he didn't want to face Sister and didn't want to be alone. Hell, where had everybody been a few years ago when he, Polecat, had been sent up after being worked over by rednecks with axe handles and then charged with attempted murder, all because of a throw-down and one white man's word over three Negro witnesses? He served bitter time just because some white floozy loved the blues. He kept his peace and the windshield wipers swooshed, swooshed, swooshed.

"Walk softly and carry the biggest stick, what I know."

"Good thing you know the road, Marcus," Bill said.

The rain fell as hard as if it had been dumped out of a giant's bucket. Marcus hugged the wheel and peered forward through the windshield clouded with vapor, and since everyone smoked, the air deep-fog thick. They got to the boat, then sat in the car for a spell. Finally, it got too smoky and they got so thirsty they decided to make a run.

They did. All made it down the slippery bank and onto the deck except Marcus, who lost his footing and slid down, then leaped somehow onto the rain-slick planks that welcomed him like a vaudeville stage, which he traversed with a grimace before he dropped in the creek.

Everyone except Marcus was howling and it would have been funny if Marcus could swim and if winter water wasn't cold. But he couldn't and it is. Polecat ran to the edge, and Bill handed a line, which he threw to Marcus, who was more than grateful.

Polecat hauled him aboard, where he flopped and shivered like a landed fish.

Bill lit a fire. He could hear Marcus out under the awning saying that he was not going to take his clothes off, all mixed with claiming that big fish had been bumping him out to the river and he heard Polecat laugh and Green say that it could be true. Bill had to chuckle in spite of himself. He realized with some surprise that he was glad it hadn't been him and that he was awfully glad this night to be alive.

"Awfully" meant a lot of things all of a sudden. He threw some kerosene into the stove and it roared. His guests slogged in and he welcomed them. Marcus was shyly trying to cover his privates with both hands. Green and Polecat carried his clothes. Bill threw a towel, a big soft one that Sarah had loved.

Marcus wrapped up and shivered next to the heat. Polecat slumped down into a chair. Bill put a bottle of whiskey in the middle of the table and a bucket of ice.

"What's with the flower?" Green asked, pointing to a yellow thing in a jelly jar.

"Damned if I know," Bill said and then poked his head under the flag that separated the cabin from his private quarters. He was wondering if Amelia had somehow snuck in, but the room was empty. When he looked back at Green, he shrugged before he saw the pie sitting on the table right beside the whiskey. Polecat noticed at the same time.

"Ruby's been here," both he and Polecat said simultaneously.

Polecat's smile was infectious. "You got forks?" he asked.

The chocolate pie was so tasty rich and complementary to whiskey that only Marcus noticed his utensil was a spoon. When he mentioned this, he was shamed. It was a fine pie that produced sounds of satisfaction. They ate straight from the tin.

"Good God! That woman can cook," Polecat said, slurping down some whiskey.

"I'll say," said Green. "What kind of crust is that? I can't put my finger on it."

"Those pastry strips crisscrossing the top had a bite," Marcus offered.

"Yes, well," Bill said, as he swirled his ice and straight bourbon. "I've seen her sprinkle a dash of cinnamon and nutmeg and, oh yes, almond extract into her pastry dough just before dusting it with powdered sugar and hot paprika."

"Paprika!" all said at once.

Bill nodded and took a swig.

"Well, you were there," Polecat said.

"I was," Bill said.

"What's with the paper dandelion?" Green asked.

"Her daughter, Amelia, must have brought it."

"Most likely," Polecat said.

"I could have sworn that was cayenne," Green said. "The bite, don't you know?"

"I hardly think so, with all respect, Mr. Green," Polecat said. "Not on a chocolate pie."

"Well, of course, but such a bite. Is she available, Polecat?"

"What you mean? Is she available?"

Green scooped one last bite and stuffed it in, shook his head.

"I mean, do you think she would make some pie?"

"Will you pay?"

"Well, how come Bill rates free?"

The rain poured down in one final torrent and then slowed to a trickle. Everyone looked at Bill, who shrugged.

"Why does she bring you pie?" Green asked.

"Nothing I did, Green. She looks after me for a host of reasons. You know the worst."

Green looked embarrassed. Bill looked at Polecat and Polecat nodded.

"All right, there is more," Bill said. "God help us—happened a long time ago."

Polecat broke the silence with the kind of resonance that could.

"For some damn reason, Bill's grandpappy didn't take a shine to slavery. He was part of what was known as the Underground Railroad. He done risked his life to help her people. That and the awful shame from the terrible tragedy that her own son brought on. That's it in a nutshell."

"And I did give her son a job after he stole my truck," Bill added.

"Yeah, and look at how he paid you back," Polecat muttered. "You spared life; he took one."

Bill was looking into his glass.

"That boy is evil," Polecat said. "I don't care what anybody says. People don't believe in evil like they used to do, but they damn should."

"He never seemed that way, tough as it is to say," Bill said.

"That's the way. You don't see it coming till it's going away."

"The boy was insane," Green said.

"You call him what you want, if it helps you sleep. I calls him evil."

"But we have to get beyond that," Green said.

"Nice if we could. Nice if we could, sir."

"What about treatment? Hospitals and the like," Green asked.

"If it makes you feel good, give it to 'em. But what you treating the devil for and what you treating the devil to?"

"We have to get beyond these superstitions," Green reiterated.

"Hope you do, but the boy is bad to the bone like a dog gone mad. You can figure on it, but you will never cure it out."

"That is not our job here," Marcus said.

Everybody looked at him and he shrugged.

"Well, we have to try," Green said. "What else can we do?"

"Good luck." Polecat shook his head sorrowfully.

"You need a lawyer," Green said.

"One more, then it's curtains," Bill said.

"Gladly," said Marcus and they had another round.

Bill was feeling wobbly, but he was game enough that when Green asked Polecat what he meant about "this underground railway," as he put it, that Bill pointed out that lots of critters worked undercover.

"What you mean?" Green asked.

"What the hell you think we were dealing with? Those bogus cops? Damn nation! They were about as underground as hell. The Underground Railroad was about as opposite in intent as you could get. Don't you see? Freedom on one hand and handcuffs and murder on the other. What could be more clear than that?"

"So there really was an Underground Railroad?"

"Come on, Green, don't play dumb. Is there a Klan?"

"You think those cops were Klan?" Green asked.

"Mr. Green, if they weren't, they were kissing cousins."

"All right, I know a little about the railroad and something about the Klan, but I can't figure two things. One, why Bill's family had any interest in the first, and two, why the second would have any axe to grind with you, Polecat."

"Maybe it's getting late," Bill said.

"I'll take it," Polecat said. "Listen, Mr. Green, I can't speak for Mr. Bill's grandpa, who maybe thought people should have a chance, who knows? One thing's sure, those SOBs at the joint tonight damn didn't. I am certain you can appreciate the contrast."

"Sure. They handcuffed me," Green agreed.

"Yeah, that and killed my nephew."

Marcus looked nervous and started slipping into his clothes. Though Bill knew they were still damp, he kept his mouth shut. Something told him not to let the conversation, or whatever it was, go too far too fast, so he said he was tired. They left. He fell into bed with shoes on and stared into dark wondering what was directing his mind. Something told him not to worry so much. Just listen.

CHAPTER 9

MADDOX MUST DIE

Midmorning, Bill hit the deck with morning coffee. He had loafed in the sheets, flopping this way and that. He had no sooner hunkered down into his chair when Crabby walked up with his batch of bad news. The first took the form of a question. "Paid your taxes?" Second: "Slips 1, 3, 6, 5, 9, 8, 2, and 10 need repair if you want to rent 'em." Third: "Some young chickadee was here late afternoon yesterday, but I didn't like her looks, so I run her off."

Bill overlooked Crabby's humor.

"Was the woman alone?"

"She weren't exactly alone, but she weren't with a baby in swaddling garments, if that's what's worrying you."

"Damn your ass, Crab. Who was she and who was she with?"

"I want to keep my job, Bill. I don't want you mad at me. Have you paid your taxes?"

"Who damn cares?"

"You know they can shut you down? I've seen it."

"No doubt you have. Now who was here?"

"That one you was running with. That's who. She was with some older fella that didn't look bad enough. Could have been a gentleman."

"What do I pay you for, Crab? To tell me everything's going to hell and I need to pay taxes?"

"I didn't take a good look, but suspect inside that cooler there, they might have dropped something."

"Fix the docks. I'll take care of taxes," Bill said.

As Crabby was shuffling back to his concrete-block hut, Sneed rolled up. Bill acted like he didn't even notice. Sneed rolled down the window. Bill stared downstream. Sneed revved. Bill took no notice.

"Your ass is grass," Sneed sneered.

"Top of the morning," Bill replied. "God bless you, son."

Sneed rolled off. Bill popped the cooler and found an envelope. Inside he found a police badge and two notes. One was from Valerie.

"Florida didn't work. I'm back. Uncle Joel drove me to see you. Some guy I met had this badge in his ashtray, plus this note. Noticed your name, so I snatched it. This happened night before last. After you read the note, you will understand why I tried to keep him busy and did for your sake. —Valerie."

Bill looked at the police badge and scratched his head. Then he un-crumpled the scrap of paper that Valerie called a note.

"Maddox must die."

Bill fired up a smoke just as Sneed passed back by grinning. Bill waved.

The rocking of his boat sent Bill into reverie. He flipped his Pall Mall into the drink and laughed when a fish spit it out. He didn't have much on Sneed; just a couple of pictures of something not all that abnormal. He shut his eyes and opened his ears to the creaking lines that secured his boat. Something else, something else, not that, something else.

Nothing occurred to him. He had nothing against anybody. He knew he should have hated Ronald, but what he felt was not hatred; it was far beyond that. It was all so horribly burned into his being and there was no emotion to silence or explain it.

He wrapped his pistol in a towel and kept it beside him until he got sick of the thing. The weight annoyed and poisoned his mind, focused him on what he didn't want to think about.

First in February, then in March, he expected something to happen. Maybe Datillo would follow up or Valerie might stop by, but nothing broke the lazy rhythm of early spring. He went fishing in his skiff, but all he caught were bluegill. He saw bass nesting, but they weren't biting. He puzzled. Lethargy amazed him.

He ran out of beer and ice, which motivated him to head out. He ran into Fred at the liquor store. Usually jolly, Fred seemed almost standoffish. The clerk behind the counter, the one they called Don Jr., rang Bill up without his usual lighthearted nonsense.

Something was brewing. Bill felt the cold shoulder. Driving down River Road, he saw Amelia walking alongside her brother, and they didn't wave. He scrunched down his own road; his inner voice said: Be alert. Listen.

He pulled in where he would normally park, and something told him to keep going. He had one eye on the river and the other in the rearview mirror. A following car rolled up slowly and pulled beside him. It was Valerie and her Uncle Joel.

"You all right?" she asked.

"Never better," Bill replied. "And you?"

Dr. Joel motioned at the boat and led the way.

Once inside, everybody seemed less wary. Bill offered them beer and whiskey, and both accepted.

"Look, Bill," Joel said. "I sure didn't want to come here."

Valerie interjected. "I made him bring me. They're going to kill you and Polecat Green. Don't ask me how I know, but you got to get out of here."

"Who wants to kill me?"

"I would rather not say."

"Well, Valerie, why do you trouble warning me, if you won't tell me what? And who the hell would kill Polecat?"

"Who knows why?" Valerie said. "I just know I know."

"Who?"

"Look, Bill," Joel interjected. "Valerie overheard stuff she shouldn't and be glad. We can't prove anything, but it seems a family member spouted things."

Bill studied Joel. He looked totally sincere. Valerie was nodding.

"When? Why?"

"Don't know when and don't know why exactly," Joel replied.

"Well, how about why not-so-exactly? You got a clue?"

"Close as I can figure, a faction is trying to take over the police, and that group also shakes down joints like Polecat's. You're seen as a threat and Polecat is, too. He knows too many players."

"What are you talking about—players?"

"Folks he deals with maybe know too much? Myself, I wouldn't know crooked cops. Would you?"

"Nope."

"Listen, Bill, they are out there. They want control and use fear to get it. Turn black against white, white against black. Do you believe that? Understand what you did when you pleaded mercy for Ronald was a direct threat? All they've got is fear."

"What did I do ever to make them want to kill?"

"You offered hope," Joel said.

"Hope?"

"What do you think?"

"Damn, if I know. My wife was killed."

"They wanted to use you, Bill, but you were bigger."

Valerie nodded her head.

"Bigger than what?" Bill asked. "What the hell do they think I am? I did nothing for or against. I did what I did."

"Bill, they want you out of the way."

"Out of the way?"

"Imagine if Sneed's kind could have stirred up enough fear to take this district? What if they control and stack the deck?"

"Bad news."

"People like you can stop them. People like Polecat, too. Don't you see?"

"Not exactly."

"Look, they want control. You are trash, so is Valerie, and me, and Polecat, and whatever Negro can make it is black trash. They play us. Can't you see? Bill, you ain't squared up."

"To what?"

"You don't fit the plan."

"I didn't like when I heard what I heard," Valerie said.

"That's why we're here," Joel said. "Trying to help."

"Well, damn," Bill said. "I don't know what, do you?"

"Nope," Joel said. Valerie shook her head.

"Watch yourself," Joel said as they walked away. Valerie winked as she stepped onto the shore, but as he watched taillights disappear, he knew it probably wouldn't be anytime soon before she returned, but he was wrong.

Before two hours had passed, there was a knock. Bill grabbed his pistol and called out, "Who's there?"

Valerie answered.

"What the hell?" was the first thing out of his mouth. She kissed him and told him to hush. She had more.

He tried to kiss her for real, but she gave him a look that reminded him of his mother.

"It is supposed to look like an accident."

"How do you know this?"

Valerie said it was too embarrassing to tell. Bill asked her to try. Apparently, she was as much concerned about being supposedly passed out when she heard than the circumstances that placed her within earshot. She was at a river camp working for five partying fisherman; she teased and occasionally pleased them with special favors. There was another girl who recruited her, but she heard nothing because she had been busy. Valerie had slipped off and pretended to sleep.

"What did you hear?" Bill asked.

"They were like kids, they were so excited. Each one had a plan. Four were playing poker. The other guy was busy. Well, one wanted to set your boat on fire; another one wanted to hook up a bomb to your car; another guy said that those guys were looking for trouble and that the best thing would be an accident. After some discussion, they all agreed that would be best. Some wanted to drown you. One guy wanted to make it look like a gun-cleaning incident, but then another joker asked how would anybody know you had one. They went around and around. Finally, they settled on a car wreck."

Bill started laughing in spite of himself, but Valerie was serious and shushed him.

"Don't forget they have Sneed. This one guy said with a radio he could tail your movements, like a fish in a bowl. The one who said this drives a gravel truck. He was willing to do his part for the cause."

"What cause?"

"They hate you, Bill, deeper than you know. They wanted Ronald to fry in the electric chair. They wanted to send a message loud and clear. You messed that up."

"This is crazy. Where they planning to nail me?"

"Bottom of the hill, right before Creek Bridge, when you're on your way to pick up your ice and booze."

"You're kidding."

"Wish I were. You're pretty regular, Bill. They got you pegged and they got the lawman—that's how they put it."

"You're not making this up, are you?"

"No, I heard it plain as day."

"Who are these people, Valerie?"

"What difference does that make?"

"Okay, what about Polecat?"

"A bullet in the back. Easy, they said."

"So how did you get here?" Bill asked.

"What do you mean?"

"I mean what I asked," Bill replied. "Who brought you and how do you plan to get back?"

"Thought maybe you, when the sun comes up."

"Who brought you?"

"My sister."

"Why?"

"I asked her. What's wrong? Are you mad? I'm trying to help."

"Then tell me who they are."

She mainly only knew nicknames. Stringer. Slouch. One fellow's name was John and he was tall and one guy they called Grease, but it sounded like Greason sometimes and his first name might have been Jim, but she wasn't sure.

"That's all?"

"Well, I'm sure it was Stringer owns the dump truck."

"Damn," Bill said. "How the hell did you get involved?"

"Told you I was recruited by this girl."

"Well, who the hell is she?"

"She ain't from here. Goes by the name of Michelle and I think she's from near Covington."

"Double damn." Bill shook his head.

"Guess I ain't much help."

"Would you tell this to the cops?"

"Oh, Bill, you know I can't."

"Suppose not. Well then, I'll mend my ways or take a different route. I don't suppose you've told Polecat?"

Valerie shook her head.

"Well, don't you think that might be the right thing?"

"I hadn't thought, but I guess now you mention."

THE RIGHT THING TO DO

They set out at twilight. The pistol, wrapped in a towel, sat between them until Valerie scooted over, reached down and placed it on the floor just beneath Bill's seat.

"We might need that."

"That thing makes me nervous."

"Me too, angel, but we might need it, so put it back on the seat."

Valerie stroked Bill's thigh instead and then told him he could reach.

"I better duck down through Creekside," she whispered.

If anyone was looking as Bill passed through the intersection at Creekside, they would have seen Bill, eyes hot on the road. Things got bumpy when they turned off onto the two-lane that led to Polecat Green's but smoothed when they parked beneath a locust tree.

"Here's your pistol, Bill Maddox. I just wanted you relaxed. I heard that's the best way."

"Can't argue; owe you one, I suppose."

"Well, that's a thought," Valerie said. "Remind me later."

"Think I'll have to?"

"Most likely won't," she said, as they crunched toward the open dark doorway of Green's place.

Polecat was behind the bar reading the *Racing Form* by candlelight. When they walked in, he looked surprised. There was only one other guy at the end of the bar, slumped over a crossword puzzle. Although Bill felt relaxed, he patted the pistol in his pocket.

"Top of the evening," Polecat said.

"How's it going?" Bill asked.

"Fair, considering." Polecat's voice was about as dark as his joint.

"I hear you," Bill said.

"Can I get you something?"

'Sure, if you'll have one. Can we sit down and talk privately?"

"That's my half-brother."

They sat down, and Polecat lit a candle in the middle of the table that made everybody look instantly ten years older and spookier to Valerie. She clutched Bill's arm. He patted her knee, trying to comfort her.

Without revealing too much, which Bill realized he couldn't if he wanted, he informed Polecat that both of them were marked. Polecat sat stone-faced. His eyes didn't move.

"So?"

"She heard them," Bill said.

"Dates and times?" Polecat asked. Valerie shook her head and Bill felt like an idiot.

"I'm sorry," Bill said. "I was not thinking straight, I guess."

"Understandable. If I was you, I might not either, but what can we do but watch our asses? Maybe ask the lady to listen a little closer." He nodded at Valerie.

"You got any ideas?" Bill asked.

"Nah, except for guard the back as well as the front. I'll listen close. You'd be surprised what I hear. Some of my girls got big ears, too. Watch it when you go out fishing, for example. Don't ask me how I know. Think about getting a dog with teeth," Polecat said.

"A dog?"

"Next to what you're packing, it's the best thing. Look, I talked to the good cop and that's the best he could do for me. What else we got to talk about?"

"I'm going to talk to Mr. Green. You want to?"

"Would love to, but I still don't believe he understands. It's a bad dream he'll wake up from. You and I won't."

———

"Want me to take you home now or in the morning?" Bill asked, as he meandered out toward River Road. For an answer, Valerie scooted closer. Bill steered the car.

"Well, you're real friendly," Valerie said.

"Feel like a damn fool. Go tell a man he's in danger. His nephew just got buried and I can't offer anything."

"You tried to do right."

"What's the damn point when you don't know right?"

Bill reached for a smoke, but Valerie already had one lit. She handed it to him and dragged on another herself.

"Well, since you didn't take a left," Valerie said, "I guess we're going back to the boat. Maybe I can show you what right is."

"Maybe so," Bill answered.

"You got a bad attitude, Bill Maddox."

"Don't mean to."

"You know you owe me."

Bill smiled in spite of himself. What if they killed him? Dump trucks? Who gave a damn? He couldn't figure why she was here or even if she was. He followed his soft low beams and realized there was nothing to know right then anyhow.

Of course, Valerie was flesh and blood. Phantoms, from what he'd always heard, declined to be clearly photographed. But sometimes the way she popped in and out spooked him like a curious dream.

Back aboard, Bill fixed whiskey but couldn't relax. She rubbed his neck so hard it hurt.

"Damn, you're tight, Bill."

"Not yet, but I soon will be."

"I'm talking about your neck. Take a deep breath."

Bill took a deep drag on his Pall Mall.

"You want me to go?"

"No."

"Everything's going to work out."

"I would like to believe."

"Try to just for tonight, all right?"

Bill tried and pretty much succeeded. Valerie's unabashed encouragement seemed to put possibilities into play. He woke up alone, but the spot where Valerie had laid was warm. He squinted and saw what he hoped was her shape. He placed his hand on his pistol and whispered. She shushed and tiptoed over.

"Someone's out there."

Bill slipped to the small window. The moon was dim, and he couldn't see anything but vague shapes.

"You hear something?" he whispered. She nodded and pointed at the car.

"Thought I saw light underneath it, then a clinking sound."

Then they both heard metal touch metal and a slight scrunch. Bill handed Valerie the pistol. The next thing she heard was two clinks and the sound of a shotgun locking shut. Bill crept out of the room, and she felt the boat sway as he moved forward to the bow. The boat rocked as Bill stepped ashore; next she heard the crash of glass breaking. A dark shape jumped and started moving like black cloth vanishing in a strong breeze. Bill growled so loud it was barely covered by the roar of the shotgun and a high-pitched yelp. The bright flash and pitch black that followed made it impossible to see anything. Bill ran back in and started to jump into his pants.

"What are you doing? You run them off?"

"I'm going to run down the son of a bitch and kill him, that's what."

Valerie pleaded with him to stay with her, but he didn't listen until he was almost out the door. They heard a car peel out and he still would have gone, but she made him realize he better check out his car. He was furious and shaking, but knew she was right.

"Bill, you need a phone."

"I hate phones."

"You could call the cops."

"All they do is talk."

Bill decided to walk to Crabby's little shack by the boat ramp, turn on the power, and light up the son of a bitch, as he put it. She didn't want to be left, so she went with him. They traded weapons. The pistol scared her.

"What was the glass?"

"Threw a beer bottle against the side of the car. Might have been kids."

She stuck close and carried the shotgun like she knew how. It felt good to be walking, breathing cool air, and even though it was dark, both were more excited than frightened. Bill had brought the wrong key, so he broke a window pane, reached inside and flipped the switch, which flooded the creek shore with light for a hundred yards.

"It is a relief, ain't it?" Bill said.

"My hero," Valerie said with a laugh, but both were genuinely relieved. Nothing looked unusual. The shadows were steady as they strolled toward the car.

"You see anything?" Bill asked.

"Nothing I could describe."

They saw broken glass on the ground beside the car and smelled beer.

"Bet that scared the son of a bitch," Bill said.

"Not as much as buckshot backside, I'll bet."

"Hit him?"

"Sure as hell. Didn't you hear him scream?"

"That damn cannon is so loud, my ears still ringing."

"Pretty sure, way he hollered, but what did you hit him with?"

"Hard to say. These shells Green reloaded. Duck loads, but some seem to pack more wallop than others. He reloads at night, you see."

Valerie looked puzzled.

"Well, I been kicked by a mule and suspect Green might have upped the ante and dumped in more gunpowder than the recipe."

"Lucky the gun didn't blow," Valerie said.

They both saw the crescent wrench at the same time and then pliers sticking out from under a New York Yankees baseball cap. They grinned at each other.

"Well, look what we have here," Bill said.

"Let it lay; don't touch it," Valerie said.

"Hell no, sweetheart, sun will pop soon. Let's have a nightcap."

On the deck, they listened to early morning sounds before turning in with drinks soon forgotten as they drifted into comfort of lazy drawling small talk, little jokes, and such. They dozed and were awakened by duck yakking on the roof. There were a couple of wood ducks nesting beneath what had been a functioning bell. Beneath quacks strident, ducklings hollowly chirped. Bill crawled out of bed.

"You know, Bill, I've been thinking," she said. "Maybe we should get out of here."

Bill grunted.

"No, I'm serious," she said.

"Me, too, but I'm seriously not awake."

He turned on the hot plate and started his coffee routine.

"These people are dangerous, Bill. What's the point?"

"Who knows? Let's have coffee. I'm curious to see what they were trying to do."

Crabby drove up as they were having a look.

"What are the damn lights on for?"

"Intruders," Bill said. "Call this cop and tell him to get out here." He handed Crabby a business card. "Give him my name. Tell him it relates to the shooting."

Within an hour, Datillo was under Bill's car. He got on his radio a few minutes later, then explained that a mechanic and a detective were on the way.

The mechanic determined the brake line had been jimmied and that the steering linkage was loosened to the point it was barely connected. He also found something else that troubled. The wrench had his own initials etched on it.

"This wrench was stolen, along with the rest of my tools, last winter."

"Where was it stolen from?"

"Right out of my bay."

Made some notes, took pictures, and snooped around. Before they left, the mechanic tightened things and replaced brake fluid.

"Good as new now, but somebody wants you hurt bad, brother," he said to Bill as he wiped off his wrench.

"Don't forget your cap, mister," Valerie said, pointing to the NY Yankees cap still on the ground.

"I'm a Dodgers fan. Wouldn't be caught dead wearing that thing."

"I do think you hit the fellow, Mr. Maddox," the detective said, as he chewed his pencil, "but I would warn you that the law frowns on shooting a man running away."

Bill replied. "I couldn't see anything."

"Just be careful and watch yourself is all I'm saying."

Bill nodded.

"We'll check emergency room records. You got an example of the ammo?"

Bill fetched him a shotgun shell. The detective examined it. The fact that it was a reload did not please him.

"Won't help. We'll let you know."

Nothing turned up. Datillo dropped by a couple of days later and urged patience. There was a man treated at General Hospital for the extraction of shotgun pellets, but he had been admitted as John Doe and all anyone could remember was that he couldn't sit, didn't talk, and was tall and skinny. Bill believed Datillo was sincere, but he couldn't resist pointing out that it was a bit frustrating sitting around waiting for the next shoe to drop.

The truth was that his mind had plotted all kinds of revenge. At sundown, now armed with information that the son of a bitch was tall and thin, he headed up to the Pine Bar, poked his head in, drank a beer, and felt stupid. There was nobody in the place of any interest, just a couple of guys slurping beer.

He drove to the Point and thought better. What was he supposed to do? Hang around looking for somebody who couldn't comfortably sit? He went back to the boat, kicked off his shoes and watched water flow. Part of him wanted to kill the son of a bitch, but that would only suck him in deeper.

CHAPTER 10

BIRDSEED

Sarah would have had an answer. Valerie, as flighty as she was, might have one. But he, Bill Maddox, watched springtime water curl past the bow and had none.

For one thing, the cop was probably right when he said they wouldn't try anything else, but what did anyone know? Why shouldn't he try to kill them first? But who were they?

Two mallards across the creek looked at him inquisitively.

They quacked. He quacked back and chuckled in spite of himself. He heard a car crackling toward him. He took a slug of his drink and patted the pistol beside him. It was Fred Ruby's car.

"Heard you had some excitement last night," Fred said as he approached.

"You know something?"

"A little."

"Come aboard. Want a beer?"

"Sort of early, but why not?"

After they settled down on the deck, Fred let on that his nephew had been washing cars and doing his janitorial work, when some guys came in the garage and wanted to know if anyone knew how to lift stains out of upholstery. The owner put Fred's nephew on the job and the young man did his best, but the stains were soaked in and didn't clean. One fellow cussed him up and down for being a fool.

The boss came to the rescue, which eased the boy's mind. The boss sent them packing, no charge, and nobody thought about it much until mid-morning.

Some roustabout braggart pulled in and said that while he was giving his girlfriend what's what in the back of his Chevy, he'd heard a shotgun blast and said some man ran by screeching like the devil, jumped into a Ford sedan, and squealed away

"He said it was on your road that it happened."

"Did he see the man?" Bill asked. "What color was the car?"

"The man was tall. He couldn't see the car except for taillights."

Bill sighed.

"Yeah, it ain't much, so what happened here? Down at Creekside, some guy said there was a killing. Said he heard it on the police radio."

"Not so lucky. Who are these fools?"

"The same as always, I reckon," Fred said.

"Most likely, but what color car was your nephew working on?"

"I asked and all he knew was that it was a Ford, tan or gold or gray."

"Damn!"

"I told you it wasn't much, but there is another thing. One guy has a snake tattooed up his arm. My boy said it was a mean-looking snake."

"That's something, I guess."

"Not much, I reckon."

———

When Bill dropped Valerie off at her sister's, she said that she would try to get back later, and he hoped she would, but she didn't. He skipped meals and cussed her at each. The first two he was joking, but by dinner, he was serious. What the hell was she doing treating him this way? Then he realized he was comparing her to Sarah, and that made him realize that there was no comparison. He checked his trot line, but there was nothing on it but hooks. Too weary to drive, he ate some pickles and retired.

Early to bed, early to rise. He woke up about four and took his pistol to the deck and smoked until dawn before setting out to Barb and Fran's Creekside Diner for breakfast. He was ravenous. He ordered the regular, but Fran kept looking at him in an irregular way. She seemed nervous and he asked why. She smoothed down her apron and smiled a proprietary smile and slid away. When she returned with coffee, he punched in his question again. She told him that she heard that he had been shot. Bill spread his arms and said not yet. She laughed nervously and told him that she hadn't seen him since . . . and then caught herself.

"It's okay," Bill said. "What are you getting at?"

"Nothing," she replied. "Just something I overheard."

"That's a lot of 'hears' without specifics; why not?"

"Bill, I'm scared. I would tell what, but I'm scared. That's no kidding."

Bill nodded and took a sip. Fran tugged on her apron.

"You in with them?" Bill asked.

"Gracious sakes, no, Bill Maddox."

"Then what did you hear?"

"Order up!"

"Wait a second; your breakfast."

When she put his plate down with bacon sizzling, there was a note sticking out the napkin side.

"Here's your check. Enjoy."

He tucked the note into his pocket and sopped up the eggs with his honey crust bread. Out in the car, he gave the note a look-see: "Farm manager, Green."

Afternoon Bill went fishing using worms he collected from underneath a board. He was pleased when the outboard motor started and slid about a mile upstream past the bridge. He baited, drifted, and caught three largemouth and two bluegill. Not bad eating.

As he was putt-putting back, he let his mind drift. There was almost no breeze, so the water was glassy. Trees arched the creek and light flickered. The whole world glistened bright, sparkling, but then some glint up ahead caught his eye. He squinted and peered but saw nothing unusual. He saw a john boat approach and before they were close enough to acknowledge each other, the man waved nonchalantly. Bill figured he was waving at him. Bill could see he was an old fellow he knew from the post office, a big talker about old-time weather. The man looked startled as they drew closer. He corrected course.

"Sorry, partner, I didn't see yer!"

"Well, who you waving at then, you old rascal?"

The man grinned and cupped his ear. Bill repeated his question.

"The Green man, you know? What's his name? You catch anything?"

Bill held up his string.

"Hope you ain't feeding a family of five," he hollered as he snaked upstream.

Bill scoured the bank as he glided past and he didn't see anyone at all. He got a funny feeling in his gut and goosed it, made sure his course was a bit unsteady, and approached his own boat warily with his pistol cocked. When he stepped aboard, he carried his pistol and left the fish behind, but nothing had been disturbed. Everything was dandy except for his mood, which was foul. Someone had been out there. His bones echoed Polecat's warning.

Cleaned fish on the bank and dropped the filets in a bowl of salted water. The sun was close to cocktail hour and he wanted an ocean of booze. He fixed a drink and plopped down in his chair on the deck. He sat and stared into the cool part of the sky. He needed to talk to Green, but what could he say? Show him a scribbled note from Barb and Fran's? He looked at it again. Then tell him some half-blind character on the creek said, "The Green man," when asked who he had been waving at.

A car rolled up. Bill tensed, but it was Ruby and Amelia. Ruby was carrying a casserole dish covered with a red-checkered cloth. She didn't look all that friendly, but Amelia clung close, grinning. He smiled back; he couldn't help it. Then Marcus got out of the car. Soon the four of them were on the deck and everybody except Amelia seemed serious.

Bill hugged Amelia and thanked Ruby for a scrumptious smelling cheese grits casserole. Marcus stood to the side. Ruby studied Bill's face. She shook her head.

"Bill, I got to tell you that I am worried sick. Somebody took a shot at Polecat. They missed him, but a wood splinter went into his eye and put it out, I believe. He's home, but he told me to tell you that you're next. They're out to kill and I feel sick to death."

Bill patted the pistol in his pocket and winked.

"Bill, you can't be watching all the time."

Amelia jumped into his lap. Ruby insisted the little girl get down. She hopped off like she had been slapped.

Marcus said, "Mr. Green is who I would talk to, if I was you."

"Why so?" Bill asked.

"Just would, that's all. He'll be home soon as I pick him up."

"Do you know something I should ask or tell?"

"Not much, no more than you. But might be something's happening under his nose he don't see. Ask him to walk down to the barn with you. Maybe have a drink in the tack room."

"Is Mrs. Green home?"

"She is, but they are on the outs. She is indisposed this evening."

"So, Green wants company?"

"Yes, sir, 'bout nine o'clock, give or take."

When they left, Bill was more puzzled than ever. He put his fish in the cooler and took one bite of casserole and dropped it into the cooler, too. He plopped on his bed and took a nap. When he woke up, it was almost nine. Someone was knocking on his door.

"Put the gun up; it's me," Valerie said as she stepped in.

"You sure come and go, don't you?" Bill said.

"Now, don't you start in. I swear to God."

"All right, I won't. I've got no time anyhow. Will you go with me somewhere?"

"Depends."

She had always wanted to see the big house, so they went. Green himself answered the door, bigger than life. Valerie was looking good and a pretty girl always fired him up. Marcus served drinks properly on the patio. Bill felt his stomach turn a little as he watched the interaction between Valerie and Green. She milked him like a cow. Bill was irritated until she seconded his suggestion to walk down to the barns. She winked at Green and involuntarily, Bill had winked back.

Armed with freshened cocktails, they entered the pungency of the barn enclave. Green was in his element. He pointed out various improvements. Cedar doors, brand-new windows. The horses were hunters and seemed spirited when the visitors peered into the stalls.

"Isn't there some place where we can sit?" Valerie asked.

"Let's get back to the patio," Green said.

"Don't you have a tack room?" Valerie asked.

Green patted his girth and laughed.

"I haven't ridden for five years. Let's check it out."

Smelled musty. There was tack hanging from pegs on the walls, but much of it was moldy.

"The kids don't ride much anymore, as you can see."

The three of them sat around an old beat-up table.

"What's that?" Valerie asked, pointing to a radio type of contraption. "What's that have to do with raising horses?"

Green slurped his drink but had to shrug. Valerie turned it on.

"Roger. I'm reading you loud and *crackle . . . crackle snarl.*"

"Proceed then, 101, just be . . . *snapple pop po crapkle.*"

"Roger, over."

"Well, I'll be damned," Green said. "That's a citizen's band radio. You can listen in on goings-on."

"No, sir, this is a police radio. Listen to this," Valerie said.

"Uncle . . . *crackle* . . . this is Birdseed, hit twenty-eight, over *pop*!"

"Birdseed, this is Uncle over, twenty-eight, roger, over."

"Watch this," Valerie said, as she turned the dial to twenty-eight. There was a cacophony of screeches, hisses, and pops.

"Hello, Birdseed. Birdseed, read me, over."

"Uncle, Uncle . . . *bleghh crackle!*"

"Birdseed? Birdseed?"

"Blah *boink jabble julocrackle!*"

"Come again, Birdseed. Uncle, over?

"117 proceed as planned . . . *crackle* . . . Never say Uncle, roger."

"Never did, sir, over."

Bill started grinning at Valerie and she grinned back.

"What's going on here?" Green asked, looking from one to the other. "What do you know that I don't know?"

"Know nothing," Bill said.

Both of them looked at Valerie. She closed her eyes and smiled.

"What is this?" Green asked. "What does this mean?"

Valerie, with eyes closed, just nodded.

"If you know something, speak up, girl!"

"If I was a girl, I would not be here, Mr. Green," Valerie replied, eyes still shut.

"Okay, so what gives?"

"Some you trust, you don't really know, and that's all I will say."

"Who?"

"You heard me," Valerie said. "Who manages your farm?"

"What does that have to do with anything?"

"Ask yourself. I'm sure I don't know, Mr. Green."

"What do you know, Maddox?" Green asked.

"Nothing certain, but my ears are open. I hope yours are."

Green looked perturbed. He glanced from Bill to Valerie and shrugged.

"I feel it in my bones," Green muttered, slowly opened a drawer, and pulled out a scrap of paper and said, "Bingo!"

Bill grabbed the paper and saw that it had two call stations as near as he could figure. "Birdseed" and "Uncle." He handed it to Valerie.

"Curious, isn't it?" she said.

"Let's listen again," Green said.

They heard nothing. Nothing at all and finally walked back to the house for a drink.

After poppers, Green was ready to call the mayor, but Bill suggested he call Datillo. When Green found out the mayor was out of town, he called Captain Datillo and got him. As soon as Green said that he wanted to set up a meeting, Datillo cut him off and said he would be right out in an unmarked car.

They met in Green's home office. The cop accepted a beer and asked for assurance that the conversation would remain confidential. He looked more troubled than he had at Polecat's. Dressed in khakis and a sport shirt, the only thing about him that looked cop were shoes: black and shiny.

He stared hard at Valerie, said, "She all right?"

Bill nodded.

"I know a little about Valerie, enough to know she is fond of money. You can help or hurt. What will it be?"

"I know some stuff," she said. "I want to help."

"You will vouch for her, Mr. Green?"

Green looked at Bill and nodded.

"All right then. Mr. Green, I want to move into your empty tenant house down by the barn and want to hire on as a laborer."

"Why on earth?" Green asked.

"I don't want wages and the county will pay rent if you insist, but it will make it easier to keep an eye on things."

"What things?"

"Mr. Green, I might ask the same. Say this place is under surveillance. I am reasonably certain you don't know why. Correct?"

Green was used to being the man in charge and wasn't sure he liked Datillo's tone of voice.

"I assure you I don't," Green said. "On the other hand, we discovered some peculiar things in the tack room that may deserve scrutiny."

"That would be the radio, correct?"

"Yes, it would, sir," Green said, as if robbed of a punch line. "It would, indeed."

"Mr. Green, how well do you know Lang Delf, your farm manager?"

"I knew his daddy and grandpa. He's worked here three years. He hasn't done bad. Weak on maintenance, but good with stock. Seems okay."

"Well, he's not, Mr. Green."

The cop let this sink in.

"Did you know that he tried to join the force five years ago and was turned down? Did you know that he was kicked out of the US Army for beating a Negro recruit near to death? He didn't like the boy's 'attitude,' as he put it at his hearing. Were you aware of the fact that he is a ranking do-dah Ku Klux Klan?"

Green shook his head.

"Look, here, I can't tell everything. Don't know everything. But we do know that he and some others are trying to make inroads into our department. The people who harassed you at Polecat's were his and whoever shot Polecat's nephew were his and whoever shot at Polecat were most likely his people. You understand? We got a problem."

"I thought Sneed shot the boy," Bill said.

"No, his weapon hadn't been fired. Forget Sneed. He was there, that's all," Datillo said.

"How can I help?" Green asked.

"Just hire me."

"You're going undercover?" Green asked.

"No, not exactly. That wouldn't work. But it's not unusual for cops to have second jobs, you know? Besides, we aren't sure how far they're into us, but obviously deep enough to get uniforms and a car or two. But they don't know we know. At least I don't think. I won't hide I'm a cop. I'll act like some poor slob who needs money. My wife's expecting. My mother is sick. I'll have a cover; don't doubt.

I'm good at maintenance, by the way, and I can drive a tractor, take care of livestock, do carpentry, painting, you name it."

"Hell's bells," Green said. "Hired on the spot!"

"Remember, it won't cost."

"Hell, no. I'll pay."

"Only if you want, but one thing you might not like."

"Like what?"

"I am going to be a son of a bitch. One sneaky, mean SOB. Your colored folk aren't going to like me. Your man, Marcus, is he around? Can he be trusted?"

"Marcus is smart. You need to talk to him?"

"Your call, Mr. Green. I need to convince the farm manager and others I'm hateful and don't have much time to do it, so I'm going to be rough. I'm going to stir things up, you understand?"

Green pointed to a buzzer beside his foot, hesitated, then pressed the buzzer. Within seconds, Marcus appeared.

"Yes, sir?" he said with a demeanor reserved for strangers or special guests.

"It's okay, Marcus," Green said. "Captain Datillo needs to talk to you as soon as you bring another round." Marcus looked nervous. Green laughed and waved his hand. "Everything's all right," he said.

Marcus didn't look too sure until he returned with the drinks and the cop stood and thanked him, shaking his hand. The cop asked Marcus to take a seat. Marcus looked at Green, who nodded, so Marcus sat.

"Wait a minute, Marcus; you look dry as a bone. Go get yourself a beer, for God's sake."

While Marcus was gone, the cop asked Green if he had a fishing boat. Green nodded. The cop told him he had been a guide and promised Green the trip of his life. Green looked puzzled.

"Bill," the cop continued, "you like to fish, don't you?"

Bill nodded. Green said that Bill sometimes captained when he went out with friends.

"Bill, these Klan folks have tried to join you up, haven't they?"

"Not successfully," Bill said.

"I suspect not, but what if the three of us started to act chummy?"

"Chummy?"

"I told you, I want to stir doubt. What if Delf thinks his job's in trouble? What if he thinks that I'm his replacement? Thinks you, me, and Mr. Green are having so much fun that his days are numbered and he's losing his perch?"

Marcus walked in, sat down, smiling east to west.

"Back to that in a minute," the cop said. "Marcus, you know of the Klan. Would you like to help me kick their ass?"

Marcus looked baffled, took a swig of beer, and grinned.

"Marcus, if I called you a bunch of names and yelled at your butt just for the hell of it, could you take it?"

"Sir?"

"Look, what I'm trying to tell you people is that Delf and a couple of the hands here have got this place to their liking. They have it figured out. Delf has a certain respectability, the manager of a fine farm. Lots of outbuildings to stash stuff in, to stash people in, but he's gotten careless. The Klan is dying, and these folks are desperate. That's why they tried to recruit Bill. That's why they're trying to infiltrate the police department. They've been forced under. They have no power anymore and I am here to say I want to make sure that they have less."

"You think they're responsible for Polecat's nephew and for putting out Polecat's eye?" Bill asked.

"Almost 100 percent. See, they hate Polecat and any black man makes money. Nephew got in the way. They wanted Polecat. Polecat knows too much. He's got a lot of feelers out. He's told stuff but could tell more. He will if we bust this bunch, I bet."

"People scared," Marcus said. "Not even Polecat's bigger than a .45."

"What do you know about Lang Delf, Marcus?"

"Don't like the man, tell the truth."

"Care to tell why?"

"He talks foul to people. Just plain mean-spirited. He killed a young child's dog right in front of him two weeks ago. Broke the poor child's heart. Scared him to death. He's a bad man and that ain't half."

"You talking about Cracker?" Bill asked.

"No sir, Mr. Bill, the other one, the fatter one."

"Hell, those dogs wouldn't hurt a fly."

"Why wasn't I told?"

"Mr. Green. Nobody wanted to bother you over some dog, and besides, Mr. Delf told the boy was Mrs. Green's orders."

"Horse manure! I'll fire the SOB tonight!"

"I wish you wouldn't, Mr. Green," Datillo said. "We'll get him. Marcus, is that boy, Joshua, pretty smart? Think he can keep a secret?"

"He's plenty smart. He knows most of the Bible by heart. Almost scary smart."

"Marcus, will you help put this man in jail?"

"Show me how!"

"I'm going to have to treat you the worse way in front of everybody. Call you things, make you look stupid. Can you take it?"

"Who you think you are talking to, Captain?"

"Mr. Green, will you agree?"

"I think so."

"Just let me move in the little house and then you tell me which building you need painted or fences, preferably out of the way, so that they know where I am, but can't be close. Another thing, I want Marcus several hours a day. Maybe the kid Joshua could bring us out water or sandwiches. His mother, Laura, is your cook, isn't she?"

Green nodded. "What if Delf asks me who you are."

"Your show, isn't it?"

"Damn right, but how did I hear about you? Do I tell him you're a cop?"

"Keep it simple. I did odd jobs for a friend who knew I needed a place. Something like that. He will know I'm a cop because sometimes I show up in a patrol car. What can he say? You're the boss."

"When do you start?"

"Day after tomorrow."

That was the plan: Captain Datillo would work on the farm. Valerie was to keep her ears open. Green was to play dumb. Bill was supposed to be on call to take Green fishing, so that he would be off the farm. Marcus was supposed to act like he hated Datillo, and Datillo was to give him lots of reasons to despise the onset of spring.

He did.

CHAPTER 11

KILL IT DEAD

The first day of May, while Marcus was loading a box into the tenant house, Datillo kicked him in the ass and cussed him for being a dumb monkey. When Marcus turned defiantly, Datillo stared him down. Out of the corner of his eye, Datillo saw one of the farmhands notice and muttered to Marcus that he was doing fine.

Delf called on Datillo that night, standoffish, and he stared at Datillo, who leaned on the door frame and stared over Delf's shoulder, focused on the red-streaked sunset clouds.

"I know who you are," Delf said.

"Tell me."

"No, you tell me."

"Look, I know the boss man I'm beholden to," Datillo said.

"What you doing here?"

"Work, Mr. Delf. Police department don't pay. Wife is giving me stuff, not good. I need money. Was I supposed to turn it down?"

"I'm in charge here. Do you understand?"

"Mr. Green told me that fact."

Delf stared at the back wall of Datillo's room and coughed.

"I was hired to paint the barn, Mr. Delf, and two outbuildings. I'm doing it for next to nothing with nigger help, but I suppose you know what that means."

"No, but you listen; I am in charge. You got that?"

"Sure do," Datillo answered. "I never was led otherwise. You are the man. That's what he said. Mr. Green's just trying to give me a hand."

"Why you? Why he hire you?"

Datillo shrugged. "I need cash and work cheap."

"I know you're a cop, right?"

"I told you that," Datillo said. "Got something against cops?"

Delf said nothing. He almost looked like he was laughing but wasn't.

"Mr. Delf, like I said, I need money. Mr. Green was kind to offer me this place. All I want is to be left alone. The damn Korea mess and the wife, I can't even talk about. Look, all I want is work."

"Think you're smart?" Delf said.

"If I were smart, would I be here?"

"Want money? And a place to hole up?"

"Would you have a big problem?'

"Who said I had a problem?" Delf asked.

"Nobody," Datillo said.

"You talk to me before you take on more projects, understand?"

Datillo nodded and Delf left. Datillo went to bed satisfied.

Bill was puzzled because Valerie had not left, and she was dozing when a car crackled and slurred to a stop. At first, Bill did not recognize the man until the man held up a pint of whiskey. It was Valerie's Uncle Joel.

"Where's my niece?" he asked.

Bill motioned him aboard and pointed inside.

"She all right?"

Bill nodded.

"Look, I heard something. Can you keep it close?"

He held Bill's gaze tight.

"Valerie is in danger. So are you. I hear things, you hear? They're planning to kill you both."

Bill invited the man inside. He offered Bill a swig. He looked around for Valerie. Bill explained that she was in the bedroom.

"What do you know?" Bill asked.

"I know I wouldn't stay, if I were you. I know Valerie better get her baby and her ass back down to Florida."

"Sneed?"

"No names. I'll take her home if she'll let me."

"Well, ask her."

"No," Valerie said as she slid through the flag.

"For your own good, honey. Your safety and the baby's."

"That's a crock. You don't even know where Alexandra is, do you?"

"Sweet girl, I didn't come to fight."

"I'm no girl and you got no fight. Take your ass away."

The man left. Bill asked Valerie why she had been so hard.

"Calling that man a worm is stretching. Besides if he knows something, why won't he say?"

"He's scared."

"He's scared, but you can bet yours he has covered his or he wouldn't be seen here."

"Might be in on it?"

"No, too weak. He'll play both sides if he can, just like Sneed."

"Where is your Alexandra?"

"With Grandmomma in Owensboro visiting my aunt."

"Joel didn't know?"

"Didn't sound like it."

"Maybe we should take a drive."

"Why don't you make me hot and sweaty, so I can appreciate a breeze?"

She pulled with something stronger than rope. Later both laughed about that in the car, when Bill asked what her secret was, and she wouldn't tell. After breezing, they stopped at the Prospect store and bought hot dogs and buns. The proprietor didn't even offer to bag the stuff. When Valerie asked him to, he was so obviously flummoxed Bill asked what the problem was.

"No problem."

They stopped off at Polecat's to buy beer and ended up having one. Polecat's eye was bandaged, but he had good news. The doctor thought he might recover his sight. Polecat had a pistol on the bar and asked Bill if he was packing. Bill nodded. Polecat grinned and nodded toward the only two occupied tables in the joint.

"That makes it about unanimous," he grinned. "What about you, young lady?"

To Bill's surprise, Valerie reached in her bag and pulled out a .38.

"Damn!"

"Present arms!" Polecat bellowed; at once, nine pistols were in the air and two double-barreled shotguns poked out of the kitchen behind the bar. Polecat grinned. "At ease," he chuckled and at once the place resembled a quiet watering hole.

"Do you know who these bastards are?" Bill asked.

"Some might be neighbors," Polecat said, "but I ain't talking. Don't want trouble from nobody and as you see, I have my own security and as long as you are here, you are welcome to take part, but I don't want nothing leaving this room, understand? Polecat has been put in the corner."

"I hear that," Bill said, "but they're after us, too."

"Yeah, but you could sign in, and I can't."

"But haven't and won't, you know that."

"Time, Mr. Bill. Work out one way or other. What I know won't help anyway. SOBs are headed for the cooler they set foot in here."

Bill looked Polecat in the eye.

"If it comes to that, but don't you think we can work together otherwise?"

"What's otherwise, Bill?"

"What's going on is wrong."

"What the hell *is* going on exactly?"

Bill shrugged. "Hoping you could tell."

"Well, I can't, and even if I could, that ain't the heart. Tell me where the heart is located, so I can kill it dead."

"Wish I could."

"See, all we agree is we don't like it, whatever it is, and takes more than that to stop it. Where we go from there, if we do? You ever been in prison? Where you start when you don't know where you are and don't know where you need to be?"

"Wish there was some way."

"Me too," said Polecat as he stroked the grip of his pistol.

———

WEATHER VANE

A little later, while Bill and Valerie were roasting hot dogs over hot coals on the bank of the creek, poor Marcus was sitting on the peak of a barn roof howling at the sun. Datillo had left to fetch more paint. Somehow the ladder, which they had secured with strong rope and which provided Marcus, who was anything but fond of heights, with what seemed to be a secure platform, slipped the knot and slid. If Marcus hadn't become part cat, he wouldn't have snagged the rope with one paw and pulled himself up to the peak, which he now straddled, petrified with fear.

When Datillo got back, Lang Delf was standing at a safe distance like he was watching a show from the cheap seats, trying to make up his mind whether to stay or leave.

"What's your boy doing there, besides making a mess, playing crow?"

For some reason, Datillo hadn't noticed the predicament that Marcus was in. He stepped back a few paces to where Delf rocked on his heels, looked, and fought the urge to murder Delf right on the spot.

"Ain't much of a painter, is he?" he said pointing to the red paint that had slathered down the steep pitch.

Datillo gritted his teeth.

"Why you got a house coon up there anyway, Datillo? Don't even have calluses."

Marcus let out a moan that ended in "help me."

Delf turned to walk away. Datillo cleared his throat and shouted, "Stay put."

Delf turned around. "You talking to me?"

"No," Datillo said. "I'm talking to the monkey, but could you help me get him down?"

"You got him up. You get him down. I got chores."

Delf climbed into his truck. Datillo yelled to hold tight and then climbed to the loft and out onto the roof through a hatch. He crawled behind Marcus who still clutched the rope, talked softly, asked for the rope. Finally, he had to pry it from Marcus's fingers. He told Marcus that he was going to tie the rope around him—double tight and double strong—but he had a hard time slipping the rope between Marcus's rigid arms and body. He told Marcus to breathe easy, that he was going to get him down. With coaxing and some cussing, he edged him back to the hatch and, with great difficulty, got him through it and onto the ladder into the loft. Marcus collapsed in the straw and shook.

"Guess that's enough painting for one day," Datillo said.

"Not real funny," Marcus shivered. "Where you learn to tie knots?"

"You can tie tomorrow, Marcus."

"Ain't enough rope," Marcus said.

"Let's slip off and have some beer."

"Yes sir. Just untie. My hands not working just yet."

They started out at Bill's and ended up there, too. Drank some beers, then ate some hot dogs with mustard.

When they first pulled to a stop, Bill had said, "We were wondering how you two would be doing." That led to laughter that required explanation. As Datillo told the story, Marcus shook his head and seemed to be pushing something away with his hands.

"Please, dear God, don't even talk. I looked down."

A few beers later, they were talking about Delf. Marcus was so grateful to be alive he was the only one not to call the man a son of a bitch. That is until he was pressed.

"All right," he yelled out. "The man is a son of a bitch!"

"Marcus," Datillo said, "in the morning, I'm going to cuss your ass right back up that ladder."

"You and your uncle, the devil man! I ain't gonna fight no Klan from no rooftop, hear me! I mean it."

He spoke so emphatically no one could deny.

"Who tied the knot?" Valerie asked. "And when?"

"We moved the ladder right before we left for lunch," Marcus said. "Then Mr. Datillo went for paint. I went back up and that's when."

"Good plan," Valerie said.

"You think . . . ?"

"I'm a girl. I don't think?"

Bill was inclined to believe that Valerie was on to something, but Datillo said, "So what?"

"Can you tie a good knot or what? That's all I'm saying."

"It worked all morning," Datillo said.

Raindrops started slapping the leaves and hissing the fire. Bill invited everyone inside, but Datillo and Marcus rolled off.

After they left, Valerie said, "Hard to know."

"You mean Datillo?"

"Something don't add up. I hope I'm wrong."

———

Thunder shook the air and rain busted loose. Marcus and Datillo were ascending Green's hill when they spotted Joshua dragging his dog with a belt. The dog was dug in and the boy was tugging to no avail.

They stopped, and Marcus got out and ushered them both into the backseat. He actually had to hoist the dog and throw him in.

"What you doing out here, boy?" Marcus asked. "Can't you see it's raining?"

"Yes sir, Mr. Marcus, but I had to catch him. Something scared him, and he run off, and I didn't want Mr. You-Know-Who to shoot him."

"What was he running from?" Datillo asked.

Joshua shrugged.

"What scared him, Joshua?" Marcus asked.

"I don't want to say."

"I understand but understand me. We need your help, do you hear, boy?"

"I think so."

"Have your momma pack us lunch in the morning and you bring it down to the barn that Mr. Datillo and I will be painting. We want a jug of lemonade and two glasses. Will you do that? And bring this wet, shaggy, slobbering dog, hear me?"

"Cracker don't mean any harm," Joshua said, pulling the dog to himself.

"No one will harm Cracker. Bring you some lunch and some for Cracker, too. We'll have a picnic. Keep it to yourself. Wear old clothes."

"That's all I have is old clothes, Mr. Marcus, you know that."

Datillo dropped Marcus off and drove to his little house. He was bone tired and was looking forward to a bath and bed. When he flipped on the light, everything looked exactly the same, but something didn't feel right. He pulled out the little back-up that he kept holstered to his calf and sniffed around. Something literally didn't smell right, and his nose soon led him straight to the source. There was a dead barn rat lying on his pillow. The thing had been dead long enough to bloat. He grabbed it by the tail, carried it over to the door and gave it a heave. He half expected a dead fish in the bathtub. There wasn't one, but there was no hot water either. The pilot light was out on the water heater and since he didn't smoke, he didn't carry matches, but he found some over the stove and tried to light the thing. There was no gas coming through the line. He got a beer out of the fridge and walked out back. There was no propane tank.

FIGHTING A FISH SURROUNDED BY FOOLS

"Will you miss me when I'm gone, when I'm really gone?"

"What are you talking about?" Bill asked.

"Will you think of me?"

Bill said yes and suggested bed. Valerie said she'd join him in a minute. A little later, he found her sitting out on the deck. He sat beside her without saying anything. He let his toes dangle in the cool water. He offered her a drag. She shook her head. She offered him her drink. He accepted. Neither said anything.

A canoe glided in shadows on the opposite bank; the man in it crouched low like he was hiding. Bill decided to sit tight and watch. The canoe snagged a low-hanging branch that dipped the current, hung a moment before slowly swinging ass-end downstream. The man aboard did not move. Bill called out, "Hey there!" Bill called again. No response. He dropped his drawers, slid into the creek, swam over, and guided the canoe to the boat.

"Get a light," he said.

When Valerie held the beam on the man's face, Bill saw it was Hawk, drunk as a pig. The light also revealed a swollen bruise on the side of Hawk's forehead and about four empty half pints of bourbon floating in crud sloshing his feet.

"Is he dead?" Valerie asked.

"Out cold. Hit his head awful."

"Or somebody hit him."

Bill hauled himself out of the creek. The whole damn thing was peculiar.

"Is he gonna die?"

Bill slipped back into his clothes and tried to calm Valerie. His attempts were aided when Hawk snored sonorously. The crickets and a few cicadas chimed in and soon Valerie asked Bill what he was thinking.

"About what?" he asked.

"That's what I want to know, Bill Maddox. What do you think about? Am I a nothing? Will you go to Florida?"

Hawk snored. Bill squirmed.

"You still love her, don't you?"

"I don't know how to answer."

"Don't bother, baby cakes."

As was often the case with Valerie, her mood shifted from serious to flirtatious. Hawk's snoring deepened, challenged by the cicada chorus, whose chanting vibrations intensified. Clouds veiled the moon and Valerie whispered she wanted it on the deck. Instead, they landed in bed where Valerie pushed him back and proceeded to rock the boat.

They returned topside to breathe early spring air and Valerie said she was sorry she had been pushy about Sarah. Bill shrugged. She grabbed his arm and told him she knew he couldn't talk yet. Then Hawk woke up.

"Ow. Ow. Yi, yi, yi."

"Hawk, Bill. Need a drink?"

"Damn, need something. Can you spare one?"

Bill was glad to slip into the cabin and grabbed a couple of beers and some whiskey. Sometimes he couldn't figure Valerie. Acted like she didn't have a care, then hollered for aspirin. Young, but reminded him of a kid trying on masks. When he stepped back onto the deck, she already had Hawk sitting in a chair. She was shining the flashlight, checking if he had a concussion. She decided he probably did not. Bill handed her the aspirin bottle.

"Good job," she said.

He handed Hawk a glass full of ice and started pouring. Hawk didn't say when until the glass was full. Hawk said his head hurt awful.

He washed down the aspirin, lit a smoke, and then asked how he got there. Bill started laughing.

"Suppose you tell. Found you drifting—out like a light."

"They're bad folks up creek. They're no good. Saw a campfire. I was tucked in, fishing the bank, minding my business. Then heard what they was saying, at least enough to make me grab a limb and duck.

"God Almighty this and God Almighty that. Niggers gotta pay. Jews gotta burn and all sorts of stuff that made no sense to me at all. Then they cussed Polecat Green, how the man was a dead man yet. Bill, they mentioned you and the crazy boy took your wife. Said he had to burn, that you were a disgrace. Then one screamed, 'Want your daughters breeding nigras?' About that time, a fish hit my bait and damn he didn't slap water loud; everything got quiet except the drag on my zinging reel. Next thing, I'm fighting a fish and surrounded by fools."

"You recognize anybody?"

"They held flashlights. All was shapes. Probably half a dozen but can't be sure. They asked how long I been snuck in. What I heard and all. I told 'em I was too busy fishing. The damn fish was running this way and that, then this one guy snatched my rod. Then another guy jumped in and said, 'nigger's lying,' and I told 'em I was Cherokee, and one of 'em said, 'He's married one and got a bunch of kids.' That bullshit and the son of a bitch with 'Gawd amighty,' when he dragged my fish up the bank pissed me off. I made the mistake of objecting. Next thing I hear is a pistol cocked and one says, 'Who don't have what right?' They laughed, then this guy says, 'Let's give Injun whiskey and let him kill his own self.' All laugh and fella had a shiny nightstick wades over a half pint and says drink. So I took a drink. Then they yelled 'All, redskin." They got more and made me drink. Then they just stood there. I didn't feel so good, but whiskey weren't the worst. This one guy said, 'Quit wasting good whiskey.' Then they started in again. I said something they didn't like. Next thing I'm here."

Valerie was for calling police. She didn't mention Datillo by name, which impressed Bill, but he wasn't sure it was a good idea. Hawk was dead certain it wasn't.

"For all I know, they were police."

With the canoe lashed to the roof, the pistol and refreshed beverages, all three bounced up Happy Hollow Road to the shack where Hawk lived. As they approached, there was a strong smell of smoke. When they came into the clearing, the headlights lit up a smoldering cross. The house was dark. Hawk struggled out before Bill stopped and fell, then staggered to his feet and called for his wife. The door opened, and a sturdy brown woman stood in the doorway with a double-barreled shotgun pointing at the ground.

Kids hugged their daddy's legs, arms, and shoulders. There were only four but seemed like ten. The wife stood back and wept.

Valerie wanted to call the cops, but beside the fact that there was no phone, Hawk and his wife wanted nothing to do with cops.

"Missy, they just as bad," she said as she wiped her husband's head with a damp cloth. "Seen them do worse for fun."

"They're about the same bunch," Hawk said. "We'll be all right."

"But why do they do this?"

"Hate don't need a reason," Hawk's wife said.

On the way home, neither spoke until the highway.

"We were poor, but you see that place? Did you see those clothes? It ain't right. Where you going?"

Bill turned onto River Road and headed back to Polecat's. Something told him to go there. He parked and told her to stay put. She nodded.

In dingy light, Bill saw four or five folks sitting around a table with Polecat standing at the head. Then a man slipped behind Bill and the door, and that man was holding a shotgun.

Polecat looked at Bill intensely, then spoke. "Believe we done found your mechanic. This skinny weasel crawling around the parking area. Pockets full of tools. What you make of that?"

Bill walked over and looked down at a bean pole of a trembling, sunken-cheeked white man, whose eyes squirmed like field mice.

"Seen him?"

"It was dark. Weasels like dark," Bill said, feeling rage that surprised. "Have you stripped him and had a peek at his backside, Polecat?"

"Lord have mercy, Mr. Bill."

"May I?"

"Suit yourself."

"Stand," Bill said. "*Stand up!*"

The man seemed to slither erect. He looked down and his lower lip trembled.

"You got a wallet?"

The man shook his head vigorously

"That's too bad," Bill said. "Your name?"

Man shook his head.

"Turn around," Bill said. "Hold still." Then he took out his knife and cut the man's shirt from collar to waist. "Damn, Polecat, this serpent breathes. Must have aimed low. Drop those trousers or so help me I'll cut them off."

The man whimpered and dropped his pants. Bill sliced through the waistband of his underpants and away they fell.

"There we go, Polecat. I did shoot low. It's hard to tell buckshot from acne scars, but these are fresh. See the pattern. Shot him right in the ass. Looks like the doctors missed a couple. This knife's real sharp, boy; want me to slice 'em out?"

The man started crying but didn't say a thing. He pointed at his throat and grunted. He shook his head and moaned. Nothing could make the man speak. Who sent him? Who he work for? The man wiggled and shrugged. Finally, they made the man strip raw and threw him into the dark—a gangly specter. Polecat had one of his men put the tools and clothing in a bag and told him to stash them in the shed.

"That was pitiful," Polecat said. "Couldn't even talk."

Bill told Polecat what had happened to Hawk and about the cross burning.

"Hawk's tough."

When Bill climbed into the car, he found Valerie holding both pistols.

"Bare-ass man ran across and into the woods."

"See anything unusual?"

"Don't think that's unusual? He was white on top."

"Recognize him?"

"Moving fast and it's dark, but if I'm not mistaken, he was Jep Greathouse, the fellow that raises quail and pheasants on Mayfair. The man who can't speak."

"Second time I heard that. What you mean?"

"Just that. He can't talk. Not sure, but I think so. He was a class ahead. He always ran bent over and sideways looking back. I would swear it was. Was he naked in there?"

Bill explained after she had un-cocked, when they were gliding down River Road and for some reason, things started to seem funny. All he wanted was to live and let live. Hawk didn't have any war against anybody, neither did Polecat, nor Marcus or Green, or Ruby. Everybody was trying to survive the best they knew. These idiots were trying to do what? For what purpose? Why? Burning crosses, screwing up brake lines, playing cops, playing dirty tricks, shooting people for nothing. What loser cowards! Sending some poor bastard that couldn't talk to do their dirty work. Pitiful, but it made Bill laugh.

"What's so funny?" Valerie asked.

"Nothing's really funny," Bill replied, "but the bastards are losing. There's no way they can win."

"Win what?"

"That's the point. They have no point to win. Bunch of sneaky losers. They're history."

CHURCH-GOING MAN

When they got back to the boat, Ruby was in the process of driving off. She was standoffish. Bill asked her in, but she declined and said that there was an invitation taped to the casserole dish. She nodded and eased away.

"Always bring you midnight supper?"

"You know better," Bill said, lifting the lid and smelling chicken potpie.

"Hungry again?"

"Hell, you're the reason why. Aren't you a tad?"

"Depends. Lady in my position has to watch her figure."

"Nothing wrong with your figure."

"Well then, quit looking at that invitation."

He folded the paper and hustled Valerie inside. She protested that night air was so uplifting. She pressed her backside playfully into Bill and feigned surprise that he found it uplifting, too.

After a while, he convinced her that her shape was perfect, and she decided she might have potpie after all. They ate by candlelight stark naked at the oak table. Valerie agreed it was delicious but was curious. Bill told her it was a long story. Valerie went down to use the head. Bill reread the invitation, written in Ruby's beautiful hand. The gist of it reminded him that there was more to life than sensual pleasure and she underscored that he had promised to attend church. She ended by saying the next Sunday would suit her fine, and in a postscript said, "Lord knows we both need it."

Valerie walked through the curtain before Bill put the note down. Bill hoped she wouldn't take it the wrong way.

She held the thing next to the candle and puzzled.

"Who is this bitch? Who the hell does she think she is? What does she mean you promised? What she mean you both need it?"

Bill started laughing. He was enjoying the fire in Valerie's eyes.

"What have you been doing would cause God to notice?"

"Nothing."

"Better hope nothing; I got teeth. They're sharp, and these ain't dull either," she said, holding up her nails.

Bill poured a drink and handed her one.

"Ain't sharing with nobody."

"It's not what you're thinking."

Told all he could think to tell her. When he got to the Underground Railroad, she had no idea what he was talking about. She wanted to know what kind of railroad ran underground. She asked more questions than a five-year-old. She knew about slavery, but the way she had been taught, white people owned slaves, as in all white people. The idea that some white people might even have thought that owning human beings was wrong had never occurred. She knew slavery was wrong, but then again, she thought they dressed funny, talked funny, and mostly didn't seem smart.

There were so many questions mixed with opinions that Bill hardly knew where to begin. She kept asking what all this had to do with Ruby, and that led back to Sarah, and then to Ronald, and the fire and the rape and murder. A spark became a flaming pinwheel.

He took a stab.

"Let's be selfish, okay? What if you were trying to grow or make something and sell it for profit to feed Alexandra, okay? Let's say there was a bitch down the road doing the same damn thing and she was your competition. All right? You go to market and the bitch can sell her stuff for less. Come to find out she don't have to pay her workers. How would you feel?"

"Like two tons of shucks."

"Slavery was that for poor whites. Understand, wrong to begin with, but it was unfair no matter how you looked at it. Why should folks who didn't own slaves be for something hurting them financially? I don't care whether they liked colored or not. What difference would it make?"

"None."

"Okay, then. Added on to that, some folks actually knew that some folks were all right. Take Polecat, what about him? What about

Marcus? You think they should be slaves so some rich bastard can rub their noses in dirt? You don't think they should be free?"

"I want everybody to be."

"So did my granddaddy and a whole lot like him. Don't forget the Civil War. You could almost build a mountain out of white men who died. Most men who fought didn't have slaves. All were caught in notions dark as the blood they were born with."

Next morning when they woke, while Bill was still stretching with eyes closed, Valerie asked if he was going to go. He didn't know what she was talking about. She said, "Go to church on Sunday." Bill chuckled and said he might. She told him she thought he should. He asked why.

"Something's got to give. Maybe that's a place to start."

DELF'S SANCTUARY

While Bill was rubbing Valerie's flank, Datillo was driving to the barn with his fingers crossed. Marcus was already there wondering why and somehow knowing. Lang Delf was in a barn loft about a quarter of a mile away, inside a makeshift room made of stacked straw bales. He was looking through binoculars at Marcus sitting on an upside-down paint bucket and was surprised to see him.

The room he was in wasn't big. The window was actually just a couple of missing boards. It was sparely furnished, a table of planks on sawhorses, a few bentwood chairs, one—larger than the others— that was his, and a mirror hanging off one of the straw walls. In a way, it was sort of cozy, like a child's fort, only larger. Big enough for ten or twelve full-sized men who wore the sheet-like robes that hung from stakes driven into the bales. Delf was alone this morning, except for a couple of sparrows and a large spider that had strung a web in the top third of his window.

He saw Datillo park his cop car and watched Marcus jump to his feet, grab a brush, and act busy. But it was obvious that Marcus was doing nothing, and he watched Datillo raise his arms in anger and charge the man. He saw Marcus look at the ground, while Datillo's arms flapped up and down. Delf had to admit he didn't know what this cop was about. Marcus looked up as Datillo made a fist, then turned and walked into the barn.

Delf saw Marcus's head pop through the roof. When Delf left, he rearranged the bales that guarded the entrance to his sanctuary and drove over. What he didn't know was that Datillo had been watching him. After Marcus went in, he followed, and as Marcus climbed into the loft, Datillo had zeroed in on Delf's little room. The sun had glinted off Delf's binocular's lenses. Marcus had noticed and Datillo's field glasses confirmed it. He could even see the bastard smile.

Delf pulled up and blew his horn several times, pleased with himself, feeling clever, parking in such a way that Datillo would have to come all the way down to talk. He had the radio loud, tuned to farm report news. He pretended to be concentrating deeply so that when Datillo stood beside his open window, he looked surprised. He raised a finger. The announcer was talking about burley prices. He turned it down, nodding sagely.

"So, this place has a tobacco base?"

"Hell, no. My brother and I raise some out in Oldham. Thought you were a detective, Datillo."

"I never said."

"Didn't have to."

"I don't know where you get information, Delf, but it's stale."

"What you mean, Datillo?"

"*Was* a detective; why the hell you think I would take this? Patrolmen don't make squat, that's why."

"Reckon that's so. Whether fair or not, I couldn't say. Believe I heard one reason you took this was that the wife packed you out."

Datillo did not respond. He glared at the farm manager and grabbed the doorframe with both hands; he squeezed until knuckles turned white. He inhaled and clenched his jaw.

Delf was enjoying this. Part of him suspected that he was witnessing an act, but he wasn't paying much attention to that. He was enjoying watching what he believed to be his own cleverness displaying its potency.

When Datillo spoke, it was a whispering hiss.

"Bring up that nigger-loving bitch again, I'll tear your tongue out!"

He stared with such fury that Delf recoiled.

"You don't know shit," Datillo continued. "You got such good information, check out the charges. Delf, it's what they call an 'internal affair,' got it?"

Delf nodded.

"I was a detective, got it? May be again, got it? All I did was what any man would do. Check it out, Mr. Stale. She's lucky I didn't find her."

All Delf could say after swallowing unsuccessfully was, "Look, I—"

"Don't apologize, Delf. What good? You put your foot in."

Delf sputtered.

"I got work to do. Use your imagination."

While Marcus and Datillo painted the roof without anything but hot late spring sun and height troubling, Delf troubled his imagination. He had been mostly bluffing about contacts. He was tight with a couple of low-ranking officers, but Delf did not have inroads into the higher levels of command, but in his mind, believed he did. He contacted one and told him what he had heard. The man told him he would look into it. The man stressed that it might be still in internal affairs but told him not to worry. Delf backed that up with a call to a desk sergeant who had been on the right side for years. He confirmed that something was going on. Datillo was no longer a detective and that there was something peculiar. Delf asked what that might be, but all the sergeant could tell him was that it had to do with some kind of restraining order. Delf went to work and called his top dog, an uncle by marriage. He didn't want to bother him because, although they were on the same side, Delf didn't trust him. He knew how ambitious the man was.

Delf tried to pry him open. The man was as tight as an oyster. What the uncle knew full well, though Delf did not, was that higher-ups had caught a sniff of what was going on.

Green had taken it upon himself, unbeknownst to anyone, to try to solve this "little problem." Green knew the mayor. Not well, but the mayor knew that he was talking with a man who buttered his bread. The police chief answered directly to the mayor. When Green personally conveyed concerns about "renegade cops," wheels were greased and began to turn. The message "Heads will roll" slid down from the high command. The guys at the top had to save their asses, no matter what they believed. The mayor could not afford scandal. Others were caught in the middle but had to weigh the odds. Guys like Sneed and a few of his ilk with bright stars in their eyes tried to keep both ends satisfied, which led to misinformation going both directions at the highest and lowest levels of city hall and the police department.

Sneed found out that Datillo was to be charged with falsifying evidence in a botched burglary attempt. Supposedly, he had shot an innocent man. He told Delf that he thought that this was what it was all about. A sergeant told Delf that the wife was under a cloud of suspicion. Delf wanted more and finally was told that Datillo was the subject of an internal investigation and would say no more. Wherever he turned, no matter what he heard, Delf confirmed what he wished desperately to hear, but the mayor heard from the police chief that there was no real problem, just rumors. The allegation that some Klan guy was digging into internal affairs was dismissed as hogwash. The chief wrote that in a memo to the mayor.

All this went down before lunch. Delf saw the future. In his mind, the department was crumbling into his hands. All he needed was for a few more to totter so he could slide into control. He knew the vast majority of cops could be swayed to put the blacks back into their place. He knew it. He knew it like he knew the sun came up.

What Delf actually unearthed was nothing. But that's not the way he saw it. He began to see Datillo as a possible ally. He couldn't imagine any white man living with such horror. He saw leverage. His uncle's reluctance to tell much, he converted into a notion that there was much to tell. He could see it vividly: *rage against* black burning through the police department. The Supreme Court was on the verge of mixing races. It was in the headlines. The court had agreed to consider the Kansas case, the Brown case. He had a pep talk to give that very evening and everything seemed to be falling into place. He now had the inside scoop.

———

When lunchtime came around, Joshua strolled to the barn with Cracker at his heels. Joshua was doing some thinking. He wasn't exactly sure what it was about but was in the mood to talk all the same. He carried a basket with sandwiches and iced tea that his mother had made.

They saw him coming, so Marcus and Datillo climbed down. They ate beneath the shade of a freshly leafed-out maple tree. Cracker kept a close eye on the proceedings.

"Two things I've been thinking about besides the word of God," Joshua said. "One thing is how come it takes the Supreme Court of the United States of America to decide where kids go to school? Second thing, how come Mr. Delf can go wherever he wants to take himself and I can't even play in that barn. And why did he kill my dog? The Bible says love thy neighbor as thyself. Well, wasn't my dog his neighbor? Is there something wrong with that man?"

The soft spongy white bread the pork was wrapped in didn't help Marcus and Datillo answer, but it did give them an excuse to simply nod and chew as they tried to unravel the young boy's questions.

The boy wanted his elders to provide answers. They chewed and stared.

"Another thing, how come there's no peace without war?"

More bites and more chewing. Cracker nodded, wanting answers, too.

"You got to win first," Marcus said.

"Why is that?" Joshua asked.

Datillo saw Marcus jump to his feet and scream like a crazy man. Joshua and Cracker started down the road and Marcus ducked into the barn. Delf pulled up.

"What's wrong with your boy?"

"What boy?"

Delf grinned.

"You know, Datillo, you ain't right. Can't you answer straight?"

"If you stood in my boots, you might know."

"About ready to start on the sides?"

"That's next," Datillo said. "Why are you watching? I'm on time."

"Seem to be. Why is that boy running?"

"Now Delf, if I knew what was in that boy's mind, I wouldn't be talking."

"Not sure what you mean."

"How about a tank of propane at my place? Can we get together on that?"

"Been done this morning, Datillo. Hot water tonight."

"It's so dry and dusty even grasshoppers kick a cloud," Datillo said, watching Delf's eyes puzzle over a cop even noticing.

"It's worse than dry," Delf said. "If we don't get rain, it will be dustbowl over again and General Eisenhower will still be playing golf on watered fairways. He don't care about the little man. If we didn't have the creek, we would have to haul water. Tobacco at my place out in Oldham is about toasted."

"What can you do?"

"Damned I know," Delf said. "They got programs for every kind of thing, but it'll take more than a miracle."

"You said something about Ike's golf? You think the president can make it rain?"

"No, goddamn it. But I'm saying the little man ain't got a friend like FDR. All Ike does is grin on the side of niggers, you mark my words. You might be thinking about your position, needing money so bad."

"Why else you think I'm painting this rotten barn? Not all changes are good by a long shot. What you come down for?" Datillo had a guarded smile.

Delf didn't answer. He pretended to be searching for a cigarette lighter, which turned up in his pocket after all.

"You'll have good hot water. Sorry about the oversight."

"Don't worry. I was going to shower at the station anyway."

"Who's worried?" Delf said as he rolled off.

————

Green dropped in. Valerie poured him a cup of coffee with a slight dollop of bourbon. He told them he had voiced their concerns to the mayor. Since what was done was done, Bill nodded and let him continue. Green bragged of hearing the mayor lay into the police chief. Bill grimaced.

"What's wrong, Bill? I heard him tell the chief in no uncertain terms to get to the bottom."

"Did you clear with Datillo?"

"No, do you think I should?"

"Tell Datillo discreetly what you've done. Better still, let me. Drive by the barn they're painting and tell him I'm coming to fish at your fishing hole."

"What's wrong with me telling?"

"Please, Green, you don't know who might be listening. Trust me. We don't know who's who. Datillo's life's on the line. Tell him to stroll down there at six."

Green left and as a parting shot said, "You play to your strengths. I see nothing wrong in a citizen using influence."

"Green, please tell him six, all right? Don't tell the man anything."

"Think he'll keep his mouth shut?" Valerie asked.

"Think so; knows he's crossed the line."

Green pulled up to the barn in a cloud of dust and tooted. Datillo climbed down. Green stayed in the car and kept it short and sweet. Told him to meet Bill at six o'clock. Datillo looked puzzled, but just then a farmhand walked out carrying a wrench and a pulley belt. Green shook his head and said the job looked good.

Datillo went inside to his perch in the loft where he kept field glasses. He focused in on the barn about five hundred yards away. Delf stood there until Green's dusty Cadillac disappeared. Then he turned to the barn and two guys came out and unloaded wooden cases out of Delf's truck. A few minutes later, Delf waved his arms impatiently. They unloaded a case of Cokes and what looked like a block of ice and a bundle of rags. A few minutes later, they re-emerged and off they went down toward River Road. Datillo gritted his teeth and made up his mind.

He and Marcus painted until about four, stood back and admired their progress. Datillo apologized to Marcus, but asked him to clean up, put everything away, and walk his own self home. Marcus was drenched in sweat, parched, and hungry. He looked at Datillo as if to say and what about you? About then Joshua and Cracker came around the side of the barn and Joshua was quoting scripture. "How shall not the ministration of the spirit be rather glorious? For if the ministration of condemnation be glory, much more doth the ministration of righteousness exceed in glory."

Both quit looking at one another and turned to Joshua.

"You expect me to walk home?" Marcus asked.

"Told you, you wouldn't like me," Datillo said.

"That was Corinthians 2," Joshua exclaimed.

"Clean the brushes and put the stuff up," Datillo insisted.

Marcus shook his head.

"Never know who's watching," Datillo said.

"Listen to this," Joshua said, as Datillo drove off: "'But we all, with open face beholding as in a glass the glory of the Lord, are changed into the same image from glory to glory, even as by the spirit of the Lord.' Isn't the Word glorious, Mr. Marcus?"

"Help me clean, boy," Marcus replied. Afterward they walked home in near silence. Marcus told Joshua his ears hurt something terrible.

"Painting does that?"

"Today it has, no doubt," Marcus said, as they trudged uphill.

CHAPTER 12

THE LOFT

Datillo met Bill and Valerie and when Bill told him what Green had done, he cursed, but then said it probably didn't change anything much. He wanted to know why Green hadn't said anything. Bill explained Green wanted to, but that he had asked him not to because he feared it might be overheard.

Datillo asked if he could hide his patrol car for a couple of hours down on the creek. Bill told him that he could stash it in Crabby's tool shack.

"Which brings me to my second request: Could you boat me up here soon as the sun goes down but before it's completely dark and then run me back?"

"Will do."

"When can you meet me at Crabby's?"

"Shouldn't take twenty minutes."

Bill beat his estimate by a full five. His haste upset a fisherman or two. When he swung open the door into Crabby's workshop, he was troubled to see that the Crab had a motorcycle torn down and parts scattered everywhere. Datillo pulled up, saw the problem and said, "Let's go." The three of them jumped in the boat. Datillo wore a New York Yankees cap, carried a flashlight, and had a pistol in his pocket. He was dressed in black.

Before they got to Green's fishing hole, he signaled for Bill to slow. He hoarsely whispered that he wouldn't be long; he told them not to lay in, but to troll up and down the banks. He would blink his light. They watched him disappear into the dusk. Valerie tossed in her line before Bill even headed upstream.

They hadn't puttered more than a half mile, when three skiffs passed going downstream. There were nine or ten men on board. Valerie waved, but only one man raised a hand. It was dark enough for running lights, but the skiffs weren't lit.

Valerie tapped him on the shoulder. "Those fellas didn't have fishing rods."

"Good eye."

"What you think they're up to?" Valerie whispered.

"Hate to think," Bill said, laying his pistol out.

They turned and trolled. It was dark, and a sliver moon peeked between leaves. As they got close to Green's, Bill lit a smoke and saw that it had been almost thirty minutes. When they had gone downstream for a stretch, Valerie tugged his sleeve.

"See skiffs in the bushes back there?"

"Back where?"

"Right below, where we dropped Datillo off. Didn't see anybody, only skiffs nosed up the bank."

"Good eye twice. Keep fishing. You got your gun?"

"No shit."

On the way back upstream, Bill lifted his gas tank. It was light. He pulled in just above Green's and killed the motor. When he checked his watch again, it had been an hour and a half. He was hungry and thirsty. There was one more beer to split.

"You think these skeeters are bad. You ought to try Florida."

"Then, no thanks," Bill said as he blew smoke he hoped would kill some.

"You ain't coming?"

"Don't know."

"You'll never get over her, will you?"

"Damn it, Valerie, this is no time. Something going on."

"You won't talk, will you?"

Bill cranked up the boat and slushed to where he'd seen a flash. Datillo hopped aboard and they slid away. Nobody said anything. Bill drained most of the beer, passed it to Valerie, who drained the can and tossed it into the bilge.

A few minutes later, a houseboat lit like Christmas roared toward them. Bill hugged the bank. A spotlight sought and found them.

"Hey there, which way to Cincinnati?"

"Turn around quick before you run aground. Head back out to the river. Take a right. About a hundred miles," Bill drawled.

Bill moved on.

"What was that?" Datillo asked.

"Damned if I know. Happens more than you think. They're looking at maps instead of the river. Hard to figure."

When they got back to Bill's, Datillo asked for help. The police department didn't even have one outboard. He shook his head in disgust.

"Look, keep this quiet," he said, as he accepted a beer. "I snuck in not a minute too soon. What I heard will make your skin crawl. They're planning to burn down Green Castle Church and take out Polecat's at the very same time. Don't ask me why. That man Delf is crazy, but what's worse is the others are crazier. Some of them wanted to blow up the white Episcopal church.

"I could hardly believe my ears. Green has got to keep his mouth shut. Bill, you got to tell him to keep quiet. I don't know who's involved, but they got a few of us and they're working on others. They're planning to strike this Saturday night. There's only three days. We might need some boats. Bill, we can't take them over land. The creek almost wraps around Green Castle Church. At the Episcopal church, we can close in from the highway. Bill, we're going to need help on the creek."

"What about Polecat's?" Bill asked.

"You know yourself Mr. Polecat Green never trusted a cop in his life. I can't blame him."

"So, what you want me to do?" Bill asked.

"Keep quiet, first thing. Second, we need a boat or two. I'll supply the men. Next thing, I need you to talk to Polecat. We got to catch these people in the act."

"What you want me to tell Polecat?"

"Tell him to arm himself to the teeth if he wants, but stress we're on his side, no matter what he might overhear. We need to be inside and outside his joint or else those devils will slip. Give him your word that we're on his side, will you?"

"Are you?" Bill asked.

"Damn right, I am."

"Me too," Bill said.

"I've got to do some thinking," Datillo said. "Why don't you do a little fishing tomorrow?"

"What time?"

"Five thirty."

"Done."

A few minutes later, Bill told Polecat what he knew, which he realized wasn't much.

"Nothing changed?" Polecat said.

"What's changed," Bill said, "is that we've got the police force on our side and we're going to catch the sons of bitches."

"Then what? They been trying to put me out for years. I will be armed to the teeth as always. Then what? Get charged with murder?"

"Do you want to see the church burned down?"

"You know I don't," Polecat said. "I just don't trust cops one smidgen."

"I don't either," Bill said, "but if necessary, would you allow some to hide in your kitchen and some in the woods?"

"What about the church?" Polecat asked.

"I don't even know about your place. Probably know more tomorrow. Think we're going to surround the place. Catch them red-handed."

"Know nothing, do you?"

"I don't, but I do believe this is our best shot. Think it over? Will you take a chance?"

Polecat nodded and waved the back of his hand. Bill and Valerie left. Bill felt disgusted.

"He heard you," Valerie said.

"You think? Guess it's too late to call on Green."

"Tonight, it is. You can talk to him tomorrow."

They had a couple and watched the crescent moon scoot through clouds. Bill was relieved Valerie didn't feel like talking. When they crawled into bed, he cradled her head in the crook of his arm.

"You're a good man, Bill Maddox."

"You're not too bad yourself."

FLOTILLA

Before he was fully awake, Bill's mind was churning. Green had two boats: a cruiser called *Half Moon* and a large john boat used for duck hunting. If only Green could keep his mouth shut. Bill decided he could if the importance of it was properly explained. He glanced at Valerie, who was embracing a pillow.

Within a half hour, he was on his way to Green's. He kissed Valerie on the cheek before he tiptoed out. She smiled and snuggled in.

As he had hoped, Green was out walking his hill. He caught him finishing the second lap. He was huffing and not reluctant to hop in when Bill told him he had urgent news.

When Green heard what was about to happen, he agreed to help in any way. He kept his cruiser out on the river on a dock at the boat club about three miles downstream. Bill figured they could launch the oversized duck boat at Crabby's, but Green thought it would be better not to. He reasoned that cop cars at Crabby's might draw attention. They agreed that the two of them would launch Green's duck boat and stash it in an empty slip at the club where it would be unnoticed. Green promised to keep his mouth shut.

On the way back, it occurred to Bill that Green would want to captain the cruiser and lead the charge. He knew that could create a dangerous mess. Bill decided Green should follow in the duck boat, which wasn't without danger, but at least didn't draw much water. He figured he could handle Green if he reminded him of the time that he had rammed and nearly sunk two boats trying to land on a calm day. Bill coasted home looking forward to coffee, Valerie, and some kind of breakfast.

To his mild surprise, she was there, sitting on the deck, writing in a notebook, which had belonged to Sarah. She was writing so intensely that she didn't see him. He stepped onto the deck before she glanced up but kept writing.

"I can write notes, too," she said, as she handed him a folded paper. Bill smiled. He wanted to look at her, not the note.

"What's it about?" he asked.

"I've got to go, Bill. They're coming right soon."

Bill laughed, but when her face turned serious, he asked, "Now how do you know? Smoke signals? Or is it female intuition?"

"Grandmomma's coming any minute, but you and I can go. It's your choice."

"You're kidding."

"Why would I?"

"How do you know?"

"I know."

She jumped to her feet and hugged him and gave him a kiss just as an old DeSoto pulled up, dragging a tail pipe and with windows so dusty he couldn't see a driver. Bill remembered thinking they needed rain. She pushed free, shook her head, kissed him, then jumped off the boat. A heavy door slammed shut and off they went. The engine's sound grew fainter. Bill was left standing with a piece of paper.

Bill, Dear Bill,

You are my true soul mate and before you laugh, think on this. We have made things happen that never could have. Good things, no matter what. I wish you would join me, but I trust that what will be will be. You are special. I believe I am special to you. I must go be a Florida girl. I guess you have decided to be Riverboat Bill. No matter what, you are in my heart forever. May God bless you.

Love, Valerie

P.S. You saved my life

Bill thought about how many times she had left before and turned up again, then realized that she had never looked him in the eye and said now or never. He didn't know what to think. He dragged down to Crabby's and found him in his shack drenching cycle parts in kerosene. Bill said he needed him Saturday night and Crabby nodded, no questions asked, no explanation offered. The man had a sweet deal and knew it.

Back on his deck, Bill watched a proud wood duck paddle back and forth while his mate scurried up the bank to hide. His eyes were all the way shut when something pulled at his sleeve. At first, he didn't even open his eyes. He was hoping whatever it was would pull him into the water and awaken him. But what pulled him apparently had no such plan.

"Tell me a story, Mr. Bill."

"Where the hell is your mother?"

"Right behind you, mister." She laughed.

Sure enough, there she was, smiling indulgently.

"Well, at least you have an escort," he said.

Ruby said, "I'm sticking my nose in, but I believe I know you better than most."

Amelia tugged on his sleeve.

"Something told me to come and bring Amelia. Lord knows I don't understand His ways, but you got to come to church Sunday. You wouldn't be alive if it weren't for the love of God. Nobody can live without somebody and you owe me. You said you would and you will."

Bill had to laugh, then chuckled and gently gripped Amelia's hand. He looked and all he saw were leaves curling up. He looked into the glistening moisture of Amelia's eyes. He thought of Valerie saying something had to give and that she thought he should go to church. He nodded, looked up at Ruby, standing sternly, and said, "Yes, all right. I'll go."

"Promise?"

Bill nodded.

"Then my house at nine thirty."

"When are you going to tell a story, Mr. Bill?"

Bill told her after church. She made him promise. Then they left and when they did, Bill wondered at the funk he had fallen into, so deep that they had been able to slip aboard without him hearing. That woke him up. He poured himself more coffee to complete the process.

Still, the cloud hung on and he found himself squinting, trying to shut out whatever light remained. He walked to Crabby's and didn't know why, and saw Green pull up in his fifty-foot cruiser. Bill started running just as Green blasted a trio of chrome-plated air horns, loud as a barge. Crabby was already on the gas dock waving his arms for Green to slow, which suddenly he did. Backwash rolled forward, splashed through planks of the dock, and soaked Crabby, almost causing him to fall into the creek. Bill jumped onto the dock and grabbed Crabby and pulled him upright, and they wrestled and shoved Green's vessel off.

"Fill her up, Crab," Green said jovially.

"Damn, Green, what the hell you doing?"

"No damage done," he said. "Any landing you walk away from, you know?"

Bill decided to drop it. He winked at Crabby. They filled her and sent him on his way. Green looked at his watch, held up one finger, and nodded.

As Green swung off, Crabby asked Bill what he was needed for Saturday. Bill didn't know what to say at first and then said, "A party. We're taking them out. You're the pilot."

"Thank God for small favors. They paying good, right?"

"You'll get your reward in heaven, Crab," Bill said.

"Very funny."

For a couple of hours, Bill repaired docks till Green roared up trailering his eighteen-foot skiff. Once it was launched, Bill drove to Green's club to pick him up. He passed Sneed on the way and gave a cheerful wave. He helped Green tie up the duck boat and then secured the cruiser, which was pounding the dock. Green said nothing. Driving back, he wanted the details. Bill told him he didn't know. Green didn't like that. He loved to revise.

Bill replaced more dock planks. Green hung around, then excused himself. Bill wasn't sorry. He loved the man and he trusted Crabby pretty much but was acutely aware that neither could keep their mouth shut. Bill told Crabby that he had to dress sharp Saturday night, because it was a big wingding, and that he, Crabby, was going to be captain. He gave him twenty dollars, told him to get a shirt and to spit shine his shoes. As Bill walked away, he knew Crabby would talk, but mainly about how important he had become.

———

He met Datillo at the creek. Datillo climbed aboard, dropped his line in the water.

"You got boats?"

"Green's skiff—that'll hold eight; mine—that'll hold four, maybe five; and Green's fifty-foot cruiser that can hold as many as you want. I got a pilot for the cruiser thinks he's taking Green out for a party."

Datillo nodded.

"What's their plan?" Bill whispered.

"Fair enough but keep it to yourself. They can't drive to Green Castle or to Polecat's, but we have the same problem. What they plan is to come downstream and land near that little Happy Hollow Creek, then slip through the woods, come up from behind, out of sight. What we want to do is place officers in the church and then have a few in the woods where they can see the clearing.

Those same men can also watch Polecat's, which is dogleg. I can't put men in yet. Don't want talking. The rest of us will fan out. Green's cruiser will block the creek if they try to escape, but hopefully, they never get that far."

"Where do you want me and Green?"

"Right where you drop us."

"What if I were to disable their boats?" Bill asked.

"Okay, cruise down and have a look, but I don't recommend it. These guys are crazy. Hard to imagine. You tell Polecat to close up on Saturday like always, but to keep four or five men back, but no cars in the lot. Ask him if he wants us in there with a radio; he will be covered, roads blocked and the creek. It's up to him."

"What about the Episcopal church?"

"Both ways in and out are easy. We're not worried."

"How many?"

"Not sure. Three teams. Probably fifteen, more or less."

"When do we load?"

"Midnight, but I'll be precise later. They plan to strike around four."

"Long night."

"Yeah, but we'll bag 'em, God willing," Datillo said.

"Want us armed, of course," Bill asked.

"I'll look the other way. We're asking for transportation. Additional force shouldn't be necessary, and I can't deputize, so when time comes, please use your head. This ain't the Wild West. Though sometimes, I wish it was."

Bill cruised home and sat on his deck awhile. He had had plenty of crap in the war. He wanted peace. He wanted to enjoy a cocktail. He wanted to shed the lead blanket.

The sun was sinking and so was he, but he realized that physical exertions had worked up an appetite, so he headed to Polecat's. He ordered ribs, beans, and corn bread. Polecat spiked the order slip in the kitchen window. Bill indicated that he wanted to talk over in the corner. Polecat lumbered over.

Polecat was expressionless while Bill told him what Datillo wanted to do. Be ready and be backed up. Datillo was right. Polecat didn't want any cops in his joint.

"What you don't understand, Mr. Bill, if *you* shoot a white, that's one thing. If *I* do, it's another."

"He's on our side, I believe."

"Believe what you want, but I know from experience. They all cover their ass. I'll put a floodlight on the back of this building tomorrow and God will be my witness."

CHAPTER 13

JOSHUA

B ill had the food wrapped up. When he got home, Green was sitting on deck with Marcus. Bill wasn't in the mood for jocularity. He carried his brown paper sack onto the boat and tried to act cordial. But Green and Marcus were serious. They weren't there for fun.

Joshua was dead. Drowned in the creek; found by a fisherman.

"Good God, what do you make of it?"

"His dog is missing," Marcus said and Green nodded. "His mother found his Bible beside his bed. That's what made her think something was wrong. That boy always carried his Bible, so she went to calling for him and Cracker. Some old man found him down by the bridge snagged in branches."

"What do you think?" Bill asked.

"There was a note in the Bible," Green said. "It said, 'an eye for an eye.'"

"When?"

"While ago. His father's pistol's missing."

"The cops on this?" Bill asked.

"Sure," Green said, "as far as drowning. But the boy's mother handed me the Bible and pointed to the note and whispered about the gun."

"What you mean?"

"God knows," Green said. "You seem to be connected up. That boy didn't drown; was like a fish. Caught him in the pool number of times."

"And the dog is missing," Marcus said. "That dog is dead, too, I guarantee, else he would be back at Miss Laura's. Delf's hand's in this."

"We can't prove that."

"I think it's pretty obvious," Green said. Marcus shook his head.

"We can't jump to conclusions. I'm inclined to agree, but there's a lot at stake. I know it's hard, but I guarantee we'll be hearing from Datillo. Wait for him. I know what you want, but there's time. This blood won't wash off. We'll get to the bottom."

They had a drink together and though it was welcome, none enjoyed it. They all felt sick. They sat on the deck in failing light. Bill saw Marcus studying the water, which for lack of rain, was sluggishly dragging. Marcus stood and pointed.

"Mr. Bill, you got a boat hook?" he asked, as he pointed at something whitish in the murky water. They hooked and raised it: Cracker. He had been shot in the hind quarters and through the head. He was still limp.

"Mark the time," Bill said. "I'm heading up to the Pine Bar. I'll call Datillo from there. Stay put."

In the car, Bill lit a smoke and flipped on the radio to take his mind off things and heard a crackled version of "That's Amore." As he pulled into the parking lot, he heard the first bars of "How Much Is That Doggie in the Window."

He slammed his door shut with such force that it brought him to his senses. He had to be calm, didn't know who might be watching. Bill decided he did need a phone installed, maybe down at Crabby's. He walked into the bar, bought a beer, and went straight to the pay phone. There was hardly anybody in the place. He tried to talk quietly, but he couldn't get past the switchboard. She had to know the nature of the call, etc. and no matter what Bill said, it wouldn't satisfy. "I'm sorry, sir, I can't. It's against regulations." Finally, Bill told her to tell Datillo that Riverboat Bill was going to slaughter three white men and hang their guts off a telephone pole on River Road as soon as he'd fed their hearts and livers to his dogs. He finished by saying, "Thanks so much, sweetie."

Bill did not know if this tactic would work, but knew he had to get back to the boat before Green and Marcus had better ideas. But it did work. He hadn't been parked for a minute before Datillo rolled up. Turns out, he had been alerted to Joshua's murder an hour before. He had told the dispatcher not to worry, that it was a crank call. When he saw the dog, he lost his composure.

"The boy's jaw was broken. He was dead before he was thrown in. We'll get the bastard."

"Cracker washed up at what time, Green?" Bill asked.

"About eight thirty."

"We'll find where it happened," Datillo said. "Understand something, please; these people stop at nothing. Can't let this take us off course. The police force is slow, but right now, that's good. We're going to call it accidental drowning. All present know it wasn't unless he ran real hard into a tree before he fell in. None of us can let on."

"Do you know about the gun? And the note in his Bible?" Green asked.

"No, sir."

"Talk to his mother."

"Will you go with me?"

Marcus nodded.

Before they left, Datillo said same place, same time. Bill nodded. Marcus and Datillo left Bill and Green sitting on the deck. Datillo got a run-around. Laura, even with Marcus, wouldn't say much except that her boy wouldn't hurt anybody and no matter what anyone said, she denied there had been a gun. She said the note meant nothing, so that went nowhere.

Datillo drove down the road to his tenant house. All was quiet and peaceful, the sky full of stars. There was a rich taste of summer in the air and he felt sick to his stomach. He wanted to call his wife and do all sorts of crazy things but knew to keep to his role. He was on the outs.

For years, these fools called the shots, but their influence was shrinking, county to county, and although they were almost nothing, they could still kill, almost with impunity. Who would question a judge who would look the other way and let them off? The cops were the first line, but who hired them? Who fired them?

He parked, and everything looked peaceful. He walked into his place and everything was as it had been left. Still he kept his pistol on his shaving stand while he showered in the crappy old bathtub without a curtain. Nothing unusual happened. He fell asleep with his pistol under the pillow.

Back at the boat, Green was energized. He wanted to tear the bastards down. Bill asked him how. He never had an answer, except that it had to be done and Bill urged patience, but Green had reached a point where patience was not only impossible to comprehend, but impossible to pronounce.

He said, "Screw 'paychens.' Where do 'paychens' end but bigger 'paychens,' answer me that. We gotta kill 'em!"

Bill, recognizing that Green was too far gone to go anywhere, but knew he would try, fixed drinks that could be described as "Good night Irenes." They worked like a charm and somehow Bill awakened the next morning in his bed and Green was partially on the floor.

Bill didn't ponder long how Green could slumber; instead he made coffee and went about his morning routine. While Green filled the air with snores, he stretched, as he had learned to do in the corps. He did sit-ups and jumping jacks, a few push-ups. Then his coffee was ready. He sat on the deck and indulged himself while he listened to Green drown out tree frogs and crickets.

Green's Cadillac sat there like an indictment, but Bill in his foggy state of mind, couldn't figure what kind. Was it rich vs. poor? Tawdry vs. tacky? His own car with a window busted out and a few bullet holes was defiantly running for something, but in his drowsy state, he wasn't sure what.

It was Friday morning. He knew that. Green snored. A duck quacked. There was something going on across the creek. He saw a white kid waving.

"What you want?" Bill growled. "Why are you waving at me?"

"I'm scared."

"Stay put."

Bill fired up his little boat and crossed the creek.

"What's scared you?"

"Crazy man was chasing me."

The boy's eyes darted side to side; he kept jerking his head to look back. He was dressed okay, but his shoes and pants were muddy. Bill got the boy on his boat, sat him down. He fetched a glass of water. Told him no one was going to harm him. He asked what happened.

The boy said he'd been digging worms and then had heard something rustling. At first, thought it might be a dog or a cow going down to drink, but then heard cussing. Not loud, but he knew it was a man coming, cussing louder. He said he was reaching for his fishing pole when the man came crawling out of a patch. The man started talking. "What you looking for, boy? What you think you're after?" The boy said he dropped everything and took off running. He said the man wasn't fast but would not give up.

"Won't show his face here," Bill said. "Say the man is crazy? You seen him before?"

"Don't think so."

"Can you tell what he looked like?"

"Big. Scary. Eyes like ghost eyes, real blue. And bald headed. He was wearing a cap, but must have got knocked off, because once I looked back, I could see sunlight off his head."

"You saw him again, think you might recognize him?"

"If I see him again, I'm running."

Green rambled onto the deck rubbing his eyes.

"Now what?" he said. Then he looked at the boy. "Robbie—is that you?"

"Yes sir, Uncle; it's me."

"Everything all right?" Green asked, as he tried to straighten himself by tucking in his shirttails and standing more erect.

"Some fool chased the boy down the creek and he was only digging for worms."

"You know who?" Green asked.

"More I think, it might be Mr. Delf if he has a bald head. Mr. Delf have a bald head, Unkie?"

"Son of a bitch," Green said. "I don't know, but I sure as hell will find out. You all right?"

"Now."

"Bill, I don't got the patience for this."

"Me either, Green, but try. Datillo's painting this morning. Go inspect his work. Tell him what happened, but whisper."

"Robbie, I'll drive you on home and we'll tell Mother you slipped and fell in the creek or something, but you got to keep this quiet."

Green reached into his wallet and pulled out a fifty and handed it to the boy.

"I'll give you three more of these in five days if you'll go along. Your mother will panic if you tell the truth. We can't have that, can we? Never let you out of her sight."

"Three more in five days?"

"Maybe sooner," Green said.

"Okay, but I got an idea. Better let me make the story. Yours are complicated."

"Deal," Green said, looking at the bright-faced kid as he stuffed the fifty. "That was just a first stab, my boy; I was working it up."

"Let me finish. I've had more practice."

"So, where were you digging worms, exactly?" Bill asked.

"Sir, it was the same place. Unkie knows where, don't you?"

As Green nodded, Bill could see the resemblance. Something about the thrust of jaw. He was a big kid. Bill would have figured him at fifteen or so, but he was only thirteen.

A GATHERING OF STONES

After they left, Bill popped a cold beer and planned to fight the blues. Everything seemed ugly and pointless. He was surprised when a black Cadillac pulled up. Polecat Green, Mr. Traylor, Miss Hayes, and Fred Ruby stepped out. As they walked toward him, Bill felt naked. Their eyes searched him like they were looking for lice. Polecat suggested they step inside and Bill waved them in. They sat around the table. The only one standing was Fred.

They weren't there more than five minutes. Polecat spoke first.

"My joint is covered, but Mr. Traylor and Miss Hayes have convinced me that having an officer or two would be to my advantage. As long as they slip in the back when I close. Tell Datillo we will be armed, but we won't shoot no cops, long as they're in the back door before lights go out at two. Nobody but me will know they're coming."

Polecat extended his open hand to Mr. Traylor, who said, "We have a prayer meeting tomorrow night and we are not canceling. It will last until it's over and I cannot judge when that will be; however, there will be some of us remaining in the church. We will stay there until dawn. Not only do we have regular services on Sunday, we have young Joshua's visitation scheduled for Sunday afternoon. God help me, both will go on."

"Amen," said everyone around the table.

"Fred Ruby is in charge of a small group of men, all veterans," Traylor added. "They will be armed inside the church. Miss Hayes is in charge of the ladies' auxiliary. At the first sign of commotion near the church, a number of porch lights will be lit at once and if there is a successful capture of these murderous devils, for those willing or able, there will be coffee and cookies and cakes served at the Green Castle Church. Please convey our best wishes to Officer Datillo."

They filed out solemnly after Miss Hayes shook his hand and Mr. Traylor nodded.

In this way, it was like the war. So damn much waiting. He didn't know what to do. He gassed his boat. Drank a beer. Drank another beer. He was cracking another when Green rolled up. After he had taken the boy home, he spoke with Datillo. There were a couple of men combing the creek. Green saw Delf, who had been directing the unloading of feed. He hadn't spoken to him but noticed his right hand was bandaged. Datillo told Green that he was fearful that the whole thing might be called off. Green told Bill that Datillo wanted as many of the scum bags as he could get, but if they didn't move the next night, he was going to take Delf Sunday morning and book him for murder.

"Does he have men he can trust?" Bill asked.

"I hope. He says he does, but God, it seems dicey."

"Let's go fish," Bill said.

"Should go into the office."

"Yeah, well I should go to confession. Let's go fishing. Drink some beer. We can't change nothing now anyhow, so let's drive 'em nuts and relax."

They stocked up on beer at the liquor store, then dropped in the Point and had ham-and-cheese sandwiches made. Then realized they didn't have bait, so they drove to a bait shack close to town that served as a beer depot, where they drank a beer and ate pretzels, until they forgot about fishing and started watching baseball on a television set that broadcast mostly fuzz.

They did end up fishing before the afternoon was over and ate sandwiches, too. Started at the same old spot on the creek where they almost always went, but this time they were whispering instead of laughing.

Neither was a serious fisherman, not that day or any other. They enjoyed beer and company. Fish were a dividend, as Green called them. Still they made a show and put lines in the water. They were slowly drifting downstream when Bill switched from worms to a minnow then cast into the bank next to a broken branch that still had green leaves. A fish took his bait, broke the surface, splashed, and struggled to get away. Green was whooping because it was a big one, but he noticed Bill was staring at something more interesting than the fish.

"Give me your rod if you ain't going to fight."

"I'll land him," Bill said, "but I'll bet you a dollar to doughnuts that's where it happened, right on that bank. Get the net."

Bill steered the fish close and Green scooped a fine healthy largemouth. Green slipped him on a stringer, cleated it, and lowered the fish into the creek.

"What you see?"

Bill didn't say anything. He picked up the paddle and worked over to the bank. Green didn't see anything but mud.

"That broken branch? Look right where it forks."

"Could be a boot print. Well, wait there's two."

"Good eye, Green. I didn't spot that, but I believe you're right. Look just below and to the left about three foot. Something shiny?" Bill whispered.

Green, who was in the bow and closest, said, "Yeah, it's a wristwatch with one of those expandable bands."

"Don't touch it," Bill said, in the nick of time. "Can you see the dial?"

Green nodded affirmatively.

"What time does it show?"

Green leaned close and the stringered fish thrashed. Green had to wipe his glasses before he could look again.

"It's reading about quarter past three and the second hand's moving, Bill, but the band is broken."

"What time you got?"

"Quarter after."

"Haul in the fish. We got to find Datillo."

They puttered downstream for a few hundred yards, then Bill opened her up and they carved their way back down creek. Bill was thinking that from the shore no one could have seen what he had. The breeze of motion brightened his eyes. Looking down from the bank above, all you would see is mud and the branch wouldn't have looked broken. It was still fresh. The wristwatch was tucked into a boot print. He had only noticed after the flashing wake of the eager fish had sunk. Against the copper-colored creek, the watch face had kept sparkling like water that wouldn't sink. The light caught and held it just so.

Green alerted Datillo to what they found and within an hour, Bill transported two detectives to the spot. They were careful to make Bill land downstream after they agreed that the place held promise. They photographed everything, and one made a plaster mold of a boot print. The watch was collected. One cop plucked some material off the tree trunk that the branch had been torn from. The process didn't take more than an hour. They scribbled in their notepads, then got in an old Ford and drove off. Bill didn't know if Datillo would be at the appointed meeting or not, but he fixed a tall one and headed back. Datillo was there, pacing the bank. Bill was five minutes late.

———

Briefly, Bill told him what Polecat had offered. Datillo said, "Done." Bill told him Fred and his crew would stay after the service. Datillo shook his head and said, "There's no way to stop it."

"Do you think they'll still try?"

"We're ready."

"When will you know what you found?" Bill asked.

"It's Delf's watch, I'm sure, and there's more to come. Please keep that to yourself."

"What time tomorrow?"

"Eleven o'clock. All of us meet at Green's club. Let's keep it simple. I don't think we need your boat, but if we decide we do, we'll get it on the way."

"You got people?"

"Think so," Datillo said. "The chief's all right. The mayor's all right. I don't think Green hurt us. Some of those in between I'm not sure, though most are. I've drawn on young cops I personally know. About half are working double shift. Not even supposed to be on tomorrow night. A couple called in sick and two guys who are brothers reported a death in the family, so we're under the radar, I believe."

"You don't think Delf will run? If that's his wristwatch, we got him cold, don't we?"

"No twice. No, I don't think he will run. He's too arrogant and crazy. This deal is a steppingstone for state-wide bragging. As to your second question: in Delf's mind, he's done no worse than swat a fly. Besides, what if that boy really did pull a gun? We haven't heard Delf's side. Don't forget, a watch is a watch."

"I don't believe that boy would have ever shot anybody," Bill said.

"I believe the mother," Datillo said. "I personally don't believe there ever was a gun involved."

"Why would Marcus have said there was?"

"Don't know, but he didn't support me when I asked, and she denied it. He got quiet. Out of respect for the mother's grief, I didn't push."

"That's kind of important."

"It's important. And yes, I trust Marcus as long as he's on the boat with Green tomorrow serving drinks. Those boys are going to light up Green's boat like Christmas and tell your man I want the music loud and lots of laughter. I want him to head up the creek and not slide back until about four thirty. Want them to act stupid drunk. If it's a little misty and it probably will be, guess we will need you in your boat. Maybe you can guide us. The big duck skiff won't need lights and if you want to screw up their boats, feel free. We can use Green's monster to turn sideways and block their escape in the event they get away with trying that. You asked about Marcus? I think he's a good man, but I'll bet you a dollar, if there is a missing gun, it's in his pocket tomorrow night."

"That puzzles me."

"Me too," Datillo said, "but concentrate on the other stuff. Eleven o'clock."

"Seriously, what about the gun?"

Datillo turned, walked back, and said, "The boy's note wasn't written yesterday. The paper was soiled and crinkled like he had carried it, struggling with it or something. I suspect Marcus tried to save the boy from doing something stupid some time back. Just a gut feeling. I think the mother is covering for Marcus, and I bet Marcus was somehow trying to point the finger at Delf. You know how that kid would always seem to come out of nowhere? Well, what if he popped up on Delf inconveniently?"

———

As he was cruising back, Bill pictured Joshua as he first appeared to him in Green's garden, now more than a year ago. Poof, there he was, full of curiosity. "Who are you? Why you here?" The kid had been persistent and unintentionally annoying. "Do you believe in the Lord? Isn't the Word good? What are you doing here?" Bill then imagined what Joshua might have said to Delf and in what circumstances. He wasn't the kind of kid you could buy off with treats or scare. Bill felt sick when he passed where it happened.

———

Marcus did not know what to do. He hadn't meant to but had implied to Green that the pistol was missing on the same day that Joshua was drowned. In fact, it had happened weeks previously, but before he could explain anything to Mr. Green, the man assumed all kinds of stuff. When he tried to interject, Mr. Green kept talking until Marcus didn't care anymore, being as upset as he was.

If he could have trusted someone enough to tell—someone who would not have been confused by the truth and who would not have taken it the wrong way—he would have said that one afternoon, Joshua walked past him on the way to the creek. He had Cracker with him but had looked dour and angry. Marcus had spoken to Joshua, but all he got was a nod. Marcus tagged along and noticed that the boy kept his hand in his pocket for the entire time and that the pocket was bulging.

"What you got in that pocket, boy? A big frog?" he asked.

Marcus remembered Joshua's funny averted glance. The boy finally pulled it out and showed him. It was a snub nose .38, loaded. He asked the boy what he aimed to do. He got the same strange look, so Marcus told him that he would teach him to shoot.

"How do you point it?" he remembered the boy asking.

"I'll show. We'll pick a target."

"I got a target in mind," Joshua had said.

Without the boy saying anything, he knew who he was talking about, but Marcus thought it important to play along. He ended up carrying the pistol and they went down to the creek together.

Marcus found a log and stood it on end. Then he found an old paint can and placed it on top. He showed Joshua how to hold the pistol and brace it right. He told him not to be scared because it was awful loud.

"You shoot first," Joshua said.

"No, you shoot first. Just aim like this. Lower it down and squeeze."

The boy would have none of it, so Marcus fired at the can to show him that it wasn't a joke, but he clean missed the can. The bullet slogged in the creek. He, himself, was amazed at the loud blast from the little cannon. He was laughing, in spite of himself, for having missed. When he looked at Joshua, he laughed even louder because the kid was holding his ears and jumping up and down.

"How do you shoot that thing with both ears closed?" he asked.

"You can't unless somebody holds them shut. Your turn."

"I don't think so," Joshua answered, crumpling a small scrap of paper.

They walked back, and Cracker rejoined them after a while. They decided that Marcus would hang on to the gun for safekeeping. Joshua told Marcus he would think of something and Marcus gave Joshua a hug outside his mother's front door, then went home and stashed the gun. How could he explain all that? Especially after Mr. Green had spun his version?

––––––––

Datillo was on patrol. He wanted to think but didn't have time. He was cruising the streets, waiting for the radio to send him here or there. The neighborhood he was in wasn't all that bad, not like some he had been assigned to when he was first on the force. The main problem in this neighborhood was domestic disturbances. One party would call the police. When you tried to straighten things out, often both parties would turn. Out of the corner of his eye, he saw a figure duck down behind a car, then the fellow abruptly stood up and tried to walk calmly away. A kid had been siphoning gas. Datillo pulled up, switched on his lights, and the kid took off, so did he. So much of what he did was nothing at all. How could he tell anybody?

A few nights before, some guys were closing in on a liquor store, casing plain as day, so he drove around the block several times, until they changed their minds. What could he have charged them with? Thinking?

What a ragtag crew occupied much of his time. Delf was a different story. He knew in his gut the man was a cold-blooded murderer. It was an ugly, lonely business. Many people Datillo was sworn to protect hated his guts, and so did the ones he wanted to catch. It made him weary sometimes.

––––––––

Fred got antsy, told his wife he was going for a drive and drove his old Buick down River Road to Bill's. What he couldn't have known was that Miz Ruby was delivering chicken and dumplings. Fred got there first, didn't know why he was there and didn't know Bill wasn't, so he stepped on the deck just as Miz Ruby drove up. She was as surprised to see him as he was to see her. Amelia loved Fred and she ran and jumped to hug him.

"What you doing here, Fred Ruby?"

"Ruby, I could ask the same."

"I want to hear a story," Amelia said. "Where's Mr. Bill?"

Fred knocked, but there was no answer. He looked at Ruby.

About then, Bill's boat rounded the bend and bore down on them whining like a mosquito. He sloshed to a stop, excused himself after lashing a line, and rushed inside. Amelia looked confused. Fred patted her head. Bill came back out with a full drink.

"Tell me a story, Mr. Bill," Amelia insisted.

"I brought you this," Miz Ruby said, handing him the dish. "Sunday?" she said with a probing glance.

"I want to hear a story now," Amelia demanded.

"I told you after church, child," Bill said as he took the casserole dish from Ruby. "Thank you, Ruby. Please, won't you all come inside?"

Only Fred accepted the invitation and a splash of whiskey. Both ate some of Ruby's food. Fred fired a cigar and looked Bill over like he was seeing him for the first time.

"Bill, I got to ask; I don't want to, but I've been sent to."

"Ask away."

"Why the hell are you getting involved in this? There are folks don't understand, and they don't trust it. I feel like I know you, but some don't. All they know is the likes of Sneed and Delf. Can you give me something to take back?"

Bill shook his head, lit a smoke, and the weight of the question sat on his brow. He poured a shot into his glass, shoved the bottle over to Fred, who poured himself one. He tried to smile. He had no idea what to say.

"Not likely anything they want to hear. I don't know the why of anything for that matter. Nothing makes a whole lot of sense right now. I can tell you that, but that probably won't give them comfort. I'm only doing what seems right, but for no particular reason. I'm here. I do what I do. I am going to be where I need to be and if they need reasons, they can talk to somebody else. I can't answer that kind of question."

Fred's amusement was comforting. They clinked their glasses together.

"I told them there was no special reason, but some of them wouldn't believe. Trying to keep everybody together, that's all."

"Fred, you tell them that Bill don't like to see folks burn the wrong stuff down."

"That'll work right there. I'll tell 'em and you want to know something funny. Sneed ain't written a traffic ticket on anybody in the neighborhood in over a month, not even a taillight or a license plate."

"Yeah, I saw him yesterday. He ain't real pleased, is he?"

Theodora Green sat behind her martini as cool as the ice that chilled her glass. Her husband was polishing firearms. He cleaned two pistols and a shotgun, but still was not dressed for their party. She glanced at her watch as he primped his weapons and decided to give him five minutes. She tried to encourage him to remember that he was one of the guests of honor, but all he had done was smile. He was in another world.

He surprised her when in four minutes and forty-five seconds, he smiled at the gleam of the polish on the stock of his shotgun and said, "Suppose I better get a move on, hadn't I?"

She had nodded with a big grin and hit the buzzer beneath her foot, which was the signal for another martini for her, not him. She didn't finish it, of course, and when he had walked out of his dressing room, had handed it to him. He quaffed it, while she dabbled with his cummerbund until she got it right.

On the way to the club, he rolled up the glass that separated the passenger seats from Marcus, who was their chauffeur this evening, and had told her some fragments of what was going on and explained why he had been tending to firearms.

"Burn down the people's church and our church, too? Why didn't you tell me sooner?"

"I didn't want to trouble you, dear."

"Who's behind this?"

"You wouldn't believe me if I told you. Look! There are the Robinsons and the Houghlands. Darling, this can wait. Promise me you'll keep it under your hat." Green opened his own door and jumped out to wave at his friends.

———

Miss Hayes walked from house to house. She had a telephone. Mr. Traylor did, too, but Fred Ruby didn't. Most didn't. All she wanted to do was alert about five or six people on two different streets to be watching her house between four and five in the morning the next day. She also asked them to make coffee and cookies and to have both ready by five a.m. She had such credibility in the neighborhood that not one woman asked her to explain, though some did look at her funny, but she didn't care, she was used to it. It had been Mr. Traylor's idea. Cookies and coffee? The way she looked at it, nobody was going to have time for that, if what they said was going to happen actually happened. But what did she know? Mr. Traylor had been a shining star for so long. She had faith in his good judgment. She was looking forward to a brighter day.

———

Polecat was making some girl feel stupid out back of his kitchen. She had promise, but she hadn't learned the score. He told her, you get that money first, no matter what. Even if the man is so drunk that you know he's blubbering. While he's talking smart, take the money and run.

His girls were more like entertainment than whores. Some of them turned tricks, but he could do nothing about that. He never took anything except for a cut of the drinks they sold. Sometimes they let a guy run it up on the cuff, turned their backsides, and the man would be gone. Looking for a bigger score, they would lose a sure thing. He was pissed off, because he assumed that's what had happened.

"I heard something scared me," the girl said.

"What's that?"

"I was out next to the car and these two fellas in the backseat was talking while I was loving on the john, trying to talk him back in. One said, 'This place will be ashes Sunday mornin' and I know my man heard that and he hugged me hard. That scared me, Polecat, I ran."

"Were they white?"

"Man I was with weren't; couldn't see. He hurt my ears."

"Keep quiet about this. I'll make it up. Go home now. Keep your mouth shut. Go now, girl! Go."

———

She had no idea why she was, but she was. Valerie was making cookies. She was mixed up and confused. She wasn't sure how she felt about motherhood. She was pretty sure about going to Florida. She had been glad to see her grandmother and her daughter, but she would still have had to admit there was something she loved about Bill. Everything felt topsy-turvy, but something came over her that afternoon of her twenty-seventh year. She had an overwhelming desire to bake cookies. Her grandmother, eager to help, pulled out her recipe box, and with no small amount of coaching, Valerie baked cookies from scratch.

Valerie made peanut butter cookies and chocolate chip with raisins. When the baby woke up, she had let her lick her fingers, and still did not know why she had made them. She was leaving sometime the next day as soon as her cousin showed. She knew that, and she knew the cookies were for Bill, Riverboat Bill, as she thought of him.

———

Delf didn't drive down to the hay barn, he walked. The broken bone in his hand throbbed, and he held it above his waist. Why he was going, he didn't know. There was restlessness in him. The stuff needed for the next night had already been put together and moved to the place they were using for a base. No practical reason to go existed. That puzzled him. As he scrunched along, the night coolness settled on his shoulders. What was a man to do?

Screwed. Screwed. And screw them back. There was no way things could go on like this. The little man was doomed before he was born. Doomed by the unholy alliance of the Negro, the Jew, and the rich white. This left no choice. As he walked, he felt his stature grow and stretch like his shadow cast by the moon. He had the message. He had been heard. Delf felt blood pound his temples. He would show the way. All of the talk of freedom and commingling was devil work, which he had sworn to reassign back to hell. What about the little man? God help him get to the top where he could do some damn good.

Datillo's headlights hit before he heard him. The cop had been driving slowly. Delf figured he could duck into shadows because the lights were dim and far away, but stubbornly he didn't, and Datillo cruised past without slowing down. Delf watched the cop's lights fog out in the dust. When he got in his little house, Datillo wrote down that Delf's right hand was bandaged. He liked to keep notes.

Delf went into his barn. He knew the stairs by heart. He crawled into the meeting space and sat at the head of the table and, in his mind, composed an acceptance speech. He saw churches in flames. He saw first one and then the other. It excited him. He imagined Polecat's joint smoldering. There he was, nodding with eyes resolute, the mantle of ascension descending onto his shoulders. He was breathing deeply, so lost in reverie that when the moon cast light through the missing boards that served as window, he assumed it was an anointing. When an owl swooshed, scratched, and perched there, he believed it to be further affirmation.

He left satisfied, even though he misjudged the bottom stair and stumbled. Exactly what had happened when he heard the kid laugh. The boy had been over in the corner behind some junk.

Delf had heard the kid muttering. Though, as he thought back, the kid wasn't muttering, but speaking straight out. For some reason, Delf started walking down toward the creek. The boy followed, saying things that made no sense. Down at the creek, they squared off.

"What you following me for, boy?"

"I ain't following you, Mr. Delf. I'm following someone greater."

"Well, where is he, boy?"

"Need to turn around and look."

In spite of himself, Delf did. Of course, he had seen nothing and laughed about that as he walked the road home and saw the break between the tree line and the field where his own house sat, tin roof dusted by moonlight. The kid had been crazy, no doubt.

"There's nothing here, but you and me," he had said.

"I heard something, Mr. Delf."

"What you hear?"

Joshua laughed. "Want to meet me again? How about tomorrow, Mr. Delf?" Then he took off running.

"Where you want to meet, son?" Delf hollered.

"Here."

Delf had been practicing his acceptance speech. He didn't know what the kid had heard. He had said nothing specific.

The boy showed up spouting Jesus. Delf nonchalantly sat, half-heartedly listening. The boy came closer. Wham! He hit him with every muscle in his body. It shut him up. The boy rolled down the bank, out cold. Delf made sure he stayed that way. He was light as a feather pillow. He shoved him under. Shoved him off. Then the damn dog bit. Delf grabbed, shot him in the ass end, then squarely between the eyes and threw him in.

"War is hell," he said under his breath as he climbed freshly painted steps.

"What you say, dear?"

"What you doing up?" Delf responded to his wife, who was sitting in her rocker in shadows.

"Just taking in this moon and breathing air, Honey Lang. Heard on the radio Yankees won the series again. Can you believe? Five times straight?"

"Dodgers never had a chance. I'm going to bed."

"Don't you want to sit a bit and tell me what's what?"

"You and your Yankees. Congratulations."

"Well, don't forget, you owe me a quarter."

———

About five o'clock in the morning, Valerie found herself in the back of a Chevy. Grandmother had got her up because her cousin was waiting on the porch. He wanted to get an early start. The baby did not awaken. There was a man on the passenger side smoking a cigar. His name was Cleve. He had a gold tooth and she found both tooth and cigar repulsive. She told them she had to make a quick stop before they left town.

Her cousin protested. "No point in arguing, she's sitting on the assets," Cleve said and laughed like he thought he was the funniest man alive.

She tiptoed onto Bill's deck, intending to leave the wrapped-up cookies on one of his chairs. When she heard Bill snore, she carried them into the cabin and placed them on the old oak table. Valerie took a note out of her pocket and laid it on top, then took a deep breath, felt like there should be something else, but could think of nothing. She peeked at him sleeping and tiptoed out.

When she got back in the car, Cleve was holding the child.

"What you doing with Alexandra?"

Her cousin dropped it into gear. "Cousin Bartlett had to relieve himself, little lady. I was being helpful."

"You could have burned her."

"Could have," he grinned. "But didn't. Look here, still sleeping like a lamb."

"Next time, ask," Valerie said, accepting the child. There was something about the man that gave her heebie-jeebies. She didn't speak to him again until they were crossing the Florida line.

CHAPTER 14

TEN-GAUGE

The day passed slowly for everybody except Cleve, who felt certain that the way to Valerie was through her child, and hell, he had nothing else to do, so he made faces and funny sounds. Determination to get into Valerie's pants kept his day stimulating.

Miss Hayes's group was well focused. Some wondered what their wives were baking for. *All* involved were sworn to secrecy. Some folks were in the know and most were not. That's the way it was.

Polecat stocked up on ammunition. Fred did, too. He had a list from his troops of the different calibers needed. The white man he bought the stuff from laughed and said, "You sure got a lot of different guns, boy. Ten-gauge, sure don't sell many of those."

Fred nodded, grinned, and paid in cash.

Polecat had one of his guys rig up three floodlights: two aimed into the woods and one spraying across the field at the church. He wasn't looking forward to having cops in his joint, but he had to in case something went wrong. He needed witnesses. He was resigned to the idea, but he felt sick inside. The whole business stunk. All day long he felt low, but as night fell, his blood started pumping.

It seemed like everybody felt that way. At first dull, then resigned. Everything seemed small compared to what was coming.

When it was time to go. Bill, Crabby, Green, and Marcus in a starched white uniform, were the first on the dock, but within minutes, the cops streamed down the steps. They were all carrying identical little bags; however, none of them looked like cops. They were all dressed in slacks and shirts; some even wore coat and tie.

There were fifteen altogether. Datillo pointed at Green's cruiser, and the guys in coats and ties climbed aboard. The others, in dark casual clothes, were directed onto the duck hunting skiff. Datillo climbed aboard with that group and sat in the bow. Bill took his place in the stern. At the last minute, Green announced that he would be captaining the *Half Moon*. Crabby called down to Bill, who forwarded this information to Datillo, who jumped onto the cruiser. Within minutes, they were backing out into the current and swinging upstream. Bill looked back and Green's cruiser was lit up inside and out. Crabby was at the helm. He wondered to himself what Datillo had said to change Green's mind. After all, it was Green's boat and he was stubborn as hell.

Bill stayed out of the channel, hugged the shore and cruised slowly upstream. Music started blaring from the *Half Moon* and Crabby began to meander in the duck boat's wake. If Bill hadn't known better, he would have sworn it was a Saturday night poker game run amuck. There was very little drift because of the drought, so the trip upstream was relaxing. Nobody in the duck boat said a word.

They slipped into the creek, slid past the stone ruins of what had been Bill's grandfather's tavern. A duck jumped up. One of the guys beside him pretended to draw a bead on him and then grinned without saying a word.

As they approached his boat, Bill pointed to shore. They landed. Datillo climbed off.

"You take three upstream in your boat. Keep 'em quiet. We'll hang down below. Just act like you're fishing. You lead us up, then we'll hang back, you go on. You'll see 'em coming down. Stay put until they pass."

Bill jumped into his boat with three men, who all of a sudden looked like fishermen. They were followed by Datillo running the duck skiff. Green's boat lumbered along with Benny Goodman blaring on the record player, clarinet needling the night. You could see Marcus all in white serving cocktails, bowing and smiling. They were barely moving, but still inching along.

Bill landed, and his men jumped off and slipped into the woods behind Polecat's. He shoved off and continued for a few hundred yards, pulled into the bank and anchored, dropped a line in, pulled out a pint. It was going to be a long night.

Datillo slipped in below the bend that surrounded the church. He and his men dragged the skiff all the way up on the shore and cut branches to cover it. Then they disappeared. They could see the church lights dim and then go dark. They hunkered down.

Green's boat was making almost too much noise to suit Datillo. He could barely see it pass as he stared back through the thicket. Sounded like a raucous party for damn sure. You couldn't hear a natural sound, not even a cricket, only lusty chants. Whoopee! Whoo-hoo! One of the officers must have had a high-pitched voice because every now and again, Datillo could hear something almost lurid teasing them on. After they rumbled past, the stridency diminished.

Two of the men slipped into Polecat's. One hid about a hundred yards away behind garbage barrels next to the church. The rest spread out along the edge of the woods.

Polecat's got dark. Bill watched the *Half Moon* go past and suffered its wake which was considerable, even at no-wake speed. The *Half Moon* kept meandering for near half a mile. He heard splashing that sounded as giddy as a skinny-dipping party. He had some worms, so instead of faking, he baited. He sat for the longest time. Suddenly there was a tug on his line and Bill was fishing for real, fighting a monster that fought with fury, tugging this way and that and then jumping. Bill was so distracted that he didn't immediately notice two skiffs without lights idling past.

"My gawd, he's hooked a son of a bitch."

Bill kept playing the fish and pretended not to notice. He heard somebody say, "Shush!"

The fish broke the line just as he watched darkness enclose the ripples that trailed the two boats. He waited for at least ten minutes, then raised anchor and started drifting. He listened for anything and everything but heard nothing except for racket from the *Half Moon*. He lit a smoke and saw it was ten to four. He was drifting close to where they should have pulled in. With his stern light, dim as it was, he could see boats tucked together up on the bank. He dropped anchor, half expecting to hear a voice tell him to move, but nobody said a thing. He sat and noticed that the *Half Moon* was quite a bit closer than he would have expected.

The creek was narrow on this bend, so Bill hoisted anchor and paddled over to the nearest beached boat. He coughed loudly and lit another smoke, but no one challenged him. He expected a guard of some kind. He laid his pistol on the seat beside him, then took the stern line of the nearest boat and tied that to the cleat of the one beside. The *Half Moon* slid past silently without lights. After they passed, Bill slipped into shadow across the creek.

Music blared up again off the *Half Moon*, but this time it was Glenn Miller and was so loud it drowned out the fact that she had turned around, headed back upstream. Bill didn't even know it: out of almost pitch black, her spotlight glared and brightened things emphatically. Music stopped.

What he didn't know was that before turning around, Crabby had nosed in and all of the cops had gone ashore. He watched Crab spin the cruiser, and for all practical purposes, plug the creek. The spotlight blinked out and everything went ink black.

Bill felt like another smoke, then realized he had one. He reached into his pocket and pulled out a chocolate chip cookie and popped it in his mouth. He washed the sweet with a slug of bourbon.

Suddenly light fragments lit the right flank, then a brighter sliver from the church filtered through, then more flickering lights on the left flank and then spotlights from Polecat's flashed. Bill imagined the open field that lay between the woods and the church and Polecat's joint would be at present a most unpleasant place to be strolling with devilment. He was chuckling when a shot sounded. He picked up his pistol and heard raised voices. A dog howled. Another shot. Dog silent. Could hear voices but couldn't make out meaning. He dropped his cigarette in the water and waited. Red flashing lights. Cussing. He listened. What he heard sounded like a beast crashing through undergrowth. He waited until he could see what looked like black cloth, blocking light, messing with the skiffs. He heard a grunt and a boat slid into the creek. Bill was about to call 'Hit the spotlight,' but the cloth shape wasn't going far, so he took a satisfied swig and hoped nobody had been hurt. He raised his weapon and took dead aim.

Boat's engine fired and roared amid a clanking, crashing grind. Green's spotlight lit the bastard like a blot on a slide. Delf. Bill chuckled as Delf hit forward and reverse, getting nowhere but tangled. Bill kept him in his sights and didn't laugh aloud until two cops stood on the bank with guns steady. Delf sat, arms spread, staring at the heavens with disbelief. The cops hauled him up the bank, cuffed and marched him through the woods.

Datillo showed. Bill motored over.

"We got 'em all, I think."

Bill saw something out of the corner of his eye, but at the exact same moment, *Half Moon's* spotlight turned to the precise spot. He heard Marcus cry out, "Stand still or I'll shoot."

Datillo ran down the creek yelling, "Hands on your head. Get down!" His gun was drawn.

The man fell to the ground and Datillo put his foot in the small of the man's back and called for help. A few minutes later, the church organ sounded. It was a hymn Bill had never heard before. The steeple was lit. Bells started ringing. Then Datillo came back and said, "They're offering coffee and cookies, if you want some. We got all of them now. Green can run his skiff back; I'm bushed."

"Good job, Datillo," Bill said.

"Better have a cookie."

The paddy wagons rolled. Crabby wanted to stay with the boats. Nobody tried to dissuade him."

Bill walked around a dead dog lying in the field behind the church.

"What's with the dog, Datillo?"

"Damned if I know. Thing jumped out at their lead guy. Drew blood. The man panicked and fired. A stray; doesn't even have a collar."

Worked like clockwork but seemed to Bill almost everyone acted strange. Miss Hayes hadn't; in fact, none of the women, but most of the men—black and white—seemed awkward to the point of bashfulness. The minister thanked everyone for helping and said, "God bless you," but even he sounded restrained. Mr. Traylor spoke up as everyone was dispersing. He was a sturdy little man with a voice twice his size.

"This is a historic moment, ladies and gentlemen, and from the bottom of my heart, this witness sincerely thanks you. May the Lord God bless you."

Even those walking away turned to see the small man, black as coal, eyes shut, and fists clenched at his side, nodding.

After everybody was dropped off and boats secured, it was dawn. Bill hit the sheets, and, like the church bell, the memory of Ruby's voice clanged, "Church, this Sunday. Breakfast at nine thirty." He groaned and pulled the pillow over his head. Ruby hadn't let him off the hook. She had nodded when she served Bill a piece of cake after the long night. "A deal's a deal, Mr. Bill Maddox."

He owed her his life, but damn, was he tired. He didn't dream but woke up laughing. What awakened him was probably the barge on the river chugging upstream, but what he was tickled about was the sight of Delf, snarled, shaking fists at the sky.

He had an alarm he never used. It was a quarter till nine. Time, if he just kept moving.

When he arrived, he was awake. Ruby poured coffee and the kids sat around, full of curiosity. The boys acted shy. Amelia never did.

She jumped into his lap and got scolded for helping Bill spill coffee.

"Tell me your story anyway," she implored, eyes full of mischief.

"Told you after church, urchin."

"What's an urchin?" she giggled.

Bill grinned.

"I'll tell what you are right after. Not a moment sooner, hear?"

"Don't have to yell," Amelia complained.

"Breakfast is ready and ain't anybody yelling in this house," Ruby said.

There was corn bread, sausage, and eggs. Lots of food. Before they left for church, Ruby led Bill into the small alcove off the living room. Once again a sewing room, but there was still a small fold-out bed in the corner. She pointed. Bill nodded.

"You've come a long way. Yours any time you have need."

Bill shut his eyes. She touched his arm. He gripped her hand, gently, he hoped.

"Let's go to church," she said.

They walked. It was only a few blocks, but there were no sidewalks or signs to delineate where they had begun or where they would end. It was so foggy that you couldn't see twenty feet and that was odd to Bill, because when he had driven over, it had been clear.

"Wind must have shifted," he said.

"What did you say?"

"Nothing, Ruby. Foggy, that's all."

The kids, all except Amelia, hung back as they walked into church. Amelia was holding Bill's hand and he was glad she was. The fog was spooky, even to Bill; after all, it was almost eleven o'clock. They sat down in one of the front pews and Bill was praying that this whole thing wouldn't take too long. He also asked the Lord for a story and was surprised when his brow inexplicably lit up, although he had no clue as yet what the story might be.

"Don't fret," Ruby said.

"Who's fretting?" Bill replied, but the timbre of his voice was such that everybody within three rows heard him.

"Hush yourself," Ruby said.

"Hush your own damn self, Ruby. I'm whispering."

"You wouldn't know whispering from a dead possum."

"Listen, this here was your idea, not mine. I'm quiet as a mouse, understand?"

"Please hush; preacher's about to speak," Amelia implored and everybody within five rows tried to suppress laughter. The minister took the pulpit and didn't say much as far as Bill was concerned. There were a few amens, but they weren't that hot. Bill realized that the preacher was probably as tired as he was.

Finally, the preacher acknowledged just that.

"For some, it has been a long, hard night. It is tempting to go into biblical references, but I won't. I was up all night, half fretting, then praying, and the rest, thanking God for our deliverance. I suppose most everyone knows what went on here last night. Dark forces, wicked forces, tried to destroy our church. They were stopped outside the gates and yes indeed, thank God Almighty, we are still here to praise our Lord.

"Before we continue, let me please acknowledge Mr. Maddox, Mr. Green, Mr. Polecat Green, Mr. Fred Ruby and his regulars, Miss Hayes and her ladies. Finally, I will ask Officer Datillo to say a few words."

Datillo walked up and looked over the crowd.

"We heard about this no-good bunch. We put a stop to it. Forgive me, I want to be brief. I'm tired; so are many here. Nobody gets credit. Everybody knows good folks were involved, but I can't go further without saying something else."

He looked down and wiped his eyes.

He cleared his throat and with a voice shaking with emotion said, "There was a boy killed last week. Name was Joshua Baker. Was no accidental drowning. The man who we suspect did it faces a charge of murder in the first degree. We suspected who the day it happened, but we wanted to catch them all. Now we've caught them and they'll all be charged and prosecuted to the fullest extent of the law. Thank you. It is an honor to serve you and to be a guest in your church."

First Mr. Traylor stood. Then Miss Hayes stood and then various folks that Bill didn't know.

"Mr. Datillo, as one of the deacons of this church, I want to assure you of our gratitude and promise you that our prayers are with you always."

Datillo nodded and then everyone stood. The minister led the congregation in a prayer that was so long and heartfelt that Bill, tired as he was, got annoyed. He opened his eyes and to his surprise there were folks all around looking the same way.

AFTERMATH

"That weren't no miracle, Bill Maddox. That was plain hard, dangerous work, that's what it was. I ain't saying the Lord's hand wasn't in it, but you all done it. We done it together. You can't leave the people part out. That puts too much burden on the Lord. You want more coffee?"

"Yeah. Sort of hard to draw the line."

"I don't think so," Ruby said, responding to Bill's nod with a full cup. "We need a new preacher. This man goes on and on like he's trying to sanctify."

"What's an urchin? I didn't forget," Amelia said.

"About like you and your brothers." Bill laughed aloud when they poked their heads around the corner. "They hide around corners, under things, behind things. They're difficult to see sometimes. They are mischievous, standoffish and bristly."

"What's 'bristly' mean?" Amelia asked. Bill tickled her ribs and she folded to the floor and curled into a ball and stuck out her hands to push him away. Bill laughed.

"That's what it means. You're like a porcupine. You become all stickly and push things away or not let them get real close."

"Oh."

"Anyway, there was a baby porcupine, who had a friend who told stories, and nobody ever told her that her friend was old and wrinkled and ugly. She loved his stories because they made her see pictures of things that she hoped she would one day see. Well, one day, one of her friends saw her with him. She didn't hear his story, but she thought he was ugly, because he didn't look like any porcupine she had ever seen. Everything was wrong about him—head to toe—and the very next day she told her friend so. She told the baby porcupine how ugly she thought her friend was."

"She didn't?" Amelia exclaimed.

"She did and went with her the very next day and said she would prove it. She carried a mirror and when they had got close to her friend, who was leaning back against a log, said, 'Look at yourself, little porcupine. See your beautiful quills? See your eyes bright and shiny? Now, just look at your friend.' But when they both looked up from the mirror, there was nothing there but a log."

"Where did her friend go? Was he hiding?"

"Not exactly hiding," Bill said. "He was standing behind them. The porcupine holding the mirror looked into it and saw the old one's face and for a moment thought it was her own and that scared her so badly she threw the mirror into the bushes and, without turning around once, ran all the way home."

"What about the other little porcupine? What did she do?"

"What do you expect she would do?"

"Well, if I were her, I would tell that old ugly friend to sit right back down."

"Well, Amelia, that's exactly what happened. The baby porcupine said, 'Sit back down,' turned around and then saw that her friend was there like always."

"I knew that already," Amelia said, nodding her head.

"Of course, you did," Bill said.

As Bill was leaving, Ruby thanked him for keeping his promise. Bill thanked her for having him.

"You ain't ugly, Bill," Ruby said.

"He's my friend," Amelia said.

"You know Joshua's funeral's tomorrow? The visitation's this afternoon, four to eight. Thank God and everybody else. At least the church didn't burn."

Bill hugged Amelia and went straight to Polecat's. He found him behind the bar, drinking a martini. He offered Bill what was left in the shaker, but Bill declined and asked for a beer. There were a couple of guys sweeping last night's mess.

"What did you see, Polecat? How did it play out from here?"

Polecat had to laugh.

"You was on the creek, I heard. Well, first thing I saw was these two nervous cops, more scared of us than of them, I would bet. They hunkered down in that corner over there and didn't say a whole lot until about quarter till four. Then they got bossy. It worked out though, didn't it?" He chuckled.

"Yeah. When did you first spot the bastards?"

"First thing I saw was this mangy-ass dog that I been running off for getting in my trash. I seen that dog turn into a blur, disappearing into pitch-black dark. Then I hear snarling and barking. A ways off, I hear a man cussing, a gunshot, and a dog wailing. I didn't need no signal. No matter what the coppers said, I hit the lights and sure enough, there they were with their soda bottle gasoline and what all. Their eyes got big and instead of fanning out, they bunched up. Then they commenced to running, but when flashlights come out of the woods, they turned to running toward the creek and the police scooped 'em up like fireflies. Fred tells me the church situation was about the same."

Fred walked in from out back.

"Damn," Bill said. "It's General Fred, who won the battle without firing a shot."

"Way it's supposed to work," Fred said with a broad grin.

"Often doesn't," Bill said.

"Well, it's helpful to have the right crew."

Polecat set Fred and Bill with another beer. Fred insisted on buying.

"My only regret is, I didn't get to fire granddaddy's ten-gauge. I had duck loads."

"Probably would have broke your shoulder," Bill said.

"That's a fact."

"You were ready, weren't you?" Polecat said.

"Had his belly dead to rights."

"Thankfully, didn't come to that. They'll put those guys away. They're marked now."

"I ain't holding breath. Hard to hold a white man for threatening niggers."

"Polecat," Bill said, "they got Delf on first-degree murder. That man will squeal like a pig, I guarantee. That kind of man has no loyalty. Rest just as bad. They're ignorant cowards. Men you don't want on your side, for sure."

"I ain't even for certain they'll press charges," Polecat said.

"I bet they will," Bill said. Fred shrugged.

When Bill got back to the boat, Green was there drinking whiskey. Marcus was sitting at the table drinking nothing and looking morose. Bill didn't feel all that great but tried not to let it show.

"Hey, what's going on?"

Green said, "I called the mayor again, and this time I ain't backing off. I also called the newspaper and I had one of my guys down at the office put it on the wire. This cannot be swept under the rug. Mr. Traylor is right. This is a historic moment and I'll chance screwing up, but the word has to get out that both races together stopped this thing. Delf needs to be executed for what he did. Do you agree?"

"I hadn't thought that far yet . . ."

"Think that far, Bill. Do you agree or not? Delf should be executed."

"If he's found guilty, I suppose."

"Excuse me, but what about Ronald? What about him?" Marcus asked.

"Delf had reasons for what he did and wanted to do. I never thought Ronald did. They're both crazy, but I don't believe Ronald knew what he was doing. I believe Delf did. Let a jury decide, I say."

"Fry him," Green said.

"Mr. Green, I need to go to the church soon, sir."

"We're all going. Bill put your necktie back on. It's important. Theodora's going, too."

Bill knew there was no way out. You couldn't argue with Green when his mind was made and deep down inside, he agreed. It would be sad, but he knew sad.

Laura's face lit when she saw them, and she walked over and thanked them for coming. The casket was open. Joshua's countenance was fixed on the ceiling, his Bible in his clasped hands. Bill walked through the line that led past what was left of the kid and he lost it.

Green and Marcus took Bill out into fresh air, where Miss Hayes was welcoming arrivals. The mayor, the chief of police, and Datillo were walking across the lot. Miss Hayes walked over to Bill, touched his hand and his neck right beneath his ear and whispered, "The Lord is with you, Bill Maddox, if you will listen."

Green and Marcus steered Bill so that he wasn't blocking the entrance and Miss Hayes greeted the mayor and thanked him for coming, and he nodded solemnly and then glanced at Green who nodded. Bill felt like snarling. There was something he couldn't describe, so hollow and twisted all he could do was lean against the column that Marcus braced him against.

"Bill, calm yourself. Take deep breaths," Theodora said.

I'm not here, he felt like saying, but couldn't, because he wasn't.

Ruby was. He could see her face. It was Ruby all right. She was looking deep into his eyes. He knew Ruby.

"Bill, come here. It's all right. Bill, come all the way. Come this way. Come now. Come on," she said and with a stern look to the others, wrenched him over to a step and sat him down.

"Bill, damn you, we've been through this. This ain't doing good. Don't go. Damn you. Hear me! You don't go back there."

Bill's head rocked his whole body and Ruby put her arm around his shoulder and his breathing became audible. He swallowed like he couldn't, and Theodora was already there with water, which Bill drank while Green and Marcus looked on.

As he was drinking, the women present nodded. The men shook their heads.

"Got to go home," Bill rasped.

"Let's go," Green said.

Bill didn't say anything all the way back. Theodora sat in the backseat with him, while Marcus and Green listened to statistics about the World Series. Theodora was worried about Bill being left alone. She urged him to come with them. Bill shook his head.

When they got to the boat, she walked him in, and he thanked her for all she'd done. He slumped down at his table and fumbled for the lighter that was right in front of his eyes.

"Bill, give me a drink," Theodora insisted.

Bill went to the ice chest, filled a glass with chunks, set it in front of her, and then poured.

"Ain't in the mood for a cocktail party, understand?"

"Neither am I, but what happened?"

"Can't say."

Theodora, encouraged to see him responding, asked for a smoke.

"Got to stop," Bill said. "Don't care how, but it's got to stop. These lies, this distrust. This hatred got to stop."

"Bill, it's going to."

"In whose lifetime, Theo?" Bill said. "Not mine, not Joshua's, not Laura's."

"I don't know."

"Forgive me. I know you don't, Theo, and I don't. Time is way past. I know that much. It's nice the mayor came and chief of police, and I'm glad that you want things better, but when, in God's name?"

"Why are you challenging me? I didn't do this. You know that."

"Who did, damn it? Who did?"

Theodora started backing away from Bill, just as Green and Marcus stepped onto the deck. The boat listed. Theodora stood her ground; Bill hadn't moved an inch, surprised at how terribly frightened she looked. Green burst in the door with a puzzled expression. He looked back and forth from Bill to his wife. Marcus stayed outside, peering in the door, and watched Bill's anger and pain, Mrs. Green's self-righteous disbelief, and Mr. Green standing there like a judge without a robe, ready to lay down the law.

"What is this about, Theodora?" Green asked, as he headed toward the whiskey bottle.

"Don't touch it," Theodora snapped.

Green retracted like he had been shocked. Bill sat down, looked up and saw Marcus observing. The Greens were locked into a staring contest. Bill broke the spell.

"Sorry. Damn, I'm sorry. Thanks for bringing me home. I don't know what came over me."

Green said, "It's not you."

"Oh, yes, it is. I have imposed. Forgive me. Let me fix a dividend."

"One more," Theodora said. "That's it."

CHAPTER 15
SING THE FISH INTO THE BOAT

When Bill was alone, he stretched out and felt the boat sway. Air was cool, the sun low, but shining; when he closed his eyes, it felt like midnight.

Bill woke a few hours later, had no idea what time and didn't care. He went to the ice chest, fished out a beer, lit a smoke, and padded to the deck. It was not cold, but the deck was nippy to the touch and he elevated his feet onto the empty chair.

He felt small in an enormous room. He was surprised by how light he felt. Coolness seemed to be sculpting his features so that he could sense every curve of his face.

He could see the North Star, although he couldn't see the Big Dipper through the trees. Autumn was on its way and Green would come by in the morning to take him to Joshua's funeral. He exhaled a long deep breath and couldn't believe he was going to church three times in two days.

As he sat, the breeze picked up and leaves rattled; some fell on him and Bill brushed them off. Sky to the north was turning gray. Wasn't looking forward to another winter. Valerie entered his reverie. How could she have been so there, and yet so absent, all at the same damn time? He went back inside and fixed a whiskey.

A car drove past, but as he looked out the window, it turned around and left. Bill went back out onto the deck. The North Star was covered by a cloud bank. He missed Valerie's warmth and laughter.

He threw his last smoke of the night into the creek and bet that the next day, he would hear both the twenty-third psalm and "Amazing Grace." He wondered if Sarah was looking down. He wondered why he was looking up. All he knew to do was to keep holding on.

———

There was hardly anything in the paper. There was something about Delf, but it was buried deep in the second section. There was nothing about cooperation between the police and citizens, or determination between blacks and whites to stop the Klan. There was nothing like that. Just a blurb, hardly a paragraph, about Delf's alleged murder of Joshua Baker. There was no mention of the churches, neither black nor white. Nothing about Polecat's. Green was outraged. Bill was resigned.

The service was simple. They did not sing "Amazing Grace," but it was predictably maudlin, until Joshua's mother, Laura, stood, interrupted the preacher, and walked forward with a stick of sandalwood.

"Please light this."

She pulled a saucer out of her pocket and handed the preacher a book of matches.

"He liked it," she said.

The preacher lit the stick and it was amazing how quickly the scent filled the church. Ruby wasn't happy; she shook her head, but no one else seemed concerned. On the way out, she whispered that it was what Catholics do. Bill smiled and looked away.

"I'm telling you, Bill, we need a preacher. One who stands for truth and glory."

Bill drove back to the boat, surprised to see Fred there. That was not so unusual, but then, it had been unusual to see Sneed directing traffic on River Road. That gave him a chuckle. Bill had waved, and Sneed pretended he hadn't seen.

"Let's go fishing soon, Bill."

"No reason not to, I suppose."

"So, let's go tomorrow. I get off around three thirty. What do you say?"

Fred left and then a huge beer truck pulled up and squealed to a dusty halt. Bill covered his glass with the palm of his hand to keep dust out of his whiskey. They needed rain. He squinted and could see dusty footprints on the deck, dust beiged plants on the shore. A burly man with a huge belly walked toward him carrying what looked like a case of beer in each hand.

"You Bill Maddox?" he asked in a deep voice that seemed etched with humor.

"Sure am. Who might you be?"

"The name is Roscoe and I been sent by Mr. Polecat Green to bring you some beer. Permission to board, Captain?"

"Hell yeah," Bill said. "Come on with it."

"Got two more earmarked," Roscoe said. "Need ice?"

The man was huge. Stood about six four and his weight rocked the boat. Bill figured a little ice wouldn't hurt. He cautioned the man to bring it on gently so as not to capsize the situation.

"Aw, Mr. Maddox, I ain't all that huge. You ought to see my wife."

Bill's eyes got wide thinking about the two of them.

"Just kidding, she's petite. Says I'm her full-grown teddy bear."

He dropped off two more cases and fifty pounds of ice, then asked if this was a good time to stop by. Bill must have looked puzzled. The man asked again, eyes twinkling.

"What you talking about, Roscoe?"

"What about next Monday I just leave it on the deck if you're not here? Polecat told me to deliver until you got sick or died."

"Damn! Well, bring it on. If ice melts, that's my fault," Bill replied, chuckling.

"Ice won't be melting much for long. Winter will be moving in."

"Don't you know," Bill said, thinking of sunny Florida and Valerie. "See you next week, Roscoe."

While Bill was breaking up the block to ice down the beer, he didn't know why, but felt like something was behind him. He kept chipping with the ice pick and fought the feeling to look, then felt a tug on his pants leg. He turned and at first saw nothing, then looked down to see Amelia beaming.

"What in blazes are you doing here, young lady?" He looked for a car but didn't see one.

"I came to see you. The circus is coming. I want to tell you about it."

Bill rolled his eyes.

"You look like the clown I saw in the picture. You're funny, Bill."

"What picture are you talking about?"

"Take me home. I'll show you. He's on my street."

Bill iced down the beer, fixed a stiff one, and drove the child home.

"Don't you understand it's dangerous to be walking on these roads? Where's your mother?"

"Don't yell. You're my friend."

"Okay, I agree. I'm your friend, but where is your mother?"

"She'll be home soon. She went to Miss Laura's."

"Your brothers, where are they?"

"They had something important to do!"

Bill was furious, but didn't want to scare the child, so he drove slowly and thought what he might say if Ruby was home and what he might need to do if she wasn't. He was thinking so hard, he almost passed the turnoff.

"You almost didn't stop," Amelia said, giggling. "Look! Look! There he is! See the clown?"

Bill looked up and saw a poster tacked to a telephone pole. It was Emmett Kelly, the clown. The Ringling Brothers Circus, under the big top. Amelia was bouncing on the seat.

"I want to go see him. Want you to take me. Will you take me, Mr. Maddox?"

Bill sighed. "So, it's Mr. Maddox now, is it?"

"Will you take me? You don't have to take my brothers."

"I'm not inclined to, but may take you, if you promise to quit walking this road."

"What does that mean?"

Bill saw them. The brothers were throwing a football with other kids in a vacant lot. He stopped and honked, but they ignored him, oblivious to everything but their own heroics. He took Amelia by her tiny hand and walked over to where the boys were caterwauling and stood there until he was noticed. He stared at the boys with undisguised contempt. Both looked down, while the other kids looked restless and confused. Bill pointed to the house, turned and walked away, climbed back into the car. He drove Amelia home.

The boys ran up all out of breath, but Ruby was already there, glaring with her hands on her hips. Bill left before brimstone scorched down, but winked at Amelia who clapped her hands, bounced on her tiptoes, and grinned ear to ear. All right, he was going to the circus, most likely.

He couldn't figure out how the child did it. It was a good two miles. On the way home, he stopped in at Polecat's. Polecat wouldn't take any money for the Falls City beer Bill ordered up. Bill thanked him for the gifts. Polecat laughed and said, if it wasn't for him, his joint would be burned to the ground. He told Bill he had taken care of Datillo, too. Bill asked him how. Polecat just smiled. What about Green? Bill wanted to know. Polecat nodded yes and then indicated that he wasn't going to go into that either. Bill had more questions to ask, but realized there was no point in it, so he got ribs and left.

He was driving down River Road and there was Marcus walking along. Bill stopped and offered him a ride. Marcus was obviously out of sorts, flustered. Green had fired him for getting in his business. Green was at the Point, but Marcus grinned and pulled out the car keys and rattled them. Bill had to laugh, so did Marcus. Green would now have to deal with Theodora. He dropped Marcus off at Green's. Marcus said he was going to pack and leave. Bill asked where he was headed. Marcus looked at him like he had never thought of that before, shrugged, and went toward his door.

By the time Bill got around to eating the ribs, they were cool, and he was tipsy. He realized the boat seemed nippier than the air outside, so he gathered some dry sticks off the bank for kindling, and with the few logs he had left from the winter before, built a fire in his stove. As it crackled, he poured himself another drink that he probably didn't need but wanted and laid the ribs on the burner plate. After dinner, he crawled into his bed and something tickled his nose. He sought out the cause and found a long fine hair. It was Valerie's. That made him smile.

At the post office the next morning, Miss Robeson handed him his mail with a wink. There was a postcard on top. In the car, he looked at a picture of various vivid shades of blue, with Daytona Beach in bold gold. He flipped it. "Everything is fabulous! Hope you are. See you Christmastime. Valerie."

When Fred's car pulled up, Bill was bailing out his boat. Fred had Hawk with him and Hawk was carrying his guitar.

"You going to sing fish into the boat?" Bill laughed.

"Naw. The kids break strings, get peanut butter and jelly all over it. Hope I can keep her inside."

"Maybe, if you'll play something later," Fred said.

Fred had the luck, but they were all bluegill, then Hawk caught a cat. Most of the time, they just drank Polecat beer and jawed about what had just happened and what might be in the future. Bill found himself in the unaccustomed position of defending cops. He didn't like most either, but Hawk had stories to tell that would scare the devil. Fred had a few that weren't pretty, so Bill focused on fishing. All agreed stuff that had happened might come to nothing but disagreed about what nothing might be.

Finally, Bill hooked his bass or at least one that fought like the one he had hooked the night of the clash. They landed him. The damn thing was eighteen inches. Then he caught another not much smaller. Then Hawk caught one that had some size. Fred's big grin turned somber when he slid them on the stringer and saw his bluegill competing for air, but then he hooked one with some obvious heft and his smile flashed again. They landed a large crappie and called it a day.

Later, Fred cleaned the fish, dredged them in cornmeal, then spooned lard into a skillet. There was beer to drink and the evening was warm and while the moon ascended, Hawk strummed his guitar. Bill went into the boat to fetch his harmonicas. They were among the few of his possessions that had escaped the fire. They had been his solace when he'd been hauling out on the road away from Sarah. His favorite one had been in his pocket that night. He plucked them out of the drawer quickly, as if they were chunks of dry ice. He heard Fred's chuckle turn into song. He searched the shadows of what had become a home and felt his way toward the cabin door. He swallowed hard, shook his head, took a deep breath, and closed the door tightly behind him.

On the creek bank, Bill paused and peered through the sweet sting of ground-hugging wood smoke, before he strolled slowly back toward Hawk and Fred, and the flickering fire.

ABOUT THE AUTHOR

Ed Middleton was born in Louisville, Kentucky, and with the exception of exploratory years, has mostly always been blessed to live there. Aside from publishing poems and short fiction in mostly forgotten rags, he has worked in many capacities to pursue his quest to be forever learning and studying about and from the timeless world that surrounds us and the courageous ones who bear witness.

ACKNOWLEDGMENTS

The author would like to thank Susan Lindsey of
Savvy Communication LLC for her tireless and astute editing.
Further, Shellee Marie Jones deserves praise for
thoughtful and sensitive design work.